INCOGNITO'S MI: ASSASSINATE LEADERS OF THE CONTINENTAL CONGRESS IN 1776.

As the colonies begin to talk openly of political separation from England, a coded letter is deciphered. It suggests that an assassin, code name Incognito, is headed to Philadelphia to assassinate key leaders of the Continental Congress. The assassin may have co-conspirators in the city, and in the Congress itself.

Will Harrell, the young man who decoded the letter, is tasked with investigating the matter, uncovering the identity of the assassin and his confederates, and foiling the plot. While he works feverishly against the clock, he must deal with some skeptical and uncooperative delegates, an abundance of suspects but a scarcity of hard evidence, his own self-doubt, and a widening plot that includes a planned assassination of General George Washington in New York.

Will is determined to thwart the assassin, but his adversary is creative and resourceful, a master of disguise, handsome, charming, and thoroughly ruthless. The price Will must pay to stop him may prove too dear.

Praise for Incognito

"*Incognito* is a heart pounding thriller, well-researched and brilliantly interwoven... an instant classic!"—*James D. Shipman, author of Irena's War*

"...a compelling story of intrigue, politics, and the fragility of our nascent rebellion against the British Crown..."--*SR Staley, award-winning author of The Pirate of Panther Bay series and St. Nic, Inc.*

"...fast paced, exciting spy...a fun way to experience the American Revolution. Highly recommend!"—*David Proctor, Ph. D., Professor of History, Tallahassee Community College*

"...a brilliant, historical, suspenseful page-turner...the work of a seasoned novelist at the height of his powers."— *Michael Lister, New York Times bestselling author of the John Jordan Mystery Series*

"A well-researched thriller that seamlessly blends fact and fiction...a crackling good read."—*V.S. Alexander, author of The Traitor*

Excerpt

John Hancock gaveled the session of the Continental Congress to order and then recognized Richard Henry Lee.

The thin, long-limbed delegate from Virginia rose slowly from his seat. He pulled down on the sleeves of his shirt, adjusted his coat and looked around the room. "I have two related resolutions to offer." All eyes were on him and a penetrating silence invaded the space as he removed the notes from his vest pocket, opened them up and began to read.

"That these united colonies are, and of right ought to be, free and independent states, that they are absolved from all allegiance to the British Crown, and that all political connection between them and the state of Great Britain is, and ought to be, totally dissolved."

Everyone in the room knew this was coming, some with great anticipation, some with a cold dread, but only a select few were privy to the exact timing, or the exact wording. Will suspected that Tim was in that number. He was not. And now, even those who had done everything in their power to bring the body to this point sat in stunned silence, as Lee's sparse, eloquent words hung in the air. A low murmur began in the chamber, and Lee waved his black silk-gloved hand to indicate he was not finished. He glanced at his notes and began again...

About the Author

Terry Lewis was a trial judge from 1989 to 2019, presiding over a variety of civil and criminal cases. He is now a private attorney specializing in arbitration and mediation. He lives in Tallahassee with his wife, Fran, and their Border Collie Mix, Pepper. This is his fourth novel.

terrylewisbooks.com

Acknowledgment

Several people read early drafts of this novel and gave me valuable feedback. They include: my wife and daughter, Fran Lewis and Angie Barry, Liz Jameson, Patrick Murphy, Lisa Blackwell, Sam Staley and Jim Jones. Thanks to my agent, Evan Marshall, always the professional and gentleman, and to the folks at Moonshine Cove for guiding me through and making this novel as good as it could be.

Boston, April 26, 1776

Chapter 1

Ian McKeever was keeping a close eye on the man, his suspicion fueled by several pints of ale and by several nagging, unanswered questions. The man who called himself Henry Belmont had no occupation, yet he dressed well and never seemed to lack for money. He had arrived in Boston less than two months ago, a complete stranger, yet had managed to worm himself into the inner circle of the Sons of Liberty very quickly. Even now, he was seated at a corner table with John Weathers, the two men leaning in, deep in conversation.

Weathers was a ship builder. He was also a smuggler. His interest in independence for the colonies was as much personal as it was political. But that didn't matter. What mattered was that he was ruthless and committed, and so were the men under his charge. He was no fool, for sure, but perhaps, thought Ian, a little too trusting of this stranger.

A blacksmith by trade, McKeever stood over six feet tall, with broad shoulders and bulging muscles that strained against his buckskin shirt. These physical attributes had proven helpful in his role as enforcer for the Sons of Liberty, as had the subtle menace just beneath the surface of his quiet, calm voice. He had proven quite persuasive in convincing reluctant citizens of the rightness of the patriot cause and of the advantages of adhering to the Sons' directives. Ian was normally not overly suspicious, but these were not normal times, were they? And his instincts were telling him that something about Henry Belmont was not right.

The Green Dragon Tavern was crowded, thick with conversation, some quiet and some loud. The air was dank and warm, aided by an unnecessary fire in the stone fireplace, and it smelled of sweat and spilled ale. A dense cloud of smoke hung in the air, clinging to everything and everyone it touched.

McKeever signaled with an uplifted chin for another ale from his friend, Alfred, owner of the Green Dragon. The man obliged, filling the pewter tankard from a barrel beneath the bar, then sliding it over to Ian's waiting hand. With the foam rising above the brim and over the sides, Ian turned it up to his mouth and drained half the contents in two large gulps. He set the container down on the bar, wiped at the foam with the sleeve of his shirt and let out a large belch.

"Hey, Alfred?"

The man looked up, his soft grey eyes curious, obliging. "Yes?"

Ian shifted his gaze toward the corner table. "What do you make of Henry?"

Alfred shrugged as he sopped up some spilled ale with a large rag. "What do you mean?"

"He's done got real cozy with Weathers; don't you think?"

Alfred shrugged again but said nothing.

"And real quick like, too." McKeever took another large swig of ale and looked at his friend.

Alfred gave him a small smile. "You jealous?"

Ian did not respond but continued looking at his friend.

Alfred frowned. "Well, yes, I suppose. No question John's taken a liking to the old fart. But what's not to like? He's friendly and gracious in his manner, and quick with a joke or a good story. And you got to admit, he's been helpful to the cause, Henry has. Remember, he's the one who found that extra store of ammunition the lobster backs had hid in Benton's warehouse, and came up with the plan to steal it, right under their British noses."

"And how did he know where it was hidden?" Alfred didn't wait for a response before adding, "Good way to get in with the Sons too, weren't it?" He drained the rest of his ale and slapped the empty tankard down on the bar. "For all we know, he could be a British spy."

8

Alfred snorted a laugh. "Henry? Really? I mean, yes, we don't know a whole lot about him, but he's got the bloodlines of a patriot. He is, after all, a cousin of George Washington himself."

Yes, Ian thought, looking over at Henry. He claimed to be a Virginia planter, a cousin to George Washington, come here to Boston to oppose British tyranny. "If it could happen in Massachusetts," Henry said, "it could happen in Virginia." He was too old for the army, but perhaps, he suggested, he could help in other ways. His accent seemed authentic, but they didn't get many Virginians in Boston, so it was hard to tell.

McKeever looked back to his friend. "We only have his word for that, don't we?"

Alfred shook his head.

"And remember last month, after Washington chased the Redcoats out of the city, and he stopped in here for a pint and to meet with Weathers? Henry wasn't here was he?" It was a rhetorical question and Ian didn't wait for an answer. "You'd think a fellow Virginian, a relative, would've been on hand to greet the general."

"Well, it wasn't like it was a planned thing," Alfred said, but there seemed to be a flicker of doubt in his gray eyes now.

"I heard he was coming, and I was here. Henry got the word too. You can bet on it. You think it was just a coincidence he didn't show?

Alfred said nothing.

"Too bad someone didn't think to ask the general about his supposed cousin." Alfred flicked his eyes toward the corner table. "Look at him, Ian. He's an old man. He can barely get around with the help of a cane."

Yes, Ian thought, Henry was an old man, maybe in his late sixties, his long, grey hair pulled back and tied with a white silk ribbon, his posture stooped, his cautious, uneven gait aided by an elegant wooden cane. He seemed harmless enough. "But you ain't got to be young to be a spy," he said.

"My, but you are a suspicious sod."

Ian shrugged. "I just think it would be a good idea to keep an eye on old Henry, try to find out a little more about him."

Alfred frowned as he wiped down his bar again, but Ian could see that his friend was warming to the idea.

"He stays in a boarding house on Treamont Street," Alfred said, "run by a widow, Mary Stevens. Maybe she, or one of the other boarders has noticed something."

"Yes," Ian said, nodding, "maybe."

"You'll want to be discreet in your inquiries," Alfred said, folding his arms across his chest, which made his large belly seem larger. "If Henry is a spy, and I ain't saying he is, but if he is, you don't want to spook him. He could lead us to bigger fish."

"Oh, yes, yes, I understand." Ian said, turning back to look across the room again, a little annoyed at the suggestion that he didn't know how to handle things. "Discreet," he repeated, as if the word left a bad taste in his mouth.

Alfred looked at him for a few seconds but said nothing more about it.

The two men fell back into a more relaxed conversation and Ian eventually wandered over to another table on the opposite side of the room where some friends were playing Whist. He sat off to the side and consumed another pint of ale and continued to focus on the object of his suspicions.

Shortly before midnight, Henry rose from his seat. He bowed slightly to his companion and headed toward the front door. He paused at the fireplace, retrieved a lighting stick from the edge, re-lit his pipe and placed the stick back in its place next to the fire. Henry took his coat from the rack by the entrance, put it on, and then shuffled out the door. McKeever looked over toward the bar and caught Alfred's eye, nodded once, and also got up from his seat. He walked to the door, hesitated for a couple seconds, opened it and stepped outside.

The air was wet and cool, a fog beginning to fall over the city. Despite the late hour, Union Street was still thick with people. Ian stood for a few moments under the symbol for the tavern, a sculptured copper dragon, green from corrosion, which hung above the entrance. He looked to his left and his right, fearing for a moment that he had lost the man in the crowd. But then he saw the glow from Henry's pipe and noted the slight limp of his walk as the cane tapped on the cobblestones. Ian followed, making sure to keep some distance between them.

The coolness seemed to sober him up a bit, but he still felt a little unsteady on his feet, and he widened his stance to accommodate. Occasionally he would place his hand on the wall of a building for a little extra support. Soon, the pedestrian traffic dwindled and most of the businesses they passed were closed. Illumination came only from a pale sliver of moon and the occasional torch lamp. Henry passed through Dock Square and turned right on Queen Street. McKeever dropped back a little, staying in the shadows.

So far, Belmont had done nothing suspicious as he headed in the general direction of his lodgings, and Ian began to have second thoughts. He could have been at the Green Dragon having another pint instead of wasting his time. But his instinct told him to keep going, and he trusted his instinct.

Another man approached from the opposite direction. The elegantly dressed gentleman looked familiar, but Ian couldn't see well enough in the dim light to be sure. When the man drew close to Henry, the two of them veered off onto Brattles Street as if on cue. They walked a short distance down Brattles, moved into the darkness of a building's shadow and began talking in low, whispered voices.

McKeever stopped, straining to make out their words. He edged a little closer, careful to keep to the shadows. When his boot crunched a clump of gravel, the two men stopped talking and looked in his direction. Ian froze and held his breath. After a few seconds, the men resumed their conversation. He eased forward again, slowly, padding as lightly as he could.

The other man shifted, and the moonlight offered Ian a brief glimpse of his profile, enough for Ian to now identify him—Alexander Lewis, the secretary to the former governor of Massachusetts. Ian thought he had fled Boston with the other loyalists when the British evacuated the city in March. Obviously not. He watched as Lewis removed a document from his coat pocket and handed it to Henry. The latter wordlessly examined it, turning it over in his hand, then broke the seal with his thumb.

"Godspeed," Lewis said, then turned and continued walking down Brattles.

Henry watched the man retreat before unfolding the paper. He quickly read its contents, then shoved it into his coat pocket.

Perhaps there was some innocent explanation for this clandestine meeting with a known Tory, a puppet of the British Army, but Ian couldn't imagine what it might be. His instincts had been correct, his suspicions justified.

Should he confront the traitor now or report his observations to Weathers and let the council decide? Perhaps, as Alfred had suggested, it would be more valuable to keep this discovery a secret. Perhaps the man who called himself Henry Belmont, whoever he really was, if watched closely, might reveal a larger network of spies. On the other hand, the document itself might be very valuable, and Ian felt certain he could get the old man to talk. The blacksmith was quite skilled at getting information from people who didn't want to give it. If he waited, Henry would no doubt destroy the paper.

Ian walked out of the shadows.

"Hello, Henry."

The older man appeared startled, but only momentarily. He turned to face him. The distance between them was thirty feet. "Ian McKeever, fancy seeing you here." As he spoke, Henry began walking toward him, tapping his cane lightly on the ground.

"Hand it over, Henry."

"What?"

"The paper in your pocket."

Henry stepped closer. They were now less than ten feet apart. "What are you talking about?"

"I saw you, Henry. I saw you with that Tory. I saw him give to you what you now have in your coat pocket. I'll have a look, if you please." He took a step forward and held out his hand.

"Suspicion always haunts the guilty mind. The thief doth fear each bush an officer."

"What?"

"Shakespeare, Ian, from *Henry VI.*"

"What?"

"Never mind," the old man said. He retrieved the paper from his pocket and held it up. "This is private correspondence, Ian, from my nephew in Virginia. It is of a personal matter and I'm afraid I can't allow you to see it." Henry had the paper in his left hand. In his right, he held his pipe and his cane. He touched the note to the glowing embers of the pipe and a very small flame began at the edge.

"Can't let you do that," Ian said, and started to close the distance between them.

Henry dropped the document to the ground, and the flame began to grow. Ian stepped forward quickly, preparing to bend down to retrieve it. In what seemed impossible speed for an old, crippled man, Henry brought the cane up horizontally across his waist and, with his left hand gripping the end, pulled it apart, revealing a double-edged blade about six inches long.

The thin steel blade glimmered in the moonlight as Henry swept it backhanded toward Ian. With the instincts of a tavern brawler, Ian pulled back just as the blade whizzed by within a hair of his throat.

The blacksmith may have been surprised by the attack, but he was not afraid. He had disarmed many a knife-wielding drunk before and then beaten them senseless. And this little piece of dung would be no different. No, he was not fearful; he was angry. He reached for the hand holding the blade.

He didn't feel it at first. A small pinch, some slight pressure. He looked down, surprised to see that Henry had buried the blade to the hilt in his gut. Before he could react, Henry had pulled it out and thrust it again. Ian grabbed for the arm but missed. He put his hands around his attacker's throat and squeezed with all his strength. But that strength was ebbing, and the choking didn't seem to faze the old man. How could that be?

Henry continued his assault, stabbing him again and again. Ian let go of Henry's throat and stepped back. He placed both of his hands over his stomach and felt the blood ooze through his fingers. Then he heard the swish of the blade slicing through the air, felt the prick along his throat. He moved his hands from his stomach to his new wound. This time, the blood spurted through his fingers.

Ian fell to his knees, grabbing at the old man around the waist, but he couldn't get a good grip. He slid slowly down the man's front, his surprise replaced by an overwhelming sense of frustration, and then humiliation, and finally by a strange peace as the life ebbed slowly from his body. His last thoughts were of his wife and children as he lost his grasp and fell face first into the gravel.

* * *

The man who called himself Henry Belmont stepped back a couple of feet and looked around quickly to make sure there were no witnesses. He watched as the last of the paper disappeared in flame and turned to ashes, which he then spread with his boot.

He wiped the blood from the blade with the sleeve of the blacksmith's shirt, picked up the other half of his cane and sheathed the weapon. He retrieved his pipe from where it had fallen and inspected it. It was still intact. He took a couple of puffs to get the fire going again, looking down at the big man, searching for any signs of life, and saw none.

Confident that the blacksmith was dead, Henry reached down, grabbed him by his arms and drug him behind some nearby shrubbery. He then stepped back a few feet, checking to confirm that the body was hidden from sight.

He took one more quick survey of the area. He used his cravat to wipe the blood from his face, hands and clothes as best he could, then put it in his coat pocket. He felt sure that, in the darkness, the stains wouldn't be noticeable to anyone he passed. Henry straightened his shirt and coat and pulled down on the sleeves. He then walked slowly away, puffing on the pipe and tapping his cane lightly on the cobblestones.

Boston, April 27
Chapter 2

The men walked quickly, and with purpose. Alfred struggled to keep up. The work of a tavern keeper was grueling sometimes, but it didn't require this sort of vigorous, fast-paced jaunt. He had grown fat and soft over the years, he realized, and was finding it difficult to catch his breath.

John Weathers spoke over his shoulder to Alfred, "Are you sure that Ian followed him out of the tavern last night?"

"Indeed, I am. As I told you, when Henry left, Ian did as well."

"That's not quite the same, now, is it, Alfred?" At this, Weathers glanced at the tavern owner briefly, then looked straight ahead again. "Did he tell you he was going to follow the man?"

"Not exactly."

"Well, what exactly did he say?"

"He didn't say anything, really. He just gave me a look, which I took to mean that he was going to follow him—like he talked about earlier."

Weathers kept walking but turned his head toward Alfred again, his black eyes hard. It made Alfred uncomfortable. Weathers muttered something under his breath, but the tavern owner couldn't make it out, nor did he want to ask. He had learned that it was best to avoid irritating the man, even a little. He gave Weathers a small grin and shrugged.

The men walked in silence until Alfred spoke again. "You think the old man could have done that to Ian, such a vicious attack?"

One of the other men, Oliver McKeever, a brother of Ian, shook his head. "If he did, he must've taken Ian by surprise. Ain't but a handful

16

of men in this town who could get the better of him in a fight—a fair one anyway."

No one contradicted him.

"And there's also the pendant they found near his body," Weathers said. The others nodded. They had all seen it before—around Henry's neck. It was unique, and coupled with what Alfred had observed, it made the case against Henry compelling.

"When I get my hands on that son of a bitch," Oliver said, "I'm gonna rip him from limb to limb." This was no idle threat. He was, like his brother, an imposing physical presence, and he was accustomed to using his size and strength to mete out his idea of justice.

Oliver had been unemotional earlier when he described his brother's body, the multiple stab wounds to the torso, the throat sliced from ear to ear. He immediately informed Weathers of the murder, who in turn called an emergency meeting at the Green Dragon to consider the matter. It was here that Alfred offered his observations of the preceding evening.

It didn't take long for suspicion to spread over the room. Weathers selected Alfred and the others to accompany him to the boarding house. Now, as they rounded the next corner, it came into sight. Alfred forgot his fatigue, his legs propelled by a sense of excitement, mixed with foreboding.

At the entrance, Weathers opened the front door and walked in without bothering to knock or call out. The others followed, crowding into the hallway. Mrs. Stevens, the proprietor, was chatting with a couple of guests in the dining room off to the right. She came forward to greet the men, her face registering surprise, and a little concern. The guests became silent, watching, listening.

"Mr. Weathers?"

Weathers bowed in the direction of the woman. "My apologies, Mrs. Stevens, for the intrusion."

She nodded. "How may I be of assistance to you this morning?"

"We would like to see one of your boarders, an elderly gentleman who goes by the name of Henry Belmont."

"Mr. Belmont? He is one of my boarders, but I believe he is still sleeping."

"So much the better as the boys would like to surprise him. And which room did you say was his?"

"I didn't."

Weathers stared at her with those black eyes, waiting.

She pointed a finger up the stairs. "He's in number three, to the right."

Weathers nodded at Alfred and the others, and the three of them quickly made their way up the stairs. He followed behind. When they got to the room the men stood to the side of the door listening. Then on a signal from Weathers, he opened the door and the men rushed in.

Mrs. Stevens, who had lingered at the bottom of the stairs for a few seconds, then followed the men, now entered the room, looked around quickly and voiced the conclusion that the others had quickly reached. "He's gone."

The men searched the room, opening drawers, looking behind the dresser, under the bed. It became obvious very soon that the occupant had not only vanished, he had carefully removed any item of personal property as well, leaving no evidence of his crime, or of his real identity, or of his current whereabouts. But any doubts they might have harbored as to the man's guilt in the murder of Ian McKeever had also vanished.

Oliver expressed the common sentiment. "Damn."

The landlady looked at Weathers, shock and worry etched on her face. "Will someone please tell me what's going on? Why would Mr. Belmont leave so suddenly, without even saying goodbye? He is paid up through the week."

Weathers ignored her. "Boys, our quarry is on the run. He can't have gotten far. Spread the word, distribute a description of the man and scour the city, station men at the docks, cut off any way of public or private transport out of Boston. We must not let him get away."

The men filed out of the room and Weathers turned his attention to the woman. He touched the brim of his hat. "Again, my apologies for the intrusion." He paused, then said, "Your former guest is suspected of a most vile murder, Mrs. Stevens. His victim was a fine citizen and patriot."

The woman put her hand to her mouth. "Murder? Mr. Belmont?"

Weathers nodded. "The evidence against him is most convincing, and his flight confirms his guilt, I'm afraid. I trust that you will notify me if you spot him or come upon any information as to his whereabouts or intended destination?" It was a statement more than a question.

She nodded absently, "Of course." Then she said, "Here in my own home, a murderer." She made the sign of the cross over her chest.

Weathers nodded. "I shall now take your leave, madam. We have a killer to catch."

* * *

John and Annabelle Fleming were waiting in the Red Rooster Inn, taking a spot of food while their driver watered and fed the horses, and made last minute preparations for their journey. They were eager to get on their way. It would be a long trip from Boston to New York, a full two days if they really pushed it—and Annabelle wasn't in the best of physical condition. The pregnancy had been a troubled one from the beginning and it had gotten worse in the last few weeks, so much so that she prevailed upon her husband to accept the offer of her parents to continue the rest of it in their home in New York.

They had no extended family in Boston. John couldn't afford to leave his law practice for long and didn't have the time to care for her as she needed. He could hire someone, of course, but no one could provide the sort of care a mother could. And he very much liked his in-laws. So, after posting a short note to Annabelle's family advising of their decision, they hired a coach and loaded it with the necessary

19

supplies for the trip. John would get his wife settled in, then return to Boston.

John looked up to see a man walk through the entrance and stop just inside, searching the room. After a few seconds, the man approached their table.

"Excuse me, sir, madam," he said, bowing slightly, "I understand that you are travelling to New York?"

He was of average height, with a sturdy frame, and long black hair which he wore pulled back and tied with a scarlet ribbon. He was dressed elegantly in matching velvet pants, coat and vest, with a ruffled white shirt underneath.

"Yes, that is correct," John said.

"I was hoping you might have room for one more in your coach. I am anxious to get to New York myself. I have received word that my aunt is very ill and has requested that I come to her bedside. You can understand the urgency. I could hire my own coach but that would put me back a day, maybe two."

John looked briefly at his wife then turned back to the man. "I'm afraid my wife is a bit ill. Company would not be best for her at this time, under the circumstances."

Annabelle put her hand on her husband's arm. "Now, John, don't be so quick to presume what would be best for me," she said, smiling at the man. "I think a little company might be nice."

The man smiled back at her, then looked at her husband. "I am willing to pay the cost of the entire trip. After all, if I had hired my own coach, I would have paid the same. You would be doing me a great service."

John studied the man again. He seemed pleasant enough, and judging by his manner and dress, was certainly not the type who might want to rob them once out of the city. Indeed, the offer to pay for the trip was very generous, if unnecessary. Still, John didn't know the man at all and something about him made him uneasy. With nagging doubts still clinging to him, John said, "I will accept your pro-rata share of the cost Mr....."

"Howe. James Arden Howe."

"Well, Mr. Howe," John said, extending his hand, "Let us get your things stored on the coach. I believe our driver is just about ready to depart."

* * *

Minutes later, the man formerly known as Henry Belmont settled into the seat opposite the Flemings and peered out of the moving coach. His ultimate destination was Philadelphia, not New York, but he would not look the proverbial gift horse in the mouth. One had to be able to adapt to changing circumstances. What he needed now was a quick exit out of Boston, and fortune had given it to him in the form of this lovely couple. Philadelphia could wait. Besides, he had matters to attend to in New York as well. He would just adjust his schedule, that's all.

James Arden Howe, as he was now calling himself, made it a point never to panic. It still rankled him that he failed to notice that he had been followed last night. He had trained himself to be more observant. He fancied himself as having a heightened sense of smell, touch, and hearing, of being able to sense danger. But not last night. He had been careless. He was not too proud to admit that. He recovered quickly, however. He stayed calm, did not panic, and handled the matter.

Even when he noticed the next morning that his pendant was missing, and that it must have come off during his struggle with McKeever, he remained calm. The pendant was a gift from his father on his 18th birthday and he treasured it. It was an unusual piece and certainly, some of those criminals and vagrants who called themselves patriots would have noticed it. If the pendant was found, clutched in the dead man's hand, or nearby, it would eventually lead to him. It was too late to go back to the scene and try to recover it. He could afford to tarry no longer.

He quickly packed his few personal items, took one last look around the room, grabbed the satchel, and made his way downstairs. He preferred not to have to explain his sudden departure to his landlady, and fortunately, he heard her bustling about in the kitchen area. No other guests were up yet. He stepped to the front door, peered out in both directions and saw that the house was not being watched. He then casually, but steadily, walked toward the river, beginning to formulate a plan to escape by way of the sea. Perhaps he would steal a boat.

Along the way, he stopped behind an empty building next to a water trough. The makeup on his face and neck which he had expertly applied each day to give him the appearance of a much older man, he now wiped away. He washed out the gray coloring from his hair, revealing his natural, dark mane. He disassembled the wooden cane, removed the blade and placed both in the satchel, then continued walking.

And, just as his cane had disappeared, so did his limp. He stood upright now as he strode easily and quickly down the street. He was almost to the river when he spotted the coach outside the Red Rooster Inn--and began to revise his plan of escape.

Yes, he thought now, as he peered out at the passing countryside, fate had interceded on his behalf again. He turned his attention to the couple seated opposite him in the small coach. They were a handsome pair. He was short and slight of frame with dark hair and eyes. She was small, petite, with very white skin and large blue eyes.

Those eyes now met his across the coach and he smiled at her. She smiled back and darted her eyes to the pamphlet which he had retrieved from his satchel and placed on his lap. He held it up so she could see the title-- *The Tempest.*

"Do you fancy Shakespeare, Madam?"

Philadelphia, April 29
Chapter 3

William Harrell was sitting at counsel table, in the court of Common Pleas, poised to make his very first legal argument, when his body gave its first hint that it was about to betray him—a little lightheadedness and a slight tingle about the lips. He tried to ignore it, but his alarm gauge involuntarily ticked up a notch.

The late afternoon sun slid in under the half-drawn blinds, providing soft, filtered light and gentle warmth to the small courtroom. Will watched as tiny dust motes, suspended in the still air, settled slowly on the surfaces around him. As he listened to the Plaintiff's testimony, his attention was drawn to the painting behind the witness, a large portrait of His Majesty, King George III.

The artist's rendering was of a tall, slender monarch with a soft, boyish face, resplendent in his royal finery—white silk shirt and scarf, gold brocaded, fur-lined cape, cinched with a blue velour belt. Will was imagining how awkward it must be for the young king to move around so encumbered when the unmistakable odor of sulfur, strong, and with no apparent source, briefly filled his nostrils, then dissipated. It was his body's second warning.

He would not get a third.

He fought against the panic that began to sweep through him. It could be worse, of course. Sometimes the attacks came with absolutely no warning. He would simply black out and awake seconds, or minutes, later with no memory of the event at all. At least now, with some warning, he would have time to adjust, to prepare.

Will turned the chair next to him sideways, pulled it close and leaned against it. If he were to lose consciousness, perhaps it might prevent him from falling to the floor. He glanced briefly over his shoulder and was relieved to see no spectators in attendance. Relieved, but not surprised. The lawsuit involved a dispute over an easement, of importance to the litigants, but not the sort of case to draw an audience.

The plaintiff was represented by James Wilson and the defendant by John Dickinson, the latter being the lawyer to whom Will had been apprenticed to study the law. When Dickinson informed Will that he was to make the argument on behalf of the client, he had been nervous, but excited to reach such a milestone. His excitement receded now in the face of this new physical crisis, and he was relieved not to have a lot of witnesses if a seizure came.

He willed himself to remain calm, as he thought it might help. He had no empirical proof of this, but he believed it to be so. He closed one eye and focused again on the painting of King George, this time narrowing it down to the blue velour belt. He began to breathe deeply, slowly taking in air, expanding his lungs, holding it for a couple of seconds, then letting it out, not in a rush, but slowly, under control. Gradually, he returned to automatic, unthinking, normal breathing. But despite his efforts and his wishes, his muscles suddenly and involuntarily stiffened. His whole body became rigid. Then everything went black.

* * *

The next thing he knew, Will found himself still sitting upright, though leaning a little more against the chair. The plaintiff was still on the witness stand and the attention of the others was focused there, not on him. No one else seemed to have noticed anything out of the ordinary. Good. It must have been a very brief seizure, just a few moments in that nether world, and without the convulsive twitching that sometimes accompanied an attack. He had the beginnings of a headache, a familiar hot flash of pain behind his eyes, but he could deal with the physical discomfort. He was just glad he had not made a spectacle of himself.

Will's affliction created a risk of physical harm, to be sure. He could easily fall and injure himself during an episode and had on occasion. Worse than the physical risks posed, however, was the embarrassment, the humiliation he felt when others witnessed one of his attacks. He hated being so completely out of control and vulnerable.

He knew that some people saw his condition as a sign of some serious character flaw, or even a demonic possession. He knew this because people said it to his face, or in whispers loud enough for him to hear. And those too polite to say it out loud, still thought there was something unnatural about him, something fundamentally defective at his core. And he couldn't blame them, as he thought so as well. It was as if God had meted out a punishment at his birth for a sin yet to be committed.

The sound of the witness chair scraping against the wood plank floor refocused Will's attention on the plaintiff, who had concluded his testimony and was stepping down from the witness stand. The floorboards creaked in protest as the extremely rotund man waddled over to the opposing counsel table and took his seat.

The judge blinked slowly, thick-fleshed eyelids closing over large bulging eyes. He leaned forward. "Mr. Wilson, closing argument?"

James Wilson rose slowly from his chair, moved to the podium and faced the judge. The young, Scottish-born lawyer was taller than average, at about six feet, and his lean frame and erect posture made him appear even taller. A few years earlier, Wilson had studied law with John Dickinson, just as Will was doing now. He had a lucrative practice among the Scotch-Irish settlers in Carlisle, a hundred miles to the west, and enjoyed a sterling reputation among his peers. His duties as a delegate to the Continental Congress, and the occasional case, brought him to Philadelphia often these days.

He adjusted his thick spectacles and bowed slightly in the direction of the judge. "May it please the Court."

The jurist gave him an almost imperceptible nod.

"Our claim is a simple one, Your Lordship. My client, Mr. Johnson, lawfully erected a fence enclosing his property on Fifth Street. This man, Mr. Rockwood," he said, pointing at the defendant, "intentionally tore it down." He paused for a couple of beats and retracted the accusing finger, but still looked at Rockwood as he continued. "And, when my client repaired the fence, Mr. Rockwood tore it down again."

Wilson turned back to face the judge. "Mr. Rockwood claims that he has the legal right to remove the fence because it blocks an easement he has for access to his own property." He paused again briefly. "But as the evidence has shown, he has no such easement."

Wilson lightly gripped the podium with his hands. "As Your Honor well knows, an easement, to be enforceable, must be in writing. Mr. Rockwood has not, and cannot, produce before this Court such a document."

Wilson bowed again toward the judge and returned to his seat. The judge looked in the direction of the defense counsel table. John Dickinson patted Will on the knee once and rose from his chair.

Dickinson was in his mid-forties but looked much older. His thin frame and ashen pallor gave him a frail, sickly appearance. Indeed, he had suffered from chronic health issues throughout his life. But he had a focused energy that belied his physical appearance. Intelligent, eloquent and persuasive in his arguments, polite and gracious, he was one of the most respected attorneys in all of Pennsylvania.

Dickinson was known throughout the colonies as "The Farmer," the author of a series of essays that challenged the right of Parliament to tax the colonists. *Letters from a Farmer in Pennsylvania to the Inhabitants of the British Colonies* was published almost a decade earlier in *The Pennsylvania Chronicle,* the newspaper owned by Will's father, Patrick Harrell, and had arguably sparked the growing resistance in the colonies. Ironically, Dickinson was now viewed by many as one of the most conservative members of the Continental Congress, a strong voice for reconciliation, and against separation from the mother country.

Although he and Will's father, whose paper had endorsed the independence movement, had grown apart politically in recent years, they remained friends. Will was sure that it was due in part to that friendship that Dickinson agreed to take him under his wing.

Dickinson cleared his throat and addressed the judge. "If it pleases the Court, Mr. William Harrell will argue on behalf of the defendant."

The judge cocked his head and arched an eyebrow at Will. "Very well," he said, leaning back in his chair and folding his hands in his lap. "You may proceed, Mr. Harrell."

Will stood and moved to the podium, nodded in Wilson's direction then faced the judge. It was natural that he might feel nervous, speaking for the first time in court on behalf of a client. He had expected it, had anticipated it. But he hadn't realized until this moment how truly nervous he would be.

Beads of sweat seemed to materialize instantly on his forehead, and he tried to unobtrusively wipe them away with the sleeve of his coat. Something near panic again swept over him. What if he had another seizure? He began to feel nauseated. His gut seemed to twist even tighter. He took a deep breath and willed the calm to return, but he was gripping the podium so tightly his knuckles were turning white, and he was aware of the quiver in his voice as he began.

"May it please the Court."

The judge nodded.

Will cleared his throat, then cleared it again. When he spoke, his voice registered barely more than a whisper in volume, but he managed to order his words in an organized fashion. He explained that the parcels of land owned by the respective clients were once part of a larger tract, and that the owner, Robert Clinton, had sub-divided the land into two parcels, selling one to his client, Charles Rockwood.

"It is true that, as a general rule, an easement must be in writing to be enforceable. There are exceptions, however, to this general rule." He licked his lips and looked down briefly at his notes, patted his brow lightly with the back of his hand. He opened the book in front of him to the page he had marked.

"As Mr. Blackstone has observed in his *Commentaries on the Laws of England*, 'Where a common grantor conveys two parcels, one of which is landlocked, the law presumes the grantor intended to convey an easement, a way of necessity as it is called, over the remaining parcel, and will recognize and enforce such an easement.'"

Will closed the book and looked up. "True, our client does not have a written easement, but under the facts as shown by the evidence, he has an easement implied in law, and we ask that this be confirmed by decree of the court."

Will returned to his seat, his face burning with the fear that he had mangled the presentation. He felt confident that he was right on the law, but had he effectively communicated it? The fact was, he had never felt comfortable speaking in public. He was not gifted with oratorical skills, as was his mentor, and probably never would be. At that moment he was wondering why he ever thought he could be a lawyer

After a brief rebuttal argument from Wilson, the judge paused only a few seconds before announcing his ruling.

"The Court finds that an implied easement by way of necessity exists over the lands of the plaintiff in favor of the defendant. The exact location of said easement, and its precise dimensions shall be determined in subsequent proceedings, absent an agreement between the parties in this regard. There being no further business before the Court, we shall stand adjourned."

Everyone stood as the judge rose from the bench and left the room. As his client looked on, frowning, Wilson turned to Dickinson and Will, bowed slightly and said, "Congratulations, gentlemen."

They all shook hands. Wilson suggested to Dickinson that they meet soon to "resolve the remaining issue" and the men agreed to confer the following week. And with that, Wilson and his client packed up their documents and accessories and headed for the exit. Dickinson, Will and their client remained in the courtroom, letting the opposing side put some distance between them before leaving. As they waited, Dickinson confirmed his client's understanding of what the judge had ruled and Rockwood smiled broadly.

"Masterful, simply masterful," he said, shaking Will's hand. Then he took Dickinson's hand. "Well done."

"Thank you, Mr. Rockwood," Will said. "I am glad you're satisfied with the results."

"Satisfied? I am more than satisfied, my boy. My obstinate neighbor has received his comeuppance and been suitably humbled, and I continue to have a way to get to and from my property. The drinks are on me, gentlemen," he said. "Shall we stop in at the London Coffee House? It is on the way, after all."

Despite the advice of his doctor to avoid excessive alcohol consumption, Will was not one to turn down a beer, especially if someone else was buying. Experience had convinced him that the medicinal value of beer outweighed any risks. Besides, he liked it. He looked at his mentor. John Dickinson was a serious man who eschewed frivolities, but the lawyer was also a skilled politician who knew the benefit of maintaining goodwill with his clients, which sometimes required more than winning a case for them. "Perhaps one," he said.

* * *

The gout made his gait noticeably stiff and awkward, but John Dickinson set the pace as the three men walked briskly down Market Street toward the tavern. As they walked, the conversation inevitably progressed to the topic that was on the minds and tongues of most Philadelphians, the election for the Pennsylvania Assembly scheduled for two days hence.

As a rule, Philadelphians didn't get too worked up about their elections, too busy making money to worry much about politics. This election, however, promised to be different. Voters would not only elect a new colonial government, they would, in effect, decide whether Pennsylvania would continue its policy of reconciliation with England, or join a growing movement toward separation from the mother country.

Pennsylvania's geographic position between New England and the southern colonies made it not only an economic power, but militarily strategic. And its delegation in the Continental Congress held sway over the other middle colonies of Delaware, New York, New Jersey, and Maryland, which formed a solid voting block against independence. Seventeen seats were up in all of Pennsylvania, but Philadelphia was the key. It could swing the election.

And the vote was expected to be close.

The Moderates who had run things in Philadelphia for years, and who favored reconciliation with England, were being challenged by a group who advocated not only independence, but also other liberal reforms, including an expansion of the right to vote. They called themselves the Independents. The Moderates called them, predictably, the Radicals. Passions were running deep and the usual tolerance for differing political views was strained of late.

"They are a just bunch of ruffians and anarchists, Rockwood complained, "who would bring chaos to city politics." He told Dickinson he was getting a little nervous. "You don't think those traitors have a chance, do you?"

Dickinson shook his head. "You are too harsh, Charles, to call them traitors. They are, I think, simply misguided. They also overestimate the support for their cause," he said. "It will be a close vote, no doubt, but I fully expect the Moderates to remain in control of both the local Committee and the Assembly."

Will suspected that his mentor was not nearly as confident as he sounded, as he had been campaigning vigorously the last couple of weeks, something John Dickinson had not found necessary in the past, he was sure.

"Well, let us hope that a good showing Wednesday by the sane citizens will end this thing and send those radicals back to their lairs to lick their wounds and shut up for a while."

Dickinson nodded. "Yes, we will need a good turnout of our supporters, my friend, and I am hoping you will do all you can to help with that." He paused briefly. "Our opponents will lose; I feel quite sure. And they may lick their wounds for a while, but I don't think they are going to go away for good. They are a persistent bunch." He said this with what seemed to be a hint of admiration. "They will surely look for other ways to achieve their objectives, and we will need to be ever vigilant."

"You can count on me," Rockwood said, "but be careful, John. These people will not fight fair."

This would be Will's first election, having just reached the age of 21, and he was keenly aware of what was at stake. He was also torn. His mentor was the leader of the Moderates, his father a vocal supporter of the Independents. There was also a girl in town that Will fancied, and her father was very much opposed to the notion of separation from England. Will leaned toward independence, but he could also appreciate the argument of those who urged caution. He planned to vote the Independent slate, but was not what you might call an ardent, and certainly not a vocal, supporter.

In fact, he generally kept his opinions to himself as he tried to navigate the local political landscape. Dickinson, who no doubt suspected his leanings, politely never pressed him on the subject. His father, for his part, had always encouraged independent thinking in his children and did not condemn his son's relative neutrality on the subject. As for the father of the girl, he scrupulously tried to avoid the subject entirely. If he couldn't—the man sometimes pressed for a response—he kept his comments as general and neutral as possible, and never directly contradicted the man. And Will was relieved now that their client, who did not hide his strong views against independence, had not asked for his opinion.

At the entrance, Will held the door for the two men as they stepped inside. The London Coffee House was crowded, as usual, its clientele mixed, by politics, income, and social status. The wood and stone walls were dank and dark, illuminated by the occasional oil lamp. As one might expect, the place smelled strongly of alcoholic beverages, especially beer and rum, the two favorites here. Clouds of acrid smoke hung in the air.

As Rockwood ordered a round of ales, Will was alerted to the sound of a familiar voice. It was coming from a table in the back corner. Although he couldn't make out the words, the tone and volume told him it was the sound of trouble brewing, and he headed immediately toward its source.

Philadelphia, April 29
Chapter 4

Patrick Harrell stood and threw his cards on the table, glowering at the man seated across from him. "What I'm saying, Massey, is that it takes more than blind luck for you to keep winning every hand."

The other man, a ship's captain named Clark Massey, stood and also threw down his cards. "You accusing me of cheatin, Harrell?"

Before his father could answer the rhetorical question, Will stepped between them. He faced his father, gripping his wrist, but it was the other man to whom he spoke. "No, Mr. Massey, my father is just a little drunk. No offense intended."

Will's father shook loose of his grip, but he made no move toward Massey, who looked skeptical, but said, "No offense taken then." He turned toward his chair at the table.

"In point of fact, however," Will said, "your righteous indignation is a little overplayed, don't you think?"

"What?" Massey whipped his head toward the younger Harrell, his face twisted in anger.

"Because you were indeed cheating, weren't you?" Will looked past the man to the other card players at the table, who were now plainly interested.

"Just like your father, ain't cha?" the ship's captain said, clenching a fist as he began moving toward him.

Will waited until Massey drew close, then grabbed his wrist firmly, flipped his palm up, and pushed the man's coat sleeve up. Revealed there were two cards, an ace of spades and an ace of diamonds, tucked into a band around his wrist. The men at the table emitted a collective gasp. Still holding onto the man's wrist, Will removed the two cards and tossed them on the table.

The false anger drained from Massey then, and his shoulders slumped. His eyes darted around the room as if searching for an escape route. The faces of the men at the table were a mix of anger, disgust, and disappointment.

One of the men said, "Clark, what is the meaning of this?"

Patrick Harrell stepped forward, a small smile on his lips. "The meaning of this," he said, "is that the man's a cheat, like I said. He has stolen our money." Now he looked at Massey, who would not meet his eyes.

"I swear, I didn't use em," the man said to the others. "I weren't cheatin."

The men at the table rose and circled the ship's captain. One of them motioned with his eyes to two large men who had been watching from the bar. They came forward and held onto Massey as the others took all the money he had on him and put it in a pile on the table, which they then divided as he looked on, helpless. Another signal to the two large men, and they began to haul the offender toward the back of the tavern, his whining, pleading entreaties fading into the alley as the door closed behind them.

Patrick Harrell allowed his son to direct him away from the table then and after a few feet he whispered, "You didn't have to insert yourself, boy. I had the situation under control."

"I'm sure you did, Father, but I didn't want the gentleman to get hurt."

"How did you know he was cheating? You couldn't have seen it."

Will gave him a small smile. "A couple of months ago, I watched him cheat some of his crew at cards. Different tavern, but same method. I assumed the man had no imagination, that he remained partial to the clumsy, but familiar, cards-up-the-sleeve trick."

His father chuckled. "Yes, no imagination at all." He tousled his son's hair and said, "It would have been embarrassing, though, if those cards hadn't been there."

Will shrugged.

"At any rate, I will keep your secret and not tell the others, who no doubt have concluded that you have magical powers."

"Or satanic."

His father frowned and nodded, conceding the point. "Want to join the game? Seems that we have an opening."

Will shook his head.

"Yeah, I think I'll call it as well. Buy you a beer?"

Will looked closely at the man then, seeing an older version of himself. Patrick Harrell was tall, eye to eye with his son, and lean, though he'd grown soft around the middle. His auburn hair, tied in the back with a ribbon, had grey streaks around the temples, and his once handsome face had grown slack, puffy from age and too much drink. The clothes were of high quality but were frayed, displaying the wear and tear of years, and neglect. He was still concerned with appearances, but depression and drink had worn that down too. The once piercing green eyes now seemed faded, dulled by not just intoxicants, but by a cynicism that had replaced the once skeptical but curious, open-mindedness. It made Will wonder how far the apple had fallen from the tree.

"Actually, I'm with Mr. Dickinson and a client," Will said, looking over in the direction of the two men seated at a table up in another corner. They waved. "Perhaps you'd care to join us," Will said, though without enthusiasm, certain that if the conversation turned to politics, his father would eventually say something to embarrass himself, and his son.

"No, thanks," he said, to his son's relief. "I've got to get back to the shop." He hesitated a beat, then said, "How did it go in court this afternoon?"

35

Will gave him a quick, and objective summary of what had occurred, not mentioning the seizure.

"Congratulations. You should take a moment to celebrate," he said, looking in the direction of Dickinson and Rockwood. Then he patted his son on the shoulder, placed his hat on his head, turned and walked toward the front door.

When Will returned to the table, Rockwood said, "Nasty business, there." He cocked his head in the direction of the table of card players.

Will shrugged but said nothing in response as he took a seat at the table.

Rockwood said, "I understand that you work in your family's businesses and also study law with John?"

"Yes, sir."

"Good God, boy, how do you find the time?"

Will shrugged again. "I go into the print shop in the morning, help my brother get the printing presses ready, prepare the layout for the newspaper, maybe do some writing or editing, then go to Mr. Dickinson's office. I return in the late afternoon to help with printing jobs or in the bookstore into the evening. At night, I read the law. It's not as much as it sounds." He looked over at Dickinson, "My employers are very understanding and flexible in accommodating my schedule. And, I require little sleep."

Rockwood nodded approvingly. Young men were expected to work long hours if they were to get ahead in the world. In Will's case, it was more a matter of having a variety of interests. He enjoyed obtaining new knowledge and learning new skills, and he took full advantage of the fact that he worked in the largest, most well-stocked bookstore in the colonies. His failure to light upon a single career path—law was only the most recent of his pursuits—had prompted some to label him a dabbler, a jack of all trades. It was not meant as a compliment.

Will managed to steer the conversation away from himself, but talk of family, of business and commerce eventually turned into observations of increased crime in the city, which somehow morphed into a renewed discussion of the upcoming election and the "ruffians and anarchists" as Rockwood described them, who were behind the "revolution" brewing in Philadelphia politics.

Dickinson seemed poised to say something in response when they heard his name called out. They turned to see three men approaching. Two were visitors to Philadelphia but well known in the city by appearance and by reputation. Samuel Adams and John Hancock were both delegates to the Continental Congress from Massachusetts, and Hancock was its president. Will knew them both as his family's shop was the official printer for the Congress. The other, Tim Matlack, a clerk to the Congress, he had known all his life.

Matlack was in his mid-forties, about the same age as Dickinson, but he looked a good ten years younger. He was tall and lean, with a slight paunch. His receding brown hair created a "V" on his forehead. He was one of the leaders of the Independents, but was friendly, gregarious, and well-liked, even by those who disagreed with his politics. He was especially popular with the common folk in the taverns and on the streets, due in part to the fact that, in addition to his work with the Congress and at his brewery, he organized regular cockfights and bull baits in the city.

Sam Adams was of middling height and weight and looked a good bit older than his companions. He was dressed plainly, even shabbily. He was frail looking, and Will noted the slight tremor in his hand. Hancock, in contrast, was tall, lean and handsome. He was dressed in lavish finery, befitting a man of great wealth, much of which came from an organized and extensive smuggling enterprise. He was known to be extroverted and not a little vain, and perhaps an unlikely rebel. But Adams, appealing to his self interest in protecting his lucrative smuggling trade, had recruited Hancock to the rebel cause early and the two had become loyal partners in the resistance movement in Boston, with Adams its chief strategist and Hancock its financier.

Hancock had been miffed when Adams and his cousin, John Adams, also a delegate to the Congress, had worked to have George Washington appointed as head of the Continental Army. It was a post that Hancock had coveted, and expected, but for which he was singularly unqualified. And no one else was surprised at the appointment of Washington, including the man himself, despite his feigned humility and self-deprecation. After all, the man attended the Continental Congress wearing his military uniform. Not very subtle. The friendship between Adams and Hancock had cooled a bit as a result, but they remained political allies.

The three men were on the opposite sides of the independence issue from Dickinson, but if political discord created tension between them, you wouldn't have known it from his reaction. He rose from his chair. "Sam, John, Tim, how nice to see you." He introduced Rockwood to Adams and Hancock, and then said, "What a pleasant coincidence. Please, join us."

The three men remained standing. Hancock bowed his head slightly and said, "Thank you, John, but it is not a coincidence. Actually, we ran into Patrick Harrell and he suggested we might find you here."

"I see," Dickinson said, arching his eyebrows. "I assume it must be of some importance then, for you to have tracked me here."

"Indeed, it is, an urgent and confidential matter." Hancock hesitated a moment, then looked directly at Will. "But in truth, we have come particularly to speak with your young apprentice, Mr. Harrell."

For several awkward moments, no one spoke. The silence, however, did not seem to prompt the visitors to say more. "I see," Dickinson finally said. He looked over at his client. "Charles, if you wouldn't mind."

The other man nodded. "Of course." He bowed. "Gentleman, I will take my leave. A pleasure to have met you both," he said, a little too formally to have been sincere.

The two congressional delegates bowed in return and watched silently as the man made his way across the room. Dickinson turned to face the men. "Would you like to speak in private with Will?"

"Oh, no," Hancock said. "This concerns you as well."

Dickinson nodded. "Would you like to go to my office, for more privacy?"

Sam Adams looked around the room once. "I think this will do," he said, taking a seat in one of the chairs. Hancock and Matlack followed his lead.

Adams leaned in and spoke, his volume just above a whisper, which forced Will to also lean forward to hear him. "Tim tells me that you have a rather uncanny ability to solve puzzles and decipher codes."

Will shifted in his seat and stared at the tabletop. In truth, he did seem to have a certain knack for spotting patterns, an ability to see things with his mind's eye that others struggled with. And he could do it quickly. It was not something he liked to advertise, though, as some saw it as more evidence of sorcery on his part.

"I do like a good puzzle," he said. "Gone through every puzzle book we've gotten at the store, at least a couple of times, and a book on the history of codes. I guess I do all right at it, better than most, perhaps."

"And a coded message is a form of puzzle," Adams said.

He nodded.

Adams removed from a small leather pouch a folded, two-page document, which he unfolded and placed on the table. Will couldn't read the writing on the parchment paper, but he could see that the script was elaborate, ornate, and in the style of a literate person.

Adams looked around the room, and then said, "This letter was intercepted by one of our people in Boston. It carries the seal of Alexander Lewis, chief assistant secretary to our former governor."

"The beloved Thomas Hutchinson," Hancock said with a smile and a wink to Adams.

"Yes," Adams said, returning the smile, "our dear friend, Thomas." He looked back to Will. "The letter is addressed to Lord Frederick North."

"The Prime Minister," Will said.

Adams looked at him, a little surprised it seemed that he would know this. Then he nodded. "I understand the man prefers 'First Minister,' humble to a fault he is, but yes, the one and same man most to blame for the destructive policies toward the colonies these last several years."

He fingered the document lightly and Will noticed the tremor in his hand again. "The man in whose possession the letter was discovered swore that he knew nothing of the contents and was merely a courier. After some, uh, rather intense questioning," he said, looking briefly at Hancock before focusing on Will, "they concluded that perhaps he was telling the truth." He hesitated, arching an eyebrow. "Anyway, the man was let go; the letter was kept."

Adams pushed the document over to Will, who picked it up and began to examine it.

"As you can see," Adams continued, "it appears to be a rather dull communication about their respective families. It is possible, of course, that the letter is what it appears to be. Lewis is, after all, the nephew of North, and the sentiments expressed are not unusual or unexpected. But given the present circumstances between the colonies and England, and the role of Lord North as the chief architect of the war against us, we thought a healthy dose of skepticism was prudent. The letter may carry a hidden message, and if so, uncovering it might prove useful to our cause. I'd like you to see if you can solve this puzzle, if puzzle it is."

Will nodded then, and he began to focus on the document, only slightly aware of the continued conversation at the table. After some time, he heard Dickinson say, "Will?" in a voice louder than usual.

Will looked up.

"Did you not hear Mr. Hancock?"

Will turned his attention to Hancock, who smiled at him. He, Matlack and Adams were standing, preparing to leave.

"Sorry to break your concentration, Will. I was just saying we'd leave the letter with you and check back in a couple of days. We have made a copy just in case, but please keep it secure. For your eyes only at this time."

Will looked briefly at the other men, then back to Hancock. "That won't be necessary, Mr. Hancock," he said. "I think I have figured it out."

"What?" Hancock said.

Will nodded, looking from one man to the other. "It is an example of masked correspondence." He was greeted by blank faces. He placed the folded letter on the table. "The method's been around at least a couple of hundred years, first used by the Italians, and it can be quite effective, depending on how intricate the mask used. The recipient places the correct mask over the document, and it blocks out the unwanted letters or words so that the secret message is revealed."

All four men were staring at him. Everyone took a seat at the table again.

"Fortunately," Will said, "the author used a rather simple horseshoe pattern, or upside-down U for the mask. So, although I didn't have the actual mask to place over the letter, I was able to decipher the hidden message without it." He retrieved a blank sheet of paper from his satchel. "Perhaps it would be best if I showed you, with a make-shift mask."

Using the straight edge of the table, he tore the blank paper into six narrow strips. He placed the two strips along the left side of the letter and two along the right side, so that they framed vertical columns, and the other two strips he placed across the top of the letter to form an upside-down U. He adjusted them a little, and then looked at Tim Matlack. "Tim, if you would. The words are to be read in ascending order, up the page, every fifth word in the column."

The man leaned over the table and studied the document a moment, and began to read, haltingly. "Our man is off to the snake pit to..." Will directed him to the horizontal column. "sever the heads of the snake..." Matlack looked up at Will.

"There's a bit more on the second page," Will said, "just one column, though."

Matlack arranged the strips along the left side of the other page and he read again, quicker now, having adjusted to the pattern. "Contacts directed to assist as needed."

There was silence around the table for several seconds until Sam Adams broke it. "Are you sure of this, Will?"

"Not at all," he said, then paused, letting it sink in. "I may be seeing something not intended. There may be no secret message at all. Or the message was intended to be uncovered, as a diversion." He waited another few moments before adding, "But this is what seemed to jump out at me."

Adams looked from face to face. "Well, what do we make of this message, gentlemen?"

No one spoke immediately. Finally, Matlack suggested, "A spy, an assassin, is headed to New York—the snake pit—to attempt an assassination of George Washington."

Dickinson frowned. "I've been to New York," he said, "and I would concur that it is a pit." The others smiled briefly. "And if anyone would be considered the head of our effort against the Crown, it would be General Washington."

Matlack looked at Will. "What do you think?"

All eyes turned to him. After a slight hesitation, he responded, "The author refers to heads, not head, of the snake."

"An inadvertent grammatical error, perhaps," Dickinson suggested. "Perhaps."

Dickinson folded his arms across his chest. "How do you interpret the message?"

Will hesitated again for a couple of moments. "There are a number of possibilities, but I'd say the snake pit refers to the Continental Congress, no offense intended," he said, looking around at the faces of the men.

"None taken, I assure you," Hancock said, the barest hint of a smile crossing his face.

Will continued. "The heads of the snake refer to the leaders of the Congress, more specifically, those who appear to the British Ministry to be the more ardent rebels, the ones pushing for independence." He looked at Hancock and Adams. "And both of you most assuredly fall into this category." The men nodded but said nothing, so he went on.

"A person, a British soldier, or more likely a spy, has been sent to Philadelphia to assassinate two or more of those leaders." Again, the men nodded but remained silent as he continued. "It also suggests that there are persons in this city, and perhaps in the Congress as well, who are prepared to help this man with his mission."

When the other men still did not respond, he made what he thought was an obvious observation, "Gentlemen, you may have a traitor in your midst."

Dusk had settled on the city when Will left the tavern, but the streets were still awash with activity, busy and noisy. Visitors to Philadelphia often complained of the dirt, noise, and congestion of the largest city in North America. They considered the constant activity to be an irritating, anxiety-producing distraction, and longed for the pastoral quiet and solitude of the farms and villages from whence they came. But like most Philadelphians, Will liked the energy of the city's commerce. He found comfort in the rattling of carriages, coaches, and wagons in the streets, the crowded sidewalks, the din of conversation that drifted out of the many taverns along the way.

By the time he turned onto Locust Street, traffic in the streets and on the sidewalks had lightened a bit. The dusk was turning to dark and city workers were beginning to light the streetlamps. The pain behind his eyes had lingered, and spread, like a colony of ants scurrying around inside his head, adding to the urgency he felt to replenish his supply of medication. He just hoped the apothecary would be in his shop.

Christopher Marshall was a talented druggist and chemist. He had owned and operated Marshall's Apothecary on Locust Street since 1729, though in recent years he had given his children more and more control over the business. Although they had proved capable, he quarreled regularly with them and complained to anyone who would listen that his offspring were in general an ungrateful lot who tended to cheat him and treat him with disrespect.

He had a reputation as a stubborn, crotchety old man who was a little strange, and who harbored resentments for perceived ill treatment from others. He was a devout Quaker but had been ousted from the

Society of Friends years earlier for associating with counterfeiters—though he was never found guilty of any crime. He insisted that he had been ostracized because of his faithful observance of the "enthusiasms" of the religion—such as going naked and quaking when he prayed.

Will thought he was probably correct in this. The modern Quakers had moved away from these old-fashioned practices—which had caused them much persecution in other colonies—and the Friends had become, as a result, more accepted by those of other faiths. Indeed, Quakers had dominated business and politics in Philadelphia for decades. They were no doubt embarrassed by the evangelicals like Marshall and didn't have to look too hard to find a reason to disown him.

Will had always gotten along well with Marshall, who seemed to have a genuine fondness for him, and a sincere desire to find him some relief. The apothecary had used his considerable knowledge of the mysterious world of drugs and chemistry to help address the symptoms of his epilepsy. He experimented with various concoctions in the effort, adjusting dosages, varying the types and proportions of ingredients, then monitoring the results.

His doctor, Benjamin Rush, had suggested he would grow out of the epilepsy, but he was now 21 and it was still with him. And there was no solid proof that anything Marshall had tried had really made a difference, that any variation in the number and intensity of his attacks was anything more than coincidence. But Will continued to cling to the hope that they could find just the right combination. He felt sure that the medication had at least helped with his headaches, and that was worth a lot.

Marshall was also one of the leaders of the city's Independents and had been actively campaigning for their slate of candidates the last several days. Indeed, Will had seen him earlier in the day handing out broadsides at the docks. He was thus a little surprised, though glad, to find the man there, two nights before the election, hunched over some paperwork at a small desk. Behind the counter was his daughter-in-law, who smiled at Will as he stepped through the doorway.

"Good evening, Will," she said. "How are you?"

"I am well, Mrs. Marshall. And you?"

She frowned. "Jane, please. You make me feel like an old woman."

"Sorry," he said, then added, "Jane."

"What can we do for you?"

Before he could answer, Christopher Marshall looked up from his paperwork and said, "You have had another seizure."

Will nodded.

The older man stood and moved around the desk to come closer. He was a tall man, with a wild, wiry tuff of white hair that made him seem taller. He was narrow at the shoulders and wide in the hips, and slightly stooped in his posture. He adjusted his spectacles as he studied the young man. "Tell me about it."

Will hesitated and looked in Jane's direction. She took the hint and excused herself to go off to the other side of the shop—to check inventory, she said. Then Will told Marshall about the episode that afternoon in the courtroom. The man listened intently, and when Will finished, he nodded, then smiled.

"That is real progress, though, don't you think?"

Will shrugged. "I suppose so."

"Could have been much worse."

"Yes."

"Headache?"

Will nodded.

"But no additional seizures?"

"No."

"This **is** a good sign. Any bad side effects from the medication?"

"Not really. Not that I've noticed. I have run out of my supply, though, which is why I have come to see you."

Marshall pursed his lips and shook his head. "You should always have a supply, Will. It is important to keep to the regimen." He rubbed his hands together. "I will mix up a new batch, then." He turned and began searching the shelves behind him. He selected three different containers and took them to a workstation. Over his shoulder he said, "I suspect the stress of making your first legal argument may have contributed to triggering the seizure."

Will was surprised that the man would have this bit of information. "I suppose so."

"You should avoid too much excitement or stress if you can help it—which is easier said than done, I know." He chuckled, turning to face Will. "Anything particularly stressful you might have to deal with in the near future?"

"Not really. Nothing more than the usual." The lie had come quickly and easily. In fact, his life had just gotten more complicated, but he had been sworn to secrecy.

Marshall turned and gave him a skeptical look, as if alerted to something in Will's tone of voice, but he returned to his preparation and said, "It will only take a few minutes."

Will paced while he waited, then leaned against the counter for a bit, then paced some more, deep in thought. Matters had progressed quickly at The London Coffee House once he announced his interpretation of the coded message. There was a shocked silence for several seconds as the men considered Will's suggestion that they might have a spy, a confederate, in the Congress.

Adams was the first to speak, looking around at the others. "If the snake is the Congress, whom among us would have the honor of being the heads?"

"I vote for Ben Franklin as the head of the heads, as it were," Hancock said. "He seems to get all the attention anyway."

"I'm sure that if he were here," Adams said, smiling, "he would modestly decline the honor."

"No doubt," agreed Dickinson, "Given the bounty the British government has put on both of your heads, you two most certainly would qualify." The three men chuckled softly and looked at Will, as if for confirmation.

He managed a weak smile. "Assuming the author is referring to those who may be viewed as key leaders of the Congress, potential targets would most assuredly include the men in this room, as well as Mr. Franklin."

"Well," Hancock said after a brief silence, "then Franklin chose a good time to get out of town."

Benjamin Franklin had, in fact, probably not wanted to leave the city, but had been asked to lead a team of commissioners on an important, though what would ultimately prove to be a fruitless, mission to Canada, to convince the people there to join in the fight against England."

Adams said, "I think I'd rather face an assassin's bullet than endure the physical and diplomatic difficulties of the mission he has undertaken."

"You may get your wish," Hancock said, "if young Master Harrell here has accurately decoded the letter."

"Hmm," Adams said, looking in Will's direction. He then looked over at Hancock and raised an eyebrow, as if communicating a question to him, which the other man answered with a single nod. Adams turned to Will. "We would like you to lead an investigation of this matter. As you say, it may be nothing. Probably is nothing. And Lord knows, the threat of death is something that hangs over the head of every delegate to the Congress. But if there is an assassin headed our way, and confederates among us, we need to know it, and we need to thwart their plan."

Will stared at him for a few seconds, then found his voice. "I am flattered Mr. Adams, but surely there are members of the Congress, delegates, who are much more qualified for such an assignment, and whose stature in the body would allow them the latitude to make the necessary, but delicate, inquiries of other members."

Adams looked around the room again, then leaned forward and spoke softly. "I think you underestimate your abilities, Will."

Dickinson nodded in confirmation. "He helped Sheriff Dewees solve the murder of Howard Bell's servant, and the theft of jewelry from Mrs. Peabody, and that was just this past year."

Will shrugged. "The sheriff is a cousin of mine, on my mother's side, and it's more that he was indulging my curiosity than I was of any real assistance."

Adams said, "Look at it as just another sort of puzzle to solve, and you'd be providing a great service to the cause in the doing."

"And as for cooperation from the delegates and those who have accompanied them to Philadelphia, and the authority to question them, I will see to that," Hancock said.

The four men looked expectantly at Will, who could barely contain his excitement at the prospect. Being of service to the cause was at best mild motivation, but the challenge of this real and most dangerous puzzle was very appealing. In a tone meant to conceal his eagerness he said, "Under the circumstances, I don't see how I can refuse."

So, yes, he thought now, as he watched Marshall work his magic, he had been thrust into something likely to produce stress and anxiety. The responsibility of his new assignment weighed heavily on his mind and would until concluded. But it was not something he could share with the apothecary, or anyone else for that matter.

Will watched as the apothecary measured and mixed the ingredients. He did not know exactly what was in the concoction Marshall prepared for him, and it had varied over time, but two ingredients were always present—a good amount of a bitter, reddish-brown opium mixture called Laudanum and a small amount of crushed coca leaves that Marshall had obtained from the high mountain ranges of South America.

The former, the use of which was common in the colonies, was to aid with the headaches and other physical pain associated with his affliction. The latter, much rarer, was intended to offset the fatigue, the lack of energy resulting from the former. Marshall explained that the stimulating effects of coca leaves increased breathing which in turn increased oxygen intake. It gave native laborers of the region who chewed on the leaves the stamina to perform their work in the thin air at high altitudes.

To counter the bitterness of its taste, Marshall advised that he mix the substance with syllabub, an alcoholic drink made from sweetened milk or cream and curdled wine or spirits. Will was not particularly fond of the mixture, but he had, over time, grown accustomed to the taste.

The apothecary cinched up the leather bag in front of him, walked over to where Will stood and placed the pouch on the counter. "Try this, lad, and let me know how you do on it."

"Thank you," Will said, taking the pouch, and then, as usual, he asked how much he should pay him. And, as usual, the apothecary declined payment, noting that Will was helping him with an experiment, and the information learned was of great value. It was the same question and answer each time, no matter how much Will insisted. He tucked the pouch into his waistband and said, "How are you feeling about the election tomorrow?"

Marshall looked a little surprised at the question. Indeed, Will didn't know why he had asked, except to be polite to the man who had just given him valuable medical assistance—for free.

"Very confident, Will, and excited."

"It's gotten pretty heated, don't you think?"

"Of course, it has. The stakes are very high."

The older man's eyes burned with the fire of passion and defiance, and Will had the sense that further discussion might darken what had been up to then a genial mood, so he said, "Good luck Wednesday," thanked him again and left the shop.

Once outside, he walked quickly to the nearest tavern and ordered a mug of syllabub. He mixed an amount of the powder into it and drank, downing it in three large gulps. Then he headed back out into the street.

* * *

At that precise moment, the man who was known as Henry Belmont to the patriots in Boston, and James Arden Howe to the young couple with whom he had shared a coach to New York, rode into Philadelphia on horseback. He had come from New York by way of New Jersey. It had been a long, tiring trip, but he sat erect in the saddle, his clothes a little dusty but well fitting, and expensive. The horse, a Narragansett Pacer, sure-footed and long on endurance, had been stolen from the stables of a large estate on Long Island. The clothes, fashionable and perfectly fitted, had been provided by a loyalist tailor in New York City.

It was his first visit to Philadelphia and his initial impression was favorable. The city was laid out with wide streets and brick sidewalks, flanked by lofty elms and Italian poplars, magnificent public buildings and well-kept homes of brick, both elegant and modest. The waterfront and the streets were thick with people and bustling with activity. There was an intangible energy about the place that exhilarated him, despite his tiredness. He decided he was going to enjoy his time here.

At the corner of Market and Third Streets, he reined his horse to a stop at a building which fronted Third Street. The large wooden sign above the entrance identified it as *The White Horse Livery and Stables.* It was a large, red brick structure with wide, wooden double doors that were opened and fastened against the outer walls by iron hooks. The man dismounted and handed the reins to the tall, skinny boy of about 14 or 15 who had come from inside the building.

"Board your horse, mister?"

"Perhaps, lad. What is the charge?"

He could tell that his affected French accent took the boy by surprise, but the lad recovered quickly and told the man the daily and weekly rates.

The man arched an eyebrow. "That's a little steep, don't you think?"

"Oh, no, sir," the boy said, flashing a smile as he gently patted the horse. "It is within the rate structure set by the city council, sir, and considering that your horse will be well fed and well groomed, looked after as befitting the fine animal he is, it is a good value for the price." He tendered the reins to the man. "But, if you prefer a lower rate, I can recommend some other establishments."

The man gave him a small smile and nod of appreciation and did not take back the reins. "You are a good salesman, my boy." He took some coins from his vest pocket and placed them in the lad's outstretched palm. "Here is three days' worth. I will be back to arrange more long-term arrangements when I have determined how long my business might take."

"And what sort of business would that be, mister?"

"My business," he said with a coldness that took the boy aback.

"I'm sorry, sir. I didn't mean to pry."

The man hesitated, and then gave him a smile. "Of course you didn't. I was just teasing you, my young friend. In point of fact, I am a writer, visiting in your country from France. I intend to record and publish a journal of my travels here." He gave him a small bow. "Monsieur Henri Dubois Tremont at your service."

"Nice to meet you, Mr. Tremont. I'm Richard Boutwell." The two exchanged a handshake. "Welcome to Philadelphia, sir."

"*Merci.* And since I have followed your advice concerning my horse, perhaps you might have a recommendation for suitable lodgings?"

"Oh, yes, sir." The boy pointed to a building across Market Street.

The man turned to see where he pointed. He smiled, reading the sign out in front of the building. "*The White Horse Inn*, eh?" He turned back to the boy. "I assume it is not a coincidence?"

The boy nodded. "My uncle is the proprietor. I believe you will find the accommodations and the food—"

The man interrupted him with a raised hand. "I know, a good value for the price."

When the boy nodded, the man smiled, removed the saddle bags from his horse, turned and began walking across the street.

Philadelphia, May 1
Chapter 6

On election day, the morning sky was clear, and the air a little cooler than expected, with a fresh wind blowing in from the Delaware River. By early afternoon, it had turned into one of those nearly perfect spring days that makes one forget how miserably hot it would inevitably become in the summer. Almost.

At a little after two o'clock, Will and Patrick Harrell headed toward the State House, where polling for the election had begun at ten that morning. They had both already voted but were curious to see how things were going, to observe and later report about it in the newspaper.

Will walked slightly hunched over, his head forward, eyes down, hands in the pockets of a sleeveless jacket. Occasionally, recalling his late mother's admonition to "straighten up your spine and see the world around you," he would hold his head up, his shoulders back, and walk with what he thought looked like purpose and confidence. But it never lasted. Eventually, he reverted to what came naturally.

It hadn't rained in several days and the accumulation of horse dung in the streets and rotting garbage on the sides was beginning to smell strongly. The odor was nothing, however, compared to the horrific stench coming from Dock Creek, a small stream which wound its way through the heart of the city, and which was used as an open sewer by the tan yards and stables that flanked it. Will thought that local leaders would do well to concentrate more on such matters close to home rather than trying to change the world, but he did not share those thoughts with his father.

In fact, neither had been particularly talkative on any subject. Will told his father about his new position with the Congress, and he was pressed for details, which he could not provide, he said, citing his vow of secrecy.

Patrick snorted. "What's the good of having a son on the inside, if I can't get inside information?"

Will shrugged and said, "Sorry."

Patrick smiled. "Just teasing. I know you can't talk about what goes on. But I have heard a rumor that they were tightening up on security at the Congress for some reason. Maybe you could just give me a hint?"

"Father," Will said, wagging his finger at him.

His father smiled again and shrugged, but pressed the son no further, and they fell back into a comfortable silence as they continued down Fifth Street. Now, as they turned the corner onto Chestnut and came closer to their destination, Will broached the topic of the day. "Who do you think will win the election?"

Patrick Harrell shrugged. "What do you think?"

"I think it will be close, but I think the Independents have the momentum. They're better organized and more passionate in their efforts, and they have been more effective with their propaganda."

His father nodded. "We are all patriots; they are all traitors. You say it often enough and loud enough, people begin to believe you, or at least are unsure what to believe."

"I hear a *but* in there."

His father paused. "They are promoting some fairly radical ideas—expansion of suffrage mainly—that make some people really nervous. They are losing the moderates who favor independence but don't want to change the status quo that much."

"Don't want to give up their favored political status."

"Exactly," he said, nodding and smiling. "And unlike some of our neighbors, Pennsylvania has so far been relatively untouched by the war. It remains economically vibrant and a lot of people feel that we benefit from our commerce with England and the protection of the Royal Navy on the seas."

"So?"

"So, my prediction is that the Independents will lose today."

Will pursed his lips. His father might be wrong, but he usually got it right. "We'll see," Will said, just as the State House came into view.

The building was located on Chestnut, between Fifth and Sixth Streets, and was easily the most impressive and imposing structure in the city. Forty-four feet wide and more than a hundred feet deep, it was crowned by a sixty-nine-foot-tall masonry bell tower, which made it the equivalent of a six-story building. The bell within the tower contained a biblical inscription that seemed appropriate for the times: "Proclaim liberty throughout the land unto all the inhabitants thereof." The Pennsylvania Assembly and the Supreme Court met there, as did now the Continental Congress.

A line of men extended outside the entrance for about a hundred feet along Chestnut Street, inching ever so slowly forward. The Harrells moved past the sea of tri-cornered hats and entered the building, where the line snaked down the wide hallway and into the chambers to the left. Sheriff Dewees's deputy, Thomas Barr, had stationed himself in the hallway. The mood was somber and serious, the tension palpable. Patrick spoke to a few of the men in line and received a cordial but terse response, or simply a nod.

"Thomas," Patrick said to the deputy, "how are you?"

He gave them a small smile. "Good, Patrick, Will. Nice to see you both."

They came closer and shook hands with the man.

"Looks like a big turnout," the father observed.

"Been like this since the polls opened, a steady stream."

"Any trouble?"

He shook his head. "Not in here. Not on my watch." Thomas was a big fellow, and his size alone often discouraged disorderly conduct when he was around. He looked down the line. "Nobody wants to risk being run out of here and not get to vote today." He said this last line in a louder voice, expanding his audience. The men in line looked briefly in his direction then returned to looking straight ahead.

Barr pointed with his chin toward the rear entrance. "A lot of folks have been hanging around after they vote, though, out in the courtyard. Things have been heating up a bit out there, but nothing more than the usual insults, a little pushing and shoving, that sort of thing. Nothing serious."

Will and his father made their way to the rear entrance and stepped outside into the courtyard, an enclosed space that went all the way to Walnut Street. It was a large area, but it was congested now, and too close quarters for the many divisive factions that had gathered there.

A great groundswell of noise from a multitude of voices greeted them. Men were congregated in groups by ethnicity, religion and politics. The aroma of burning tobacco wafted through the air, mixed with the earthen smells of the farmers—of mud and hogs and cows and chickens—and though not allowed at polling sites, the strong odor of beer.

Patrick ambled in one direction and Will in the other. Just outside, to the left, sitting on the corner of the steps, was an Indian of the Oneidas tribe who Will recognized. Will did not know what he was called in his native tongue, only the English name he used—George Williams. The man had engaged the services of John Dickinson early in Will's apprenticeship, and Will had found him to be likeable, honest and honorable.

George was well known for his craftsmanship with wood, not just in the frivolities of carvings but also for the beautiful and functional furniture he made for wealthy clients. He was now whittling on a piece of wood, yet unformed, and he looked up and nodded at Will, who sat down beside him.

"What are you making, George?"

He shrugged. "It's supposed to be a horse," he said, his English flawless and accent free, belying the fact that it was not his first language.

Will looked at the piece of wood, noncommittal, then looked around the courtyard. "This doesn't seem to be a great place to concentrate."

He frowned. "No, but I sold three figurines earlier, so good for business. Besides, it's been interesting, and I think it's about to get even more interesting." He jerked his head toward a group gathered on the west wall. "Cannon's been stoking the Germans, getting them riled up."

Will looked over to where George had pointed and recognized James Cannon, a math teacher at the Academy and College of Philadelphia, and a core leader of the Independents. A big burley man with intense, black eyes, which were accentuated by massively bushy eyebrows, he had the analytical and creative mind of a mathematician, which he had used effectively to organize the impoverished and un-propertied of the city slums and the backcountry into a significant political force, its members drawn mostly from the militias.

There were some thirty companies of militia formed in Philadelphia and 53 battalions of associators spread across the backcountry. The men elected most of their officers, so there was a democratic tradition to build on, and the citizens depended on their service. Cannon had recognized the potential there and formed the "Committee of Privates" which had become a formidable political force in the colony, with Cannon as their secretary and undisputed leader.

Cannon was saying something Will couldn't make out, but he clearly heard the response from another man in the group, his German accent heavy and his voice loud.

"Yes, they are content to get rich on the backs of common folk. They couldn't care less about what is good for all. They will keep us down until we rise up and take what is ours. Bunch of hypocrites who talk liberty but keep slaves and indentured servants and send us to fight their wars for them. Not much better than the English lords they rail against, if you ask me."

The group turned to follow the gaze of the man, which was focused on another small group of men across the yard. At the center of the group was a man Will recognized as Joseph Swift, who appeared to have been listening to the comments, and didn't like what he heard.

Swift was not a loyalist. He was a patriot, a well-respected citizen and businessman, on the board of the hospital and on the vestry of Christ Church. He was willing to put his fortune and life at risk in resisting the British. But he also supported moderation and had been a vocal critic of what he considered the radical ideas of the Independents. Like many people, he assumed that the Germans, or the Dutch, as they were often called, favored those radical political ideas.

Swift was portly and wore expensive clothes. He puffed out his chest with importance, though it was never enough to reach further than his enormous stomach. He spoke loud enough for the Germans to hear.

"They come here and stay for two years, pay a small fee and become a citizen. But they don't care enough to learn English, but want instead to cling to their strange, guttural language, and their strange food and customs. They don't understand our traditions. They don't share our values. Imagine not having to have property to vote. What chaos. No stake in society, only looking out for themselves. Except for that ludicrously easy path to naturalization, none of them would have a right to vote. And they shouldn't. The Dutch have no more business voting than do the Negroes or the Indians."

Will looked briefly at George, who rolled his eyes but kept on whittling.

It was as if the Germans shared some silent signal then that said, "That's it." They began to move toward Swift. And it seemed that everyone else in the yard sensed something was about to happen. Heads turned and voices lowered. If Swift assumed that the men gathered around him would protect him against attack, he was disabused of the notion rather quickly as the men fanned away from him, clearing a path.

The Germans picked up their pace and Swift, realizing his predicament, moved his large frame quickly toward the rear gate. With the Germans close behind, he began running, rather unceremoniously, down Walnut Street. Several other men, excited by this new development, ran after them.

Will decided to follow, and he was relieved to see that Swift, panting and severely winded, found refuge in a friend's house, just down the street. The Germans groused and snarled and hurled insults, but nothing else. Nor did they move to break in. After a bit, their mood changed. They laughed and joked about Swift's humiliation. Satisfied that they had made their point, they walked back to the State House, and soon left for their homes and farms. Will remained, however, for the rest of the day.

Things were quiet after that until around six o'clock when Sheriff Dewees decided he would close the polls. James Cannon and some of the other Independents who were hanging around the State House protested loudly at this move, pointing out that working-class people didn't have the leisure to take off work during the day, and that an early closing of the polls would deprive them of the right to vote in this important election. He worked the crowd up into such a frenzy that the sheriff re-opened the polls and kept them open past midnight.

Will was there when the results were read aloud about an hour later. The Moderates managed to win three of the four seats and thus, as his father and his mentor had predicted, retained control of both the local committee and the colonial assembly. This meant the congressional delegation would still be under instructions to vote against a declaration of independence and in favor of reconciliation with England.

Will was a little surprised, and mildly disappointed at the outcome of the election. But the voters had spoken and had said no to independence and the local political revolution urged by its adherents. And that was that.

Or so he thought.

Philadelphia, May 2
Chapter 7

The man who called himself Henri Dubois Tremont brought the glass to his lips and took a slow draught of red wine, peering over the liquid at the young women across the room, daughters of the proprietor of the White Horse Inn. The older sister, Rebecca, was quite the beauty, he thought, with her large blue eyes, long blond hair, and curvaceous body. The plain Quaker clothes and lack of make-up could not disguise the latent sexuality that she exuded with every smile, every graceful movement.

And she was attracted to him. He could tell by the way she cast her eyes in his direction ever so often, gave him that coquettish little smile. Yes, he could feel it. He could smell it. One would have to be stupid and unobservant not to have noticed—and he was neither. As if to prove his point, the girl turned in his direction then, locked eyes with him and smiled. She was getting more brazen, more forward.

He considered the possibility that he might be mistaken, that these perceptions were the imaginings of a slightly drunk, self-centered older man who fancied himself irresistible to the ladies. But he immediately rejected the idea. Experience, not ego, had taught him that women were attracted to him. He was, objectively speaking, handsome by most standards, articulate, educated and well read, and impeccable in his manners when he chose to be. He could be quite charming. He knew that.

Not all women had the same reaction, mind you. Some took a little persuading, presented something of a challenge. And he liked that. The other sister, for example, Elizabeth, was also pretty, but in a more subtle, subdued way. She was more modest in manner and dress. Her hair was a dark brown, which she wore tightly bound in a bun, with ringlets dangling on the sides. She had smaller breasts and narrower hips than her older sister, but equal to her in grace of movement. She was also more intelligent, a deeper thinker than her sister. He could tell that almost right away from their conversations.

She reminded him a little of the young, pregnant woman with whom he had recently shared a coach ride from Boston to New York. The lady had been attractive, friendly, and knowledgeable on a variety of subjects, including, to his great pleasure, Shakespeare. Her sensuality was there, beneath the surface, and he could easily imagine the passion he could evoke in her if given the chance.

Her husband was a bit aloof. He seemed a little suspicious of the man—which was wise given the unusual circumstances that had thrown them together. After a time, however, the husband began to loosen up, perhaps beginning to see it as a happy coincidence. After all, James Arden Howe dressed, acted, and spoke like the English gentleman he claimed to be, a person with impressive family connections in both England and the colonies. He was a cousin to none other than General William Howe and his brother, Admiral Richard Howe. It was an acquaintance, the husband no doubt concluded, that might prove helpful to a young man seeking to get ahead in the world.

And Howe, as he called himself, grew fond of the couple along the way, and he enjoyed their company. He also felt sympathy toward them for the troubled pregnancy that had prompted their trip to New York. He was not an unfeeling monster, as some thought. He was capable of empathy.

He could not, however, let his feelings for the couple affect his decision of whether to kill them and their driver. Rather, his action would, as always, have to be guided by cold logic and rationality, a weighing of the risks and benefits. And he had agonized over the decision, the arguments for and against being equally balanced.

The couple, and to a lesser extent the driver, would surely be able to identify him later, even if he changed his disguise. It was not likely, though, that they would be asked to do so. The rebels in Boston would be looking for an elderly, grey-haired man who claimed to be from Virginia, not a young, dark-haired Englishman.

And if the couple didn't show up in New York soon, the woman's family would become worried. They would make inquiries. If they turned up dead, people would remember the finely dressed gentleman who left Boston with them. Even if no one made the connection to the supposed spy, a man suspected of a triple homicide would be hunted with energy and thoroughness.

On the other hand, no one else had seen him up close in this new disguise. It would take some time before the bodies were found, and perhaps even more before it could be deduced that the killer had been the man who had joined them as they were leaving Boston. By that time, he would be long gone, in a different city, and in a different disguise.

He had considered his options, and warmed to the idea of eliminating the witnesses, planning out the murders in his head, down to the last detail of burning the coach with the bodies in it, personal items and horses taken. It would look like an Indian attack, or perhaps that of random bandits. He would kill the husband first, quickly and quietly with his blade. He would hush the terrified woman with a finger to his lips as he called out for the driver to come to their aid. The driver would never know what struck him.

Then he would turn his attention to the woman. The thought of sex so soon after witnessing the deaths of her husband and the driver would no doubt repulse and sicken her. He expected resistance, looked forward to it. And he had no intention of physically forcing her. He had found, though, that fear was a powerful aphrodisiac, and increased in proportion to the level of terror. And she would be terrified. She would feign disgust and loathing, but she would submit, and willingly,

63

enthusiastically, for fear of disappointing, of enraging her assailant, desperate to save her life.

But, in the end, logic had prevailed over passion. The risks associated with murdering outweighed the risk that they might later identify him or give information that could lead to his capture. So, he let them live, and did not regret his decision. He never did. Once he had committed to an action, or inaction, regret served no useful purpose. Indeed, he had accompanied the couple to the home of the woman's parents and met them, staunch loyalists who, he decided, might prove useful in the future.

He sensed a presence at his table which brought him back to the present. It was the older Boutwell sister, Rebecca.

"Monsieur Tremont, I hope the meal is to your liking?"

"The food and the drink, Mademoiselle, are excellent, as is your French." He held up his glass of wine. "Care to join me?"

She blushed, pleased and embarrassed. "I'm afraid I must tend to my work. Father frowns on too much familiarity of staff with the guests."

"I don't see the wisdom in such a policy. More familiarity might lead to a more satisfied clientele, at least for this particular guest."

She blushed again but said nothing in response.

"Speaking of which," he said, "I'm in need of a guide, someone to escort me about your lovely city, as I am a visitor and unfamiliar with it. I was hoping that either you or your sister might agree to help me in this regard. I would pay for this service, of course."

The suggestion that there might be competition for his attention from her sister had the desired effect. She cast her eyes downward and away with feigned modesty, though he could see her lips curl up in a small smile. "You would have to have permission from my mother and father, but if so, I would be pleased to introduce you to Philadelphia. I think you will find it to be a lovely and sophisticated city."

"I already find it so, mademoiselle, based upon what I have seen so far. Yes, quite lovely, and sophisticated." He flashed her a smile that was just short of an outright leer and the girl blushed yet again.

The man did not think the parents would object. He had made a point to ingratiate himself to both, acting the part of the lost puppy, appealing to their instinct toward kindness to strangers, especially those from a foreign land. "I shall plead with your parents then until I have the necessary permission." He then took her hand in his and kissed her wrist. "You have very delicate hands, my dear, not suited for hard labor. These are hands made for leisure, for playing the piano, painting, that sort of thing."

This time she did not blush at all. She cleared away the plates from his table, smiled, then turned and walked away. He watched, admiring the swish of her backside. When she got to the doorway, she turned toward him again and smiled one more time before leaving the room. Yes, he thought, she was a lovely girl. Her seduction would be very pleasurable—and relatively easy.

It was the younger sister, Elizabeth, who presented the real challenge. She was actually more mature than her older sister, less susceptible to his charms. But she wasn't immune. No woman was. The sexual conquest of her would be all the more satisfying, and the thought now of seducing the demure and more modest sister made him hard. Maybe he could have them both, together—a *ménage a trois*. Very French, indeed. He smiled.

The man pretended then to concentrate on his wine while he listened to the conversations around him. He was especially interested in that of the congressional delegates from New York, who were also guests at the Inn. He had been introduced to them at breakfast the morning before.

The story he gave the proprietor was that he was from France, specifically, Paris. His family was part of the aristocracy, and close to the king. He was very interested in the conflict between England and her colonies and had come to North America to see for himself what was going on. He planned to write a journal of his travels and publish it upon his return. He hinted, ever so subtly, that he had more authority than he could say, to speak for the king in matters concerning aid or even alliances.

Although the delegates were cordial and intrigued upon learning that he was French, especially the tantalizing prospect that his family had some influence with the royal family, they scrupulously, but politely, declined to discuss the business of the Congress with him. They were not so shy, however, in discussing their personal political views.

They also seemed to sometimes forget that their private conversations might be overheard. From what he had been able to hear thus far, Tremont had concluded that for the most part they were some of the more conservative members of the Continental Congress, favoring reconciliation with England and an end to hostilities as soon as possible.

As he took a final swallow of wine, emptying his glass, he noticed one of the New York delegates excuse himself from the table and walk outside onto the veranda. It was the man who had introduced himself as Philip Livingston. After about a minute, Tremont rose, placed his napkin on the table, and followed the man outside.

Livingston stood on the edge of the decking, a freshly lit cigar in his hand. No one else was there. Cigars were rare in the colonies, and in England for that matter, pipes and snuff being the more common forms of tobacco use. Tremont himself preferred a pipe, but he also liked the aroma of a cigar and had smoked a few when he was in Cuba some years back. Interestingly enough, he had been told while in Boston that it was one of the rebel generals, Israel Putnam, who was credited with first introducing them into the colonies after a trip to Havana in the early 1760s. Tremont stopped a few feet from the man.

Sensing his presence, Livingston turned to face him. "Monsieur Tremont, how are you this evening?"

"Tres bon, Monsieur Livingston. And you?"

He nodded. "Very fine, indeed, thank you." He took a draw on his cigar and blew out the smoke.

"I haven't smelled the aroma from a cigar in quite some time."

"Oh, I'm sorry, where are my manners?" Livingston reached into a vest pocket and retrieved another cigar. "Join me," he said, clipping off the end and extending it toward the other man.

"Merci." He accepted the cigar, sniffed it, and then used Livingston's proffered cigar end to light it. He puffed a couple of times quickly, then took a longer draw and exhaled the smoke. "Excellent."

Livingston nodded. "They are quite good." He took a draw himself and exhaled. "My family owns a plantation outside of Havana," he said in answer to the unasked question. "I always carry a box with me."

The two men conversed for several more achingly long minutes until Tremont thought he would explode, but he kept his face passive, feigning interest. Livingston had been to Philadelphia on many occasions, it seemed, and was free with his opinions of the city and its inhabitants. While he acknowledged the precision with which the city had been laid out, he disliked what he saw as its uniformity and sameness, and complained of the pervasive use of brick over wood, a material he saw as warmer and more comfortable, and more accommodating of individual tastes.

He admired the industriousness of the people and remarked favorably on their tolerance for ethnic and religious diversity in the city. "English, Scots, Welsh, Irish, Germans, and Africans rub shoulders in the taverns. Jews are not uncommon here, either." He took another draw from his cigar and blew a ring of smoke up into the air above his head. "Yes, regardless of your religion, there is a church here for you."

The Frenchman nodded and puffed once on his cigar, then held it down by his side. Both men had been looking toward the street but now Tremont turned his head toward Livingston. "Are all Philadelphians as courteous and hospitable to strangers as Monsieur and Mademoiselle Boutwell, and are all the ladies as fair as their daughters?"

The man looked at him now as if to make sure he had been serious before replying. "Yes, I have found many of the city's citizens to be welcoming and helpful, especially when it was good for their business." He looked back toward the door of the inn. "Some, however, I have found to be exceedingly grave, and sour, and most of them are far too sure of the superiority of the city and its citizens. Now, I hasten to add that you may find similar feelings about my home, New York, and I guess everyone to some extent feels their city is better than others simply because it is more familiar. Provencal pride, if you will. But in my opinion Philadelphians are in a class by themselves. They think all their geese are swans."

Livingston smiled then, as if to imply no hard feelings were attached to his observations and turned again toward the street. He took another short draw on his cigar and blew the smoke out in front of him. "As for the women of Philadelphia," he said, "not to be too unkind, but I think you will find that the lovely Boutwell sisters are more the exception than the rule. Philadelphia has, I dare say, more homely women per capita than anywhere else in the colonies." He paused. "I don't wish to be too harsh and hope you are not offended by my frankness."

"Not at all," Tremont replied, "Indeed, I now feel even more fortunate in my choice of lodging." Changing the subject, he said, "I assume that you are acquainted with Dr. Benjamin Franklin?"

"Of course."

"It is my understanding that he makes his home in Philadelphia, and I did so much want to meet the famous gentleman, to interview him for my journal. Would you be amenable to making introductions?"

Livingston looked a little nonplussed at the question. "I'm afraid Dr. Franklin is not presently in the city."

"Ah, I see. Do you know when he might return?"

"No, sorry," he said in a tone that did not invite further inquiry.

The man who passed himself off as a Frenchman did not push the matter as the reticence of the delegate confirmed his information—that Franklin was on a mission to Canada. He was wildly disappointed. There were other leaders whose assassination would cripple the rebellion as much, if not more, than Franklin, but Tremont had powerful, personal reasons to include the crafty old man among the casualties, and his absence complicated matters.

After a couple of more minutes of conversation, Tremont announced, "I think I shall take a stroll, explore the city a bit, and digest my supper. Care to join me?"

"Thank you for the invitation, but I have several letters I must write tonight." He took a draw on his cigar and exhaled. "And be careful where you stroll, sir, as not all parts of the city are safe for visitors after dark. There are ruffians and criminals about."

"Is there a particular section you suggest that I avoid?" When the man gave him the names of the streets that bordered what he said was generally considered to be the rougher part of the city, the Frenchman said, "Yes, I think I know this area, and will heed your advice." He bowed slightly. "Have a good evening, Monsieur Livingston."

"And you, Mr. Tremont."

The Frenchman took a puff on his cigar and stepped down from the veranda. Once outside the gate, he turned east onto Market Street, toward the river. Once there he turned south and headed directly toward the area of the city Livingston had described.

Philadelphia, May 3
Chapter 8

The scratching noise came from inside the mattress, and it stirred Will from a rather fitful sleep. But when he moved in the bed, it stopped. He lay still, listening, staring out into the darkness. Ten seconds passed, then fifteen, and then the scratching began again. It was not an unusual noise during the night, but it was always a bit unnerving, and annoying.

Will remained motionless, his breathing short and shallow. When the scratching stopped again a few seconds later, he heard a soft thud and then the pad of tiny feet on the floor beneath, then the clawing, scratching noise on the bed's wooden frame. Momentarily, the rat appeared, brazenly perched on the post at the foot of the bed.

He was rather large, his fat, grayish brown body completely covering the top of the post and extending a few inches on either side. But he appeared balanced and comfortable on the small surface, his long tail whipping and writhing about like a tiny snake. It seemed to Will that the creature was looking directly at him, taunting him.

Slowly, Will reached down toward the floor, all the time keeping an eye on the rodent. He grabbed a boot, brought it up slowly, then flung it at the creature. The boot hit the post at just the right spot, but the rat scampered out of the way a split second before it arrived. The boot fell uselessly to the floor.

"Son of a bitch," Will muttered.

The rat ran across the room, then stopped, turned and looked in Will's direction one more time before disappearing through a small hole in the base board. How such a large rat could squeeze through such a small hole was a mystery. "Clever rascal," he said aloud.

Will's internal clock, and the greyish light coming in through the dormer window, told him it was about six-thirty. He threw the covers off and sat on the edge of the bed for a few seconds, surveying the space around him. The room, which served as his living quarters, was the attic space of the building which housed *The Pennsylvania Chronicle,* Harrell and Sons Printing, and The Black Cat Stationery and Bookstore, all owned by Will's father. Entry to the room was either by way of a spiral staircase on the second floor of the bookstore, or from a set of outside steps at the rear of the building. He had moved in about six months before, agreeing to pay his father a modest sum for rent.

He had previously lived in the family home on Spruce Street, where his father, sister, Anna, and his brothers, James and John, still resided. It was a large enough place to accommodate them all, but it had been time, he thought, to establish his own place, humble as it might be, and take that step toward the responsibilities of manhood.

His new living space, though small—about 170 square feet—was adequate for his needs. It was hot in the summer and cold in the winter, but blankets helped against the cold, and the dormer windows allowed some bit of air to come in from outside to make the heat bearable. The windows also let in some light and offered a view of the city.

He had cleaned out the room of discarded furniture, boxes, papers, and other items which had been stored there for lack of anywhere else to put them. What couldn't be given or thrown away, he organized and stacked in one corner. He swept the plain heart pine floor, cleaned it thoroughly, and hand rubbed an oil finish on it.

And he had added his own personal touches—his four-poster oak bed from home, an old armoire and mirror which needed a good bit of work, purchased for next to nothing, as well as a wash table with built in basin, which fit neatly against the north wall. And under one of the dormers, he set up a reading and writing area, where he spent many an hour at a small oak desk, his text illuminated by a large candle he kept on the corner.

He stood now and stretched, then he quickly walked across the wood plank floor, cold on his bare feet, to the armoire. The early morning chill hung in the room, as did the musty smell he couldn't seem to get rid of. In the grey silence, he put on his breeches, then a ruffled white linin shirt and a braided vest. Taking one last look at his reflection in the dull mirror, he headed down the back stairs at the rear of the building.

All three businesses, which were just down from the Quaker Meeting House, shared a public entrance on Arch Street. A private entrance was located at the rear, accessed from the alley off Fourth Street, and it was here that Will entered.

His brother, James and his apprentice, Peter Warmack, were already hard at work at the printing press, and Will paused just inside the entrance and watched for a minute. James and Peter stood next to the tall, wooden flat-bed press that sat on a platform in the middle of the space. Both wore black-smeared leather aprons, but unlike his master, the apprentice's breeches and shirt were also stained with ink, as were his face and hands.

Peter was also his sister's fiancé. He was an ardent Independent, a little too ardent for Will's taste, but he was a decent fellow, a hard worker and quick study. And Anna seemed to love him very much, so Will had determined early on to like him—and he did.

With amazing speed and dexterity, James plucked the metal type, letter by letter, from the case, then locked them into the large chase. He sat the chase in the coffin, then placed a sheet of dampened paper between the tympan and frisket hinged on the coffin. He then snapped his fingers for Peter to do his job, inking a pair of leather balls and then applying the ink to the waiting type. Though the balls had handles, it was messy work—hence the sticky and smeared look of Peter.

James then clamped the sheet between the tympan and frisket and folded down both so that the paper showed through the frisket in four page-sized cutout sections, which permitted the paper to contact the inked metal. Next, he slid the coffin under the massive vertical head of the press. A screw lever was used to lower a four-inch-thick piece of hardwood on top of the closed coffin, providing the necessary pressure to leave an impression on the paper. James raised the platen, pulled back along the rails, removed the sheet of paper and set it aside to dry. A new sheet would be inserted into the coffin and the process repeated, with re-inking as necessary, until the right number of sheets had been run.

It was a process with which Will was very familiar, having learned alongside James from their father. Although a very useful skill, requiring physical and mental acuity, he was just as glad that he no longer had to practice it on a regular basis.

It was an extremely messy affair. He'd had to scrub and scrub to get the ink stains off, and even then, he could never seem to get all of it from under his fingernails. He also remembered having to wash ink from each form, using a foul-smelling alkali solution that not only removed the ink from metal and knuckles, but bits of skin as well.

Besides, though Will became competent at the various tasks involved, James had taken to it like a duck to water. And he seemed to like it. All in all, a good fit. Their father found Will more suited to the front office work, taking printing orders, selling books and stationery items, taking advertisements for the paper, writing and editing articles and other submissions, making deliveries, that sort of thing.

Finally, James and Peter looked up and noticed Will by the entrance. Both smiled and gave him a wave. As he moved toward them, he said, "Nothing like the smell of ink and the thump of a press in the morning to rouse a man awake, get him ready to greet the day."

He had been half joking but both of them nodded in agreement.

"Is Father here?"

James shrugged. "I haven't seen him, but Peter and I came right here and started the Caldwell job. He might be up front." He raised his chin, pointing with his head in that direction.

A quick survey of the front office and the bookstore, however, did not reveal the missing proprietor. Will checked the clock on the counter—quarter till seven. Just as he turned to go back to the press room, the front door opened and in walked his sister, Anne, and his youngest brother, John. Anne was carrying a large basket, the aroma from which filled the small room, and caused Will's mouth to water. She smiled as she sat it down on the counter. She gave him a quick peck on the cheek.

"Had any breakfast?"

Will shook his head and watched as she lifted the checkered cloth covering of the basket. Inside he saw two dozen or more boiled eggs, an equal number of biscuits and a large stack of sliced ham. Anne removed three eggs and three biscuits from the basket. She shoved chunks of ham into the biscuits and placed them on a plate which she sat on the counter.

"Share these with James and Peter," she said. "I'm taking the rest over to the Alms House. Then I'll drop John off at school and be back before eight."

"Did you talk to Father this morning? Is he headed here?"

"Father didn't come home last night. Again."

Will arched an eyebrow. "He'll probably come stumbling in after a bit."

"Well, if he does and is looking for breakfast, he will be disappointed," she said, but then after a slight hesitation, she reached back in the basket. She prepared another ham biscuit and egg. "Here's one for him, too. I'm sure he will not have had the sense to eat anything either."

"You are too good to us," Will said.

"Someone has to look after you." She was frowning but Will knew she took great satisfaction in mothering them all. As the eldest, and only, surviving daughter, she had assumed the matriarchal role in the family when their mother died in childbirth six years before. It was a burden too heavy, a responsibility too great, for one so young—she had been only sixteen at the time---but she had grown into the role and performed admirably. She had become the glue that held the family together.

Will's older brother, Patrick Jr., joined the Continental Army last year, shortly after his 21st birthday. He rode off toward Boston with a contingent of Philadelphia militia, right behind the newly appointed Commanding General, George Washington, from Virginia. Their father was distressed about it, but not wanting to appear hypocritical, did not voice an objection. Anne cried openly and tried to dissuade him, but to no avail.

James was a year older than Will. Though not the sharpest knife in the drawer, he was a skilled pressman and was a master at getting the jobs out at the print shop. John, the youngest, was born into this world just before his mother left it. Like Will, he took after their father in physical features, with his slender, tall frame, curly, reddish brown hair and green eyes set in an angular, thin face. Will's other brothers and his sister more resembled their mother—short and squat with square-jawed faces, their hair thick, straight and dark brown.

Though his father would never admit it, Will thought he had a hard time being a proper father to John because the lad was a constant reminder of the loss of his beloved wife. Her death hit all of them hard, but it affected their father the most, something Will resented to some degree because he felt that his father should have been the strong one, the one to comfort his children, instead of the other way around.

His father's mood became darker, his temper closer to the surface. He neglected his various businesses, started drinking more heavily, and gambling, the latter of which had resulted in considerable debt. He went into a downward spiral so severe and so deep that Will feared he would not come out, at least not alive.

He seemed to have evened out in the past year or so, but he was still not the man he was before. The family residence on Spruce Street was a substantial one and well furnished, but it was slowly deteriorating. The drapes, the linens and some of the furniture were beginning to look a little shabby, as were his clothes, and those of his children. And none of this seemed to concern him much.

Anne's mothering of her father was well intentioned, Will thought, but perhaps not such a good thing because it gave him a crutch, enabled him to slide off the rail of responsibility, knowing that she would be there to catch him. And Will had to admit that he had done some enabling himself, ignoring things, not wanting to acknowledge what was happening, and taking on more responsibility at the shop.

"Speaking of the Alms House," Anne said, "now that you are a lawyer, perhaps you will volunteer on occasion to help some with their legal problems?" It was as much a statement as a question.

Will shrugged and said, "First, I'm not a full-fledged lawyer yet. I still must be supervised by Mr. Dickinson. I would need his permission to take on any legal matter. And second, I'm pretty busy these days." When Anne frowned, he said, "But we'll see if something specific comes up."

"I'm sure you'll find the time."

She was a persistent one, his sister, and would have the last word on the subject, he knew, so he said nothing else in response. And with that, both decided they needed to go about their errands. Anne picked up her basket and grabbed her little brother's hand and headed to the Alms House. Will returned to the printing area.

To James' questioning look, he said. "He's not here yet." Then he added, "Do you have the order for the White Horse Inn?"

James smiled. "Looking to make a personal delivery, are you?"

He shrugged. "I have the time."

James' smile grew wider. "Wouldn't have anything to do with the opportunity to see Miss Rebecca, would it?" He put a hand over his heart and patted his chest.

Will could feel his face flush, but he didn't respond.

"I say to Hell with her father. You should ask for her hand anyway if that's what you want." James looked at Peter, who smiled as well.

Will could think of no response.

James pointed to a box on the shelf in the corner. Will tucked it under his arm and headed toward the door.

"Good luck, brother," James said.

Will stuck a hand up in the air, but he neither looked back nor spoke in response as he left the building.

Philadelphia, May 3
Chapter 9

In 1727, Joshua Boutwell, a Quaker, grew tired of the discrimination and outright hostility he faced from the ruling Puritans in Massachusetts and moved to Pennsylvania, a colony founded upon a principle of religious freedom. He settled in Philadelphia, eventually opening a place for lodging, drink, and meals for travelers and locals, located on Market Street, just west of Second Street. He named it The White Horse Inn.

Joshua soon established himself as a hard-working and honest businessman. He developed a talent for brewing beer, and soon he was turning out some of the finest beer and ales in Philadelphia. His wife, Mary, was a good partner and an excellent cook. She worked just as hard as her husband, taking responsibility for the cooking and cleaning at the inn. A couple who could care for your horse, give you a comfortable place to sleep, and provide good food and drink at a reasonable price, was bound to have plenty of business. And plenty of business they had.

Joshua's progeny maintained and expanded his holdings after his death. His son, Joseph, was the current owner and operator of the inn and the White Horse Stables and Livery, located across the street from the inn. In addition to the inn and livery business, Joseph also owned two warehouses on the Delaware River and a sawmill.

He and Will's father, though not close friends, had served together on local boards for the hospital and the library. And they now had something in common. Both of their sons had joined the Continental Army. Joseph was a devout Quaker and abhorred violence. He was dead set against separation from the mother country and the waging of this "hopeless war" as he called it. It pained him immeasurably when his son went against these teachings. But, like Will's father, he always encouraged his children to think for themselves, so he tried to support his son's decision when it was clear he would not be deterred.

An unintended consequence of his son's enlistment was to raise Boutwell's standing with the rebels in the city. Although most people understood and accepted the pacifist creed of the Quaker religion, some were suspicious and resentful of their Quaker neighbors. And the more polarized the city became, the more suspicious and resentful they became. Most were aware of Joseph's loyalist leanings, too. For business purposes, he staked a more neutral territory, but he would not hold back his opinion if asked. Now, it was presumed, his son had in fact brought him closer to that middle.

Will knew better and was thinking about some of the man's inflammatory and opinionated statements as he bounded up the front steps and through the door that led into the lobby area. There was no one at the front desk. To his right was the dining area, where several people were finishing up breakfast and the smell of bacon and sausage wafted through the air.

He walked back to the kitchen, where he found Martha Anne Boutwell and her two daughters, Rebecca and Elizabeth. The daughters were peeling potatoes and cutting up vegetables and dumping them into a large cauldron that was extended over the fire by a long rod. Their mother was loading up a platter with eggs, bordered by bacon and sausages.

Martha Anne Boutwell was a rather large woman, perhaps the victim of her own good cooking, but she carried the extra weight well, with an erect posture and easy, graceful movements that belied her size. She dressed plainly and modestly, as befitted a Quaker woman, but she always managed to find clothes that complimented her physical features. Her round face was dominated by a pair of large brown eyes

79

that suggested the kindness at her core. She smiled at him as she rushed past with the platter, headed toward the dining room.

"Good morning to you, Will."

"Good morning," he said, loud enough for the daughters to hear, and they each looked up.

Elizabeth was short and petite, her black hair usually worn in a bun, with little ringlets hanging down in front of each ear. She was graceful in her movements and had a modest dignity about her that exuded self-confidence. Her large brown eyes shone with an intelligence that became obvious after only a short conversation with her. She was knowledgeable in many areas, including science, philosophy and politics, and though never rude or discourteous, she did not hesitate to speak her mind—a trait some said explained her lack of suitors—though Will thought it one of her more attractive qualities. Indeed, had Elizabeth given him any indication of a willingness to go further than friendship, she may have been the object of his affections, rather than Rebecca.

It was Rebecca, however, who had, much to Will's, and everyone else's surprise, shown an interest in him, who had encouraged him with words and actions. And if Elizabeth was physically attractive, Rebecca was stunning. She was tall and slender, with a regal bearing. She had rosy cheeks, and sky-blue eyes that twinkled when she smiled. Her blond hair was a mass of soft curls. All of Will's friends assured him that she was quite a catch and couldn't understand what she saw in him.

Neither could he. She was coy and flirtatious by nature and seemed to enjoy the attention she drew with her beauty. She could pretty much have any man she wanted, and he felt sometimes as if he was in a competition, as if she were weighing him against other options. He didn't like it, but the fact that he might even be in contention for her affections was a surprise so complete that he accepted his status without complaint, holding onto what little pride he had by feigning ambivalence. She gave him a slight crease of the lips, now, the beginnings of a smile, and it made his heart race.

"Sure smells good in here," he said.

Her eyes registered bemusement. "Would you care for some breakfast, Mr. Harrell?"

He looked down at the floor. "Oh, no thank you. I've already eaten."

She looked over at her sister, then back to Will "Are you sure? You look like you could use a little extra meat on those bones. What do you think, sister?"

Elizabeth gave him a small, sympathetic smile. "I think you shouldn't tease Will so much." She focused back on peeling potatoes.

He was fidgeting, shifting from one foot to the other, trying to think of something clever to say, when Martha Anne Boutwell reappeared in the kitchen. He lifted the bundle he had under his arm and said to her, "I have your newspapers. Would you like me to leave them at the front desk?"

"If you will put them on the buffet in the dining area, please, Will, that would be more convenient for the guests."

He nodded. "I have some spare time, Mrs. Boutwell, before I have to get back. Is there anything I can help you with?" He looked at Rebecca as he said this.

"He could accompany me to the market, Mother," Rebecca said, batting her eyes at Will.

Her mother looked from one to the other, a small bemused smile dancing on her lips.

"It would be my honor, Mrs. Boutwell," Will said.

Her mother nodded once and said, "You sure you have time, Will?"

"Oh, yes, Ma'am."

Rebecca wordlessly rose and wiped her hands on the towel, then removed her apron. Her mother handed her the list she had prepared earlier. Will looked over Rebecca's shoulder, taking in the bayberry scent of her hair as he went quickly down the list, committing it to memory.

Elizabeth handed her sister the large canvas bag they often used for shopping at the market. Her teasing smile was subtle. "But don't you two tarry too long. There's lots of work to be done around here."

Rebecca ignored her sister's needling, took the bag from her, and walked out of the kitchen, with Will right behind. They walked through the gated entrance of the wooden picket fence that surrounded the inn and turned left onto Market Street. After several feet, Rebecca turned to Will and said, "How did your first legal argument go on Monday?"

He was pleased that she had remembered, and eager to tell her all about it. He knew she would be bored with the facts and the point of law, so he gave her only the essential information. He also didn't mention that he had suffered a seizure in court. Rebecca was aware of his affliction, though thankfully had never witnessed one of his seizures, and it apparently had not disqualified him in her eyes as a suitor. He could tell, though, that it was not a subject she liked to talk about, so he didn't.

"I'm sure you were wonderful. Soon, you will have your own law practice. That will be exciting."

He nodded but said nothing.

"I also heard that you were given a special assignment with the Continental Congress."

My God, if the Congress was a boat, it would have sunk long ago with all the leaks. "Who told you that?"

She gave him a coy smile. "I have my sources."

"Well, your sources are misinformed. I'm still just a clerk. Mostly an errand boy, making sure the delegates have what they need during the session, and that they are not disturbed, see to the security of the chambers and the members. Nothing special."

Of course, he wanted to tell her about his assignment, to impress her with the importance of his secret mission, but he could not. And the less said about his connection with the Congress, lest it get back to her father, the better. If he was to have any chance with Rebecca, he couldn't afford to alienate her father. Given the differences in religion—his family was Anglican—and wealth—the Harrell family's financial profile was quite modest when compared with the Boutwells—his chances were already pretty slim. Strong political differences, however, could poison the well of good feelings more easily and more deeply than any of the other differences.

Rebecca looked over at him. "I hear there is a move by some of the delegates to declare independence from Great Britain."

He started to ask her where she got this information, but it didn't matter. It was a subject of common speculation. "Well, I think the election results yesterday will thwart that move, at least for the foreseeable future. As long as Pennsylvania's delegation remains opposed to it, it won't happen."

"In your position, you are privy to all of their debates and discussions."

"Perhaps, but I have been sworn to strict secrecy as to anything I hear or learn in that room."

"Even from me?" She gave him another coy smile.

"Even from you."

She punched him on the arm. "I'm just teasing you, William Harrell. You are much too serious for such a young man."

"I can be frivolous, if the occasion calls for it."

She rolled her eyes.

He smiled. "Anyway, as I said, my job is to make sure they have quills and ink, and paper to write on, water pitchers and glasses. I doubt that I will be entrusted with any sensitive matter."

By this time, they had reached the market, which was contained in a long and narrow covered building with open ends which ran from Front to Sixth Street along Market Street. The quantity and variety of provisions offered was immense, and as usual, it was crowded and busy with vendors and customers.

Rebecca wasted no time in accumulating the items on her list, inspecting the produce, talking to the proprietors, all of whom knew her. And she selected expertly. When she said she was ready to head back, he gave her a questioning look.

"What?"

"Aren't you forgetting something?"

"What?"

"Didn't your mother want some muslin?"

She looked at the paper again, frowned, then looked at me. "How....?"

"I saw the list."

"You have a good memory."

"Sometimes."

He followed her as she backtracked to the stall she wanted. She inspected the product displayed and ordered the proper amount. She paid the vendor and turned to me. "Anything else I forgot, Mr. Harrell?"

"Perhaps, but you have now purchased everything on your mother's list."

As they walked back to the inn, he stole furtive glances at Rebecca, taking in her smooth face in profile. He loved the way her hair curled out from under her cap onto her forehead, and around her ears. He imagined her head resting on a pillow. The thought sustained him against the dismay he felt in anticipation of having to talk with her father when they returned. Perhaps the man would not be there. He had other businesses to attend to after all.

But he was.

He was standing at the front desk going over a ledger when they entered. He looked up and though he did not smile, he didn't frown either. Joseph Boutwell had the look of a much younger man, tall and large of frame, with wide shoulders and a broad chest. His hair was still jet black, with only a hint of grey at the temples. His grip as they shook hands in greeting was a little too strong, and, not to be outdone, Will met it with equal force. Neither of them gave any sign of discomfort in the contest. His hope of avoiding politics with the man disappeared when Rebecca boasted on his account about being given a special, secret assignment with the Continental Congress involving security.

Will stared at her, incredulous.

"He denied it, of course. It is after all, supposed to be secret. But I have it on good authority."

Will started to protest but Joseph Boutwell fixed his gaze on him and snorted, "Security?" He shook his head. "Will, you're a good lad, but no amount of security in the world will be able to protect those misguided souls from the consequences of their actions—which the Crown sees as treason. There are those who are more prudent, including our friend, John Dickinson, but they are but a small pistol in the face of the cannon of arrogance and stupidity. I fear they will be drowned out by the rabid mob that pretends to be the legitimate representatives of the people. Every one of them will be captured and hanged, at least the ring leaders will be. You should take care that you are not caught up in their mischief and hung with them."

"I will do my best, sir. And you make a valid point. Perhaps you should be among our delegation, a voice of reason, so to speak."

If he caught the sarcasm behind the suggestion, he didn't show it. "Humph," he snorted. "I don't have time for such things. I have businesses to run, a family to feed. And unlike some, I don't like to talk to hear myself talk. I'll leave that to the lawyers."

These last words were a barb aimed at Will, it seemed to him, but he took the stinging words in silence, simply nodding at the man. He then took his leave of the Boutwells, bowing to Rebecca, and headed for the State House.

Philadelphia, May 3
Chapter 10

Will arrived a little early to the State House to re-familiarize himself with the building, to survey it from a new perspective, examine it with the eye of a would-be assassin. He walked the perimeter, noting the double doors at the main entrance and in the rear leading into the courtyard. Two single doors allowed entry on both the west and east sides of the building, and an iron gate led into the courtyard from Walnut Street. He stood for a minute at the Chestnut Street entrance, his back to it, and searched the surrounding buildings for a sight line.

He assumed the doors to the building were locked at night, but also assumed that several people would have keys. Would the windows also be locked? They were long and tall with the bottoms only a few feet from the ground, offering easy access at night. The Pennsylvania Assembly met in the building as did the Supreme Court. When the building was open for business, anyone could walk right in. There were no guards at any of the entrances and its halls were often crowded with people.

When the Congress was in session, the doors and windows of the chambers were closed, but more for privacy than security. A doorkeeper was stationed outside to screen entrants and discourage eavesdroppers, but, according to Tim Matlack, did not stay so stationed during the entire proceedings. That would change if Will had his way.

He entered through the main entrance at precisely a quarter to ten. Off to the side, he could see into the chambers, where several members had already gathered. Sam Adams was talking to another man who Will recognized as Sam's cousin, John Adams, a short, squat man with a round face that matched his round body. Sam Adams waved him over.

It was a good bit warmer inside the chamber, the air still, and heavy, and he began to perspire more heavily, wiping his brow with the sleeve of his jacket. Sam Adams introduced his cousin, who gave Will a firm, if slightly sweaty, handshake. His calloused hand bespoke more of his life as a farmer than as a lawyer.

"Yes, Will," he said, "I have heard many good things about you from Sam and I understand you will be working with us."

"Yes, sir," Will said, wondering how much he had been told about his real assignment. Did the cousins confide in each other in such matters? He suspected so. "And I have heard many good things about you, as well, Mr. Adams."

He frowned. "That is extremely unlikely." He looked at his cousin, then back to Will. "And you should accordingly wish to question the reliability of your source, though I do appreciate your effort at diplomacy."

Sam Adams smiled. "If you will excuse us, cousin, Will and I are to meet with Hancock and Thomson before the session starts this morning." He turned to leave, motioning for Will to follow.

"Indeed. Well, welcome to the circus, Will."

"Thank you," he said quickly over his shoulder. He followed the other Adams out of the room, down the hallway to a room off to the right. Adams knocked lightly on the door and opened it before anyone inside could respond.

"Good morning, gentlemen," Adams said as they entered the room. It was a small space, maybe twelve by twelve, and spare, not even a table or chairs in which to sit, nothing on the walls, and a plain wood plank floor with no rug. Four men were standing close together, huddled in the middle of the room. They separated and looked up. The group included Hancock, Dickinson, Matlack, and Charles Thomson, secretary for the Congress.

Thomson was well known as an early leader of the Sons of Liberty in Philadelphia. He was tall and thin with an angular face. His hair, prematurely white, was short on the top and puffy on the sides. He had a look about him that was not unfriendly, but serious.

Hancock gave Will a smile. "I believe you know Charles Thomson?"

"Yes, of course," he said, stepping forward to shake the man's hand. "Mr. Thomson."

"Hello, Will."

Adams said, "The lad has a deferential attitude which will serve him well with some of the vain-glorious men in this Congress."

"None in this group could be so described, of course," Hancock said, smiling and looking around at the others.

"Of course," assured Dickinson.

Will nodded but noted that only Matlack, who was twenty-five years his senior, had insisted that they were on a first-name basis.

Hancock spoke again. "For now, this group will constitute the committee on safety and security for the Congress. No one outside the group, including other members, can know the full scope of our work."

Will raised his hand, which caught Hancock by surprise. "Yes?"

"I'm not sure that would be possible, or wise." Will couldn't believe he had been so presumptuous as to question the decision of a man like John Hancock. Nor, perhaps, did the others, who stared at him a few seconds. So much for deferential attitudes. Well, they had asked him to lead the investigation, hadn't they? Best to find out sooner, rather than later, the degree of latitude he was to be given.

Adams was the first to recover. "What do you mean, Will?"

"I believe your colleague, Mr. Franklin once noted, 'Three can keep a secret if two of them are dead.'" There were smiles around the room, except for Hancock. "While we can shore up the leaky boat that is the Continental Congress, it will be difficult to plug all the holes, or keep new ones from forming, especially if I start asking questions. Besides, if some of your members are targets of an assassin, they have a right to know, so that they can take precautions."

Will then threw Hancock a bone. "I appreciate the desire for secrecy. I'd rather not alert any confederates of what we know, or suspect, which would allow them to cover their tracks and warn the would-be assassin." He paused for a couple of beats. "I was thinking we could find something in between complete secrecy and complete disclosure."

Hancock, sufficiently mollified, said, "What do you propose?"

"Go ahead and tell the delegates the truth, that you have received intelligence that the members of the Congress have been targeted for assassination by a British agent, either individually or as a group. Downplay it, but suggest they take individual precautions, just as the Congress itself will take precautions. Explain that the agent may have accomplices and it is important that they not share this information with anyone, including family and servants."

The room was silent for several seconds. Then Adams said, "Any other thoughts, or suggestions?"

Will looked around at the faces, took a deep breath and began. "We have limited resources at our disposal, and we must assume limited time as well. We should, of course, monitor as best we can any recent arrivals to the city. And the more information we can gather about anyone associated with the Congress the better, especially those travelling with the delegates. And we should focus on those loyalists in the city who are more extreme in their views."

"I can't imagine," Dickinson said, "that any Philadelphian, regardless of his political views, would participate in the murder of a member of Congress."

"Maybe not the gentlemen, you know," replied Matlack, "but I can assure you, there are some Tories I can think of who might, especially if also motivated by money."

Will continued. "The best way to discover the identity of the assassin, I think, is to identify those in the city or connected to the Congress whom he has enlisted to help him. They will lead us to him.

In that respect I believe we can narrow down our search by eliminating the delegates from suspicion. All of you are honorable men who have sacrificed much time and money and are risking your lives by simply agreeing to serve in the Congress. Some of you are quite wealthy; some are of more modest means; but none of you are likely to be tempted by an offer of a bribe."

He paused a moment as the others nodded their agreement. "The same cannot be said, however, for those who serve the delegates. There would be varying degrees of loyalty to their masters or employers, and to the Patriot cause. Some, maybe many, could very well be tempted by an offer of money, or freedom, to cooperate with the British authorities."

There were nods from the others at this.

"We also need to consider the likely means of attack. There are four, maybe five general approaches to consider, each with advantages and disadvantages. First, he could force his way into the chambers armed with pistols and begin firing. This would have a very dramatic effect—something I think he might desire."

Adams looked over at Thomson and asked, "How many of our members carry firearms or knives on their person, do you think? Or have them secreted about the chambers?"

Thomson frowned. "Very few, I should hope. I suspect that most of our members do not see a need."

"Or perhaps," Adams said, "they are wise enough to see that easy access to weapons during the sometimes-heated debates in a hot, crowded room with people only loosely bound by a common cause is not a good idea."

The others smiled at the observation. Hancock suggested that a knife wouldn't be much use against an assassin armed with a pistol nor was it likely anyone could retrieve a firearm quickly enough to thwart a surprise attack.

Will nodded. "It would be more effective to jump on a shooter after he has fired his first volley and before he can reload. Even one proficient with a pistol would take quite some time to reload. Of course, a lone assassin could enter with two, three or maybe even four loaded pistols, in which case he could get off several rounds before anyone could react." He paused a few seconds to allow them to reflect on the scenario. "And what if he was not alone? The efficiency and resultant danger would be increased if the attack is carried out by two or three individuals, perhaps more, rather than a lone assassin."

"You think there might be more than one?" Dickinson asked.

"It would be unwise to rule it out."

Will could tell, looking at their faces, that it was not a comforting thought. "But such a terrorist is more likely to be a lone wolf, I suspect, with an ego large enough to make him adverse to sharing in the glory of such a bold attack. And this approach would almost ensure his capture, or death. At some point he would be shot or overpowered by the others. He will want to live to fight another day. I suspect that this is not the sort of man who is hampered by high ideals. He is a professional killer, neither a patriot nor a martyr."

If anyone wondered how and why he had drawn this profile of the would-be assassin, or disagreed with it, they didn't say so. After a few seconds, Matlack ventured, "What about a bomb?"

"Yes," Will said, "an explosion could inflict maximum injury at one time, and he could be a safe distance away when it goes off. A bomb, however, by its nature, does not offer precision. He might succeed in killing some members but maybe not the leaders he intended. And it would be difficult to collect enough explosive materials and place them expertly and secretly in the building to create a tremendously large blast."

He waited a few seconds before posing another alternative. "A person proficient with a long rifle could pick off one or two delegates as they entered or exited the State House. This plan offers the preciseness that a bomb does not, and the advantage of allowing the assassin to escape capture, or even detection."

Again, the others nodded.

"The disadvantage with this option is that the shooter could only hit one target, at best two, before people realized what was happening and sought cover." He paused a moment before adding, "On the other hand, two leaders of the congress killed on the doorsteps of the State House would make a statement—and instill the fear he wants."

His final suggestion was that the man might choose to make his attacks away from the State House, away from crowds. "He could isolate his targets and kill them one at a time. A man could commit several murders in a single evening, and no one would know there was a connection until it was too late."

"But that would deprive our man of the effect of a public assassination," Matlack said.

Will smiled. "Exactly. The site of the State House, or some other public place where a large number of persons are gathered, provides the opportunity of multiple targets at one time, and the opportunity to have the greatest propaganda effect, to make the most emphatic symbolic statement. And I suspect he wants very much to send a message."

In the silence that followed the men looked at each other.

"Well," Hancock said finally, "it seems that you have been giving the matter considerable thought, and I reiterate that you have our full confidence. I will proceed as you suggest with the members. Sam will chair the committee, and Tim will work closely with you. You will find both he and Charles to be invaluable resources for information about the Congress and its members, but please feel free to call on any of us for anything you need, including a sounding board for your ideas."

The others nodded their assent and Hancock said, "Gentlemen, I believe it is time to get started." He headed in the direction of the door and the men filed out behind him. Once inside the chamber, Hancock walked over to his seat at the east end, motioning for Will to follow, which he did. The members began to take their respective seats.

The room was large—about forty by forty feet with a twenty-foot high ceiling. The windows on the north side were wide and tall. A substantial fireplace, faced with marble, stood on the opposite wall. All the walls were paneled and painted a light gray, though the morning sun through the windows gave it a slight bluish hue. One wall was adorned with captured flags and a British drum, seized from Fort Ticonderoga by a colonial military force the previous year.

Thirteen round tables, one for each colony's delegation, were scattered about the room, and each was covered with green linen and encircled with hard, un-cushioned Windsor chairs. The exception was the dais where Hancock, as the president, was provided a special cushioned armchair. The doorkeeper stepped into the hall and closed the door behind him, and the congressional chambers were once again a private preserve. Hancock gaveled the session to order.

"Gentlemen, let me introduce to you Mr. William Harrell, who is an apprentice at law with our member, Mr. John Dickinson. He has agreed to serve the Congress as a deputy clerk."

He told the members that he had received reliable information suggesting a physical threat to the members and thought it prudent to establish a committee to help provide better protection, not only for the physical safety of the members but also to maintain the confidentiality of the proceedings. He hinted that some persons, "whether they be members, or persons associated with members, I do not know, have been less that discreet in this regard." He named the members of the committee, stated that Will would head it up. He requested that Will's appointment be approved and asked all delegates to cooperate with the committee.

"Do I have a motion?"

Sam Adams introduced the motion and Dickinson seconded it. Hancock asked if there was any discussion. There were murmurs of complaint from some that they didn't need security, that they were all aware of the risks of association and would take appropriate cautions themselves. Some wondered aloud as to the accuracy of Hancock's information. One member questioned the choice of "a child" for such a task and another inquired as to how the Congress could afford to pay for such services. Hancock assured them that Mr. Dickinson was providing the services of his apprentice at no charge to the Congress. This latter point seemed to be all that many needed to approve the measure. What was the harm, they thought, even if it turned out to be a hollow threat. The motion carried by unanimous vote of the members present.

"Very well, then," Hancock said, "then on to our next item of business, a request by Mr. Ned Campbell for payment of eighteen quid for two horses."

* * *

The man calling himself Henri Tremont stood on the brick sidewalk just outside the Chestnut Street entrance to the State House and took in the impressive structure—wider, deeper, and taller than anything else in the city. Despite its size, however, it blended well into its surroundings, built with the same light red brick used throughout Philadelphia and designed in the clean, plain style associated with the Quakers.

This was his third visit here in as many days. On Wednesday, election day, he had been in the company of the Boutwell girl, Rebecca. They did not go inside as it was being used as a polling place for the election, too crowded, too busy, and too boisterous for a young lady. So, they were limited to a stroll around the perimeter.

Still, it had been useful. He had made mental notes of the building's architectural features, the number and location of windows and doors, distances from street to entrances, placement of trees, walls and other items that might impede visibility of the entrances from a distance away. He had concluded that for his purposes, he should focus on the entrance off Chestnut Street. His decision had been made stronger yesterday as he observed that the vast majority of delegates to the Continental Congress entered the building here.

He had also been pleased to learn the day before that, for the most part, the building was open to the public, and he had been able to walk through the interior, getting a feel for the layout and the function of the various rooms and spaces. He understood that the chambers of the Continental Congress were closed during sessions, but it was otherwise open, and when he entered this morning, several of the delegates began to gather there. He was warmly greeted by Phillip Livingston and a couple of others who he'd met at the White Horse Inn. They in turn introduced him to others, including the infamous Adams cousins, John and Samuel.

John Adams puffed with pride when Tremont exclaimed that he knew of his "reputation as a fierce patriot and eloquent spokesman for liberty." He was clearly intrigued when he learned that the Frenchman's family published several newspapers, and that he had specifically come to record and write about the building tension between England and its colonies. But Adams snapped to attention when Livingston said, "Monsieur Tremont's family is very close to the king and has great influence at the court of Louis XVI."

"Yes?"

"*Oui,* Monsieur Adams. And our king is very interested in what information I may gain, and what impressions I may form from my travels here." Tremont, with carefully chosen words, insinuated that, though he could not say so outright, and certainly not for public consumption, he might have authority to speak for the French monarch. This nearly caused the man to salivate, and he gave an impromptu speech about the reasons why it was in France's interest to form treaties with the colonies.

What gullible fools these Americans were. People, he had observed, often believed what they wanted to believe. And the more desperate, the more easily convinced. Tremont feigned interest but was noncommittal. Leave them hoping for more, he thought, and he left Adams with the observation, "But how can France form a treaty with colonies who are not sovereign states?" And then he excused himself and exited the room and the building.

Yes, he was disappointed with the election results in Pennsylvania. He understood what it meant. It meant that its delegates to the Continental Congress would continue to advocate for reconciliation with England, and oppose a separation, and that the other middle colonies would follow its lead. And Tremont did not want reconciliation. He wanted the rebels to vote to separate from England, to declare to the world their independence—and then to slap them down like the cur dogs they were. Timing, as every good actor knows, is everything. Their arrogance and ingratitude will have earned them the ignominious death of their leaders, and the resulting chaos and confusion, and then the remaining terror as they realized their impotence and their vulnerability.

This morning he walked the exterior twice more and took another tour of the interior of the building, reinforcing images he had formed the day before, and adding new information. This time he climbed up to the bell tower and looked out over the surrounding rooflines. He would want to get a set of architectural drawings, but firsthand viewing was crucial.

He spent the last hour walking the streets near the State House, getting a lay of the land, surveying the buildings that fronted the other side of Chestnut Street, and those located on side streets. He took note of the businesses in each location and spoke with proprietors. He had many factors to consider, including ease of access, escape routes, and whether the location would be conducive to privacy, but most importantly, whether it offered a clear line of sight to the Chestnut Street entrance. He now turned his back to that entrance and considered his options once more and made his decision. He waited for a carriage to pass by, then walked across the brick-paved street.

He paused briefly at the covered entrance of 356 Chestnut Street. The sign above the open, double door entrance proclaimed, "The Philadelphia Emporium." Two mannequins posed in the window to the right, a blue satin dress on one and a beige velvet suit on the other. In the window on the left, tastefully arranged, were several household items, including candles, oil lamps, glassware, cast iron pots and pans, a floral-patterned armchair, and a chess board and pieces, displayed on a walnut side table. In this window was also posted the sign which had caught his attention earlier, "Rooms to Let. Inquire Within." The lettering was ornate, and precise.

He opened the door and stepped inside, taking in at a glance the layout and the contents of the room. Floor-to-ceiling shelves, filled with merchandise, lined both side walls. A wide staircase was positioned in the rear. Four wooden tables, symmetrically arranged in the floor space, equidistant from each other and the surrounding walls, were stacked with various items of clothing and accessories, all of high quality.

There were three people in the store. A man sat at a desk in the back, and two women stood next to a table which contained rolls of fabric. The women's conversation stopped abruptly when he came in. They all looked up, recognizing immediately a newcomer, not a usual customer. After a brief silence, the man stood from the desk and came forward. As he did, Tremont turned toward the women. Both were quite handsome, one tall, erect in posture, the other, short and petite, and both elegantly dressed. Tremont tipped his hat in their direction and made a small circle with his hand. "*Bonjour, mesdames.*" He turned to face the man. "*Monsieur.*"

"*Bonjour, monsieur,*" the man responded. "*Puis-je t'aider.*"

"Ah, *vous parlez français.*"

"*Seulement un peu,*" the man said, holding up his hand, his finger and thumb a small distance apart.

"I appreciate the effort, monsieur, but I am happy to converse in English. Indeed, the more the practice, the better, no?"

"*Oui,*" the man said. "Your English is much better than my French."
He winked then and gave Tremont a smile. Allow me to introduce
myself. I am Eric Patterson." The two men nodded at each other.
Patterson reached an arm out toward the taller of the two women.
"This is my wife, Clara, and this is one of our best customers, Mrs.
Mary Dickinson."

The Frenchman bowed deeply and then kissed the hand of Clara
Patterson and then of Mary Dickinson. "Ah, yes, the wife of John
Dickinson, I believe."

Their faces betrayed the surprise, just short of shock, that this
stranger would have this information. "Why yes," The petite woman
said, managing a smile. "So pleased to meet you, Mr. Tremont."

"The pleasure is all mine, Madame Dickinson. Although I have not
been long in Philadelphia, I have learned of the esteem in which your
husband is held. I have had the privilege of making his acquaintance
and he spoke of you by name."

Tremont turned to the Patterson couple. "What a lovely store you
have here. It is no wonder Mrs. Dickinson frequents it."

"And I can see that you are a man who appreciates quality, so you
have come to the right place. May I interest you in a new suit perhaps?
Many of our fashions come from France, as you might imagine."

"Actually, I am here to inquire about your room to let." He jerked
his head back toward the entrance, and the sign in the window. "I may
have an interest."

"*Bien sur, bien sur,*" Patterson said. "Of course," he repeated once
more, in English.

Philadelphia, May 6
Chapter 11

It had been a long and tedious session at the Congress that day and it was almost seven o'clock when Tim Matlack and Will Harrell headed to the City Tavern to compare notes and discuss strategy. They walked at a leisurely pace down Chestnut Street, with Matlack searching each passing face for recognition, and often finding it, nodding or tipping his hat in greeting, occasionally stopping to make small talk.

Will thought Matlack to be friendly to a fault. He didn't consider himself unfriendly, but he found engaging in frivolous chatter to be exhausting. He preferred in depth discussions on topics of some substance, or better yet a long walk alone to sort things out in his mind. Part of him, though, envied the man's easy social grace.

And he found that he genuinely liked Tim, and considered him a friend, though he was twenty-five years his senior. Matlack spoke his mind directly but not rudely. He had a creative mind and an air of confidence about him, but he was also modest and self-deprecating in his manner. When Will was with him, his own social awkwardness seemed less noticeable. And he had proven a good collaborator in the investigation. So, if it took them longer than it should to get where they were going so that Matlack could greet passersby and make small talk with them, Will was not going to complain.

When a man inquired as to Tim's brewery business, he told him it was doing fine, putting bread on the table for him and his family. When they resumed their stroll, Matlack's mood became reflective. He said, "My father, you know, never made much money and died bankrupt."

Will didn't know, but he nodded.

"Maybe the apple doesn't fall too far from the tree," he said. "I failed miserably in the hardware store business a few years back. I suppose, to be honest, I was more interested in cockfights and horse racing than business."

Some would say he still was, Will thought, but he held his tongue.

Tim shook his head. "Before long, I too was both bankrupt and disowned from my Quaker meeting for, as they put it, 'frequenting company in such a manner as to neglect business whereby he contracted debts, failed, and was unable to satisfy his creditors.'"

"That must have really stung," Will said, noting that he was able to recite the indictment verbatim after so many years.

"Not as much as the time I spent in debtors' prison." His smile was tinged with bitterness.

"I guess so," Will managed.

"But my point is that although I am making a decent living with the brewery, I'm always aware that things could turn in an instant. The small businessman and the workers have little protection. You never feel secure."

"And the Quakers? Are you back in their good graces?"

His mouth turned up in a wry grin. "They're a hard bunch, but they did arrange my release from debtors' prison. Thought I'd learned my lesson, I guess. But they never let up, you know. I remember one day, not that long ago, I was on my way to battalion drill in my uniform, my sword by my side, and I ran into one of my Quaker acquaintances. He says, 'Where art thou hurrying so fast with this thing dangling by thy side?'" His impersonation of the Quaker's manner and language had more than a hint of mockery to it.

"I told him I was going to fight for my property and my liberty. And he says, 'As for thy property thou hast none—and as for thy liberty, thou owest that to the clemency of thy creditors, me amongst the rest.'"

He laughed a little harder now, the humor overriding the bitterness, and Will joined him. "Some of us, ousted from our Meeting, get together, informally call ourselves Free Quakers." He was still smiling when he said it, but Will detected a trace of sadness in his voice.

At the tavern, they ordered beers and navigated past several well-wishers to a corner table at the tavern, where they began to take stock of where they were in their inquiries. By now, Will had memorized the names and faces of the delegates and the colonies they represented, and where they sat in the chamber. To the extent possible, they had made a list of the secretaries, servants, slaves, and others who may have accompanied the delegates, as well as any other employees of the Congress.

The latter category consisted of the two of them and three young men, boys really, Jonathon Zeigler, Jeremy Owens and Thomas Beall, who acted as assistant clerks, manning the doors, running errands and delivering messages and, as the title suggested, otherwise assisting the clerks, he and Tim, in their duties. Will had begun making notes as to each person, gathering additional information, and evaluating each as a possible suspect.

"Do you favor independence for the colonies?"

Matlack's question had come out of the blue and caught Will a little off guard, but he answered without hesitation. "I think that is the better course for us, though I can see why others disagree."

Matlack gave him a sideways glance. "You consider yourself open-minded, then, willing to consider all sides." He said it as if it were a serious character defect. "I suspect that you are a bit hesitant, cautious about declaring your position because of your relationship with Mr. Dickinson?"

Will thought such an observation to be obvious and said nothing in response.

"And I certainly see why you would not want to be at odds with Joseph Boutwell."

The oblique reference to Rebecca made him blush, but he held his tongue.

"You must know that the time is fast approaching when you will have to choose sides, Will, and history is on the side of independence. I can almost taste it, my young friend, smell its sweet fragrance in the air."

Will nodded again but said nothing.

"And don't get me wrong. I like John Dickinson. I serve with him in the militia. He is an honorable man, and no doubt sincere in his beliefs. But he is getting left behind by the movement he helped start."

"Perhaps he is just wary of tearing down a house before building another to take its place," Will said, repeating something he had heard his mentor say. "That seems to be a reasonable position."

Tim shook his head. "The house is falling down around us, Will. We must get out before the roof caves in on top of us."

Will shrugged again.

"Don't you see, if we can change the political landscape in Pennsylvania politics, we can change the dynamics in the Congress. And if we can do that, we can change the world."

"But you lost the election," Will said. "Mr. Dickinson and his allies are still in control of the Assembly and the delegation to the Congress."

"Yes, but not for long, perhaps."

Will gave him a long look then, wondering what he meant, but before he could respond, he looked up to see Sam Adams standing at their table.

"May I join you, gentlemen? I have new intelligence from Boston."

* * *

Adams' hand was trembling so badly, Will thought he would drop his hat as he removed it and placed it on the table. He got right to it, telling them that one of his men in Boston, a member of the Sons of Liberty, had been killed a couple of weeks before, his throat sliced ear to ear.

"He was a dear friend and true patriot, and he has left a wife and three children behind. All the evidence points to a man who called himself Henry Belmont as the killer. He is described as an elderly man in his sixties, with long grey hair. Walks with a cane. He claims to be from Virginia, and a cousin of George Washington, though that is now considered highly doubtful. They think he may be a British spy. He left Boston to avoid capture and his whereabouts are unknown."

Tim asked, "You think he might be our assassin?"

Adams shrugged. "It seems more than coincidental."

"I had pictured a younger man," Matlack said.

Will's lips started to tingle and go numb. He ignored it and took a large gulp of beer. He had been warned that alcoholic beverages might trigger seizures, but so did just about everything else he did. He placed the mug on the table. "Could the killer of your friend have been wearing a disguise?"

"I suppose so," Adams said, "but that wasn't in the message."

"Well," Tim said, "it is at least something to go on." He turned to Adams. "While you're here, we need to recruit some street lads we know to help check around the city for recent arrivals, and to follow certain people and report to us on their comings and goings. We also need teams to act as bodyguards for some of the delegates, to watch their backs. Will and I just can't do it alone."

Adams arched an eyebrow in his direction, the question implied.

"These boys can be trusted. Besides, they would not know why they were gathering the information." He hesitated, then added, "We would need money to pay them."

Adams gave him a shrug. "Who do you want followed? And which delegates need protection?"

Will answered with a question of his own. "What do you know about Geoffrey Powell Hamilton?"

He wasn't familiar with the name, Adams said. Will looked to Tim.

"He is an aide and secretary to Phillip Livingston," Matlack said, "a delegate from New York. He was a last-minute replacement for Livingston's long-time regular secretary, who apparently had taken ill and couldn't make the trip to Philadelphia."

"Nothing necessarily sinister about that," Will said, "but it does mean that we don't know much about him. And perhaps we should."

Adams nodded.

"We are also interested in the secretary for Samuel Chase, from Maryland."

"Yes," Tim said, looking at Adams. "Chase, as you know, is currently on a mission to Canada with Ben Franklin, but he left his secretary, Edward White, behind. White is a long-time servant to the Chase family, and apparently much trusted, but I have been told that he has strong loyalist views, and I have myself seen him in the company of known Tories in the city on several occasions."

"Again, not necessarily incriminating, but...." Will let the thought hang in the air, then said, "I have also heard that he has tastes that are more expensive than his financial means can support."

"He certainly dresses in fine clothes for a secretary," Tim said, "and he is not shy in gambling at a horse race or cockfight. To this I can personally attest." He grinned.

Will suggested that there were many persons in Philadelphia who might be willing to help a British spy. "Some might be motivated by money, some who sincerely believe that the rebellion is a stupid, illegal act that was doomed from the beginning. There are others who put their fingers to the wind and decide which way it is blowing. At any rate, it makes sense that the British may have recruited a few Tories to do more than just talk. Identifying the Philadelphians who might have been enlisted in such an effort will prove difficult, however, simply because the pool of suspects is quite large."

Sam Adams nodded again but said nothing in response.

"And one more suspect," Will said. "Edward Rutledge of South Carolina is known to be in favor of independence, at least privately."

"Yes," Matlack said. "The little prissy peacock is an ally in the Congress for independence, so long as you don't threaten to take away his slaves." Tim was vehemently anti-slavery and had to work hard to reign in his tongue about it when in the Congress. "Did you know they have more slaves than colonists in South Carolina?"

In fact, Will did know. He knew that slaves comprised approximately sixty percent of the population in the colony. But he thought the question was a rhetorical one, so he didn't respond directly. Instead, he turned to Adams and said, "Like other Southern delegates, he has travelled to Congress with an entourage of slaves. One of those, a Thomas Miller, has attempted escape at least once while here in Philadelphia. And there are probably others similarly situated and similarly motivated to escape their bondage—and would not feel any particular loyalty to the political cause of their masters."

"I can't say that I blame them, the slaves, but I also cannot fault your logic," Adams said. "We can't ignore the possible threat from that corner, I suppose."

"Damn slaveholding hypocrites," Matlack said under his breath.

When they told Adams that they had exhausted their present list of possible suspects, he rose and clapped each of them on the shoulder and said, "Excellent progress, gentlemen. Please keep me informed." He declined the offer to join them for a beer. "John and I have some work to do, a meeting at our lodgings, and he gets irritable when I'm late." He bade them a good evening and made his way across the room.

A few moments after Adams walked out the front door another man entered. He caught Tim's eye and Tim waved him over. He was handsome, clean shaven, square shouldered and square jawed, with wavy dark hair which he gathered in the back with a black silk ribbon. His clothes were finely tailored and spoke of wealth. Tim introduced him to Will as Henri Dubois Tremont, recently arrived from France.

The man smiled when he heard Will's name, showing a mouthfull of teeth. "Ah, but I believe I have already heard much about you, Mr. William Harrell."

To Will's look of puzzlement, he explained, "You see, I am a guest at the White Horse Inn. I believe you are familiar with my hosts, especially the two sisters, Rebecca and Elizabeth Boutwell. Both lovely ladies, so charming. Rebecca has agreed to be my personal guide to your grand city."

Will could feel his face flush at the words which, though neutral on the surface, seemed to have a lascivious undertone. He was instantly repulsed, and suspicious. Judging by his friendly manner toward the stranger, Tim did not seem to share his concern.

Will's suspicion was fueled in part by an irrational jealousy, and anger at the familiarity the stranger's words suggested. He knew that. But it also made sense to be suspicious of any new arrivals. And intuition was a powerful, if unexplainable, tool in detection. Was he really a Frenchman? He didn't match the description Adams had just given them, but they had agreed that the man in Boston may have been wearing a disguise.

"Indeed," Will said, "I've always heard that the French have a finely tuned sense and appreciation for all things beautiful."

"*Mais oui*, Monsieur. It is so. And we have also an appreciation for the passion in all things."

Again, Will sensed a lewd meaning in his words and he wondered if Matlack sensed it too as there was an awkward silence for a few seconds, finally broken when Tremont added, "Like the passion of you gentlemen for liberty. It is most inspiring."

Matlack explained that Tremont's family was also in the newspaper and printing business, and that he was travelling the colonies, writing a journal of his observations for later publication. He also said that Tremont's family had close ties with the French monarch, and much influence at Court.

Tremont bowed slightly. "I fear that you have an estimate too great of my family's influence in such matters. I assure you, however, that my father, who is close to a few ministers and to the king, would advocate a closer relationship with the colonies if they were determined to be an independent country. It is part of why I have come to the colonies to gauge the mood, the support among your citizens and leaders for such a move."

"Exactly," Tim said. "That is why independence is the logical and, I suggest, undeniable result of our efforts. I fully expect that the Congress will very soon vote to do just that, to sever all ties with that corrupt nation."

Will gave Tim a look but said nothing.

Tremont shrugged and pursed his lips. "Certainly, you are a much better judge of the status, but if I understand correctly, your fellow citizens had the opportunity recently to express their support for this proposition but declined to do so."

"We are working to find a way around this obstacle."

Again, Will gave his friend a look but said nothing.

"Hmm," the Frenchman replied, "I do hope you will keep me informed. And now, I will take your leave." He bowed and walked toward the other side of the room where he was greeted by a group of men at the bar.

"Well," Tim said, "I have a cock fight to host. Care to come with me?"

Will wanted to tag along just so he could ask him more about his new friend from France, but he shook my head. "Got to get to the store. I'm sure the Harrell family will be represented there, however, in the form of Patrick Harrell."

Tim nodded and headed for the exit, and Will followed behind him. As he walked, Will looked back and caught sight of the Frenchman across the room. Their eyes met briefly, then the Frenchman looked away.

* * *

The two roosters flew at each other, leaping three feet off the ground, attacking with a congenital aggression that made them natural fighters. These specially bred gamecocks had been conditioned by their owners for increased stamina and strength, their combs, wattle, and earlobes

107

cut off in order to remove anatomical vulnerabilities in a fight. Much time, effort, and expense had been expended in preparing them—and a lot of money was riding on the outcome.

The cockpit was located on the outskirts of town on Vine Street, just west of Eighth, behind a small barn. The fighting space was enclosed by a split-rail fence about three-and-a-half feet tall, with the spectators crowded around three deep, men craning to get a view of the action. The tension and excitement charged the air around them, fueled by the vast quantities of alcoholic beverages being consumed.

One of the men gathered around the pit was Henri Dubois Tremont. Tim Matlack, who was serving as referee for the fights, had recognized him and made room up front for the visitor from France. As the second of the three scheduled fights began, however, Tremont eased back to stand at the periphery of the crowd, searching for the individual he was to meet.

It took less than a minute to spot the man fitting the physical description he had been given, complete with the white silk ribbon used to tie his hair back. The man made eye contact with Tremont as he approached and then walked past him toward the barn. Tremont waited a few moments then followed. He caught up to him on the other side of the barn where the man prepared to relieve himself on the side of the building. Tremont stood next to him and did the same.

With his free hand, the man reached behind his back and under his shirt, retrieved a large slip of folded paper from his waistband and handed it to Tremont.

"The architectural drawings for the State House and a map of the city with the addresses for the delegates marked, as well as the location of the warehouse." He reached into the pocket of his waistcoat and brought out a metal key, which he handed over. "This will unlock the door to the attached shed. The materials you requested have been delivered there. There is no entrance to it from inside the warehouse so neither you nor your things will be disturbed."

"Very good. And one other thing...."

"Yes?"

"I will need the name of a gunsmith, a real craftsman. He should reside in a town other than Philadelphia, and he must be a man who will be discreet."

"I will see what I can do. Anything else?"

"Not from you, not at this point. There are additional materials I will need, but if you were to purchase them it might raise suspicions. I have others who will assist in this."

There was also the concern on Tremont's part that no one person should know his true mission or the details of his plan to achieve it. Only he would know how the parts made the whole. Tremont reached inside his shirt and brought out a wad of bills which he handed over. The man pocketed the money without counting it.

"The less we meet face to face the better. I will make contact in the manner agreed upon when additional services are needed."

The man nodded and began to walk back toward the cockfight.

"And remember," Tremont said, and the man turned back, "absolute secrecy."

"I understand," the man said, then turned away. He walked around the building and out of sight.

Philadelphia, May 7
Chapter 12

John and Sam Adams shared a room at Mrs. Yard's boarding house, located across from the City Tavern on Second Street. It was not a large room, and to John it seemed even smaller this evening, packed as it was with some of the local leaders of the Independents. He sat apart from the others, his back to the bay window and his arms resting on the small table that functioned as a both a writing desk and a place to eat.

He glanced over at the guests: Christopher Marshall, the apothecary, James Cannon, mathematician and president of the Committee of Privates, Dr. Benjamin Rush, and Thomas Paine, author of *Common Sense*. Of the four, John Adams thought Rush to be the most sensible of the group. He was a short man with a slender frame, an aquiline nose, a very large head, and highly animated blue eyes. He also had flattered Adams upon his arrival in Philadelphia, something that no doubt colored his evaluation of the man thereafter. Marshall was an ornery old cuss whose manner reminded Adams a little too much of himself. Cannon was a bit like his cousin, Sam, not one to step to the front as a spokesman, but terribly effective in organizing men and events behind the scene.

Unlike the others, who were long-time residents of Philadelphia, Thomas Paine had arrived in the city barely two years before, a divorced, unemployed Englishman who had failed at numerous business ventures, with nothing more than a letter of introduction from Benjamin Franklin to recommend him. Paine had planned to start a school for young girls, but never got around to it, as he found he had a talent for writing, from which he could make a decent living. His essays, in which he reflected on a number of topics including dueling and slavery, were regularly published in the local newspapers. He had also become the chief propagandist for the Independents, publishing essays and letters in the newspapers under a fictious name.

Indeed, *Common Sense* was just a natural extension of these pieces. And it had struck a nerve with the people with its simple, direct prose, and its daring but logical message. It somehow made the idea of separation from England more acceptable, more a part of main stream discussion. It was the most read publication in all the colonies, second only to the Bible.

But though Thomas Paine may have had many admirers in the colonies, John Adams wasn't one of them. He considered *Common Sense* to be a great, malicious, shortsighted, crapulous mass. The only good thing to recommend it, Adams thought, was its passionate call for independence—which, he had to admit, had proven useful.

And yes, Adams wanted independence, badly. But he didn't want a revolution of the type Paine and these other radicals were pushing for, which he saw as an abandonment of traditional forms of government in favor of rule by the mob. He believed firmly in the traditional forms and principles of government and proper society—and the stability they provided.

In this sense Adams was more like John Dickinson, his nemesis in the Congress. Dickinson likewise trusted in the strength and stability of the traditional forms of government. Adams admired Dickinson's intelligence and integrity, and his political skills. And had the times and the issue been different, they would no doubt be not only close allies, but friends as well, to the extent Adams allowed any.

The problem was Dickinson's opposition to independence, for which he used his considerable skills to great effect. In his frustration with the man, Adams had imprudently sent a letter home referring to Dickinson, declaring, "a certain great fortune and piddling genius, whose name has been trumpeted so loudly, has given a silly cast to our whole doings." The British got hold of the letter and published it. For months thereafter, the Philadelphia delegates refused to speak to him, and John Adams was an object of nearly universal detestation. For his part, Dickinson did not hold his grudge long, at least not publicly. The two men continued to adhere to exaggerated civility as they led their opposing factions. Perhaps Dickinson would eventually come around, but Adams didn't want to wait. He had waited too long already.

So, Adams held his nose and, along with his cousin, worked with Paine and the other radicals to attempt to change the make-up of the Pennsylvania Assembly, and in turn the instructions to its delegates regarding independence. They all hoped, and expected, that they would be successful in the May 1st election.

But they lost.

And now Sam had gathered them together for a post-mortem of sorts on the recent election, and to develop a new strategy—one that would discredit and topple the newly elected government.

"It's not too difficult to understand," Paine said. "It was those damn proprietary dependents and Quakers spouting testimony. And the Catholics that voted in a block. I'm sure of that." He looked around the table. "They have been enslaved so long, they are afraid of freedom, afraid to break their chains."

John Adams thought it more likely that the more moderate voters who favored independence were scared away by the radical egalitarian reforms the group had advocated, but he held his tongue. As he did when Cannon observed that, "They don't want to share the power," to which Adams thought, *Of course not. Why would they?*

Marshall nodded his agreement. "If the election was held tomorrow, I am confident we would win. Public opinion is shifting more and more each day."

"You think you would have the votes now?" Sam asked.

"Yes," Marshall said, and the other three nodded again in agreement.

"But it's too late now," Paine said. "There won't be another election until next year."

"There may be a way," Sam said. He turned to his cousin, and the others did as well.

John Adams put down his quill pen and leaned forward on the table. "Since our monarch has declared the colonies in a state of rebellion and outside his protection, we intend to offer a resolution in the Congress, encouraging the colonies to label as illegitimate any government that requires a loyalty oath to the king, and to otherwise disavow any allegiance to the crown, and to form new governments as the people deem proper to promote their safety and happiness."

There was silence for several seconds as the others took in the meaning of his words, then they started nodding. "Thomas," Sam Adams said, "You could set the tone and begin the attack on the present government with your typical eloquence, in letters to the newspapers."

Paine nodded, quickly warming to the idea. "Yes, the assembly must go because its authority is from the Crown, not the people. And, as a judge cannot pass upon himself, so that body cannot right the wrong itself. We need a convention to take the pulse of the citizens."

Sam Adams smiled broadly. "Exactly." He turned to the others. "Christopher, you and Charles and the others start organizing your supporters, so as soon as the resolution passes, you can call a town meeting and get the people to approve a new election, under a new constitution if necessary."

The two men nodded. Sam shared a knowing look with his cousin and smiled again.

* * *

The morning sky was overcast, and the air was cool and damp, remnants from the thunderstorm that had blanketed the city the night before. But the sun was beginning to peep through the clouds, and Will knew it would soon bring more of the oppressive heat and humidity that had settled over the city for the last few days. As if in anticipation, perspiration beaded up on his forehead as he walked briskly down

Chestnut Street, approaching the State House. The building stood quiet amidst the growing pulse of activity on the streets and sidewalks, citizens of the city preparing for another day of work and commerce.

As soon as he crossed the threshold, he spotted one of the assistant clerks for the Congress, Jonathon Zeigler, just outside the chambers. He was sitting in a straight back chair, bent forward, elbows on knees, chin resting between his palms, eyes closed. Will walked over and stood next to him a few seconds before calling out his name, quietly at first, then louder. Zeigler startled awake and jumped to his feet

He presented a small, embarrassed smile. "Morning. I guess I must have dozed off a minute."

"Late night?"

He nodded. "Not what you think, though. Had to help my father with a rush job."

Jonathon was a tall, gangly lad of 16, with arms longer than they needed to be. His features suggested a mix of races, with his straight, brown hair and dark eyes, and a complexion the color of copper, but nobody knew for sure. He had been left on the steps of the Alms house one morning, a small infant with a note pinned to the basket asking the Quakers to take care of him. He was later taken in by a kind and childless couple, Raymond and Harriet Zeigler, who raised him as their own. Raymond was a fine silversmith who also worked with brass and copper, or any other metal. He never lacked for business, and both his wife and adopted son helped out regularly.

Will liked Jonathon. He was a hard worker with a good attitude. The assistants prepared the chambers each morning before the sessions and cleaned up afterwards. While the body was in session, they worked in shifts, serving as doormen and errand boys, usually taking a post just outside the entrance to the chambers.

The other two assistants were Jeremy Owens and Thomas Beall. Jeremy was a little older than Jonathon, at 17. His family had business interests in farming, shipping and lumber. Thomas was the eldest at 20,

114

an orphan who dabbled at the study of law and lived off his inheritance, playing billiards and cards in the taverns, and entertaining a variety of young ladies. All three had been hand-picked by the Secretary of the Congress, Charles Thomson, and all were from good, Quaker families, but each of them went on Will's list of possible collaborators with the purported assassin. Not from anything suspicious in their background or their behavior, but because of their position. Each had access to the building after hours, and to information on the members of the Congress, and its business and schedule.

Tim and Will had met with them last week, along with Thomson, who explained the new security protocol.

"After each session closes, and after you clean up, you are to make sure that all doors and windows to the building, and the doors to the congressional chambers, are locked before you leave in the evening. In the mornings, before the session begins, you will examine the entire building, inside and out, top to bottom, for anything out of place, especially any sign that a lock has been breached. If so, report it immediately to Tim or Will, or me.

"And look closely. Look under steps and stairs, in closets, crook and crannies, and other hiding places, as an object may be hidden from plain view."

The boys shared a look and Beall asked, "What sort of object are we looking for, and why all the sudden concern?"

"Any sort of object that wasn't there the evening before," Thomson said, a hint of irritation in his voice. "Any sign that someone has been inside at night, especially into the chambers. And I should think you would need no explanation in order to do your job."

Tim put a hand on the secretary's shoulder and gave the boys a smile. "These are tense times, lads, and getting more tense every day. We just thought it prudent to be a little more careful. And specifically, you should be looking for a bomb or some explosive device."

This got the assistants' attention and almost in unison they all said, "Yes, sir."

"During session," Thomson continued, "one of you will always be posted outside the chamber doors. Keep an eye out for anyone who looks strange or out of place, or anything that seems out of the ordinary, anyone loitering around with no apparent purpose." He gave them the description they had of the elderly man suspected of the murder in Boston and told them to especially be on the lookout for anyone matching that description. "And no one gets in who is not a delegate or previously approved by a delegate. Understood?"

They all shook their heads and assured Thomson that he could count on them.

Will had gone behind them since then, reinforcing and explaining what was expected, but mostly he was pleased with their thoroughness. They rotated the duties, and it had been Jonathon's rotation this morning.

"How's it look this morning?" Will asked.

"Fine. I checked everything and everywhere, including the grounds. Nothing out of place. Nothing suspicious. And I've got everything set up in the chambers as well."

Will gave him a pat on the shoulder. "Good work. Go ahead and rest while you can. The members will begin arriving soon."

He then climbed the stairs to the third floor and up the steep narrow ladder to the bell tower. There he perched himself, leaning against the bell for balance and support, and scanning the surrounding rooflines.

A would-be assassin with a long rifle could position himself on one of the surrounding rooftops from which he might pick off delegates as they entered or left the building. Will figured it would make more sense to attack in the morning, though. Sessions for the Congress began with some regularity at ten o'clock, and most members arrived ten to fifteen minutes before the scheduled time. Though some members came in the back entrance, through the courtyard on Walnut Street,

116

most entered through the front entrance on Chestnut. In addition, the Walnut Street side had the courtyard and several trees that effectively blocked any reasonable line of sight.

Will had made this surveillance protocol part of his regular morning routine. Aside from the security aspect of it, there was also something peaceful and serene in getting above the din of activity below. And there was usually at least a slight breeze up this high that afforded some relief from the sweltering heat and humidity on the street, and from the stifling chambers of the Congress, with its doors and windows kept closed. So, he lingered there several minutes, looking out over the city and at the people on the sidewalks and in the carts and wagons on the streets, going about their day.

Thoughts of Rebecca and the Frenchman, Tremont, came to him then, unbidden. The man had gotten under his skin with his words, his insinuations. But when he suggested to Rebecca that maybe it wasn't such a good idea for her to be seen alone with the man, accompanying him around the city, she became angry.

"I don't see you complaining when it is you that I accompany in public."

"But that's different."

"How is it different, William Harrell? Do you think you own me?"

"No, I just...." He couldn't find the words that came next, no matter how hard he looked around for them.

She had lightened up then, giving him a squeeze on his arm and a smile. "I appreciate your concern, Will. It's sweet, but I can take care of myself."

He wasn't so sure. But he was sure that she didn't want to hear anything bad about her new friend. There was nothing he could really tell her, either. He couldn't say anything about a possible assassination plot against leaders of Congress, of the general suspicion of any new arrivals to the city. He had checked up on the man and, so far, had nothing to suggest that he was not who he claimed to be. People who spoke French thought his speech and accent seemed authentic, and he had a thorough knowledge of all things French. He was charming and had quickly found favor among many of the delegates, and with the Boutwell family as well.

The sound of footsteps on the ladder below brought him back to the present. A moment later, Tim Matlack's head appeared through the cupola's opening.

"I thought I might find you here." He smiled as he climbed the rest of the way up and stood next to Will. "What a beautiful view," he said, looking out.

"Indeed," Will said.

They stood there several more seconds without speaking.

"The three buildings there," Will said, pointing, "would seem to offer the best bet for a rifleman."

Tim crossed his arms in front of his chest. "We should find out who owns each, inquire of uses, tenants, maybe get permission to look around."

Will nodded. "So much to do, so little time. We also need to get up with Cecil O'Conner and see if he and his lads will help."

"Yes, we'll catch up with him later today."

"Very good."

"And now," Tim said, "I believe it is just about time for the session to begin, and I think you will want to be present, as things may become interesting."

Will gave him a questioning look, but Matlack said nothing else, just gave Will a small wink before heading back down the ladder.

Philadelphia, May 10
Chapter 13

Henri Tremont positioned the straight back chair two feet away from the window and drew the tattered blue curtains back enough to leave an opening of about three inches. He sat down and once again peered through his spyglass toward the State House. He could see through the outer doorway of the building, down the hallway to the entrance to the Continental Congress chambers, where the doorman was now closing the doors. Wooden blinds blocked his view at each window so that, despite the magnification, he was unable to see inside the chambers.

He took the watch from his vest pocket and noted the time, then replaced the watch and put the spyglass to his right eye again, moving it slowly in an arcing motion to examine the full exterior of the building. He looked up at the cupola, where minutes before he had observed the Harrell boy, perched against the massive bell, scanning the surrounding area. Had Harrell been looking for something in particular? It seemed so, but he couldn't be sure, so he was careful to remain concealed behind the curtains. Harrell was joined for a brief period by the other clerk, Matlack, then both climbed back down.

Renting this small room had proved a good choice. Indeed, he thought it nearly perfect for his purposes. It was located on the third floor of the building, and the one window in the room offered a good line of sight to the State House. On the first floor, the owner and his wife operated a general store. The second floor was divided into four rooms which were rented out for commercial or professional uses. One was used by a lawyer and another by a surveyor. The other two were vacant, and the owner of the building, Eric Patterson, had tried to interest him in one of these. He could offer a very good rental rate, he said.

"Merci, Monsieur, but it is much too large," Tremont had said, shaking his head politely. "I require only a small space. As I say, I am wanting only a quiet place to write, away from the rather noisy White Horse Inn."

The owner had frowned briefly, then quickly replaced it with an understanding smile. "The third floor we use mostly for storage, but I have a small room that is nearly empty and might be suitable for your purposes. It has no furniture or furnishings, but we could take care of that if you like the space."

And he did like it. It was small, maybe ten by ten feet, but Patterson had cleaned it up and furnished it with an oak writing table and chair, an upholstered reading chair, and even a couple of decorative paintings. He could reach the room through a side entrance off 5th Street, so that he could come and go without having to go through the store. In addition to offering a good place from which to watch and record the comings and goings of the congressional delegates, it also offered access to the roof of the building, up a narrow staircase.

"*Certainement,*" Patterson said when Tremont asked if use of the roof area would be included in the rent.

"Bon, bon, Monsieur Patterson. I like to have some fresh air, especially when it becomes so very hot, as it happens in your city, no?"

Patterson had agreed that Philadelphia was often very hot in the late spring and summer months. "And also, it offers a very nice view of the city."

"*Certes,*" Tremont said, "Indeed," he repeated in English.

And, when the time came, he would take the narrow staircase to the roof, where he would have not only more height and a better angle for his attack, but also a more effective escape route. Only six feet separated the building from its neighbor to the north, which housed a tavern. A board could be stored on the roof and used as a bridge to this other building, then pulled over and hidden there. And if necessary, he thought the distance between the two buildings was such that he could clear it easily with a running start. He had noted a metal ladder attached to the rear of this adjacent building which led down to an alley in the back of the tavern. He felt that he could thus easily and quickly put some distance between himself and anyone who might be inclined to come after him.

Yes, Tremont told Patterson, the room would work well. He emphasized that he did not wish to offend his hosts at the White Horse Inn, or make the other guests uncomfortable, so it was important that no one else know about their rental arrangement. If the owner thought the request for secrecy odd, or suspicious, he gave no indication of it, but rather gave his solemn assurances that the fact that he was renting the room would remain confidential, just between them.

Tremont now pointed his spyglass toward the street below, and took a few more minutes to observe people passing by, especially the women, dressed in their finery, strutting by—not unlike the woman last night, though the latter carried no illusions of her station in life. She hid behind no façade.

As he looked now once more through his spyglass, his attention was drawn to a gentleman who was walking hurriedly down Chestnut Street. The man rushed into the State House, knocked on the double doors of the congressional chambers and was given entry. Tremont checked his pocket watch again. *I wonder who the latecomer is.* He then folded the glass and placed it beside him as he leaned back in the chair.

He pulled from his leather knapsack the list of congressional delegates he had compiled. It contained their names, grouped by colony, together with a physical description and basic information about each one. He determined the latecomer to be William Paca, a delegate from Maryland. His notes described him as short and trim with a thin nose and mouth, but with a fleshy face and medium length brown hair. He was a lawyer and a planter, quite wealthy, about thirty-five years of age. Tremont dipped his quill pen into the ink and scratched an additional note: "Late to the session on this date, May 10th."

He placed the document to the side, then withdrew the architectural plans for the State House from the knapsack. He spread them out on the desk, using the inkwell to hold the drawings in place. He took a fresh look at the plans, scratched some notes at the appropriate places. He then looked out the window, into the distance, considering his options, fine tuning the plan he had been formulating since his arrival in Philadelphia. On a separate piece of paper, he made a list of additional information and materials he would require. This note he would leave at the designated location later that day. He was so busy writing and lost in thought that the sound of the knock on the door barely registered with him.

"Mr. Tremont?"

Instinctively, he shoved the plans back into his knapsack. "Yes?"

When he heard no response, Tremont rose, went to the door and opened it. He put on a smile. "Bonjour, Monsieur Patterson."

"Bonjour," Patterson said, looking around the room. "Is everything to your satisfaction?"

Tremont knew he was not so much being solicitous of his tenant as he was just overly inquisitive, and a bit overly friendly—despite his strict instructions for privacy. He would have much preferred to be left alone, but he also did not wish to do anything to arouse suspicion. "Oui, certes," he said.

Patterson ran his hand through his stiff, wavy hair. "Didn't mean to disturb you." He gave his tenant a smile. "Had to grab a couple of rolls of muslin we have stored up here." He turned to display the two rolls in the crook of his left arm. "Thought I would just check on you."

"No, no. No disturbance. In fact, I was just finishing up, here. He closed the knapsack and slung it over his shoulder. "I'll accompany you down the stairs if that is where you are heading." He looked behind him and saw the spyglass, quickly retrieved it and stuffed it in the knapsack. Had his landlord seen it? If he did and wondered why his tenant had a spyglass in his room, he didn't say so. Tremont investigated the other man's face and saw not suspicion, but a willingness to please. Patterson nodded. Tremont locked the door behind him as they exited the room, then he followed his landlord down the staircase.

* * *

The meeting room for the Continental Congress was a small, intimate space, the round desks for each delegation close together and the acoustics so good that delegates could be heard clearly across the room—sometimes to the embarrassment of those prone to muttering under their breaths. For privacy, the doors and windows to the chamber were usually closed, exacerbating the heat and humidity that blanketed the city.

And it was hot this day, even at ten o'clock in the morning when the session began. Will wiped a bit of perspiration from his brow with the sleeve of his shirt as Hancock recognized John Adams "for purposes of proposing a resolution."

Adams rose slowly from his seat at the wooden desk and looked around at the men with whom he had debated many issues, some important; many not, but almost all hotly contested. It was natural that tempers often flared and the delegates practiced elaborate forms of politeness to keep from throttling each other.

There were a lot of large personalities and egos in this body—and John Adams was one of its largest. He knew that. He also knew that he was disliked by many of his fellow delegates, who found him to be obnoxious. He tried to be more diplomatic, but he rarely succeeded. It was just not in his nature. Popularity would have been nice, but it was not something he strove for. He'd rather have their respect and admiration. And he had his eye more on posterity and his place in history than on the favor of his contemporaries.

Despite his confrontational style and brutal bluntness, his dogmatic pursuit of his objectives, no one could deny his intelligence or his oratorical skills. Even his political opponents begrudgingly acknowledged that he could make a compelling argument for his position.

If he were a British assassin and wanted to eliminate the leaders of the Congress, Will thought, John Adams would be at the top of his list. As would his cousin, Sam. For, if John Adams was the public face of the independence movement in the Congress, Sam Adams was the one calling the shots, the master of behind-the-scenes negotiations and manipulations. He understood human nature, grasping quickly the strengths and weaknesses of those he met, and how to use each to motivate them.

Sam recruited John to the cause in the mid-1760s, effectively appealing to his younger cousin's vanity by arranging for him to join with James Otis and Jeremiah Gridley, two of the most prestigious lawyers in Massachusetts, to argue before the Royal Governor and Council against the Stamp Act. John, a little-known lawyer from Braintree at the time, was proud and excited to have his talents recognized in such a conspicuous way.

John Adams became a fervent defender of Whig traditions of liberty and an effective voice for the rebel cause. But he also became increasingly concerned about some of the methods used by the Sons of Liberty in Boston. To enforce boycotts, they used self-appointed committees of inspection—tough gang members really—to threaten and abuse noncompliant merchants. They terrorized and humiliated some resistors, dragging them through the streets. Boston's unity was being enforced by the kind of terror and torture that John Adams saw as the height of lawlessness. He agreed with the observation of a loyalist he'd overheard after a riot in the streets by a mob. "They call me a brainless Tory, but tell me, my young friend, which is better—to be ruled by one tyrant three thousand miles away, or by three thousand tyrants not one mile away?"

Sam Adams, on the other hand, had no such qualms. He was focused and single-minded in his goal of independence, and he was confident that he could control both the methods and the men he used in furtherance of his goal. He was skilled at manipulating events and men, motivating and organizing like-minded men in resistance, and in recruiting others to the cause. And unlike his cousin, he was not concerned with his public persona, now or in the future. He was not interested in recording for posterity his actions in furtherance of the rebel cause, and indeed, took great pains to burn his notes and correspondence to leave no paper trail.

Sam now gave his cousin a slight nod. John stood before the other delegates and waited until the murmur of conversation stopped and all attention was on him, then spoke.

"Gentleman, the resolution before you for discussion and vote, co-sponsored by Mr. Richard Henry Lee from Virginia and myself, reads as follows:

'Resolved, That it be recommended to the respective assemblies and conventions of the united colonies, where no government sufficient to the exigencies of their affairs have been hitherto established, to adopt such government as shall, in the opinion of the representatives of the people, best conduce to the happiness and safety of their constituents in particular, and America in general.'"

The language was dryly procedural and seemed rather innocuous. Most of the members probably had no idea of the underlying motive behind the resolution, or its real purpose. But John Dickinson understood exactly what was happening. This was a sneak attack against the newly elected government of Pennsylvania.

But he was ready. When it came his turn to speak, Dickinson rose from his seat and waited as the room fell silent in anticipation. He scanned the members and then rested his gaze on John Adams, who returned it for several seconds before looking down, purportedly at his notes.

"I agree entirely on the necessity for such a resolution," Dickinson said, looking now around the room at all the delegates. "The colonies need stable governments to carry out the imminent summer campaign. Furthermore, such a resolution would not prevent, and perhaps may even promote, a speedier reconciliation with the mother country."

He returned his gaze to John Adams, who did his best to hide his surprise. "Of course," Dickinson said, "this resolution does not apply to Pennsylvania, which is not a royal government. It has never allowed its representative body to be disbanded as has others, and it is in a unique position to facilitate reconciliation. Thus, Pennsylvania already has a government sufficient to the exigencies of its affairs and one to which the voters have just given a mandate of approval."

Sam Adams sat stoically in his seat, his face unreadable. He glanced over at his cousin, John, who could not help but register his disappointment in the tight lips and tense lines at the corners of his mouth. So, with Dickinson's unexpected blessing, and very little discussion, the resolution was passed, and the body went into a brief recess. The Adams cousins and Dickinson shared a glance and small nods as the delegates filed out.

Dickinson admired both Sam and John Adams and respected their differing views on the merits of a separation from Great Britain. But what they had intended this morning by the resolution disgusted him. They were trying to reverse the results of an election held less than two weeks before, to thwart the popular vote of the people expressed thereby, just to achieve their own political objectives. They were meddling in the internal political affairs of his colony, trying to achieve by trickery what their allies could not at the ballot box.

He had outmaneuvered the Adams cousins, had stymied their efforts, at least for the foreseeable future. The political threat thus abated, he decided to leave town that afternoon for his family plantation on the Delaware shore.

That would prove to be a mistake.

Philadelphia, May 10
Chapter 14

Cecil O'Brien was an orphaned lad of perhaps 16 years who hired out for work when he could, the odd job here and there, and lived mostly on the streets or with the family of friends, and occasionally at the Alms House—which is where Will first met him when he volunteered with Dr. Rush. Matlack knew him, of course. He knew just about everybody, and certainly all the street urchins, with whom he traded favors from time to time. They both agreed that Cecil was the right person for what they had in mind.

The lad was smart, resourceful and had an independent, self-reliant spirit that Will admired. He had become the de facto leader of several similarly situated youths. He was not above a bit of thievery, but his victims were almost exclusively visitors to the city, and he was careful not to steal so much as to attract attention. He was loyal to his friends, and if he gave you his word on something, he would honor it.

He had done some work at the print shop from time to time and had never abused the trust placed in him. He was a quick study, and Will's father offered him more regular work, but Cecil respectfully declined. "Too confining," he said, quick to add that he appreciated the offer, but "I prefer to keep me options open."

"As if something more appealing is going to come along," Patrick Harrell snorted. But his father continued to look to him for the occasional job—which was just what Will had in mind.

After the session ended that day, Will went in search for the lad. It didn't take long to find him. At the corner of Market and Fourth, a small crowd had gathered, and Cecil was at its center. Will moved to the edge of the crowd to observe the lad work one of his favorite street games.

"It's a fun and entertaining distraction, my friends," he said as he began to shuffle three walnut shells around at moderate speed on a rectangular board supported by two posts, all the time looking anywhere except at the shells. "Are you willing to pit your skills of observation against the speed and dexterity of me hands, and to answer the question, is the hand quicker than the eye?" He looked around at the faces and settled on a well-dressed man Will recognized as a delegate from South Carolina, Thomas Lynch.

"What about you, sir? The rules are simple, and fair," Cecil said. "The question is always the same—under which shell is the pea? If you guess right, I pay you a couple of quid. If you pick wrong, you pay me." He stopped moving the shells momentarily. "This time just for fun. Which do you choose?"

There were a few shouts from the bystanders suggesting the middle shell, some for the one on the right or left, but more for the one in the middle—which is what the delegate chose by pointing his finger. Cecil lifted up the middle shell to reveal the pea underneath. He grinned. "Now, I warn you, I will go much faster when we play for real. D'ya think you can keep up? Are you willing to wager against me?"

The man presented something just short of a smile, tinged with a bit of skepticism, or perhaps suspicion. "Very well, lad, I'll take your wager." He looked around the crowd for encouragement and they obliged with claps and shouts.

Cecil placed the pea back under the middle shell and arranged all three in a line. He removed the middle shell to reveal that the pea was still there. He started off slowly, moving and rearranging the shells, gradually increasing the speed, all the while talking to the man, trying to distract him. Then he stopped abruptly and asked him to choose a shell.

Immediately the crowd erupted with a variety of suggestions, as before, this time the majority seeming to favor the shell to their left. The man again pointed to the middle shell.

Cecil looked at the man then at the crowd, then back to the man. "Are you sure?"

There were shouts of both "yes" and "no" from the people gathered behind the man. He gave a slight nod to Cecil and pointed again with his finger. Cecil lifted the middle shell. No pea. There were groans and jeers from the crowd. Cecil put his hand over the shell on the left and hovered there, letting the shouts grow to a crescendo, then he lifted the shell to reveal the pea underneath. More groans and contrasting shouts of self-congratulations arose from those in the crowd.

The delegate from South Carolina smiled, surprising many in the crowd who expected anger perhaps. He handed over the agreed sum to Cecil. "A small price of pay in order to witness your skill and showmanship, young man. You should, however, perhaps put them to better use." The statement suggested he suspected a slight of hand on the part of Cecil, but he smiled again and walked away.

"Who's next?" Cecil looked around at the faces around him. No one spoke.

Will stepped forward then and said, "I'll give it a try."

The boy looked at him, rolled his eyes, gave him a small grin and shook his head. "I may be reckless at times, but I am no fool, Master Harrell." He bowed in his direction. "I will acknowledge your superior skill to all those gathered round and most respectfully decline to lose more of my hard-earned money to you, sir."

Some in the crowd urged him on, some accused him of being a coward, trying to shame him into another game.

"You never know, Cecil," Will said. "This could be your day."

"No, sir," he said, and at this point the crowd was enjoying the show, still urging him on and hoping to see another game.

"Well, then," Will said, "may I have a minute of your time to discuss another matter?"

Cecil looked at Will appraisingly for a few moments then turned to face the crowd. "If you will excuse me, gents, I will be back shortly." As he gathered up his shells, though, and followed us to a nearby alley, they began to disperse.

"Sorry to interrupt your game," Will said.

Cecil gave him a dismissive wave of the hand. "It had run its course anyway." He looked at Will expectantly.

"I have a job for you—and some of your lads." He paused. "There's money in it."

"Well, I should hope so. Otherwise, it's a favor and not a job." He smiled. "So, what is the job?"

May 15

It was a little past midnight when Will closed the book in front of him, leaned back in his chair and stretched, then gave a big yawn. He was tired, no question about it, and he knew he needed his sleep. So, he extinguished the oil lamp on the small desk, disrobed and plopped into his bed.

But sleep would not come. He lay there for several minutes, staring at the ceiling, listening to the scratching of rats in the wall, to the argument of a couple on the street below his window, and to the distant but persistent sounds of a city still awake. It was too hot, and there were too many things on his mind. Even with a lessening of outside distractions, the peace of slumber eluded him, and sixty minutes after his head hit the pillow, he rose, dressed, and headed down the back stairs to the alley behind the shop. He began walking, with no particular destination in mind and no real preference as to direction, either. He would use the time to think, to reflect, to clear his head.

He traveled down Arch to Front Street, along the river north, then south, past the warehouses of his father and others, up Plumb Street and Shippen, past The City Tavern on Second Street. The air was thick and heavy and clung to him. Despite the late hour, the temperature was still near eighty degrees, though a bit cooler down by the river where a slight breeze gave some relief.

As he walked, he went over in his mind the pieces of the puzzle he had assembled thus far, but no clear picture emerged. He was not at all sure how, or if, the pieces were connected.

Because of limited resources, there was no choice but to sort as much as possible confederates, aider and abettors who might have some connection to the Congress, and as to those citizens of Philadelphia who would be most likely to help a British spy if asked. He'd also had to recruit Cecil to help with the task. "We need some extra eyes and ears to record the comings and goings of certain people," Will told him. "We want to know where they go and when, who they talk to, what they do—from the time they get up until they go to sleep at night." He gave him a piece of paper. "This is a list of the people with information as to addresses and description. Some you may know already."

He paused while Cecil read through the list. "We also want to know about any recent visitors to our city, anyone who has arrived in the last three or four weeks, and anyone who comes here going forward. Check with all the inns and boarding houses, private houses that have guests, anywhere a person might take up lodging. I want to know anything you can find out about them. I'm particularly interested in any information about a possible recent arrival, an elderly man with gray hair who walks with a cane and speaks with a Virginian accent."

"Why do you want this information?" Cecil asked. "Does it have something to do with the Congress?"

Will thought for a moment before answering, and settled on "Yes, but I'm not at liberty to discuss any details, nor is it necessary for your purposes. And really, the less you and your lads know, the better. And it is very important that we keep this matter confidential. Pick only lads you can trust. Be discreet in your inquiries, and don't let these people know they are being followed."

"So, sort of like spies then."

Will gave him a small smile. "Yes, very much like spies."

Recruiting Cecil and his lads was a risk. Despite the admonition to keep the assignment confidential, one or more of them might talk. It's just hard to keep a secret, and people like to brag when they think they have some special knowledge. Based on this same principle, Will had tried to infiltrate the Tory population in the city to see if there was any talk, any gossip of an assassin come to Philadelphia, better yet, who might be involved in any plot. Professionals might have the self-control, but not the ordinary citizens. If there was a plan afoot, someone in that community would know, and someone might talk about it.

He also made it a point to mix with the lower sort in the taverns and bawdy houses, at the bull baits and cockfights, keeping a low profile, but also keeping his eyes and ears open. And when he couldn't sleep, like this night, he walked, sometimes for miles, looking for what, he wasn't sure, maybe an old man walking with a cane. He made inquiries of people he knew along the way, casual like.

One good thing, he had become so immersed in his work with the Congress in general, and in his hunt for the assassin in particular, that his headaches and his epilepsy seemed to be held in abeyance, as if his body understood the importance of the challenge. It might have been strictly coincidental, but he clung to this interpretation.

After about an hour of aimless strolling he headed back to his room above the shop. At the corner of Third and Arch Streets, he came upon two women he knew, prostitutes. Cynthia Farrington and Judy Bradford were friends who worked together out of a bawdy house on Arch Street. Sometimes they walked the streets nearby, soliciting customers. Judy had been his first sexual experience when he was sixteen, something arranged by his father. Since then, he'd come back a few times. Once he had been with Cynthia. Always a pleasant time.

"Hello, Cindy, Judy."

They had seen him coming, sizing up his potential as a customer. Now that they recognized him, they both broke out big smiles. Cynthia spoke first. "Well, if it ain't William Harrell. A little past your bedtime, ain't it?"

Will smiled. "I think you're right. That's where I'm heading now, to bed."

"Maybe with me, or Judy?" she gave her friend a smile.

"Not tonight, ladies. But I do have a favor to ask."

They looked at him expectantly.

"I'm looking for an elderly gentleman, long grey hair, smokes a pipe, walks with a cane, speaks with a Virginian accent. Probably a finely dressed gentleman with money to spend. Have you seen anyone fitting that description? Or maybe heard someone mention someone like that?"

They both shook their heads. "Sounds like a man we wouldn't mind meeting," Judy said, "and a man with money to spend is a man we would remember."

Cynthia nodded in agreement. "friend of yours?"

He shook his head. "Never met him." To the puzzled looks, he said, "And I don't want him to know I'm looking for him." This clearly intrigued the women. "But if you do see someone of this description, will you get word to me?"

They pressed him for more information, but he held them off. "It's better you do not know." It was a reply that he had used to good effect before, and it worked this time as well. They promised to let him know if they saw or heard word of such a man. They also tried to entice him with an offer of "two for the price of one" but he again declined, bade them a goodnight and headed back to his room.

* * *

When Tremont first walked past her, there had been too many people around and he ignored her call. But he noticed her. She had dark hair and olive skin, a smile that shone in the darkness and a dress so tight he thought she might just pop right out of it if she moved too fast—which she didn't seem inclined to do. Later, on his return trip, she was apart from the others and he approached her.

She stood, posed, with her hand resting on the wall of the building, her right hip jutting out toward the street, a significant amount of cleavage showing at the top of that tight dress. She smiled at him. "Well, hello again, good looking. Change your mind?"

He bowed deeply. "Madame," he said, without a trace of the French accent he had adopted of late. He had assumed that night the disguise, the role, of Henry Belmont, Virginia planter, complete with stooped posture and walking cane. Good looking? No. But his clothes were expensive. Hence the friendly greeting. Tremont looked around again quickly, satisfying himself that no one was paying attention to them. He put his finger to his lips and motioned her to the nearby alley.

"I got a place close by," she said, "if you want more privacy."

He smiled and shook his head. "The public place, the fresh air, can sometimes encourage a special ardor. Don't you agree?"

"Sometimes," she said, a coy smile dancing across her lips.

The woman was no ignorant whore, he decided. He sensed that she was tolerably intelligent and articulate. She was also obviously self-assured. He suggested a price and though she tried to hide it, he could tell that she was surprised, and pleased, that he had started so high, and hoping to get him a little higher.

But she wouldn't.

"And what would the gentleman expect for his money?"

"Anything he wants."

She smiled again. "And what does the gentleman want?"

He told her what she could start with. "We'll see where it goes from there."

She held out her hand. He removed a wad of cash from a pouch inside his shirt and counted out the bills. She looked at it, frowned and noted that it was not the amount agreed upon.

"Half now, the other half when I'm done—if I am satisfied."

Even at half the quoted amount, it was a good deal for her, but she pushed for full payment in advance. "Oh, don't you worry dearie. You'll get your money's worth, and more."

"Then you will get what we agreed upon, and more."

He had intended to be cautious, conservative in his actions. He had urges, strong urges which he needed to satisfy, but he did not wish to be imprudent. He rejected the suggestion that the pox, which had been around ever since Columbus and his men brought it back from the "New World" was divine retribution for sinful sex outside of marriage. That was nonsense. He did believe, however, as did many others, that it was somehow contracted during sexual acts.

He had seen the results of the infection on those who had indulged without taking adequate precautions—though it was hard to know what constituted adequate precautions other than abstinence—and it was a truly appalling disease. There were three stages. The first stage usually manifested in genital chancre, sometimes showing little pustules, like grains of millet all over one's face. This was followed sometime later—and no telling how long—by a second stage that was more painful and sometimes resulted in hair loss. The symptoms of both first and second-stage pox generally resolved after some time, regardless of whether it was treated or not, and for most people that was it.

But heaven help the man who faced the third stage. The infection literally ate away at the body, destroying bones and tissue, and deforming facial features. And the most common treatment—a mercury-based concoction, was arguably as bad, or worse, than the disease. It produced all sorts of toxic symptoms or side effects, including spongy bones and loss of teeth. Hence the observation, "one night with Venus, two years with Mercury." It also reminded him of the statement of

Edmund Burke in the House of Commons who was being assailed by a political opponent who suggested as to Burke that, "He will either die on the gallows or of the pox!" to which Burke replied, "Depending on whether I embrace your principles or your mistress."

With that in mind, Tremont figured her mouth was all he would require to scratch his itch. But the woman was good, as good as she thought she was, and he found himself throwing caution to the wind. He used every orifice on her body in a well-orchestrated three-act play. In the final scene, he choked her, at first gently, assuring her it would heighten her pleasure, and she willingly submitted.

He gradually increased the pressure, though, and she started to struggle against him. She grabbed his arms but couldn't loosen his grip. Her legs were spread, and she could not get leverage with them to push him away. She was a small woman but strong and she struggled mightily, her eyes bulging. But he was stronger, and her struggle only intensified his desire. Although he regretted the lack of control that resulted, he realized he was powerless against it, and gave in to it.

His orgasm came at the moment of her death. As she collapsed onto the dirt of the alley, he lovingly repeated his comment from earlier that evening, to her and her friends, meant as a compliment. "This above all, to thine own self be true." And he thought she had been, true to her real self, to the very end.

He stepped back and straightened the sleeves on his shirt as he stared into her vacant eyes. He glanced around quickly to confirm that no one had been looking, then began moving toward the street. After a few steps, he stopped, turned and went back to where she lay. He fished the wad of bills out, counted out three more and threw them on the body. "A deal is a deal," he said, then turned and walked away.

Philadelphia, May 16
Chapter 15

Patrick Harrell was in his corner cubby, working feverishly on an editorial. He had not come home the night before and Will suspected that he was operating on very little, if any, sleep. He seemed full of energy, however, which was not unusual. If experience was any indication, his father might function at an agitated, accelerated pace for several days, until he crashed, either from simple exhaustion, or as might be aided by a good quantity of alcoholic beverages or drugs. Then he would grow morose and cynical, lacking motivation to do much of anything except drink and gamble.

It was a vicious but reliable cycle, and it seemed to grow harder and harder for the man to stay on an even keel, to mask his volatile and varying emotions and moods. But he was able to function fairly well and present to the public the facade of normality so that few others saw a problem. Will resigned himself to the situation, determined simply to be there when his father needed him.

While his father worked on the editorial, Will edited an article for the next edition of the newspaper. James was in the back working the press and Will could hear its occasional thump—a familiar and comforting sound. In the other corner, Will's sister, Anne, was bent over the books of accounting, scribbling occasionally. In addition to the newspaper, the print shop and bookstore, Patrick Harrell also owned a couple of warehouses on the waterfront and Anne kept track of it these books as well.

Unlike the other businesses, his father did not take an active role in managing the warehouses. Will's older brother, Patrick, had overseen this aspect of the family businesses, but with his departure, Patrick Sr.

had hired a weasel of a man named Owen Green to handle the day-to-day operations. It was a move that mystified and concerned Will. Green was involved in some shady gambling enterprises in Philadelphia and had a reputation for skirting the law when it was convenient to making money. Will suspected that his father had somehow gotten tangled up with Green as the result of gambling debts, and Green had used it as leverage.

Will also suspected that not all activities run out of the warehouses now were strictly legal. But apparently Green knew how to turn a profit and that seemed to be enough for Patrick Harrell, who refused to discuss the matter with Will or Anne whenever they broached it. Perhaps, he was trying to protect them, and himself, theorizing that the more hands-off the owner, the less likely the culpability if any wrongdoing was discovered.

Will focused on the article in front of him, dipped his quill pen into the ink bottle and scratched a few notes in the margin and made changes to the text. He looked up when Anne stood and walked into their father's office, book in hand. Will watched as she placed the book in front of their father. He could see that she was frowning but couldn't make out what was being said. After a bit she came back to her station, still frowning.

Will called to her across the room. "Something wrong, Anne?"

She shook her head, looked over at her brother and rolled her eyes, but said nothing. Will started to say something else, but before he could, the front door opened, and a man stepped inside. Tall and elegantly dressed, he moved with an easy, unhurried stride. He stopped in front of Will.

"Good morning, sir," Will said. "How may I be of assistance?"

"Yes, ahem, I'd like to place an advertisement."

"Certainly." Will grabbed a piece of paper and a pen, dipped it in the ink. "And what sort of advertisement?

"Come again?"

"What would you like it to say?"

"Oh, yes." He pulled a note from his vest pocket and unfolded it. "I've written down the essentials. It's for a runaway slave." He handed Will the document.

"I see," Will said, suppressing a frown. He was opposed to slavery, as was his father, but such ads were a good percentage of their ad revenue. He read over quickly what the man had written.

Eight Dollars Reward.

RAN AWAY from the subscriber, living in Pixton township, Dauphin county, about six miles from Harrisburg, on Friday, the 3rd instant, a Negro BOY, named SAM, 17 years of age, 5 feet 9 or 10 inches high, well made, has very large feet, large features, and thick lips, much pitted with the small-pox; had on when he went away, a brown coloured hunting-shirt, under jacket with strings to it, and trowsers of the same, a pair of coarse tow trowsers, and a linen shirt. It is probable that he will change his name and clothes. Whoever takes up said Negro, and secures him in any gaol, so that his master may get him again, shall have the above reward, and reasonable charges.

BENJAMIN DUNCAN

When Will finished, he looked up at the man. "I assume you are Benjamin Duncan?"

The man nodded.

"And is this then the exact wording you would like, Mr. Duncan?"

"I think it adequately relates the information, but I am open to suggestions."

"No," Will said, "this is fine as is." He suspected the man had done this before. "Just wanted to make sure." He inquired as to the number of times and dates Duncan wanted it to be published, then quoted him the rate. The customer handed over the agreed amount and Will wrote him out a receipt. The man tipped his hat, wished Will a good day, then stepped back outside.

Patrick Harrell came out of his cubby and stood beside his son, looking over the advertisement the man had just submitted. "Humph," he said, then turned and went through the doorway leading to the printing press.

Patrick Harrell believed that the ownership of another human being was abhorrent, and indefensible. So did Will. The newspaper had printed many essays from Thomas Paine and others about the evils of slavery, had printed editorials condemning the practice. The hypocrisy of taking money for such advertisements—and they did so regularly—could not be explained or defended, so his father tended to ignore it. After all, the business needed income to survive and do the other good things they did, and if they didn't take the business, well, there were plenty of others who would.

The father came back a couple of minutes later and stood beside the son once more. Will looked up and his father stepped back a couple of feet and leaned against the wall. "Interesting development in the Congress yesterday with that preamble. It's the talk of the town."

He was right. It had been an interesting development, to say the least. All important resolutions of Congress were dignified with a high-sounding preamble before giving them to the public. Adams used the preamble to effectively plug the holes Dickinson had exploited in the resolution passed five days earlier, to guide interpretation of the resolution itself in the manner Adams had intended. Essentially, it labeled as illegitimate any government that required giving a loyalty oath to the king. It stated, in part that,

"...it appears absolutely irreconcilable to reason and good conscience, for the people of these colonies now to take the oaths and affirmations necessary for the support of any government under the Crown of Great Britain, and it is necessary that the exercise of every kind of authority under the said crown should be totally suppressed..."

Its language clearly brought Pennsylvania within its ambit, as its assembly still pledged loyalty to the crown, the King's justice was still practiced in the courts, and the general official tone of the colony was to recognize still the king's authority. And this time, unlike with the resolution itself, most members understood the impact of the language in the preamble. With Dickinson still at his plantation in Delaware, the job of arguing against the measure had fallen to his protégé, James Wilson.

"In this province," Wilson said, "if that preamble passes, it will throw the colony of Pennsylvania into chaos. There will be an immediate dissolution of every kind of authority; the people will be instantly in a state of nature. Moreover, Congress had no authority to interfere in the internal affairs on any colony."

John Duane of New York, a prosperous, plump lawyer, slightly squint eyed, agreed with this last point. "You have no right to pass this resolution, any more than Parliament has," he said. "And why all the haste?" he asked. "Why this urging? Why this driving?" He declared that he would take no part in it and observed that, "It would not have been proposed," I suspect, "if Sam Adams had not already counted the votes and was certain of passage."

Richard Henry Lee, from Virginia, a co-conspirator with the Adams cousins, pointed out that these arguments really were against the resolution—which had already passed—and he was right. Sam Adams, who seldom spoke in Congress, rose to answer Duane. His white hair and deeply lined face, and the congenital trembling of his hand and head made him appear older than his 57 years.

"Mr. Duane urges Congress not to act until our petitions to the King have been answered. Our petitions have been answered with fleets and armies and are soon to be answered with Hessian mercenaries from abroad. The King has thrown us out of his protection. Why should we support governments under his authority?"

The vote was close. Six colonies—the four from New England plus Virginia and South Carolina—voted in favor of the measure. North Carolina, New York, New Jersey and Delaware voted against. Georgia was absent. Pennsylvania and Maryland abstained. Actually, Maryland did more than abstain. After the voting, her delegates gathered up their papers and walked from the chambers.

As the official printer for the Congress, Will's father was privy to any formal resolution that was to be published for the general public.

"What are people saying?" Will asked.

"That the Congress has all but declared independence by this preamble—something a lot of people don't like but which is just what the Independents were waiting for."

"What do you think?"

Patrick Harrell pursed his lips together and folded his arms. "I think our local radicals are being helped along in the Congress by Sam and John Adams." When Will didn't respond right away, he held up his hand. "I know, you can't talk about what happens in the Congress, but it's pretty obvious what's going on."

His son's continued silence did not deter him. "And I tell you what else I think. I think your mentor has his head so far up his arse he can't see or hear what's going on around him. He is getting out-maneuvered on this thing and he doesn't even realize it. He took off at just the wrong time, oblivious to what is happening here, and now it may be too late."

Will did not disagree with his assessment. It certainly seemed that Dickinson was entirely too nonchalant about what was going on. It also seemed that his father was disappointed at the development.

"But isn't that a good thing for you and your friends who favor independence?"

"I suppose so," Patrick Harrell said. "I just hate the incompetence, if not outright stupidity, of Dickinson and his allies, the arrogant, hubris-laden, self-satisfied approach they have taken. Oh, he'll regroup and scramble. He'll compromise. But he's running out of options. The radicals have called for a town meeting on the 20th. They will seek to dissolve the Assembly and hold a convention to draft a new constitution."

Will frowned. "Do I sense a little regret?"

His father shrugged. "I don't like bullies, and I don't like sneaky and underhanded. If you can't win on the merits of your argument, maybe it's not such a good argument."

When his son nodded in agreement, Patrick added, "Not that you'll hear me saying that in public or putting it in writing. The ship of independence has set sail, and those who don't get on board are going to drown."

Before Will could respond, the bell above the front door rang, signaling the entrance of a potential customer. They both looked in that direction as the couple walked in. Rebecca Boutwell strode in, and directly behind her, holding the door, was the Frenchman, Henri Tremont. Once both were inside, Rebecca interlocked her arm with his and they came closer. She caught Will's eye and smiled, seemingly pleased and proud to have such a fine trophy on her arm.

"Good morning, gentlemen." She fluttered her eyes at an alarming speed for a couple of seconds before continuing. "Allow me to introduce Monsieur Henri Dubois Tremont. Monsieur Tremont, Patrick and William Harrell."

"Mr. Tremont and I are already acquainted," Will said, nodding at the Frenchman, who gave him a small bow.

Rebecca looked a little puzzled as she glanced from one to the other, but then she smiled. "Wonderful."

"I don't believe I've had the pleasure, though," Patrick Harrell said, extending his hand. The two men shook hands and Tremont said, "The pleasure is mine, Monsieur."

"Mr. Tremont is visiting from France and is a guest at our inn," Rebecca explained. "I am showing him around the city and felt that a visit to Harrell and Sons was a required stop along the tour."

"We are honored," the father said. "And I will say that I would not be much of a newspaper man if I had not at least heard of the visiting Frenchman who is a guest at The White Horse Inn. Welcome to Philadelphia, Mr. Tremont. I can't imagine a better guide than Miss Boutwell."

"Indeed," he said, "she is quite wonderful."

"I understand that your family, too, owns a newspaper and printing business."

The man arched an eyebrow. *"Oui,* Monsieur, and a bookstore—along with other interests, to be sure."

"*Ou est-il situe*?" Will asked.

The man seemed surprised that Will had spoken in French, but he smiled and answered in French that the printing business, newspaper and bookstore were located in Paris. "But of course, we spend most of the time in the country." After a slight hesitation he added, "I explained to Miss Boutwell that I am also an avid reader, so she suggested I visit your establishment."

"Well, sir," the father said, "if you like to read, I'm sure you will find something in our bookstore of interest to you. We have the largest collection in the city, and the greatest variety." He swung his arm in the direction of the stacks of books.

"Yes," he said, "quite impressive. Do you mind if I peruse the shelves?"

"Please. And my son, Will, knows our collection extremely well should you need assistance. I will leave you in his capable hands. I have an editorial that should have been completed two hours ago."

Not so capable, Will thought, but he asked, "Do you have a favorite author, or a particular subject matter that interests you?"

Tremont smiled. "My tastes are rather eclectic and broad, though I have a real love for plays. And my favorite playwright by far is Shakespeare."

"The man was a genius," Will said.

"He had such insight into the human heart, don't you think?"

"Quite so. None better. I presume that you are also fond of the work of some of your countrymen?" Voltaire perhaps?"

"Indeed, and Diderot, and Beaumarchais, all are brilliant. I am particularly fond of the latter's play, *The Marriage of Figaro*. A wonderful comedy—though Monsieur Beaumarchais had difficulty getting it performed in Paris because of its political message. I understand it was quite well received in London, however."

"And in the colonies. Also, popular here is Monsieur Montesquieu."

"Ah, yes, so I hear."

"We have works by all of these, and Mr. Shakespeare, of course."

"Perhaps I will just look around a bit?"

"Of course," Will said, then gave him a quick summary of how the volumes were organized. Tremont bowed again, then began walking down one of the aisles. Will turned his attention back to Rebecca. They stood in awkward silence until broken by Rebecca.

"Are you enjoying your new position with the Continental Congress?"

Will looked over his shoulder at Tremont before facing her and saying, simply, "Interesting." When he looked back toward Tremont, the Frenchman had disappeared in the stacks. He turned back to Rebecca. "Nice of you to escort Mr. Tremont around the city," he said, but his tone betrayed the insincerity of the words, and the awkward silence returned. "Perhaps," Will ventured after some time passed, "I should assist our customer locate what he wants." But he made no move toward the shelves, but rather busied himself rearranging items on a nearby shelf, stealing glances at Rebecca, who pretended to be interested in some of the pamphlets on display.

The man who called himself Tremont did not need directions or assistance from young William Harrell. He knew right where he was going. He took his time, though, so as not to raise suspicion. After a few minutes, he had worked his way up the spiral staircase to the second floor and to the far-left corner, and the top shelf.

He looked around once more to make sure he wasn't being watched, then removed the volume from the shelf, opened it to the last page. Using a small pen knife he had stored in his pocket, he sliced the binding of the back cover. He eased his finger inside the lining and retrieved a small scrap of paper. The writing on it was very small, both sides of the paper, and in code. He slipped it into his vest pocket. He then removed the note he had made from the other vest pocket, folded it and placed it inside the book binding. He used the glue he had brought for the purpose to reseal the slit, then placed the volume back on the shelf.

When he returned to where Will and Rebecca were standing in their silence, he had in his hand a small volume of plays by Joseph Addison.

"Excellent choice," Will said. "*Cato* is very popular here in the colonies."

"I understand it is one of General Washington's favorites."

"It is indeed," Will said, thinking that the man seemed to have obtained a lot of detailed information very quickly.

"How much do I owe you?"

Will gave him the amount, and as Tremont fished in his pocket for the sum, the door opened, and Tom Barr came in. They all looked up at the large deputy sheriff who filled the doorway. He tipped his hat toward Rebecca then turned to Will, and without any preliminary words of greeting, said, "Sheriff Dewees and Dr. Rush would like a word with you if you are not too busy." After a few seconds of silence, Barr answered the unasked question. "Found the body of a young woman this morning in an alley off Arch Street. The sheriff and the good doctor would appreciate it if you would come to the scene and see what you make of the situation."

Philadelphia. May 16
Chapter 16

The woman was lying on her back, mouth open, stone cold eyes staring unflinchingly into the morning sun. Will had viewed dead bodies before, many times. And he always approached the task with a strange mix of reverence, dread and fascination, for being close to the death of another reminded him of his own mortality. The eyes said it all—those blank, staring eyes that signified the deep, dark void of death. The lifeless eyes he gazed upon now were those of a woman he had seen, had talked to less than twenty-four hours before.

Reverend Taylor spoke from the pulpit of the joy of the afterlife, and Will guessed that he knew what he was talking about. But no matter how wonderful heaven might be, Will had a hard time imagining it. This life on earth was all he knew for sure. And once it was gone, it was gone. This existence was fragile indeed, and it could end suddenly and much too quickly from the vagaries of disease and accident. But to have it end intentionally and violently at the hands of another seemed all the more tragic and unfair.

Dr. Rush was kneeling next to the body. Sheriff Dewees stood on the other side, and a small crowd of curious citizens had formed a semi-circle a discreet distance away. As Will and Barr made their way past the onlookers, Rush stood. "Take a look, Will, tell me what you see."

The onlookers may have wondered why the eminent physician would call upon this young man to examine a dead body, but there was good reason. While not a doctor himself, he had read a lot about human anatomy and medicine. And he had briefly studied under Rush, contemplating a career as a physician—until he realized that the sight and smell of blood made him nauseated, and worse, seemed to be a trigger for epileptic seizures. Not the kind of thing to give one confidence in their doctor. He thought maybe he would grow sufficiently accustomed to it so that it would not interfere with his training in, and ultimate practice of, medicine. And it did get better, but never good enough. So, he had foregone medicine for the study of law, where his affliction would be less of a deterrence.

He never lost interest in the marvels of the human body, though, nor the causes and cures of various maladies that attacked it. He had continued to assist Dr. Rush in his visits to the Alms House, where he volunteered his time. Determining the cause of death had been a part of his training, at which he had shown particular interest, and apparently some considerable skill, such that Rush continued to call him to scenes of death for his opinion. In fact, Rush also harbored the hope that Will might someday resume his study of medicine.

Will studied the body for several seconds, surveyed the surrounding area, then focused back on the woman. Cynthia Farrington was small of frame, with a somewhat gaunt look about her, and had a harsh beauty that seemed magnified now in death. He looked up at the sheriff and doctor. "This is not how you found her, is it?"

Rush and Dewees shared a look but neither spoke right away.

"I observed the bits of dirt on her face and the mild disturbance of the soil near the body," Will said in explanation. "Her clothing was not disheveled as one might expect after an attack, but neatly arranged about her body. It is possible the killer was concerned about her modesty, but unlikely."

Dewees nodded in confirmation. "She was face down in the dirt. We turned her over so the doctor could examine her. And we pulled her dress down to protect her modesty." He looked around quickly before adding in a lowered voice, "Her arse was showing."

After a couple of seconds Will said, "Her name is Cynthia Farrington."

If the other men wondered how he knew the victim, they didn't ask. Rush nodded in confirmation. "Yes." He gestured toward the small crowd behind them. "Some of the people who live nearby recognized her. Plus, I knew her from the Alms House. Came in from time to time. Not a bad sort. Just doing the best she could with what was available."

Will studied the woman's face again. "Have you talked to her roommate yet?"

Again, neither man seemed surprised that Will knew she had a roommate.

"Not yet," the sheriff said. "She was sharing a room with another tart, just down the way on Arch Street. Name is Judith Bradford."

Will turned toward Rush. "Strangled?"

Rush gave Dewees a grim smile and nodded confirmation of the decision to call on this youth for assistance. "What leads you to that conclusion?"

Will looked down at the woman. "Well, I see no blood on the ground or about the body. No obvious disfiguration of the skull. And now that the skin has begun to dry and become more transparent, you can begin to see the bruising." He kneeled down beside the body, pointed at marks on the neck. "These patterned abrasions and contusions appear to be fingernail scratches, likely caused not by the attacker, but by the victim trying to pry whatever was used to choke her from around her neck. And these," he said, lightly touching the bruising, "is the horizontal circumscription of the neck caused by the ligature, which I would guess was a scarf or some similar soft-textured item, as I do not see the burn marks you might expect from a rope or other rough-surfaced item."

Rush smiled approvingly. "Very good. Anything else?"

"Well, there are the pinpoint hemorrhages in the skin, the conjunctiva in the eyes," he said pointing, "which indicate asphyxiation."

The doctor smiled again, shaking his head. "Truly exceptional diagnosis."

"I had an exceptional teacher," Will said, shrugging and looking at Rush. He tried but could not suppress a small smile at the praise.

"You would make such a fine physician. Why you would want to waste your time studying the law when you could study medicine is a mystery to me."

Will shrugged again. "I don't know that they are mutually exclusive." Before Rush could respond, he turned toward the group of onlookers and asked, "Any witnesses?"

"No, not that anyone will say anyway," Dewees answered. "Some folks gave us her name and where she lived and with whom. A couple of people said they saw her earlier in the evening, out on the street, but just in passing. Didn't talk to her or anything, but said she was in the company of Miss Bradford when they saw her. Word is the two work the same area as well as live together. But nobody says they saw anything or anyone suspicious. And no one heard any screams or anything out of the ordinary last night."

Will rubbed his chin with his thumb. "Perhaps then, we should go see if we can find Miss Bradford."

Tom Barr and Dr. Rush stayed behind to oversee the transport of the body to Rush's office while Will and the sheriff went to the reported address on Arch Street. To say that the small house on Arch Street was modest would be an understatement. Its siding was made of unpainted wood, a good bit of which showed signs of water rot, mostly around the eaves and fascia board. What little there was of space between the street and the front door was comprised of dirt. But the dirt was raked smooth and clear of the household garbage that many surrounding buildings displayed, and the small stoop had been swept clean. Will stood on the street while Sheriff Dewees knocked on the door.

The woman who answered the door was short and stout, wearing a plain cotton dress that was a little too small for her large frame. She wore her hair piled high on top of her head. Dewees tipped his hat. "Miss Harper, Good morning."

Her eyes widened upon recognizing the sheriff, a mixture of fear and suspicion perhaps, which would be quite normal under the circumstances. She managed a "good morning," while she looked beyond him to eye Will suspiciously, trying to size up the situation. Before she could protest to him that she had no idea what her guests did in the privacy of their rooms, the sheriff assured her that he was not interested in such matters.

"I have come to inform you that one of your guests," he said, lingering over the last word as if to say he was not so sure it was fully descriptive, "was murdered last night, a Miss Cynthia Farrington."

The woman placed both of her hands over her heart and said, "No!" with what seemed to be genuine surprise and grief. "The poor girl." Then she reached out with her right hand and grasped the door frame for support. She put her other hand to her forehead. "How? What happened? Who would do such a thing?"

The questions had come rapidly, without giving the sheriff an opportunity to reply. He gave her a moment to collect herself before saying, "That's what I'm trying to find out, Miss Harper." He paused briefly, then said, "I understand that she shared a room with a Miss Judith Bradford. Is she here?"

The woman took a few seconds to reflect on the implication of what the sheriff had said, then turned to face inside and shouted, "Judy?" She waited several seconds before shouting the name again, this time louder and more emphatically. From somewhere inside the building a voice, faint, indistinct, gave a one word reply that Will couldn't make out. "Someone to see you," Miss Harper shouted. "Hurry up." She turned back to the men. "She'll be right down." From an upstairs window, a curtain was drawn back an inch or two and someone peered down at them for a few seconds, then disappeared behind the curtain.

While they waited, the sheriff introduced Will to the landlady, who smiled at him as he bowed slightly in her direction and repeated her name. Dewees asked her questions about the victim, which she seemed more than willing to answer, but her information was not so very helpful. She knew very little about her past, her family, or friends, other than the girls who lived there in the rooming house. Certainly, she said, she knew of no one who would wish her ill.

Presently, Judy Bradford appeared at the door and stood behind Harper, looking out at them through large brown eyes. They were framed by an oval face and a luxurious, cascading mane of black curls. Will's mind instantly strayed to a happier occasion with the woman. She gave Will a familiar sultry smile and their eyes locked on each other for a few seconds until Will looked away.

If Dewees noticed the look exchanged between the girl and Will, he didn't show it. He stood by quietly as the landlady explained the purpose of their visit. Judy gasped and held her hands to her stomach as she looked away. When her gaze found the sheriff again, she was trembling.

"Miss Bradford, I understand that you and your roommate were, ah, together last night?"

"Yes," she said, absently.

"When and where did you last see her?"

She hesitated a moment before saying, "It was about two o'clock, over off Third Street. I went off for a bit with a gentleman and when I came back, she was gone."

"She did not return home with you last night?"

"No."

"You didn't you think that strange? You weren't concerned?"

The woman shrugged. "No, I figured she found more suitable accommodations for the night, which would not be so unusual."

"Did you see her with anybody last night, or was there anyone or anything unusual that you remember?"

She thought about the question for a few seconds, then, looking straight at Will, said, "Yes. There was an old man with a cane who walked by a couple of times, smoking his pipe and looking our way, but he never stopped. Seemed a little weird, and it was like he was snubbing us, which I didn't like. So, I called out to him, asked him if he thought he was too good to mix with us, and he said something strange."

She had not mentioned the fact that Will had stopped and talked to the women the night before, had asked them about a man fitting this description. Good, Will thought. He didn't want to have to explain that to the sheriff. He asked her, "What do you mean strange?"

"I didn't hear it all that good, but it sounded like, 'Though the wine on your shelf be blue.' Something like that. I just figured he was a little crazy."

The sheriff asked her to repeat the phrase, then he looked at Will. "That makes no sense." He turned back to the woman. "Are you sure that's what he said?"

"No. Like I said, I didn't hear it clearly."

The words had seemed vaguely familiar to Will and he racked his brain to make the connection. Finally, he thought he had. "Judy, could he have said, 'to thine own self be true?'"

She thought again for several seconds, then nodded and said, "Could have been that, I guess."

Will turned to Sheriff Dewees, whose face registered his confusion. "It's from a play by William Shakespeare, Sheriff. *Hamlet.*"

Philadelphia. May 17
Chapter 17

The Philadelphia Emporium was housed in a three-story building that took up half a block on the corner of Chestnut and 6th Street. It was one of three buildings Will and Tim had identified as the most likely choices for an assassin planning an attack with a long rifle on the State House. Will Harrell and Tim Matlack entered the business a little after six o'clock. They were greeted by the owner, Eric Patterson, who they knew to be a loyalist in his political leanings. Business being business, however, he was solicitous of the two potential customers.

"Gentlemen, welcome. What can I interest you in today?"

Matlack smiled. "Good evening, Eric. Actually, what we are interested in is information."

The smile was still there but was tinged with wariness. "Yes?"

He got right to it. "Have you had any recent tenants?"

"Recent tenants? Why do you ask?"

Tim smiled again. "The why is not important. Have you let out space recently?"

The smile was completely gone now. "Not that it is any of your business, but no, my tenants have all been here for a while."

Tim changed to a conciliatory tone. "I'm sorry, Eric. I didn't mean to be disrespectful. It's only that it is a quite urgent matter. The man we are looking for is dangerous, a murderer we are quite anxious to find."

"If you give me a description, I will contact you if I spot him."

Tim explained that the man might be wearing a disguise but described the elderly man with a cane. Patterson said he'd seen no one matching that description.

"Have you met a Frenchman who calls himself Henri Tremont?"

The man swiveled to look at Will, who had asked the question, and was searching the man's face as he waited for his answer.

"Why yes, I have had the pleasure. Sold him a nice suit as I remember. Why do you ask?"

"I also have had the pleasure as he is a regular customer of the bookstore, and he is a very interesting person. We don't get many Frenchmen in Philadelphia."

Patterson nodded, apparently satisfied with this answer.

"One other thing, Eric. Would you mind if we go up on the roof of your building, take a look around?"

Patterson looked as if he might object, but he smiled and said, "I don't see why not. It is a nice view of the city."

And the State House, Tim thought, but didn't say. When they were on the roof, alone, Tim asked Will, "What did you think of Patterson's answers?"

"He was lying."

"About?

Will shrugged. "Maybe everything. Maybe just parts. Hard to say, but his body language, his defensiveness. We were making him very uncomfortable. He was hiding something."

"I agree." They stopped on the edge of the roof that looked upon the State House. "Maybe we should check with the current tenants. Chances are they would have noticed someone new. I know James Newsome, the surveyor. I'll come by again during business hours."

Will nodded. "This would be an ideal spot for a man with a rifle," he said looking across the street. "Any word from the local gunsmiths?"

"No one had had any orders or made any sales to a stranger."

"Of course, he could have someone buy one or more rifles for him, or go outside Philadelphia."

"Or both. Or he never planned to use a rifle. Or there is no assassin."

Will sighed. "True, true, and true." After a hesitation, he asked, "How about recent purchases of gunpowder and other materials for making bombs?"

Matlack shook his head. "Nothing."

Will gave him a small grin. "Well, at least we are making good progress.

Tim grinned back as they both turned to go back downstairs.

* * *

The street was dark, illuminated only by a pale quarter moon that was partially hidden by the clouds. A gentle breeze brought some relief from the hot, dank night, but also carried with it the stink of rotting garbage. The building stood stark and quiet on the west side of 2nd Street, a block and a half from the Delaware River. The man who called himself Henri Tremont inserted the key into the lock and turned it, producing a satisfying click as it opened. He removed the lock and slid back the horizontal bolt. He paused then, took a couple of puffs from his pipe and looked around once more briefly. Satisfied that he had not been followed, that no one lurked in the shadows, he opened the door and stepped inside.

The warehouse belonged to one of his contacts. He had offered Tremont the use of the room attached to the rear of the building—a shed really—with no questions asked. It was small but more than adequate for his purposes. He closed the door behind him and felt on the shelf for the candle he had placed there. He puffed hard a few times on his pipe again to get the embers glowing, took the thin strip of wood from his pocket and held it to the fire in the bowl. It ignited easily, and he used the strip to light the wick on the candle.

Holding the light out in front of him he walked slowly around, surveying the shelves, confirming that the supplies he had requested had been delivered. And there they were, lined up neatly in a row on a lower shelf: a container of potassium nitrate, or saltpeter, one of sulfur and one of charcoal. The iron pellets and broken pieces of porcelain in

158

their separate crates were next to them, along with the necessary material to make fuses. It was sufficient for at least four fragmentation bombs, maybe five, and it wouldn't take long to assemble them. He would begin construction soon, on his own timetable. He walked over to the corner and confirmed that his makeup, wigs and other accessories for disguise were still in place.

Tremont thought about changing his appearance and identity, donning one of his alter egos for a little tour of a certain part of the city, but thought better of it. He had gotten a little carried away two nights before and the discovery of the woman's body yesterday had put everyone there, and throughout the city really, on alert, had made people apprehensive. A stranger now would draw too much attention. He would let the excitement die down. People couldn't maintain this level of vigilance very long. There was fun to be had, money to be made.

After he closed up and headed back to the White Horse Inn, however, he reflected on the incident—he had a hard time thinking of it as murder. He knew that he had been unprofessional and careless, reckless even. He had indulged himself and ignored the risk to his mission. Part of him, however, reveled in the risk, confident that his little indiscretion would not be a hindrance. There had been no witnesses, nothing to tie him to the woman. In fact, the murder would be a distraction for the local authorities, helping to conceal his true objective.

He didn't know what, if any, intelligence the rebels had concerning his mission and what precautions may have been taken, but he had to assume they had been forewarned. No matter. They would not be able to stop him. No one suspected his true identity or his true reason for being in Philadelphia, and he planned to keep it that way.

The thought buoyed him as he bounded up the steps to the White Horse Inn. Maybe he would prevail upon the Boutwell girl to accompany him on a stroll, where he might find a discreet moment and place to advance his seduction of the girl. It had been going smoothly he thought, though he knew that it was not something to rush. She was almost there, though, and the anticipation of the culmination of his efforts aroused him even now.

"Monsieur Tremont."

He turned toward the source of the sound, recovering quickly from a momentary startle. It was the boy from the bookstore. "Monsieur Harrell, how nice to see you."

Will Harrell had been sitting in a chair on the veranda and he now rose and walked toward the other man. "I was hoping you would return before I had to leave. I wanted to deliver this volume to you personally," he said, holding it out to him.

Tremont took the item from Harrell and looked at it. A small intake of breath escaped from him as he realized what he was holding—a collection of the plays of William Shakespeare. He looked back up at Will. "This is a very rare volume indeed. I didn't notice it in your shop."

"It is indeed rare. I don't think there is another such volume in all the colonies."

Tremont turned it over in his hand, then carefully opened it.

"We don't usually keep it on the shelves, as it is not for sale, but we loan it out to our special customers, people who can appreciate it. I remembered your expressed fondness for the bard from the other day. My father agreed that you might enjoy perusing this during your stay with us."

Tremont closed the book and held it to his chest. "I am very moved, Monsieur, by your generosity, touched and appreciative that you and your father would entrust me with this rare treasure. I assure you I will take great care of it and read it from cover to cover."

"I suspect that you already know each of the plays collected there, by heart, and line by line."

"Some, perhaps," he said, "but not all and certainly not so completely. Regardless, I thank you again."

"You are very welcome."

The Frenchman's face remained passive, but his eyes were taking in the young Mr. Harrell from a fresh perspective, sensing something beneath the surface, something dangerous. He was about to excuse himself but decided to probe a little. "I read the alarming news of the young woman found dead, the one the man was talking about in your bookstore. I hear she was a prostitute."

Will nodded but said nothing.

"Was it murder, you think?"

"No doubt."

A few seconds of silence passed between them before Tremont said, "So, the sheriff seeks your counsel and advice in such matters? That's quite impressive, I must say, for one so young."

Will shrugged. "I'm happy to help if I can."

"How was the woman killed?"

Will told him, then said, "Actually, you may be interested to know that the murderer might be a fellow fan of Mr. Shakespeare."

"Oh, really?" Tremont worked hard to project a neutral expression, but his heart raced. "Why do you say that?"

A friend of the dead woman reported seeing a creepy older man who walked with a cane and who quoted Shakespeare to her. He seemed suspicious and passed by several times. It is thought that this man may have been the killer."

"Sounds like a bit of speculation to me."

Will shrugged. "At the least, the man may have seen or heard something. The sheriff would certainly wish to talk with this person. Anyway, I thought the Shakespeare angle might interest you."

"What was the quote?"

"She wasn't entirely sure, but when I asked her, she said it could have been, 'To thine own self be true.'"

Tremont did not hesitate in placing the quote. "*Hamlet, act II, scene 5.* And the full quote, I believe is 'Above all is this: to thine own self be true, and it must follow, as the night to day, thou canst be false to any man.' A wise sentiment, *oui?*"

"Certainement. Have you come across any fellow devotees of the bard during your stay in the city that might fit that description?"

"You are the only one, though you do not fit the physical description."

"I suppose I could have worn a disguise."

The Frenchman's smile was forced. "Did you?"

Will smiled back at him. "Curious about the Shakespeare connection though, is it not?"

"Yes, assuming your interpretation of what was said is correct."

He shrugged. "Yes, true."

With this thought drifting up in the air around them, the bookseller rose and professed a need to return to work.

"Thank you again for the loan of the book," Tremont said. "I promise to return it in its present good condition."

As he watched the boy walk down Market Street, the man who called himself Henri Tremont frowned and cursed himself silently. He had been careless, and now this boy suspected him. That was clear. His little cat and mouse game was not very subtle. It was also clear that he had underestimated the abilities of the boy. Did he know or suspect why he was in Philadelphia? No matter, he would deal with it. The boy was no match for him, but he offered a challenge of sorts, and he decided that was a good thing. It would help keep him sharp, and focused. Yes, he would deal with the prostitute, and find a suitable way to neutralize the young Mr. Harrell. Indeed, the seeds of a plan were already beginning to sprout in his mind as he turned and walked inside the inn.

Philadelphia, May 20
Chapter 18

Alan Grayson, clerk of the criminal court, sat in front of the judge in a wooden alcove behind a three-foot high railing. He was good at his job, efficient and knowledgeable. He had a monotone voice and the aura of one who has seen it all and is neither surprised nor impressed with anything anymore. Some of the defendants here were hardened criminals, violent, exploitative sorts who could expect no mercy from the judge. Others were basically decent men who had gotten a little too much liquor in their bellies and done something stupid. Grayson knew the difference, and Judge Harrison Dodson, who was fairly new to the bench, knew enough to pick up on his clerk's subtle signals in this regard. And Will would be counting on that this morning.

He had argued two more times in court since his legal debut in the easement case the previous month, but today he would be going it alone, without supervision. Tim Matlack had asked him to represent one of his employees, Jonathon Stoltz, who had been arrested and charged with beating his wife, and he had accompanied Will there this morning.

There were two cases ahead of them on the docket. The first defendant was a man named John Fargas. In his matter-of-fact manner, Grayson announced that he was charged with "assault and battery on one George Carson by violently and without justification biting off a piece of said George Carson's ear." The judge then asked him, "How do you plea?"

Fargas promptly admitted to the charges, but said the biting was justified, as Carson had referred to his wife as "the ugliest scarecrow he had ever seen." A few snickers rippled through the audience. The alleged victim, who was present in the gallery, began to protest but the judge held up his hand to silence him. He then looked over his spectacles at Fargas.

"I understand your desire to protect your wife's honor, Mr. Fargas, but the victim did not suggest that your wife engaged in any improper conduct, nor did he besmirch her reputation in any way. Beauty, after all, is in the eye of the beholder." Here he looked in the direction of the victim. "It was perhaps unkind, and unwise, of Mr. Carson to express his opinion to you on the subject as it relates to your wife, but he didn't deserve to lose a piece of his ear for it."

Again, there were the beginnings of laughter, which quickly ceased with a look from the judge. He turned back to the defendant. "Besides, I have seen you wife, sir, and though she may be a wonderful person, she is indeed quite homely—an unpleasant truth you will have to accept." This time the judge ignored the laughter that erupted. When it died down, he pronounced his sentence to the dejected Fargas. He did not, pointedly, require restitution to Carson, admitting that he had little sympathy for the man's stupidity to have made his comments under the circumstances.

The next case concerned a husband and wife team—Joseph and Mary Hines—who on oath of their neighbors had been charged with "being disorderly people and keeping a house for admitted street walking women, and of assaulting John Lewis and threatening to beat him." They pled not guilty and the judge ordered them held over for trial until they could post security.

Stoltz's case was called next and Will stepped forward. He had spoken briefly with Stoltz and his wife the night before and now he nodded in his client's direction, who gave him a tentative wave from his seat in the dock. Will looked over at the wife, who sat on the corner of the front row. She lowered her eyes.

"May it please the court, William Harrell on behalf of the prisoner."

"Yes, Mr. Harrell."

He moved closer to the judge, looking over again at his client. "Your Honor, Mr. Stoltz is a long-time and valued employee of Mr. Timothy Matlack."

Will waited, trying to gauge the judge's reaction to the name. Matlack was not necessarily a favorite of many city officials these days, given his radical politics, but most people found it hard to dislike him, and he had told Will he thought Dodson would be a friendly face. The judge gave a small nod in Tim's direction.

"The incident which resulted in my client's arrest was most unfortunate, fueled by an excessive amount of drink by Mr. Stoltz. He is generally a hard-working, law abiding citizen. The liquor and his temper got the better of him, is all. His wife is here today to plead for your mercy. She admits that she was at least in part at fault for the altercation. She needs him back, for herself and their two children."

Judge Dodson looked briefly at the prisoner and then at his wife before returning his attention back to Will, nodding for him to continue.

"Mr. Matlack is willing to post the necessary sum as security for the prisoner's good behavior in the future, if the court finds it agreeable to release him into his custody."

The judge looked at the wife and directed her to come forward. "Young woman, is what he says true? Are you willing to take this man back?"

"Oh yes, Your Honor," she said. "I do love him. And besides, we need his paycheck."

There were a few chuckles from the audience. The judge asked her how he could be sure something like this wouldn't happen again, disturbing the peace of their neighbors, requiring the authorities to take their attention away from more substantial matters.

"If he takes a swipe at me again, My Lord, the law will be the least of his worries."

More chuckles. The judge decided too much frivolity had been indulged and he silenced the audience again with a penetrating glare. He then turned and took a long hard look at the defendant, who wisely kept his head down, venturing only a small, hopeful look in the general direction of the judge.

"Very well, Mr. Stoltz. This is your first time before the court." He waited a few seconds, then said, "and it had better be your last." Another hesitation. "Do you understand?"

"Yes, sir."

"Defendant is released on a peace bond of ten pounds."

By the time Tim deposited the required sum with the clerk and Will got the client and his wife sorted out, it was forty minutes after eight o'clock, and he and Matlack headed straight for the State House. They had arranged to meet with Sam Adams there, and get a report from Cecil O'Conner, before the scheduled town meeting began at nine.

The rain had been coming down in a drizzle most of the morning and as they walked down Chestnut Street it began to pick up steadily, as did the wind. Will held his coat over his head, dodging the puddles along the street. When they arrived at the State House, there was already quite a crowd gathered in the brick-walled courtyard in the rear. Will knew Matlack was anxious to join them and suggested that he would fill him in on what Adams and Cecil had to say if he wanted to go ahead to the courtyard.

"No, no, I want to be there. There is plenty of time for me to do both," he said as he led the way inside. The congressional chambers were empty—the session had been cancelled that day—save for Cecil O'Conner and Sam Adams, who seemed to be enjoying each other's company. They were sitting at the table assigned to the Massachusetts delegation. Adams motioned for them to join them. They both pulled out chairs and sat.

"Thank you for setting this up, Tim. I am anxious to learn how the investigation is going. I wanted to hear Cecil's report but didn't want him to have to repeat himself." He looked at the lad and smiled. "So, he has been entertaining me with some rather ribald stories of Philadelphia while we waited for you."

"No doubt," Matlack said. grinning at Cecil, then nodding for him to speak.

"Aye, gents," Cecil said, "me lads and I have been busy. Very busy."

They waited. He looked from one to the other, then continued, focusing his attention on Tim.

"We have been keeping track of the comings and goings of the people on your list, maintaining our distance, of course, taking note of what they do and the people they meet up with. We have made discreet inquiries as well."

With prompting from Tim, Cecil gave them a summary on some of their suspects: Edward White, the aide and secretary for Samuel Chase, delegate from Maryland, Geoffrey Hamilton, aide and secretary to Philip Livingston, delegate from New York, and Thomas Miller, slave of Edward Rutledge, delegate from South Carolina.

"This White fellow, perhaps he feels less restrained in his associations while his employer is away, but the man was seen regularly in the company of some of Philadelphia's most ardent Tories. Right out in the open, mind you." Cecil paused a moment before adding, "The man has a taste for liquor and gambling, and for expensive clothes. I don't know what Mr. Chase pays him, but he seems to not want for coin."

Tim nodded. "Good, good. What about the others?"

There was nothing unusual or unexpected in Cecil's report as to Hamilton or Miller. The latter was always in the company of Rutledge— probably because of his prior attempts to escape. "He might have sneaked out at night," Cecil said. "I didn't think it an efficient use of manpower to post someone near the lodging place all night long, for any of them, really. But our boys stayed late enough to be pretty sure they were asleep before leaving."

Cecil said that Hamilton, unlike White, did not run in Tory circles, nor seem to be interested in the gambling sports or other extravagancies. "He mostly kept to himself at the lodging he shares with Mr. Livingston, at the White Horse Inn."

Which was also where Tremont was staying, Will thought, but didn't say. "Have you checked all the inns and lodging places for recent arrivals to the city?"

Cecil gave him a sideways glance. "It's only been a few days, yet, Will." He gave a small smile. "Been through a lot of places, though, specially looking for your old man."

"And?"

"We have sightings of a man fitting the description, mostly in the northeast section of the city. Some prostitutes, mostly." He paused, then said, "This is the man who murdered Cynthia?"

From the way he said it, Will thought Cecil may have been friends with the deceased. Good. Additional motivation. "Perhaps," Will said, without elaboration. "Where he is staying?"

"Nobody seems to know. Nor much else about him either, except that based on his dress, he's rich. No sightings in the last few days."

"Well, keep looking," Tim said. "I have a feeling he will show himself again."

After a brief pause, Will asked, "And Henri Tremont?"

Cecil nodded. "I took him for myself, followed him almost constantly, day and night, with one of my trusted lads to spell me on occasion."

"And?"

Cecil reported that Tremont had been seen in the company of Rebecca Boutwell, squiring her around town." When he said this, he gave Will a sideways glance, but Will kept his face passive as he waited for more. "The man has spent a good bit of time in taverns, and at the Black Cat Bookstore, where he seemed to be real friendly with your father," he said, looking at Will. "He's been down by the river a few times. Lost him there twice."

"Maybe the Frenchman noticed he was being followed and took evasive action."

Cecil seemed offended. He shook his head. "Not on your life. When I follow someone, I'm invisible. I make sure not to get too close, so as not to alert my target—which is part of the problem. It was just real crowded down by the docks and he got lost in the crowd. A bit later, he showed up again, so it wasn't that long. Probably spent some time in one of the taverns."

"Where is he now?"

"He's probably here or will be. Half the town will be, I suspect."

There wasn't much more for Cecil to report after that. Tim thanked him and gave him a wad of bills, telling him there was a little extra in there. The boy pocketed the money without counting it and smiled. "Thank you, kindly. Shall me lads continue?"

Tim nodded. "Keep your eyes and ears open and stay in touch."

Cecil left them then and Tim and Will stood to go. Adams said, "Do you have a minute more? I have some new information from Boston you might be interested in."

The noise of the crowd outside was muted by the closed windows, but it had been swelling while Cecil gave his report, and now was a definite distraction, beckoning Tim, and to an extent, Will, but they both sat back down and gave Adams their attention.

Adams looked at Will. "Tim has told me of your suspicion of the Frenchman."

He nodded. Tim had not thought much of his theory about Tremont, and his evidence was very weak, for sure. But Matlack had been willing to indulge him in the matter. Will now summarized for Adams the facts that had led to his suspicion.

When he was through, Adams nodded. "I am told that a man that fits Monsieur Tremont's general description, left Boston in a coach the

169

day after my friend was murdered. The coach was headed to New York, and the man rode with a young couple who have not yet returned. The driver did not know the man. He said he was English, not French, but as you say, our killer may be disguised."

"And might he also be the assassin referred to in the message?"

"It is perhaps worth exploring," Adams said. He looked briefly at Matlack before returning his gaze to Will. "I have sent word to Boston to ask the driver to come to Philadelphia, to have a look at this Tremont, see if he is the same person."

"Excellent idea," Will said.

Tim nodded. "We will either confirm your suspicion or eliminate him from our pool of suspects."

Adams stood. "But now, Tim, I believe you have another important meeting to attend, which, judging by the increasing noise from outside, is about to begin."

"Yes, sir. Will you be joining us?"

He shook his head. "Too much excitement for an old man like me."

* * *

There were close to four thousand persons crammed into the courtyard, drenched from the rain, but enthusiastic. A stage had been hastily erected, and on it were some of the leaders of the Independents. Matlack quickly joined them and Will took up a position in the corner to the west of the Walnut Street entrance. Shortly thereafter, the meeting began.

Daniel Roberdeau, who served with Christopher Marshall and James Cannon on the board of American Manufactory, had a booming voice and he had been tasked with reading aloud the various resolutions. The crowd was to vote by voice to accept or reject.

He started with the May 10th resolution and its preamble, then moved on to a series of resolves, written by the City Committee. The whole thing had been carefully scripted and those who deviated from the script were to be quickly corrected. This became evident on a reading of the second resolution, which resolved that the Assembly had assumed arbitrary power, lacking the authority of the people. When a grocer named Isaac Gray voiced dissent, he was made the subject of abuse and insults. John Cadwalader, who was also on the stage, moved to edit some of the resolutions, "not for substance but for clarity," he said. He was an old man, in favor of independence and well-liked, but the crowd began to shout at him, calling him not only a bore but a traitor. The frightened man quickly fell silent.

After that, people got the message and the responses were unanimous. Was the current government of Pennsylvania "competent to the exigencies of affairs," as Congress had put it? The crowd said no. Should a new government favoring independence be created by a constitution on advice of the City Committee and the authority of the people? The crowd said yes.

Will stood at the edge of the crowd, feeling the pressure of the mob but resistant to it. He kept silent when votes were taken. As he surveyed the scene, he did not see his mentor, John Dickinson, who had arrived back in Philadelphia the day before. Not a surprise, given the current mood of the people.

Will felt certain that most of the delegates to Congress who voted for the resolution and its more brazen preamble, assumed that the task of reforming the governments would go to the assemblies, where there were such who had authority to set such matters. They didn't imagine that it would be twisted to allow an unofficial town meeting like this where the demolishment of the colony's regularly elected government would be forced through on a voice vote. If they succeeded in overthrowing the government, it would be two to three months before they could put anything in its place, resulting in much confusion and uncertainty.

Daniel Roberdeau, who was reading the resolves, said that the assembly would continue to carry out its business until a constitutional convention and a new election. Will didn't see the logic there, though, because you can't destroy confidence in an institution, deprive it of public support, and expect it to continue functioning effectively.

Will had heard enough and was just about to leave when he saw Cecil working his way through the crowd in his direction. Momentarily he stood beside him. He whispered something in his ear, but he couldn't hear it above the noise of the crowd. But he followed his gaze to a second-floor window of the State House. What he saw there made the hair on is neck rise. John and Sam Adams stood, watching the proceedings in the yard below. In between them was Henri Tremont and Patrick Harrell. They were all conversing as if they were old friends.

Philadelphia. May 25
Chapter 19

Will arrived at the boarding house on Second Street, across from the City Tavern, at a little before eight o'clock in the evening. The sun had set but it still illuminated the sky. The air was warm and sticky, clinging to him as he bounded up the front steps. He found the correct room number and knocked lightly. A few seconds later Sam Adams opened the door and bade him enter.

In the room, John Adams and another man sat in spindle chairs on opposite sides of a small oak table in the middle of the space. Adams had a small pile of papers in front of him, a quill pen in his hand, and a frown on his face. When he looked up, though, he smiled and said, "Will, welcome to our humble abode."

Will nodded, thinking that those who saw only the obstinate, belligerent side of John Adams were not looking deep enough. "Thank you, Mr. Adams."

"Please, I appreciate the courtesy, and perhaps in the Congress it is 'Mr. Adams' but in my home," he said, waving his hand around, "such as it is, I'd prefer you call me John."

"Yes, sir...John."

Adams smiled, shaking his head, and returned his attention to the papers in front of him.

The other man sat stiffly, hands on his knees. He was a large, muscular man with a thick neck and short, stubby fingers, dressed in buckskin pants and vest over a plain muslin shirt. His hair was jet black, matching the eyes that were set deep in the sockets. Sam Adams introduced him as "Oliver McKeever, a dear friend and loyal patriot—as was his brother, Ian." Will was introduced and described as "the young lad who thinks the man who murdered Ian may be here in Philadelphia, disguised as a Frenchman."

McKeever stood and took Will's hand in his. "Nice to meet you, Will," he said in a soft baritone that seemed incongruous with his size.

The man's grip was firm but not overwhelming, reminding Will of his father's words: "A limp handshake suggests a weak character and a person not to be trusted; a strong grip suggests strength of character, but too much pressure is a sign of aggression." Will did his best to reciprocate with his grip and judging by the approving look that flashed in McKeever's eyes, he felt he had succeeded. Message sent and received.

Sam Adams had informed him that the coach driver from Boston couldn't come. In his place, they would send the victim's brother. "Thank you for coming," Will said. "I know it was an inconvenience."

He shook his head. "A chance to find my brother's killer? It is not an inconvenience, I assure you."

Sam Adams put a hand on the man's shoulder. "Now, I don't want you to get your hopes up too much, Oliver. It's only a possibility. We're not at all sure. But if it is the same man, we need to know, as he would pose a danger to our entire war effort."

"If he's the same man, I'll know it and I'll make sure he poses no more danger to anyone."

"Now, Oliver, I know how you feel, but it is important that we keep him alive—at least long enough to find out what his plans are and with whom he has conspired."

"I understand," he said, though his tone of voice and the frown he wore on his face made Will skeptical.

Sam Adams pulled a chair up to the table and motioned for Will to do the same. "Let's talk this over," he said. His cousin frowned but consolidated his papers in front of him to allow more room at the table as the rest of them took seats.

"Now," Sam began, "the man we are interested in goes by the name of Henri Dubois Tremont. He is staying at the White Horse Inn." He looked over at Will, then at McKeever. "The question is whether he is the same man you knew in Boston as Henry Belmont. John Weathers sent you here because first, you are the brother of the victim, and second, you were around the man many times and assured John that you would be able to recognize him—even if he was disguised."

McKeever nodded. "If I get to look into his face, I will know if it is him."

Sam Adams nodded. "We thought about going over to the inn but that would be too obvious. We want the encounter not to appear staged, but rather by chance. We want him to come to you. If this man is the same man you knew in Boston, he will be sure to recognize you as well. He is a good actor, but he might give himself away if he doesn't see you walking toward him."

John Adams leaned back in his chair and said, "You, Sam and Will are to meet with another man, Timothy Matlock, at his home. He works in the Congress and is an affable person, well liked in the city. And he is friendly with our quarry. The plan is for the four of you to go to The City Tavern, which Tremont is known to frequent most evenings. You will choose a table so that your back is to the entrance. Chances are good that when Tremont comes by, he will see Sam, Tim and Will and will eventually approach your table."

Will looked over at Sam Adams, eyebrows arched, and the older man shrugged. It was obvious that Sam had confided in his cousin about the possible assassin, contrary to instructions from Hancock. Will couldn't fault him, though, in this. It seemed cruel, and unwise, not to warn those who were most likely to be targets. And if the would-be assassin was after the leaders of the Continental Congress, John Adams had to be at the top of his list.

Sam Adams took over the explanation. "You will then have the opportunity to see the man close up." He paused a moment and put his hand on McKeever's arm. "Now, if you do recognize him, it is very important that you not let on that you do. You must be just as good an actor as he is. Can you do that?"

"Yes, I understand," the man said for the second time. "You want him to lead you to others who may be traitors. Don't worry. I was always better than Ian at hiding my thoughts."

Adams nodded his approval. "Good. Anything else, Will?"

"No, sir."

"Very well," he said as he rose from his seat, "then we should be heading out." McKeever and Will also rose from their seats. John Adams shook hands and wished them good luck. "I look forward to your report."

"What if he doesn't come by the tavern?" McKeever stood with his hands on his hips.

"He will," Sam said.

"But if he doesn't?"

"If my brother says he will come to the tavern, he will come," John Adams said, impatience in his voice, "Just you concentrate on your assignment."

Will noticed a flicker of anger pass across the visitor's face but it appeared neutral when he said, "Very well." Perhaps the man did have the necessary acting skills he professed. Will followed the other men out the door and onto the street.

* * *

Tim Matlack was in a particularly good mood, glad-handing everyone in the room before finally settling down at the table with Adams, Will, and McKeever. They played cards while they waited for Tremont to show. Things were a little awkward at first, the conversation stilted, but Matlack was good at getting people talking and making a person feel at ease. And soon, with the help of the three beers he imbibed in quick succession, the visitor began to loosen up, laughing and talking freely.

He told them about his family and the "good life" he enjoyed as a farmer and part-time blacksmith. They talked politics, including the growing anticipation that the Continental Congress might soon declare the colonies separated from Great Britain. Oliver, like his brother, was a member of the Sons of Liberty, and he took pride in the role the group had played in confronting "the tyranny of the King." And, less than an hour after they arrived, as Sam Adams had predicted, Tremont walked through the front door.

Will noted that Oliver, who had his back to the door, seemed to struggle with the urge to turn around when Matlack announced Tremont's arrival, but immediately he seemed to sober up. Adams leaned over and put a steadying hand on his arm. "Easy, Oliver."

They resumed their game of cards and conversation, with Tim serving as chief monitor of Tremont's actions. Eventually, the man looked over in their direction and locked eyes with Matlack, then walked over to their table.

"*Bonsoir*," he said in a silky voice, wide smile on his face. "How are you gentlemen this fine evening?"

"*Bonsoir*," Adams said, which Tim and Will echoed. "I must say," Adams continued, "that your command of the English language seems to improve every day."

Tremont's smile broadened. "I am learning, Monsieur. I am learning." He gave a look at McKeever, who sat stiffly, his face turning to look at the man. If either man recognized the other, they both did a good job of concealing it.

"I don't believe I've had the pleasure," Tremont said.

McKeever rose from his seat and turned squarely to Tremont. Their faces were inches apart now. McKeever did not smile but he did not frown either.

"Monsieur Tremont," Adams said, "allow me to introduce Oliver McKeever, a good friend of mine visiting from Boston."

The two shook hands. "So very nice to make your acquaintance," Tremont said.

McKeever nodded and gave a small smile but said nothing.

Will watched the two closely during this exchange, noting no change in either's expression, and was a little disappointed. He had hoped for some little sign, a flicker of recognition perhaps, to confirm his suspicion. Could he have been wrong? Or was Tremont just that good? But what about Oliver? He had harbored real doubts about his ability to keep a straight face, whether he recognized the man or not, but especially if he had recognized him. Perhaps he had also misjudged him. Maybe he had better self-control than Will had assumed.

"Would you like to join us?" Tim waved his hand over the table.

Tremont raised both hands and shook them as well as his head and smiled. "Oh no, Monsieur Matlack. I have lost too many times to you with the card games." He turned and winked at McKeever. "A little advice, my friend, watch out for this one," he said, pointing a long finger at Matlack.

Oliver looked up at the man and returned the smile. "He's been courteous so far, letting the visitor win a few hands, but I will keep an eye on him."

"Gentlemen," Tremont said, tipping his head slightly. He turned then to walk away but stopped after a step and turned back. "So very nice to meet you, Monsieur McKeever. I hope you enjoy your stay in Philadelphia as much as I have."

After Tremont left the table, they all sat in silence for several seconds. Tim began to slowly deal the cards. All eyes were on McKeever who sat still, looking down at the table.

"Well?" Adams prompted.

The man looked up then, reached over to the beer glass and took a long swig, then wiped his mouth with his sleeve. He shook his head. "Looks like I made a trip from Boston for nothing."

"Are you saying..." Adams started.

"I told you, if I got to look at him up close, I would know—and I got a good look at him. It ain't him." McKeever shook his head again.

Adams sighed and gave Will a look of mild chastisement? "Well, I suppose it was worth a try."

They continued to drink and play cards and talk politics, but the excitement was gone, the conversation subdued. In a short while, Adams rose and announced that he had grown exceedingly tired and would be heading back to the boarding house. "Oliver, can you find your way back?"

The man nodded. "Not a problem. I have been paying attention to my surroundings, and the streets in this city seemed to be laid out and numbered in a most logical manner."

"Not like Boston."

"No," he agreed, not like Boston—in many ways." He paused a few seconds then said, "At any rate, I will be along shortly, and I shall leave for home tomorrow morning."

Adams said, "But you have just arrived. And if our man is in the city, you might be the best person to spot him. At the least, you stay another day or two and rest up. It is a long ride back to Boston."

McKeever shook his head. "I appreciate the hospitality, but I have much work waiting for me back home. The sooner I get back the better."

Adams nodded, bade a good evening to everyone and ambled out the door. They took a break from their card game then and Tim and Will took the opportunity to introduce McKeever to some of the other independents who had now gathered—Benjamin Rush, Thomas Paine, Oliver Cannon, and Christopher Marshall. It wasn't much longer before Oliver announced that he too would retire and left the tavern.

* * *

Oliver McKeever waited in the shadows cast by the tannery building located about a block and a half east of the White Horse Inn, just around the corner on Third Street. It had been a little over an hour since he left the City Tavern. He didn't know how long he would have to wait, but he knew that at some point, the man he knew as Henry Belmont would make his way to the inn. Oliver had chosen a good vantage point from which to observe, and to intercept him along the way.

He had, of course, recognized Belmont. Oh, it was a good disguise—a Frenchman no less—but when he looked directly into the man's eyes, eyes that reflected a cold emptiness he had seen before but had not appreciated until that moment in the tavern, he was sure. And the man recognized him as well. Of course, he had. And, despite what Sam and the others had planned, it wouldn't work because the man was on to them. He knew Oliver had recognized him. And the man was no fool. He would have to assume that Oliver would tell the others that he was the man from Boston known as Henry Belmont. And he would flee again, as he had in Boston, and probably that night.

Oliver couldn't let that happen. If he had told Adams and the others that he recognized the man, they would have insisted on letting the man live, probably even let him move about freely in order to serve a "larger purpose." They wanted to learn the identities of his co-conspirators. Oliver understood that sentiment, but he didn't care. He wanted, needed, to avenge his brother's death. An eye for an eye. The others could worry about what else he had planned, who else he may have conspired with. That was not his concern. If the man was a threat, then he would take care of the threat—for good.

Another thirty minutes passed, but still no Belmont. Oliver paced a little, careful not to come out of the shadows. He wanted to light his pipe but didn't want to draw attention to himself in any way. He put his hand to his side, confirming that the hunting knife was still there, in its sheath. It was getting late, but there were still plenty of people walking by on Market Street—not so much on Third Street, though. He would prefer a quiet spot, but if he had to do it in front of witnesses, then so be it. The man must die—and by his hand.

This was not a reckless decision on his part, not hubris or arrogance. He was aware of the danger, the risk. His brother had been one of the craftiest fighters he knew, yet Belmont had managed to slice his throat nearly in two. Oliver had to think, though, that the man must have caught Ian off guard. He could see how his brother might have underestimated the threat, from an old man who walked with a cane.

This time, though, it would be the other way around. The man would not know what hit him before the life began to run out of him, from the end of Oliver' blade. It bothered him a little, seemed just a little cowardly to not confront him, let him know what was going to happen to him and why. But he couldn't take the chance that Belmont might find a way to defend himself. So, he had settled on a compromise. After he struck the first blow, the one which would incapacitate him, he would hesitate, look him in his eyes before he finished him off—and Belmont would know. And that would be good enough.

Two hours later, at a little after midnight, Oliver spotted Belmont coming up Third Street, to his rear. The street was deserted, and dark. Perfect. He slowed his breath, began to move toward the man, trying his best to appear nonchalant. Belmont moved easily, smoking on a pipe as he walked. He gave a glance in Oliver's direction but gave no indication of recognition, either of Oliver or any potential danger.

At about thirty feet, Oliver rested his hand on the knife handle and kept it there as he moved forward. At twenty feet, he slowly pulled the knife out of its sheath and held it down by his side, a little behind him, hidden from view. At ten feet he began to worry that Henry would be able to see and recognize him, but Belmont continued to amble slowly, his eyes downward. Eight feet, six, four. Oliver gripped the knife firmly and prepared to thrust it. He heard himself say, "Hello, Henry."

He didn't know why he had spoken, why he had deviated from his plan. Perhaps he just wanted the man to look up, to meet him eye to eye just before he struck. He probably would have kept his silence had he been given the luxury of second thoughts—but he wasn't.

With a swiftness and a ferocity that took Oliver completely off guard, Belmont grabbed the wrist of the hand which held the knife, pinning it to Oliver' side. At the same time, he stepped inside close and stabbed Oliver with a knife of his own, three times in quick succession. Indeed, Oliver wasn't quite sure it had been a knife until Belmont backed away a couple of feet and he saw the dagger blade glimmering in the moonlight, felt the rush of blood through his fingers when he put his hand to the wounds.

And now, their eyes met. Oliver had expected to see that same cold emptiness he had seen earlier and was surprised to see that they shone with excitement and intensity, and perhaps even glee.

"Oliver," he said, "thank you for not giving me away earlier, telling the others that you recognized me." He smiled, not a friendly one. "I know, you thought you would handle the matter yourself—just like your brother." He shook his head back and forth a few of times. "Not a good idea, though, was it?"

Oliver made a move toward him, thrusting with the knife, but he had been weakened, and slowed, by the rapid loss of blood, and Belmont easily sidestepped out of harm's way. His vision was becoming blurred and it seemed that he barely had strength enough to remain on his feet.

"Yes," Belmont said, "very foolish indeed." He had turned his back to Oliver now, looking off down the street, dismissing him as a threat. Oliver wanted to go after him but his body would not comply.

"But," Belmont said, turning his head to look over his shoulder at Oliver, "As the bard would say, 'I'd rather have a fool to make me merry than experience to make me sad.'"

Oliver could barely make out what the man had said, much less understand its meaning. Belmont then whirled around quickly and buried the blade of the dagger to the hilt in Oliver's gut. The blow took his breath away. When Belmont finally removed the blade, Oliver fell back against the building, then to his knees, and finally, face down into the dirt.

* * *

The man who now called himself Henri Dubois Tremont had a vague sense of de ja vu as he bent over the still body and checked for a pulse. When he was certain the man was indeed dead, he wiped the blade of his knife on McKeevers' shirt sleeve and returned it to the sheath which he had attached to his waistband, underneath his coat. He then emptied McKeever's pockets and removed what little money or other items of value he found. He placed the items in a handkerchief and folded it over.

He didn't want the things, of course. He would dispose of them later. But now the death would look like a robbery gone bad. He would rather it not have occurred so close to the inn, and he thought about trying to move the body, but that wasn't feasible, or worth the risk. They might be suspicious—already were if they brought Oliver from Boston to see if he could identify him. But they would have no proof. He stood, looked both ways down the street, then began walking slowly toward The White Horse Inn.

Philadelphia, May 27
Chapter 20

From his hidden position across the street, Will watched Henri Tremont walk out of the front entrance to the White Horse Inn. The man paused for a few seconds, took a few puffs on his pipe, then headed down Market Street. Will waited until Tremont strolled out of sight before making his way over to the inn.

He paused at the doorway, newspapers under his arm, and glanced inside. As he had hoped, no one was at the front desk. Most of the guests were taking supper in the dining room, and the focus of the Boutwells and staff would be there. The newspapers were his prop, and his explanation for coming to the inn, if Rebecca or any of her family were to notice him. Plausible, he thought. He crossed the room quickly to where the room keys hung on little iron hooks behind the wooden counter. He removed the one for number three and headed up the stairs. He had been paying attention the other night when Tremont collected it upon his return, and he knew the room was on the second floor.

At the door to number three, Will paused and looked up and down the hallway one more time to be sure no one was watching. Then he unlocked the door, opened it and eased inside, closing and locking it behind him. For several seconds, he stood, surveying the space, and willing his racing heart to slow. He needed his wits about him.

Will believed that the man who called himself Henri Tremont was not who he said he was, that he was English, not French. He felt certain that he was the man who had killed Ian MacGregor and his brother, Oliver, and also Cynthia Farrington. He believed he had come to

184

Philadelphia with the intent to assassinate leaders of the Continental Congress.

But no one else shared his belief, at least not with anything close to his certitude. And he couldn't blame them. He had no real evidence of it. Tremont was new to the city and no one could confirm that he was who he said he was, but that was true of dozens of people who came through Philadelphia every week. He had received no suspicious mail, and yes, they had been monitoring his mail. He'd received just one letter from a merchant in New York. The merchant was a Tory, but so were a lot of businessmen in New York, and Philadelphia as well.

Will really had little more than a bare suspicion, founded upon one rather ambiguous clue—a quote from Hamlet given to a prostitute by an elderly man who walked with a cane and smoked a pipe. As unsupportable as it might be with logic, Will's suspicion of the man ran deep. He could feel it in his bones.

Or was it just emotion clouding his judgment? Was he being led by jealousy and a vague distrust of the man? It didn't really matter. Either way, he still needed proof. The Frenchman had managed to charm not only the Boutwells but also key leaders in the city and Congress, insulating himself somewhat from suspicion with the very people Will would need to convince. Tremont would remain in that fairly large pool of possible suspects unless he could find more convincing evidence of his guilt.

So, with the assistance of the fading sunlight that filtered through the window, Will began to conduct a quick search of the room, looking for that evidence. Maybe the man had secreted here materials for disguises, alternate papers of identification, weapons, or tools that could be made into weapons, and, if not actual messages concerning his mission, perhaps journals or notes that would connect Tremont to the assassination plot. Will was not particularly optimistic. He didn't think the man would be so careless, but he had to check it out.

Will took out the travel bags and looked through their contents, carefully, as he did not wish to alert Tremont that anyone had been sifting through his belongings. He felt for hidden compartments in the sides and bottoms. He felt inside pockets of the clothing kept inside the armoire, checked the drawer of the small desk. He looked under the bed. Nothing. He was about to check under the mattress when he heard footsteps in the hallway.

Will froze, listening, waiting, his heart thumping loudly and quickly against his chest. The footsteps were light, steady—those of a woman, not a man. They stopped just outside the door. The door handle wiggled slightly as the person outside tried the door and found it locked. It could be Rebecca, or her sister, or one of the employees of the inn, maybe coming to clean the room or change linens. If so, she probably had a master key to every room, and Will would have only a few seconds before that key was fetched from a pocket or pouch, and the door opened.

His mind raced through the possible scenarios, his options, trying out plausible explanations for why he was in Tremont's room. *The gentleman had asked me to come and wait for him in his room.* With the door locked? Hmm. *I was just dropping off another volume from our lending library. The guest was not in so I thought I would just leave it in his room.* And where is the volume? And why did you lock the door? Damn.

Will looked over at the window. Not enough time to escape that way. The armoire was too small for him to hide inside it. Under the bed? Possible, but if his explanation for being in the room was weak, being found hiding under the bed would eliminate that option completely. Hide behind the door and sneak out undetected when the person came in? Not likely to be successful, but maybe he could move fast enough that the person would not be able to identify him as he rushed past.

With reluctance, he concluded that he would just have to bluff his way through with an explanation that seemed best when he had to give it. Will moved quickly to the chair at the small desk, sat and waited for the door to open. He heard the click of the lock opening and the knob began to turn.

But the door did not open. He heard voices then in the hallway, female voices, one next to the door and one a distance away. The footsteps at the door moved down the hallway several feet and stopped. The voices resumed their conversation. He couldn't quite make out what was being said, but perhaps the brief exchange might give him the time he needed for a better option. He rose from the chair, moved quickly to the window and opened it. He squeezed through the opening and, while balancing on the small bit of roof just below it and holding onto the frame with one hand, managed to close the window with the other. He edged over a couple of feet to the left just as the door opened into the room.

Will could not see who entered and hoped she could not see him. He inched a little more along the roof and looked around. The window faced the street and he was visible to anyone passing by if they were to look up. Fortunately, there was no foot traffic on the street at the time.

If his luck held, the person inside would complete whatever chore had brought her to the room and leave quickly. He could then enter back through the window, complete his search and leave the way he came in. But then the person inside the room closed the window completely and locked it. In this weather? Did they think someone would climb in the second story window? Will cursed silently again and looked around for another option.

He eased himself along the roof to where it joined with that of the veranda and walked as softly as he could across its roof to where a trellis, covered with Honeysuckle, ran up the side. He stepped gingerly on the makeshift ladder, hoping it would hold his weight. After a few feet, he dropped the rest of the way to the ground, dusted himself off and walked back inside the front entrance. Fortunately, no one had spotted him, and still, no one was at the front desk. He contemplated another try to complete his search but thought it better not to press his luck. Just as he hung the room key back on its rack, a voice from behind him made him twitch involuntarily.

"Monsieur Harrell."

Will turned to see the man just inside the entrance, walking toward him, smiling. What was he doing back so soon? More importantly, what had he seen? "Monsieur Tremont," he said, and followed his gaze to where the room key for # 3 swayed on its hook for another second, then settled.

Tremont's face registered surprise and then, it seemed, mild amusement. "You have still another job? You also work for the Boutwells?"

Had Tremont seen him placing his key on its hook? "Just delivering some newspapers," Will said, throwing a glance to the stack on the end of the counter." That, of course did not explain why he would be behind the desk.

Tremont arched an eyebrow at Will but said nothing.

"I was replacing a key I noticed had fallen to the floor," Will said as further explanation, and instantly regretted it. There was really no need for further explanation, and it just made him seem guilty.

"And coincidentally, it happened to be mine. Room number three?"

Will looked back at the keyboard, as if to confirm, then turned back to face him. "Yes, it was number three. That is your room?"

Tremont held his nose up as if sniffing an incredibly stupid lie. "Yes," he said, smiling, "that is my room number. Perhaps I clumsily failed to adequately place it on the hook on my departure."

"Perhaps," Will agreed, hoping desperately for some merciful end to this conversation. And it came, in the form of Tim Matlack, who just that moment entered the inn and called out to them.

"Monsieur Matlack," Tremont said, bowing toward him.

Tim gave a bow of his own, greeted him with, "And a good day to you, sir." Then he turned his attention to Will. "I've been looking all over for you. Your sister said I might find you here," Matlack said, a little rush to his voice.

"Yes?"

"Excuse us," he said to Tremont, who gave another bow and a wave of his hand. Tim took Will by the arm and led him out onto the front porch area. He looked around and leaned in, lowered his voice and said, "General Washington is at The City Tavern, taking his supper, meeting with Hancock and some of the members of Congress."

Will waited. There must be more. He knew of Washington's planned trip to Philadelphia to consult with Congress. Indeed, most of the city knew about it. It was not information widely disseminated but was not officially a secret, either, and it was the sort of thing that got around quickly. The details of his itinerary and schedule while in the city were confidential, but as the deputy clerk most responsible for security at the Congress, Will was privy to it. He knew when the general was to arrive, where he was staying, and when he planned to depart to go back to New York.

"Yes?" he asked again, prompting.

"The general has specifically asked for us, well, for you specifically, to join them. Sam Adams sent me to fetch you, post haste."

* * *

General George Washington raised his pewter wine goblet and took a sip of Madeira. He sat at the head of the long table, stoic, outwardly calm and unruffled, but inside, raging against the idiocy that surrounded him. They all had advice for him on how to wage war against the mightiest army in the world, safely ensconced in their lodgings here in Philadelphia. They praised him and second guessed him at the same time. They had no real appreciation of the situation he faced in New York—completely outnumbered and defending an indefensible position—enamored as they were with an optimism detached from reality. Perhaps, he conceded, this was due as much to his failure to adequately communicate the situation as it was to their willful deafness. Perhaps.

Members of Congress had paraded in and out over the last three hours, some partaking in food and drink, some just paying their respects and leaving. The core group that remained included John Hancock, John and Sam Adams, John Dickinson, Benjamin Rush, Samuel Chase, Richard Henry Lee and a newly arrived young delegate from Virginia, Thomas Jefferson. Also present was Joseph Reed, a young Philadelphia lawyer who had served for a time as Washington's personal secretary, and who had now been recruited by Washington to serve as Adjutant General for the Continental Army.

Washington took another swallow of Madeira and placed the pewter container on the table. He removed a small sheet of paper from a pouch by his side, unfolded it and placed it in front of him. "Gentleman," he said, reading from the paper, "we have at present a total of 8,880 men, 6,923 of whom are fit for duty. The British have upwards of 30,000 men, 17,000 of which are Hessians, preparing for an attack on New York."

"Surely you exaggerate the troop strength of the enemy," a voice called out. It was Samuel Chase, from Maryland, whose face tended to flush red when angry or excited—hence his nickname of Bacon Face. He also tended to speak his mind without an adequate filter. He had just returned from an arduous and ultimately unsuccessful mission to Canada with Benjamin Franklin and others seeking an alliance and could perhaps be forgiven if he had not yet recovered physically and mentally from the experience. Indeed, Franklin was confined to his house, trying to recuperate from a severe case of the gout he had contracted on the return trip. Otherwise, he certainly would have been present for this meeting.

Washington gave Chase a withering look, which had the intended effect, reducing the other man to silence. Chase's face turned bright red and he seemed to have developed a keen interest in the condition of his fingernails. In fact, Chase, like every other man in the room, knew that George Washington was not a man prone to exaggeration, and to suggest otherwise was very close to accusing the man of lying—a very dangerous move indeed.

"What I mean," Chase stammered, trying to recover, "is that we can't be sure of the exact number of the enemy forces, can we?" Chase looked around the table now rather than directing his question to the general, and it was John Adams who gave an answer.

"True, Sam, but even assuming approximate numbers, the disparate troop strength is rather alarming." He looked at Washington, who nodded slightly in agreement. "I think what the general is trying to tell us, gentlemen, is that he needs the colonies to send more men, and more supplies. New York, I think we all agree, is crucial real estate in this struggle. Our army has done an excellent job of setting up defenses and fortifying their positions in the city, but the geography of the area, the fact that it is surrounded by water, plays into the strength of the British navy. And if the British take New York, they will have divided New England from the other colonies."

Washington did not nod this time, but he was pleased that at least one of them grasped the situation. Not that he really thought the assistance would be forthcoming in the numbers or quantities he needed. No matter, he knew that he would be directed to do the impossible, with whatever troops and arms he had.

And, in fact, Washington was himself a victim of an optimism unjustified by his circumstances. He really believed that their forces had an intangible asset not possessed by their enemies. Theirs was a righteous cause, he felt certain, and Providence would no doubt guide them to victory, if not in New York, and not right away, eventually, and completely. This was not just a motivational speech for his troops and the politicians gathered in this room. It was what kept him focused on the task before him and committed to its ultimate success.

Tim and Will made it to the City Tavern in less than three minutes. They were escorted by two of the general's personal guards to a private dining room upstairs. The room fell silent when the door was opened. Matlack made eye contact with Sam Adams who nodded for him and Will to come in. The guard closed the door behind them. Washington took note of their arrival with the slightest of nods to Sam Adams, who then said, "General Washington, I present Mr. William Harrell, as requested."

Will stepped from behind his friend and bowed toward the general.

Washington's mouth curled up in the barest of smiles. "Mr. Harrell, it is good to make your acquaintance. I have heard a great deal about you."

Will had in fact met the general before, when he was just one of the delegates from Virginia who frequented the bookstore. He would not have remembered Will but Washington, on the other hand, made an impression on everyone he met. It didn't hurt that he walked around in a military uniform, or that he towered over most everyone—Will was six feet tall and had to look up to meet his eyes. As he remembered, the man was a fan of the play, *Cato.* Regardless, Will was not about to contradict the man, so he said, "The honor is mine, sir. And I, too, have heard a great deal about you."

This brought a few chuckles around the room and made Will blush. Of course, he had heard a great deal about General George Washington. Who hadn't? But if some in the room were amused at his naïveté and surprised that the general would have requested his presence at such a high-level meeting, they must have been shocked when Washington said, "Gentleman, this might be a good time to take a break and stretch your legs. I'd like to have a few words with Mr. Harrell—in private. If you could give us the room for a few minutes?"

Philadelphia, May 27
Chapter 21

It was not really a question, and the stunned members seated around the table and in chairs against the wall hesitated only a few moments, then rose as one to leave, eyeing Will with a mix of grudging respect and jealousy. Washington told his guards, too, to wait outside the door. When the room was cleared, the man rose and walked over to the side table where he poured himself more Madeira.

Will noted again how tall the man was, easily three or four inches taller than his own height of six feet, and a good bit larger in frame as well. He was dressed, as usual, in his military uniform of blue and bluff, an imposing figure that moved with surprising grace across the room. Without asking if he wanted any, the general poured a glass and handed it to Will.

"Thank you, sir."

Washington took his seat again and motioned for Will to take the chair just to his right. He followed his host's lead in taking a sip of the wine. The general placed his wine off to the right and folded his hands together, leaned back in his chair and studied the young man, who sat still, hands in his lap, uncomfortable in the silence, yet determined not to fill it. Eventually, the general said, "Mr. Samuel Adams told me that you deciphered a coded letter in a matter of minutes."

Will shrugged. "Well, assuming my translation was accurate."

Washington frowned. "Oh, it was accurate, all right. Men on my staff also decoded it, and concur in your interpretation of its meaning," he said, the hint of a smile creasing his lips again, "although it took them considerably more time to come to the same conclusion."

Will could think of nothing to say that wouldn't appear to be false modesty, so he said nothing.

"It could have been a fortunate coincidence, a one-time event, but I suspect that instead you have a considerable talent that could be of great use to our glorious cause. Accurate and up-to-date intelligence will be a key to ultimate victory. My sources also tell me that you are a person of integrity as well, a man who can be trusted."

Was the general recruiting him to be a spy? To join him in New York? He was awash in mixed emotions at the thought of it, but Washington dispelled that notion with his next statement.

"For the time being, your work here with the Congress is most important, and you have the full support of not only the leaders of Congress but of me as well. The assassination of any of our congressional leaders would be a severe blow to morale. I would not want to distract you from your mission here. I would, however, very much appreciate it if I could from time to time send you messages that we may intercept and get your advice and opinion."

"I would be honored, sir."

"Mr. Adams has informed me in general as to the progress of your investigation here, but I would appreciate hearing directly from you. Tell me what you have found thus far, what theories you are pursuing and any conclusions you have reached."

Will nodded, and then summarized as concisely as he could everything they had done, what precautions had been taken, what they thought they knew, who they suspected, and of what, and concluding with an assessment of the risks and potential benefits of pursuing certain theories over others, given the limited time and resources available.

"I understand all too well the impact of limited time and resources on attaining ones objectives," Washington said. "Tell me about this Frenchman, Tremont."

Pleased, and a little surprised at his apparent interest, Will gave him the details, including the suspected connection to the murdered prostitute, even his recent search of Tremont's room. He tried his best not to embellish the scant evidence he had to support his suspicion of the man, and to give the counter argument.

Washington seemed amused at the recount of his close call at The White Horse Inn just minutes before coming there. He rose, went to a window and looked out. "That was quick thinking on your part, Will, but next time, have an exit strategy *before* you start."

He turned back to face Will. "I have not met the man, but some of the delegates spoke of him this afternoon. Some of our leaders in Congress are anxious to seek the aid of the French, and they seem to think this man's family may be of assistance when the time comes. Perhaps it has blinded them to the possible danger he poses."

He frowned. "Of course, France will never consider allying with us if we do not declare ourselves an independent nation, something some in Congress seem reluctant to do." There was a hint of disgust in his voice when he added, "some still are content to dine on the dainty food of reconciliation."

Will said nothing in response but nodded ever so slightly.

Washington walked back to his chair and sat, then leaned forward. "For some time now, we have received reports of a British spy, code name Incognito. He is said to be well-financed and well-connected, with ties to Tories throughout the colonies. Although he is given assignments and gets direction from England, he seems often to operate on his own initiative. Very smart, very resourceful, knowledgeable in all kinds of weapons, skilled in the art of close combat, and extremely vicious. He is also apparently a master of disguise. Descriptions of the man are as varied as the reports of his exploits. Perhaps he is a myth created by our enemy to distract us. Perhaps several agents use the same code name, and for the same reason."

"Incognito," Will repeated.

Washington looked at his hands briefly, then directed his gaze toward Will again. "But if he is one man, you will not be able to rely upon one description of him. It is possible that the man who fled Boston, an elderly man pretending to be from Virginia—my cousin no less—may be the man known as Incognito, the same man who has organized a spy ring in New York, and the same man who now has taken on a new and completely different identity here in Philadelphia. Could he be the Frenchman?"

He paused, as if considering his own question, then said, "Perhaps. And if he is, you must take all appropriate precautions for the safety of yourself, and the members of Congress, whether they realize the danger or not."

Will started to respond but couldn't seem to form the words. Washington was looking at him and speaking again but his voice seemed to be coming from across a vast ravine.

And then, his whole body stiffened.

* * *

The next thing he knew, General Washington was sitting next to him, holding onto both of his arms, looking at him and saying "You are all right, my boy. I have you."

Will gradually became more alert and aware of his surroundings, realizing that he'd had a seizure, not a partial, but a full one, and it had come on without any warning. He was embarrassed beyond measure, mortified. "I'm so sorry," he said.

"Tut, tut," Washington said, his voice rich with compassion. "You have nothing for which to apologize, my boy. Are you feeling better now?"

He nodded and the general tentatively removed his hands. "Are you sure?"

He nodded again, stretching and moving his arms and legs, confirming that normal range of motion had returned. The familiar flash of pain originating behind the eyes and extending to his temples had arrived, but it was more annoying than debilitating. "I am fine now," he said, still embarrassed. "Thank you for your assistance."

The general stood and moved back to his chair.

"I have an affliction which causes me to have fits, or seizures, from time to time," he said. "Sometimes I black out for a period. It is quite inconvenient, to me and those who are present at the time. I am truly sorry to have burdened you with having to come to my aid."

Washington shook his head. "As I said, it is not something for which an apology is needed. I was informed of your medical condition and have had some experience with it. I recognized what was happening right away and was more than glad to have been available to assist." He hesitated for a few seconds, then said, "The French have a term for it, roughly translated into English as epilepsy."

He nodded. "Yes, sir."

"My dear Patsy had it for all of her short life, and it finally took her from us." He studied his folded hands for a few seconds. "It has been three years now, but it seems like only yesterday."

In fact, Dr. Rush had told Will the sad story of Washington's stepdaughter. "I am so sorry," he said.

Washington gave a wave of his hand. "I didn't mean to become morose. Tell me, what medications or treatments have you tried, and to what efficacy?"

Will told him of the various combinations of drugs that his apothecary had experimented with, of the exercises and diet modifications. Washington listened attentively, nodding often. When he finished, the general told him about the various treatments he and his wife had attempted with his stepdaughter, Patsy, and the frustration of not knowing what, if any, effect they had, and the frustration of being unable to find any real relief for her. If the opportunity arose, he assured Will, he would assist in procuring necessary medications for him.

Will was dumbstruck. "You are too kind, General Washington. You have many important matters that demand your attention, and I would feel guilty if you spent any of it on such a trivial matter as my medications."

He frowned. "But you didn't ask it of me. I offered, and I meant it. I would like to help if I can, and I would welcome the distraction. You would not deny me this satisfaction, would you?"

"Well, when you put it like that. Thank you."

Washington stood then and said, "We had best bring the others in, lest they get too suspicious of us." He gave him a hint of a smile as he moved toward the door.

* * *

The man whose code name was Incognito was disguised this night as a sailor of Irish heritage. He wore a plain shirt of broadcloth, brown leather breeches, and white stockings, and sported a full beard. His long, reddish brown hair, which hung to his shoulders, was kept in place and out of his eyes by a red and black checkered bandana. To complete the role, he puffed on a clay pipe, and affected a slow, almost tottering gait, as if he was still onboard ship and trying to maintain his balance amidst rough seas.

He had made his way from the warehouse on the river, down Second Street, a little after sundown, stopping at The City Tavern, where he sipped on a beer and made a mental note of the surroundings. He confirmed, by the presence of several guards stationed near the stairs and on the second-floor landing, that General Washington was indeed present, upstairs. After his beer, he stepped outside, and he now leaned against the wall of the building across the street, concealed in the shadow of its awning. Perhaps, he thought, opportunity might smile on him.

He had intended to seek out the general in New York, once he had things set up in Philadelphia, part of a coordinated operation that would crush the rebellion before it could get started, deprive it of its preeminent leaders, both political and military. But a good assassin had to be flexible. He could adjust his plans if needed. Besides, he had little confidence in the New York operatives. They were sloppy, careless. But he had to deal with what he was given.

He added a bit of tobacco to his pipe to keep the fire going and puffed a couple of times. He removed the flask of whiskey from his pocket and took a swig. Just as he replaced it, a group of men began exiting the tavern. He recognized several as delegates to the Congress, some of whom were high on his list of possible targets, though not the one he most wanted in his sights. Not Franklin. He'd heard that the man was back from his mission to Canada but was laid up at his house with a bad case of gout.

Then, the man the delegates had all come to see stepped out of the doorway. There was no mistaking General George Washington. He was noticeably taller than the others and dressed in a fine blue and buff military uniform. He came down the steps with a confident stride, flanked by his bodyguards. His bearing was commanding, even regal, as he stopped briefly at the bottom of the steps and shook hands all around.

Incognito observed the man with not a little admiration, and regret. The cause for which Washington fought might be glorious in his eyes, but it was hopeless. He could not defeat the most powerful military force in the world with his rag tag rabble that called itself an army. In a sense, Incognito would be doing them all a favor by concluding the farce sooner rather than later.

Yet, he had to admire the man's commitment, as misguided as it was. One of the richest men in all the colonies, George Washington had put all he owned, and his very life, at risk for an idea, and Incognito felt sure he would inspire those around him to rally for the cause. Such a man was a dangerous and worthy opponent. Yes, he would regret taking his life. But he would, and without hesitation.

It would not, however, be here, not tonight. There were too many people, too many obstacles, and too much of a risk of being caught even if he was successful. And that was not an acceptable risk. It would require planning. Perhaps before the general left, he would think of something.

Then he caught sight of the boy, the meddling book clerk who was too clever for his own good. William Harrell descended the steps of the tavern onto the street and was greeted warmly by Washington. For a reason Incognito could not quite explain, the sight angered him.

Harrell had been in his room earlier that evening, searching it, of that he was sure. The boy had been careful, but he could tell. He always took care to note the position of his clothes and personal items to be able to ascertain if they had been sorted through in his absence. It could have been a maid or other employee of the inn, perhaps, but somehow, he knew it was the boy, looking for something to support his suspicions, no doubt. His little lie about the room key had sealed it in his mind.

Harrell had not found anything. Of that he was also sure. There was nothing to find. But that was beside the point. It displayed a lack of respect as much as a lack of skill on the boy's part. Did he really think he was as smart as he was, that he could match wits with him? That in itself suggested either arrogance or hopeless naiveté. But it also demonstrated a willingness to take risks in a dogged pursuit of his suspicions. And that could make him a real threat.

"Well, Mr. Harrell," he whispered, "you seem to be everywhere you shouldn't." But no matter, he thought, he would deal with the troublesome boy, in his own way and time. After all, neutralizing an opponent often had a psychological aspect, one that was sometimes much more satisfying than the simple physical removal of the obstacle. In this case, he had decided it would involve the seduction of the lovely Rebecca Boutwell. Yes, two birds with one stone. He smiled.

And he was almost there with the Boutwell girl. Indeed, if not for his own restraint, they would have consummated the act two nights before, on the rooftop. She had been willing, eager even, but he knew that delay would make it sweeter, bond her even closer to him, and make her more pliant. The memory of the encounter was still fresh, and strong.

They were out for a stroll after a light supper at the inn. He persuaded her to join him on the rooftop of the Philadelphia Emporium for a view of the city at sunset and early evening. He told her he had made friends with the owner, who allowed him access. She smiled with guilty pleasure at the idea, and giggled, following him through the side entrance and up the stairs

On the roof, she placed her hands on the top of the wall and peered out over the city. They watched as the sun dipped below the horizon, painting the sky a deep scarlet. A gentle breeze off the Delaware rustled the leaves in the trees and cooled the air around them, bespeaking a pleasant, temperate evening to come.

Incognito moved behind her, placing his hands on her waist. She didn't flinch, but rather acted as if it were the most natural thing in the world. She turned her head to look back at him. "What a lovely view. I understand why you like to come up here. You can see clear down to the river from here."

He noted a small line of perspiration on her upper lip. "Yes," he said, "it is, how do you say, my own little sanctuary." He moved his face close to hers and kissed her lightly on the neck. She murmured softly but otherwise gave no indication that anything unusual was happening as she continued looking straight ahead. He moved his hands from around her waist and cupped her breasts, and now her moan was audible. But still, she kept her hands on the roof wall, out in front of her. She made no effort to remove his hands or move away from him.

Now, as he continued to kiss her neck, he moved his hands lightly over her breasts. He felt her nipples harden underneath the material and he moved even closer, until there was nothing separating them but their clothing. He slowly removed one strap of the dress off her shoulder and let it rest on her arm, then the other. Her breasts heaved underneath her dress as she took short, shallow breaths. He slipped his thumbs inside the fabric and eased the dress down and over the firm, young mounds. She reached up with both her hands and caressed his neck, arching her back and thus exposing her breast more fully to the cool night air, and the nipples hardened even more. With his right hand, he pulled up on the light brown muslin dress and slipped his hand underneath, finding her sweet, moist center with his finger.

Her whole body shuddered, her knees buckled, and a small cry escaped her throat. He held her up and pressed his hardness against, while he continued to work the finger of his right hand. Her skin burned as with a fever and she moaned more loudly now, her body limp and willing. He was just about to bend her forward and enter her from behind when the door to the roof rattled open.

The girl quickly pulled up her straps and adjusted the dress. By the time the building's owner stepped out of the opening, the two were standing by the roof wall, faces turned toward him, the picture of innocence.

"Monsieur Tremont," he said, walking toward them.

"Monsieur. May I present Miss Rebecca Boutwell," Tremont said.

"Ah, yes, I know Miss Boutwell. Nice to see you, miss." If he thought anything improper with the scene he had come upon, he didn't say so, either in words or facial expression.

"Mr. Patterson."

The man gave Tremont a knowing wink. "Enjoying the view?"

"Exactly right," he said.

"Well, I'm sorry to intrude upon your quiet, but I needed some merchandise, hand tools, I have stored up here." He raised his chin toward two boxes stacked under a covered area on the side of the door.

"May I be of assistance"

"No, no. Just need one box. I can handle it easily." And with that the man quickly retreated back through the opening, box under his arm, closing the hatch behind him."

As soon as he disappeared, they both giggled. Rebecca placed her hand over her heart. "Oh, my. That was close."

He sensed both embarrassment and regret in her tone. He placed his hand on her shoulder and drew her close. Then he kissed her, stroking her hair. Her lips parted and he tasted the sweetness of her tongue. She probably could have been easily convinced into continuing where they had left off, but he also sensed that the mood had changed. Best to stoke her anticipation. "Perhaps we had best go back down ourselves."

"Yes," she said, looking downward. There was definitely a hint of regret in her tone then. "Do you think he suspected anything?"

"No, of course not," he said, as he led her to the stairs.

And now, re-living the moment in his mind, he grew hard, and he smiled as the plan began to take shape in his mind. No loose ends. Then he turned and shuffled off down the street.

Philadelphia, June 5
Chapter 22

At a little before eight o'clock in the evening, the man who called himself Henri Tremont approached the residence at 323 Market Street, a small, two-story red-brick structure between 3rd and 4th streets, and the home of Philadelphia's most famous citizen. He stepped onto the stoop and rapped the large brass knocker twice. The door was opened momentarily by a tall, thin African, dressed in black knee breeches, a white linen shirt, silk stockings, black buckle shoes, and a black waistcoat. His face registered neither friendliness nor hostility, but rather the neutral expectancy of one who has ushered many a visitor through the door of his master's home.

"Good evening, sir," he said, giving a small bow.

Tremont gave him a nod. "Henri Dubois Tremont to see Mr. Franklin."

The servant bowed again. "Yes, Mr. Franklin is expecting you." He eased to the side and held his arm out, entreating entrance. Tremont stepped inside and stood in the foyer. "If you please," the servant said as he turned his back to Tremont and began walking.

The visitor followed, past the stairwell that led to the second floor, down a narrow hallway that opened onto a living area to the right and dining room to the left, back to a small study, where Benjamin Franklin reclined on a chaise lounge in the center of the room. His left foot was elevated on a pillow and appeared quite swollen. His neck was wrapped in a thin, white towel. On his lap, on a small wooden writing tablet, were a few sheets of paper, a quill pen and bottle of ink. He placed the pen to the side and looked up, managing a smile. "Monsieur Tremont?"

The visitor had quickly taken in the sparsely furnished room and its occupant upon entering, noting with interest the wooden chess set on a small table against the wall to his left, and on the opposite wall, one of Franklin's inventions, a glass harmonica similar to the one he had first heard in London more than a decade before. The wood paneled walls were plain and unadorned, save for a couple of paintings. A curtained window centered the far wall.

As for the room's occupant, the old man looked smaller and feebler than Tremont had expected, his skin pale and ashen, with a couple of puss-filled sores on his face and neck. He was aware that the man had taken ill on the arduous trip to Canada and so had not expected a robust Franklin, but he was not prepared for the wasted figure before him. He felt a pang of sympathy for the man, but it passed quickly.

Tremont bowed. "It is truly an honor, Monsieur Franklin." He walked over and took Franklin's outstretched hand in both of his, kissed the hand lightly, then released it and stepped back. "I hope you do not mind the intrusion, especially given that you are, I understand, a bit under the weather. I prevailed upon my new friend, Monsieur Samuel Adams, to solicit for me an audience. He sends his regards and hopes to see you soon in the Congress."

Franklin nodded. "Any friend of Sam's is a friend of mine, and welcome in my home." He pointed at the elevated foot. "It's the gout, I'm afraid. It has hit me hard this time. I have also contracted some disease that has manifested itself with these fairly nasty sores," he said, placing a hand on the towel that covered his neck. "I think the heated, moist wrap helps in the healing process, but regardless, it makes me more comfortable. And I plan to return to the Congress within a day or two, carried if necessary." He motioned to the straight back wooden chairs on either side of him. "*S'il vous plait asseyez vous.*" To his servant, he said, "Othello, some tea, please."

Tremont eased himself into one of the chairs. "In my country, sir, your writings, your public-spirited innovations and scientific achievements are well known and very much respected. I couldn't come to Philadelphia and not avail myself of the opportunity to spend some time with such a great mind, and I thank you for seeing me."

"Tut, tut, young man, you will cause my head to swell like my foot." He smiled. "And I must say, you speak our language very well."

The man nodded. "I continue to learn."

"I understand that you have recently arrived in the colonies and are engaged in writing a journal for publication on the status of our, ahem, political situation."

"That is correct. As you once did, here in Philadelphia, my family has interests in printing and newspapers, mainly in Paris, and has underwritten my quest."

"Did you come first to Philadelphia, or have you visited elsewhere on the continent?"

"I arrived in New York, about a month ago, to handle another family business matter. Not so interesting, but financially rewarding. I must say that I found the city and its people not completely to my liking. Not nearly as, how do you say, civilized, as here."

The servant returned with the tea, served both men, then left the room.

Franklin took a sip, then said, "You would not be alone in that evaluation, sir, of New York. Still, the city is important to us, and as inhospitable as it may be, we do have an interest in keeping it out of the hands of the British." He smiled again. "Sam tells me that your family, specifically your father, has the ear of King Louis XVI. He says that perhaps you may be willing to intervene on behalf of the colonies with the king regarding our dispute with England."

"You wish to have the King of France assist a rebellion of British subjects against their king? Not a particularly good precedent, I should think. And though I find you patriots to be passionate and sincere, I wish to remain objective. Besides, Mr. Adams' assessment of my family's influence with the king has been greatly exaggerated. I hope I have not implied more than is warranted and am sorry for any confusion. Still, there is the power of the pen, you know."

Franklin looked at the Frenchman appraisingly. "Ah, yes, indeed, though our need for support is a little more urgent than such as might result from your final publication—assuming, of course, that it will be favorable to our cause."

Tremont arched an eyebrow but said nothing.

"Just as a matter of speculation, no obligation at all on your part, but do you think your king might be persuaded to join our cause against the British?"

He shrugged. "If I may speak frankly?"

Franklin nodded. "Please."

"There is no love lost between the French and the English. I'm sure my king is, or will be, sorely tempted. But in addition to the distasteful idea of encouraging rebellion of subjects against king that I have mentioned, there is also the concern that you will lose. The English have one of the mightiest armies in the world."

"Arguably the mightiest."

"And certainly, the mightiest navy. So, why should the French extend their blood and fortune for a stateless, loosely organized group of colonists in a cause that is opposed by half of your fellow colonists? From what I have seen and heard in New York and here, there are many who are against separation from England, who profess their loyalty to the king and wish ardently for a reconciliation. It is not that long ago that we fought the British here in North America, and it didn't turn out so well." He paused a moment, then added, "Of course, I have no idea what the king thinks. I am just speculating, as you requested."

"*Bien sûr,*" Franklin said. "And you make some astute observations in your speculations. I would only answer that independence of the colonies from Great Britain is inevitable. It will come sooner or later, and my bet is that it will be sooner than most people think. The gentlemen behind the movement are determined, organized and tireless in their efforts. So, very soon, France will be dealing with thirteen united colonies."

Tremont pursed his lips. "It is one thing to wish to be independent, but quite another to make it a reality against a government that does not consent."

"Yes, that is true. But military victory is also inevitable, and for the same reason that political separation is inevitable. A small island country cannot logically hope to forever rule a larger, more populous continent three thousand miles away without the consent of its people. And even the mightiest army in the world cannot secure forever an entire hostile country. They will have to take and hold every city, town, and village in the colonies indefinitely. It is a burden which can be shouldered only so long. The colonists have shown, at Bunker Hill, that they can match up with the trained soldiers of the British. We outsmarted them in Boston and forced their army to evacuate. No, sir, we will win the war sooner or later. With France's help, it can come sooner."

Tremont nodded and expressed his admiration again for the idealistic and committed patriots he had met, which most assuredly included the renowned and wise Benjamin Franklin. He then steered the conversation toward a discussion of some of Franklin's scientific discoveries and inventions, and his political and philosophical writings.

The old man was good at hiding his feelings and he projected humility and modesty in the face of Tremont's praise and the near worshipful tone he employed in inquiring about his host's many accomplishments. Franklin made sure to seek a balance in the conversation, inquiring of Tremont's background, seeking his opinion on a variety of subjects, but Tremont could sense that Franklin was falling for, and basking in, his feigned adulation. Vanity, he had long discovered, was the most common sin, and a most reliable trait to exploit in getting close to someone. Everyone loved praise and everyone loved to talk about themselves. Franklin was no exception. The man, he sensed, was clearly taking a liking to him.

"Do you play chess, Monsieur Tremont?" Franklin asked, throwing a look over at the set against the wall.

"I do, though not very well, I'm afraid."

Franklin chuckled. "Then we shall be well matched. Would you care to give it a go?"

"It would be an honor, but are you sure you are up to it?"

He smiled. "*Pour* echecs? *Toujours.*"

As they played, Franklin said that he had, in fact, been introduced to the French monarch once. "Yes, I visited Paris with my friend and frequent travelling companion, Sir John Pringle, in 1767. I was much impressed, with both the city and the king."

"Then you will not need anyone to intercede on your behalf with the government of France."

Franklin waved his hand. "That was a long time ago and for a very brief time. I met many other interesting people—scientists and politicians, including some very fine chess players. I would often go to the Café de la Regence to find a game. Perhaps you have played there as well?"

"I know it well, and the men who frequent it for chess are some of the best chess players in the country. Alas, as I have suggested, I am not of that caliber. I am afraid that I will be embarrassed now in the face of your obvious advanced skill."

"I didn't say I won." Franklin smiled, moving a piece on the board.

Eventually, the conversation centered on Franklin's time in London. "My family's business interests have taken me to London on occasion," Tremont said. "I'm surprised that our paths never crossed before."

"Yes," Franklin said, concentrating on the chess board.

"You spent many years among the British, enjoying the culture and amenities of London, socializing with politicians, scientists, artists, and only recently have you returned. How did you come to now so despise your brethren across the sea?"

"Yes, I was in London on and off for nearly 20 years, as the agent for several of the colonies. I very much enjoyed my time there. Until I didn't. And I don't despise my brethren. I'm just disappointed in them. They do not understand us colonials, and what is worse, do not wish to. I returned to Philadelphia for good this past year."

Tremont moved one of his pieces on the board. "Yes, I remember a couple of years ago reading about a controversy in which you were involved—something about some letters, wasn't it?" His tone was casual.

Franklin looked up then from the board, the slightest crack in the old man's otherwise composed, inscrutable face.

"Yes, letters from the Massachusetts' governor as I recall. What was his name?"

"Hutchinson," Franklin said, looking down at the board again and moving a piece.

Tremont studied the board as he spoke. "Yes, that's right, Hutchinson. Somebody got possession of private letters he had written asking for the Crown to crack down on some troublemakers in Boston. It was rather embarrassing when the letters were circulated in Boston." He moved a piece and looked up. "People apparently thought you were the culprit."

"You seem to know a great deal about the affair." Franklin's tone was neutral, but a slight frown creased the corners of his mouth.

"Oh my, yes. It was in all the newspapers, including ours, *Mercure de France.* I was fascinated by the story. You were summoned to appear before the Privy Council as I recall, in the place appropriately called the cockpit."

"Yes."

"And you were systematically ridiculed and humiliated for ninety minutes by the Solicitor-General, what was his name?"

"Wedderburn."

"Yes, a nasty man by all accounts. And I for one felt that you were treated shabbily and with a disrespect completely uncalled for. It was despicable. And it was this bully, Wedderburn, who came out looking bad, not you."

Franklin nodded appreciatively. "It was not an entirely pleasant experience I must admit."

"And by all reports, you took it all without saying a word. You just stood there stoically, never flinched, refusing to give them the satisfaction of knowing that it affected you at all."

"J'espère bien."

"You are an amazingly strong-willed and disciplined man. I don't know that I could have stood there and taken such abuse."

"It was illuminating for me, quite frankly. I realized just how arrogant and corrupt they are. Not only do they not understand their fellow subjects in the colonies, they don't want to understand us."

"Still," Tremont said after a brief pause, "I wonder whatever happened to Governor Hutchinson. Thomas, I believe was his first name. This no doubt caused him and his family much embarrassment, probably ruined a promising career. We sometimes lose sight of the effect on the innocent members of the man's family. Do you know what happened to him? Or his family?"

"I must confess I do not, but I suggest that whatever adverse consequences he and his family may have suffered were the result of the Governor's own actions and words."

Tremont shook his head slowly, saying "private letters" in a whisper so low that Franklin did not hear.

"Pardon?"

His visitor waved a hand. "Nothing," he said. Tremont studied the board and quickly realized that he was one move away from victory. He should let the old man win, massage that ego a little more and thus discourage suspicion. But he couldn't help himself. He moved a chess piece on the board and looked up. "I believe that is checkmate, Monsieur Franklin."

His host looked at the board for a few moments, then reached over and laid down his king in capitulation. "So, it is. It appears that you have underestimated your abilities or overestimated mine. Either way, I congratulate you on a well-played game. Perhaps you will grant me a rematch in the near future."

Franklin gave his visitor a bemused smile and Tremont had the sudden, disconcerting thought that perhaps Franklin had let him win. He quickly dismissed the idea, however, and said, "It would be my pleasure. I am sure this unexpected result will not reoccur. Perhaps you were not quite yourself yet, not recovered from your illness, or perhaps you were a bit distracted by my talk of the cockpit. I apologize for bringing up what must be a sore subject for you."

"Nonsense," Franklin said, "you just out-played me—this time." He gave his visitor another smile.

Tremont shrugged and returned the smile, a smile born of self-satisfaction, certain that he had in fact distracted the old man with his questions about the Hutchinson letters. And that would be enough, for now.

A few minutes later, Tremont was escorted out by the tall, thin African Franklin called Othello. The man had paused to chide his master softly for "trying to do too much, too soon" which Franklin had dismissed with a wave of his hand. On the front stoop, the servant gave the visitor a small bow. "Good evening, Mr. Tremont," he said, and then closed the door behind him. Polite but not overly friendly, Tremont concluded. Much like his master.

As he made his way down Market Street toward the river, Tremont reflected on his visit with the famous Benjamin Franklin. What a hypocrite. All his talk of liberty and independence, and all the while the owner of slaves, and this one named Othello, no less. Franklin appeared amiable, even charming, in his own parochial style, trying to

212

appear sophisticated and humble at the same time, but Tremont had not been fooled. He knew the man had been mining for information, testing him, trying to get a bead on the newcomer to his city.

He had almost gotten carried away with his talk of the cockpit episode, exposing himself to discovery if Franklin were to put it together. But observing the old man's obvious discomfort at having to recount the event had been very satisfying, and worth the risk. Besides, he was confident that Franklin had not recognized him, and would never make the necessary connection. Until it was too late.

* * *

Benjamin Franklin accepted the fresh towel from his servant and placed it on his neck. "What did you think of Monsieur Tremont, Othello?"

"Didn't think anything about him, Mr. Franklin, sir."

"Oh, come now, Othello. You must have formed some impression."

The African shrugged, hesitated a moment, then said, "For a Frenchman, he seemed to know a lot of what happened in England."

"You were listening to our conversation?"

The slave arched an eyebrow at his master. "I had to remain close in case you needed me."

Franklin nodded, a small smile forming. "Yes, of course you did." He looked up toward the ceiling for a few moments, then said, "You know, there was something about him that was familiar, as if I had met him before, or at least have seen him." He brought his gaze back to the servant. "Oh well, I'm sure it will come to me eventually."

Philadelphia, June 7
Chapter 23

Richard Henry Lee was in a deep sleep, dreaming of hunting geese on his plantation in Virginia when his servant, Tom, called out softly. "Massa." Lee frowned and stirred but didn't open his eyes, his subconscious clinging to the pleasant image of the dream.

"Massa Henry," Tom said again, this time a little louder.

The dream faded and the veil of sleep lifted. Lee opened his eyes and took in the kind, but somewhat scolding countenance of the man he had owned since birth.

"You need to get yourself on up now," the black man said, as if to a child. "Don't want to be late."

"What time is it?"

Tom gave him a frown. "Like I done said, time to get up. Big day today—least that what you told me last night when you said not to let you sleep too late this morning."

Lee pushed the covers off and sat up in the bed, his legs over the side. The room swayed and his head throbbed with pain. He sat still, trying to get his bearings, seeking some equilibrium. After several seconds, the room was still, and though his headache remained, the pain had eased a bit. Tom stood a couple of feet away, ready to assist his master if necessary, but Lee waved him off and rose to his feet.

"A little too much whiskey last night," he said.

Tom nodded as he frowned. It was not an uncommon occurrence. Lee's ability to consume large quantities of intoxicants and still function reasonably well had amazed some of his fellow congressional delegates, even if some disapproved.

"Drank John Adams under the table, though."

"You drink everybody under the table, Massa Henry."

Lee smiled at the man. The use of his middle name was a familiarity reserved for certain family members and trusted servants—which most assuredly included Tom. "True, very true indeed," he said with some pride, and checked the pocket watch he kept on the bedside table. Plenty of time before the Congress convened, but no time to waste, either.

He walked over to where Tom had laid out a set of clothes for him—burgundy velour breeches and coat, gold silk vest, white ruffled shirt with flared sleeves, and snug, black leather boots that rose high on the calves. With the practiced assistance of his servant, Lee dressed quickly. The last adornment was a black silk scarf which he wrapped around his left hand as a custom glove. Years before he lost the four fingers of this hand in a shooting accident, and the black silk served to both hide and emphasize his disfigurement—a powerful, dramatic prop for the gifted public speaker who frequently gesticulated with the hand during speeches.

After a small breakfast, and a glass of burgundy, Lee left the house on Second Street and walked briskly toward the State House, Tom in tow, following a route he had taken six days a week for nearly a year now. He passed what were now familiar sights. There was Christ Church, an impressive example of simple and elegant Georgian architecture which, with its steeple, was one of the tallest structures in North America, the Laurel Hill Cemetery, several coffee houses and dram shops, the outdoor market, and the Walnut Street Jail.

But he was oblivious to them, as well as to the rattle and rumble of commerce around him. His mind was elsewhere, anticipating the momentous event that was about to play out in the Congress, and his pivotal role in it, which would secure his place in history, and perhaps on a scaffold, hanging from a rope. He patted his vest pocket, assuring himself that his notes were there. He did not need them, as he had memorized the words, but pulling the paper from his pocket would lend an additional air of drama.

Lee was aware that some people back home in Virginia considered him overly ambitious. He didn't think so, but even if true, what was wrong with ambition? It was the ambitious who got things done. He was proud that it was Virginia, not Massachusetts, that was taking the lead now in the push for independence, and proud that it was he, as the most respected member of the Virginia delegation, who had been chosen to introduce the resolution.

He left Tom outside as he entered the State House, and into the chambers of the Continental Congress, a little before ten o'clock. He was greeted warmly by Sam Adams and they conferred in whispers in a corner. The two were unlikely confidantes—the tall, elegant Virginian and the short, disheveled Bostonian—but they had become fast allies and friends. Sam's cousin, John, had been a little frustrated that Massachusetts' assembly had not given the go-ahead to offer a resolution for independence, and that Virginia had beaten them to the punch. Sam, though, recognized the advantage of having Virginia lead the way, a point his cousin eventually come around to.

Matlack and Will took their seats on each side of the dais as John Hancock gaveled the session to order and the members took their places. The doorkeeper closed the double doors to the chambers, and they got down to the business of the day. The Congress had a full schedule. It began by agreeing to compensate a Mr. Charles Walker for a sloop and other goods taken by a commander of the continental fleet—such as it was. Next it considered a committee report on resolutions passed by the convention of South Carolina concerning battalions raised in that colony and received complaints about the quality of gunpowder manufactured at Mr. Oswald Eve's mill. A committee was set up to investigate. Then Hancock recognized Lee for the purpose of moving certain resolutions.

The thin, long-limbed delegate from Virginia rose slowly from his seat. He pulled down on the sleeves of his shirt, adjusted his coat and looked around the room. "I have two related resolutions to offer," he said. All eyes were on him and a penetrating silence invaded the space as he removed the notes from his vest pocket, opened them up and began to read.

"That these united colonies are, and of right ought to be, free and independent states, that they are absolved from all allegiance to the British Crown, and that all political connection between them and the state of Great Britain is, and ought to be, totally dissolved."

Everyone in the room knew this was coming, some with great anticipation, some with a cold dread, but only a select few were privy to the exact timing, or the exact wording. Will suspected that Tim was in that number. He was not. And now, even those who had done everything in their power to bring the body to this point sat in stunned silence, as Lee's sparse, eloquent words hung in the air. A low murmur began in the chambers and Lee waved his black silk-gloved hand to indicate he was not finished. He glanced at his notes and began again.

"That it is expedient forthwith to take the most effectual measures for forming foreign alliances. That a plan of confederation be prepared and transmitted to the respective colonies for their consideration and approbation."

The resolutions were immediately seconded by John Adams, after which an uneasy silence fell over the room. After several seconds, James Wilson, a protégé of John Dickinson, rose and cleared his throat. When recognized by Hancock to speak, he moved to postpone discussion of the resolutions for at least a few weeks.

"As many of you know," he said, looking squarely at those seated at the Massachusetts table, "Pennsylvania has been subject to a bit of political turmoil as of late." He turned to face the rest of the room. "This has been caused in large part by the resolution of this body last month. I opposed it because I anticipated the chaos that would result if it were thought to justify an attack on the government of Pennsylvania, a government which had just been approved by its people in a lawfully held election." He then directed his gaze once again to the Massachusetts table. "And this is just what has happened."

Wilson stopped to take a drink of water and let his words sink in a bit. "At any rate, a provincial convention has been scheduled to take place later this month, on June 18th, and purportedly will allow the people of this colony the opportunity to decide what government will exist here and, relevant to these proceeding, may provide new instructions to the delegates to this body. The people of this colony should be allowed to consider the matter at the convention. The efforts of the Pennsylvania Assembly to give new directions to our delegates have been blocked for lack of a quorum and, accordingly, we have no authority to vote in favor of the resolutions that have just been offered. It seems prudent to wait, not only for Pennsylvania, but also the other middle colonies, to consult with their colonial assemblies."

Prudent it did seem, and a pragmatic John Hancock cleared his throat and said, "Gentlemen, I note that we have several other matters on the agenda today that require our attention, but may not require an inordinate amount of our time. I suggest that discussion of Mr. Lee's resolutions, which might occupy a significant block of time, be delayed until tomorrow morning—which will also allow the respective delegations an opportunity to consider the matter amongst their members overnight."

Both Lee and Adams nodded in agreement and a general murmur of consent rolled through the room. No one raised a voice in objection.

"Very well, then," Hancock said. "Let us then take up the next item on the agenda, a report from the committee charged with investigating an attempt to counterfeit Congressional bills of credit. Mr. Morris?"

And with that, the debate on Lee's resolution was effectively delayed to the following day, a Saturday. The body addressed the resolutions then in a session that lasted until 7:00 p.m., but without a decisive vote.

The debate resumed on Monday, June 10. John Dickinson and his allies took a new tact, acknowledging that it was now impossible to "ever again be united with Great Britain" and assuring the proponents that they were "friends" to Lee's resolutions, but opposed adopting them "at this time." Delay was now his best, perhaps only, option.

"In the past," he said, hand on chest, "Congress has followed the wise and proper policy of deferring to take any capital step until the voice of the people have driven us into it. And this is because we understand that they are our power, and without them our declarations could not be carried into effect."

He looked around the room and waved a hand toward the tables assigned to the middle colonies. "The provinces of New York, New Jersey, Delaware, and Pennsylvania have not been empowered by their home governments to vote for independence. It is my considered opinion that such authorization may be forthcoming. But if a vote is taken today, their delegates must necessarily retire from this body—and possibly their colonies may choose to secede from the proposed union that is so important to our success. Surely, this would hurt our cause more than a foreign alliance might help it. Indeed, division amongst us would make foreign powers less willing to join themselves to our fortunes—or allow them to insist on hard terms for their help."

Others who spoke in support of putting off a vote also questioned why either France or Spain would be inclined to join with the colonies against Great Britain. What was in it for them? These countries also had colonies. Would they really like for them to be encouraged by the American colonies' example of declaring independence? Wasn't it more likely that France would form an alliance with Britain to divide North America between them? Little would be lost by waiting for some more concrete inclination from the French in terms of an alliance. Even if an alliance was obtained this day, there could be no practical assistance in the war effort until next season anyway.

On the other hand, if France might be tempted to join them against her old enemy, England, the colonies' bargaining power would be greater while reconciliation with the mother country was still a possibility. Once independence was declared, however, and that option was off the table, the need for foreign help would be all too plain and would shift the bargaining power accordingly.

Richard Henry Lee responded. "We would only be declaring a fact that already exists. We have in fact, from the beginning, been independent of the British people and the Parliament. All we do now is absolve ourselves from an obligation or allegiance to a king who has declared us out of his protection and is waging war against us. I offered this resolution not out of choice, but of necessity. Until we declare our independence, no European power can negotiate with us, receive an ambassador, or even allow our ships to enter their ports."

John Adams, part of a tag team with Lee, rose to add his voice in support of the resolution when the latter paused in his argument. "Surely, it is in France's interest to help sever the connection between Britain and the American colonies. But let us assume that France proves unwilling to support us. We will be just where we are now. The point is we shall never know until we ask. And let there be no mistake, France could be of considerable assistance immediately, if only by interrupting the shipment of military supplies, or by obliging Britain to divert its resources to defending its possessions in the West Indies. Isn't it better to form an alliance before Britain has the opportunity to suggest some division of North America with France?"

He turned now to Dickinson. "As for the middle colonies, it is clear to anyone with eyes and ears that the people favor independence in all colonies. It is their representatives who lag behind their constituents, dragging their feet like petulant children. If necessary, I for one am willing to forego our longstanding struggle to reach consensus, as it is perhaps unlikely that all men shall ever be of one sentiment on any question. It would be vain to wait for an unanimity that might never come."

But unanimity was a prized goal of most of the delegates and ultimately prevailed in the debate. The Congress decided to give the colonies some time to get on board, postponing the question again for three weeks, until the first of July. But, upon the motion of Lee "to avoid delay if the resolution were to find favor" and perhaps as a signal of the inevitability of passage, a committee was appointed to draft a declaration of independence. The members appointed to the committee included John Adams, Benjamin Franklin, Roger Sherman of Connecticut, and Robert Livingston of New York. Surprisingly, Lee declined appointment to the committee and recommended a fellow Virginian who, he declared, had demonstrated a fine talent as a wordsmith—Mr. Thomas Jefferson.

* * *

The man who called himself Henri Tremont took a left at Front Street and walked briskly for about fifty yards to arrive at the warehouse. He had been lost in thought as he walked, but now, as he approached the storage shed attached to the side of the building and began to fish for the key in his vest pocket, he sensed eyes on him. He paused for a few seconds, puffing on his pipe, and then abruptly turned and began walking back in the direction from which he had come.

He scanned both sides of the lane as he walked, looking for anyone who stood out, who seemed out of place, but he saw nothing suspicious. Perhaps he had been mistaken. Perhaps he had not been followed. But, best to make sure. He continued walking. After two blocks, he crossed the street and entered The Brass Monkey Tavern. He was familiar with the layout of the place, and its owner, a sympathetic Tory.

He walked through the entrance and directly to the rear of the building, nodding at the owner behind the bar along the way. He checked once to make sure no one had followed him inside, and then he stepped out the back and walked quickly down the alley that ran along the rear of the buildings, backtracking again. After a block he came out to Front Street, easing himself to the edge of the building and peering out, scanning the area around the entrance to the Brass Monkey.

And there he was, across the street from the tavern, partially hidden in the shadows. Tremont recognized him as a young street urchin he had noticed on more than one occasion over the past several days. This was not a coincidence, he knew. The lad had been following him. He would figure out why, and for whom, later. For now, he would be content to evade him. He went back down the alley until he was a safe distance from the tavern, and then made his way to the storage shed. He quickly changed to his seaman's disguise, locked up, and headed back along Front Street. As he walked by The Brass Monkey, he got a good look at the boy, who was still stationed across the street, and confirmed his earlier identification. He resisted the urge to approach him and walked on past.

It was a short walk back along the river to Arch Street, where he turned left. Soon, he was in familiar territory, passing and flirting with some of the prostitutes along the way, but declining their offers. His was searching for one particular woman.

The dark-haired prostitute had seen him that night. She had heard him speak. That was his mistake, and he would have to fix it. He had donned his Henry Belmont disguise that night, and he didn't think she would be able to identify him in his Frenchman persona. But it was a risk he didn't want to take, and one of the reasons for the completely different seaman disguise this night.

About thirty minutes later, he spotted her, at the corner of 6th and Arch, standing with another woman, blond, large, who dwarfed the dark-haired prostitute. He hadn't realized before how tiny she was. He waited in the shadows for an opportunity to approach the girl when she was alone. He did not want the complication, again, of another witness.

And it didn't take long. An obviously drunk man, short and slight, stumbled up to the two women. He seemed to be most interested in the blond, and after some apparent negotiation, the two walked off down Arch Street. When the blond whore and her customer were out of sight, he ambled over. She looked him over, as he did her, and, apparently satisfied, gave him a big smile.

"Hello, sailor."

"Evening, lass, can we go somewhere more private and discuss some business?"

The girl looked up and down the street, gave him another smile, took his hand, and then led him toward the nearest alley.

Philadelphia, June 9
Chapter 24

At quarter past seven o'clock that same evening, Cecil O'Brien opened the front door of the bookstore and stepped inside. He was sporting a black, tricorn felt hat and smoking a long-stemmed pipe. He gave Will a deep bow and then a big grin. "Cecil O'Brien, master spy, at your service."

Will looked at the clock on the wall and then back at Cecil. "Nice hat."

Cecil removed it and held it out, examining it. "You like it? I won it off a man from New York." He placed it back on his head. "And the pipe as well."

"Quite elegant," Will said, motioning for him to come into the small alcove.

Cecil pulled a wooden stool from the side of the wall, placed it on the opposite side of the desk and sat down. "You want to find out what we found out?"

Will nodded.

Cecil took a couple of puffs on his pipe. "The Frenchman, I suppose, you are most interested in?"

Will shrugged, his hands out, palms up, suggesting it made no difference to him. It did, of course, but the less Cecil knew, the better.

"I took him for myself and have dogged him day and night for the last several days."

"And?' Will prompted.

Cecil took another puff on his pipe then held it in front of his chest, his arm bent. "If he rises early, he doesn't venture outside before he's had his breakfast. Once he gets going, though, he can cover some territory. He has walked most of the city, talked to a lot of people. Seems to be friendly with a lot of those Congress folks. Sometimes he has sat on a bench in the commons, appears to be writing in a book. He visits the taverns in the evening, mostly The London Coffee House or The City Tavern. He's gone down to the waterfront the last two nights."

"Where did he go?"

"I don't know. I lost him."

Will raised an eyebrow. "Again?"

"Well, the fog's thick sometimes near the water, and there was a lot of people, and I didn't want to risk getting too close or else he'd see me and know he was being followed."

"He probably did spot you following him, especially if you were wearing your not-so-subtle outfit there." Cecil started to protest but Will waved his hand. "It doesn't matter."

In fact, though, Will was thinking that if Tremont knew he was being followed and took steps to lose the tail, it probably meant he was going somewhere he didn't want to be seen. "Can you show me where exactly you lost him?"

"Sure."

Will packed up his papers, collected his waistcoat, locked up the shop and the two of them stepped out into the night, headed toward the Delaware River. "So," Will said, "what else do you have for me?"

Cecil said there had been no unusual or suspicious activity from the slave of Edward Rutledge, Tom Miller. Samuel's Chase's secretary, Edward White, continued to associate with known Tories and attend many gambling events. At one bull bait, he was seen in the company of the Frenchman for a few minutes. Geoffrey Hamilton, the secretary to Philip Livingston, had received mail from persons in New York with obvious loyalist sentiments and he too, had been seen in the company of known Tories in Philadelphia.

"Oh," Cecil said, "something interesting about them all, including the Frenchman. They have been frequent visitors to the Black Cat Bookstore."

Will arched an eyebrow at him. Not so unusual. They did offer one of the finest collections of books and writing materials in the colonies, and so had plenty of customers.

As if reading his mind Cecil added, "But only very rarely did they purchased anything, just walked around the store. Hamilton bought some stationary, I think, but that's all."

"Were they ever there together?"

Cecil shook his head.

"Who was working the shop at the time?"

"You were there some, your father too. Didn't get a report of any big conversations, though. As I said, they wasn't buying anything."

A silence fell between them after that. At Front Street, they turned right and walked about a hundred yards until Cecil stopped in front of the Brass Monkey Tavern, a small, run-down drinking place favored by sailors and others who worked the docks.

"He went in here?" Will's face registered his surprise.

Cecil nodded. "I waited across the street for quite a while, then took a chance and went inside, but didn't see him anywhere. He must have slipped out the back."

"So, he probably did spot you. Did he make any stops before he went inside here?"

"Well, it looked like he was heading to one of the warehouses down that way," he said, pointing with his pipe southward, "but all of a sudden he stopped, turned around and headed back the way he had come. Then he went into the tavern."

Will nodded. A warehouse made sense. If the tools of his spy trade were not kept in his room, Tremont had to have a place to store them. And many of those warehouses were owned by loyalists. It was possible that Tremont had doubled back and headed north, but unlikely. It was also unlikely that his destination had been a building one or more blocks west of the river, as he had walked all the way to Front Street before turning southward. Will looked southward down the street. He was familiar with the entire area as his father's two warehouses were just up the street in the opposite, northerly direction, and he knew many of the owners of the other warehouses along the river. Most were friends of the family. "Show me exactly which warehouse," he said.

Will followed Cecil down the street. He stopped in front of a warehouse that had a small attached shed on the north side of it, with a separate entrance, the door to which was locked.

"This is the building he was headed toward?" Will asked.

Cecil nodded. "Sure looked like it."

There was nothing necessarily unusual about an attached shed, Will thought, but it did seem ideal for someone who needed a small private space to store things without others in the general warehouse space having access. And, most interestingly, Will knew who owned this warehouse.

* * *

It was a little before eight o'clock in the morning, and a fine mist hung over the docks and buildings along the Delaware River as John Dickinson and Will Harrell approached the Essex Shipyard, its signature blue and yellow flag gently flapping above the door of the small office next to the yard. The business was one of several successful enterprises owned by their client, Charles Rockwood, which included shipping, glass manufacturing, warehousing and general merchandising. The shipyard, however, was the one which seemed to give him the most satisfaction, and to which he devoted a substantial amount of hands-on time. Dickinson had suggested they might find him here this morning and his intuition had now proved correct.

Rockwood was on the deck of a boat-build in progress, pointing and gesticulating to some freshly cut timbers for masts as he spoke to the workers. The swampy, decaying odor of river mud and wet sawdust lay like a blanket over the scene. He turned toward Dickinson and Harrell when some of his men looked their way. His face registered surprise, but pleasant surprise it seemed, mild curiosity at the presence of his lawyers at his shipyard. Out for a morning stroll and happened to stop by? Some pressing legal business? He smiled and motioned for them to come closer. He walked forward and extended a hand as the workers, taking it as a cue, got back to their assigned jobs.

"John, Will, how nice to see you this fine morning."

They exchanged handshakes, the other two men confirming that it was indeed a fine morning. Rockwood did not ask right away why they had come, nor did they offer.

"Looks like a fine ship," Dickinson said, looking around.

"It will be."

"What sort of ship is it, Mr. Rockwood?" Will asked.

"Call me Charles, please, my boy." He turned slightly to look at his project. "It's a slaver, built for a group of investors actively involved in the Transatlantic Triangular Trade."

He said it proudly, without a hint of shame or defensiveness. Will wasn't sure why he expected otherwise. His view was that trading in human beings as property was immoral. It was not, however, the majority view by a long shot. Certainly, most people had no qualms about owning slaves, including his mentor.

It was especially prevalent in the southern colonies, where slave labor was an integral and essential part of the economy, and thus the culture, of the region. Not so much in the middle and northern colonies, though, and it was this reality that made southern owners more vigorous in their defense of the practice, Will thought, rather than some higher moral ground held by those in the other regions.

"It's quite profitable," Rockwood said, perhaps sensing Will's disapproval, but probably simply stating a fact. "Cheap trade goods to Africa, iron products, cloth, trinkets and beads, guns and ammunition; exchanged for negroes, gold and spices, but mostly negroes, who are then carried here, or to the Caribbean, and then sold; tobacco from the former and sugar from the latter, purchased to be resold in England. A thirty-ton sloop will carry seventy-five negroes, and one slave in good condition will make you a profit of twenty-five pounds, sometimes more---enough to pay the wages of ten men for two months on the sea— and ten men can sail her."

Will made a quick calculation based on the size of the ship and the number of slaves intended to be carried and concluded that it would be very cramped quarters, indeed, even with a small crew. He kept his observation to himself, though, as their client led them through a short tour of the almost-finished project. Rockwood proudly emphasized the quality material being used, including the local oak used for the recently fashioned masts. The sails, he said, would be made of the best hemp flax available. "Can't skimp there," he said, "or it will all be for naught." By the end, though, Rockwood's curiosity finally overcame him, and he asked them what had brought them to his shipyard that morning.

Dickinson asked if they could talk in private somewhere. Rockwood suggested the office in the small building adjoining the yard and led them there. As they walked, Will noted several gulls gliding overhead, their grey and white plumage blending with the glimmering, slate-grey water of the river and the overcast sky.

The office was a rather small room, but uncluttered, centered by an oak desk and chair which allowed an unobstructed view of the yard. It smelled faintly of that same decaying odor that permeated the yard. Rockwood offered them tea. They declined. He shrugged, poured himself a cup and motioned for the two visitors to take the chairs opposite him as he took his seat behind the desk. They did. He again asked the purpose of their visit. Dickinson responded.

"I'll get right to the point, Charles," he said, sitting forward in his chair slightly. "We have been on the trail of a British spy we believe has come here to Philadelphia, and we have reason to believe that he may be receiving assistance, knowingly or perhaps unknowingly from some of our citizens. He may be using space in one of the warehouses by the river to store materials."

He leaned back in his chair but continued to study his client, who began to perspire and fidget a bit. It was certainly obvious to Rockwood now where the conversation was headed, and he became stiff in his seat.

"I am not at liberty to divulge all the details but suffice it to say that it is important that we determine the identity of this man and capture him before he can do irreparable harm to our cause."

Rockwood snorted, "Our cause? And what exactly is our cause? Open rebellion? Independence?" He looked from one man to the other.

Will wasn't sure if the questions were rhetorical or if he really wanted an answer. Neither he nor Dickinson responded.

"Yes," Rockwood said, "I know the Congress is debating a resolution to declare independence from England. It is all over town. And I know you are against this madness, John, this treason, but I believe you are a candle in the wind over there. You know better than most of the reckless, unethical tactics the Independents have employed in their efforts. They are little more than a lawless mob."

Looking at Rockwood now, Will was reminded of a weasel that had been cornered, snarling, teeth showing. He was defensive, wanting to vent, to justify his actions—and Dickinson let him do so without interruption. "In the end, they will lose. You both know that. They can't win against an army the size of Britain's. And the sooner the rebellion is crushed, and we can return to sanity, the better. Best to avoid further bloodshed, if possible."

Dickinson waited a few seconds before responding, choosing his words carefully. Will could tell he was struggling to keep his temper under control. His mentor was one of the most polite and temperate men he knew, but Will had learned when he was reaching a boiling point. There was a subtle change in his body language, redness in the face, stiffening of the jaw as he struggled to control it. Dickinson lowered his head and shook it slowly, as if wondering what to do with a wayward child. Then he looked up at Rockwood.

"Charles, you know that I have been a stalwart advocate for reconciliation. I firmly believe that this talk of declaring independence is foolhardy."

Rockwood nodded his head as his lawyer continued.

"No one has been more steadfast in opposition to the more radical elements in the Congress—and in our own city. And I too abhor the tactics that have been employed by the opposition. But the fact of the matter is, we are at war with England, or more precisely, she has made war on us. And, despite our differences, we must stand united in defending ourselves, even while we attempt a reconciliation. And just as the British government may very well view our resistance to be treason, so too, many in Congress would consider aid to a British spy to be treason."

Rockwood did not seem convinced, but he gave a small shrug of concession.

"You need to trust me on this, Charles. It is imperative that we identify this man and capture him." He waited a moment or two, then said, "Has there been a visitor who has asked for your help in some way? Specifically, have you given him use of space in one of your warehouses?"

The specificity and directness of the question got his attention in a way the more general and theoretical discussion had not. He looked at Dickinson, then Harrell, then back to Dickinson, the arrogance and certainty beginning to drain from his face, which registered the unasked question racing through his mind. How could they know this? His eyes darted up to the ceiling and back. He took a sip of tea and set it down, stalling it seemed to Will, as he formulated his answer.

Finally, he folded his hands in front of him on the desk and said, "A few weeks ago, I received a letter from a friend and business associate in New York, a man whose political views are in line with mine. He advised that a gentleman would be arriving in Philadelphia who would require my assistance, specifically, to provide a safe place for the gentleman to store some materials, away from prying eyes."

He took another sip of tea in the silence that followed. "Yes, I understood that this man was loyal to the King, and that he wished to keep his activities confidential, especially from the rabble, and I didn't hesitate to agree, especially as I was offered a fair sum for the rental."

The defiance and arrogance had crept back into his voice as he gave them a small smile. "So, yes, in answer to your question, I did in fact rent space to the man, an attached shed at one of my warehouses."

"Who is this man?" Dickinson had fixed his eyes on the client.

"I don't know. I was not given his name."

"What did he look like?" Will asked.

If Rockwood was thrown off by the change in questioners, he didn't show it. "I only met the man once, and it was at night, in the shadows. I could tell he was an older man, slightly stooped, and he walked with a cane, but that's about it."

Dickinson and Will shared a look, then Dickinson said, "Take us there."

Rockwood did not protest. He nodded, took one more sip of tea and stood. The warehouse, he said, was just down the street. "Let me get my coat."

On the walk there, their client pressed his defense, his rationalization, again. "You know yourself, John, that the colonies have not a chance in hell against the King's regulars. We can't afford to be caught up in this Massachusetts madness. Our only reasonable course of action, our only hope, really, is to pursue a quick reconciliation. Those of us who have resisted the foolish course of open rebellion will be spared the inevitable and justified wrath of the King. And those who assist in bringing matters to a quick close will no doubt be rewarded."

"It is one thing to press for reconciliation, Dickinson said, "to argue against the precipitous actions that would plunge us into a protracted military struggle, but quite another to aid the enemy in time of war, because that is what this is, sir, and the man you have assisted is a cold-blooded assassin."

Rockwood did not press his case after this and while they walked, Will tried to get more information about the man, without much success.

"When, exactly, did you meet with him?"

"The day after the election."

"Who was your friend in New York that requested your assistance?"

"I'd rather not say."

"Do you know where the man is staying?"

He shook his head. "No."

"Who else in Philadelphia is assisting him?

"I don't know."

"What has he been storing in your shed?"

"I don't know."

"What are his plans?"

"I don't know."

"Do you know a Frenchman who goes by the name of Henri Dubois Tremont?"

He looked up again, whether to concoct a lie or to search his memory, Will wasn't sure. "Yes, I have met him."

"Could he be the man to whom you rented the space—in disguise, of course?"

The man seemed to consider it for a moment, but then dismissed it. "No, and I can't imagine why you would think so."

"The man we seek is said to be skilled in the art of disguise."

He considered it again, but still shook his head and said, "As I say, I met him one time, and it was dark, but it was not Tremont."

Will didn't know if he believed him or not, but he sensed he was telling the truth. Didn't mean the man was not Tremont, of course. Or maybe Tremont and the old man were two different people, working together.

The warehouse was not directly on the water, but across the street from it, and the shed to which Rockwood had referred was on the western side of it, accessed from Front Street. They cut through the alley alongside the building then turned onto Front Street. At the door, Rockwood fished in his pocket and retrieved a ring of keys, sorted through them and selected the one for this lock. It clicked open and he stepped back, motioning with his arm for them to enter. Dickinson entered first with Will close behind.

The windowless room was dark, the only illumination the indirect light from the overcast, grey sky that came through the door. Will opened it further to allow more light inside, but it wasn't much help. He stepped inside further and let his eyes adjust to the dark interior. It was not a small room, perhaps fifteen by twenty feet. After several seconds, Will was able to see well enough to make out its dimensions and note the shelves that lined the walls. He scanned them quickly and saw nothing there. Nothing on the bare ground, nothing on the shelves.

The room was completely empty.

Philadelphia, June 11
Chapter 25

The Alms House was located on Tenth Street, between Spruce and Pine. The two-story rectangular building was accented by a large turret of about thirty square feet at its entrance. It typically housed about sixty residents with a variety of physical, mental and economic problems. They were farmed out for labor and were lectured regularly on how to improve their lot in life. It was sometimes called the Bettering House, but mostly as an epithet of contempt by its beneficiaries.

Will was here at the request of Dr. Benjamin Rush, who had tended to a recent arrival, a woman who had been severely beaten, but was reluctant to say by whom, and why. "It was Judy Fleming," Rush said, "the girl whose friend was murdered. You remember?"

Of course, he did. The image of the small, dark-haired girl with her shy smile instantly formed in his mind.

"She wouldn't tell me anything," Rush said, shaking his head. "She's obviously terrified of someone, and it may be our killer, given that she could be the only eyewitness able to identify him. I thought maybe you might have better luck."

Will nodded. Sheriff Dewees cared about solving the case, but it was not likely to be a priority. The death of a prostitute rarely was. Rush cared for these people, and he had a strong sense of justice, as did Will. But Will had an additional motive he couldn't share with Rush—the tie to the plot to assassinate leaders of the Congress. And he felt a little guilty that he may have inadvertently divulged her as a witness when he tried to play the little cat and mouse game with Tremont.

He was not surprised to find his sister, Anne, just inside the entrance. She smiled.

"So, what brings the rising star in the Philadelphia legal constellation to the Alms House? New client?"

"Perhaps, in a manner of speaking. I'm here to see Judy Fleming."

Anne knew right away who he was talking about. "That poor girl. Do you know what happened to her?"

"Not yet." He paused. "Perhaps you can help. I think she'll feel more comfortable if you come with me to speak with her." Will explained the connection to the recent murder.

Anne nodded her approval and led him back to the woman's room, which she shared with three others. The room was approximately ten by twelve, with a brick floor and plaster walls. But it was clean. With prompting from Anne, the roommates gave them the desired privacy. Judy Fleming was sitting on a cot that was flush against the wall, on top of a coarse wool blanket. She was dressed in a modest, full-length dress, no doubt provided by the House. Her face was a collage of purple and yellow bruising and was swollen considerably.

"Hello, Judy."

She managed a weak, crooked smile. "Hello, Will." Her breaths were shallow, reminding him that she also had a couple of broken ribs, according to Rush.

"Will is my brother," Anne said.

The young woman gave Will a look that suggested this connection had raised him up a bit in her estimation. He asked her to tell him what happened to her.

She frowned. "I already told Dr. Rush; I fell down some stairs." When both Anne and Will gave her a skeptical look, she added, "A little too much to drink, I'm afraid." Their looks of skepticism remained, but she said nothing more.

Will sat on the edge of the cot and took her hand in his. "I'm afraid that no one believes you."

She gave him a look of defiance but said nothing.

"It is easy to see at a glance that your injuries are inconsistent with a fall down some stairs, drunk or not. They were inflicted intentionally. The question is who hurt you so badly, and why. Was it a disgruntled customer or was it perhaps someone who wanted to keep you quiet about what you witnessed the other night? I think the latter is more likely."

She cast her eyes to the floor but didn't respond.

"I understand that you are frightened, Judy. I don't blame you. Whoever did this to you is cruel and dangerous. But the only way to protect you from future injury, or worse, is to tell me what happened and help me capture and punish the person who did this to you, and who murdered your friend, Cynthia."

She looked up.

"Yes," he said. "I think he's the same person."

She shook her head.

"I want to keep you safe."

"I don't feel safe, Will."

"Then help me help you."

Anne spoke up then. "Judy, you can trust my brother. He keeps his word, and he is very smart and capable. If anyone can find the man who did this, it's Will." She looked over at her brother and gave him a smile and a wink. He nodded his thanks.

Judy sat in stoic silence for several long seconds as Anne and Will waited patiently. Then she collapsed into Anne's arms, sobbing. Will waited as the two women embraced and Judy gradually regained her composure. Eventually, she blotted her eyes with the handkerchief he extended and looked at the opposite wall as she spoke.

"It was not the same man who I saw the night Cynthia was murdered, but I suspect he was sent by that man, to give me a message." Her description of the man who had beaten her was nothing like Tremont, nor of the elderly man with a cane, but rather of a sailor of average height and weight, with red hair and beard.

"I should have been suspicious," she said. "He was handsome, in a way, I suppose, if a little rough looking, but he had a cruel smile. There was no warmth to it. He seemed harmless, though, and so insistent. I felt helpless to deny him. So, I followed him into the alley way, off of Spruce, just down the way from here actually."

She got very quiet for a few moments, looking down, then continued, her voice lower. "We stopped about halfway down the alley. He looked around to make sure we were alone, then he got up real close and said, 'I heard what happened to your whore friend. A real pity. What would be even more of a pity is if the same thing were to happen to you.' He weren't polite no more, now, and now I was really scared. I started to walk away, but he grabbed me by my shoulders and spun me around. Then he started hitting me in the face, not with an open hand but with a closed fist. The blows would have knocked me down, but he held onto my dress front with his free hand."

After another brief pause, she continued. "I don't know how many times he hit me but I blacked out at some point. When I came to again, he let go of me and I fell backwards to the ground. Then he kicked me a few times in the side. After that, he leaned down close to my face and whispered. 'How is your memory now, my sweet? What do you remember of that night?' Nothing, I told him. He asked me the name of my friend and I said I didn't remember. This seemed to satisfy him and he turned and walked away, but not before he gave me one more kick in the side and said, 'Good, let's keep it that way, or I'll have to come back and finish the job.'"

She looked back up at them then. "I don't want him to come back and finish the job." She started to cry again but stifled it.

Her fear was reasonable. There was no guarantee the man wouldn't start having second thoughts about just scaring her off, that he might want to tie up this loose end. "Judy, could this person perhaps have been the same man you saw the night Cynthia was killed? Could he have..." She started to shake her head, but Will put up his hand. "Let me finish. Maybe he was wearing a disguise."

She seemed to consider this possibility for a few moments. "I don't think so. I mean, I didn't get a good look at the old man with the cane, but no, I don't think so."

Will considered that maybe she was right, that it was a different man. And if so, it meant that the spy had allies willing to do his dirty work for him. But it also made him more vulnerable because it meant there was someone else who knew his business, someone in whom he had sufficient confidence to delegate such a task.

"You can't tell nobody else what I told you." She looked at them both.

Will nodded. "Anything you tell me will be kept in strictest confidence."

Anne nodded her agreement as well. "Did he say anything else to you? Anything else you haven't told me? It could be very important in identifying the man. Anything?"

She thought about it, looking up as if to find the answer on the ceiling, then turned to Will. "He said something about silence bringing me joy, or some such shit. It didn't make any sense, but of course he was beating my brains out at the time." She gave him a weak smile.

"Silence is the perfect herald of joy. I were but little happy if I could say how much."

Both Judy and Anne stared at him.

"From *Much Ado About Nothing*, by William Shakespeare," Will said.

Judy gave him a blank face.

"It's a play. Could that be what the man said?"

She thought about it some more, all the while staring at Will. Finally, she said, "I don't know. Could have been, but I don't know."

* * *

239

Will left The Alms House a few minutes later and made his way toward The White Horse Inn at a quick pace. Regardless of what Judy said, he knew that the man who had beaten her so severely was the same man who had murdered her friend, and the same man who had been sent to assassinate leaders of Congress, the man who called himself Henri Tremont. He didn't know exactly what he would say, but he had to warn Rebecca and her family. They were housing a killer. The thought of Rebecca walking down Market Street on the arm of the smiling, charming Henri Tremont nauseated him. It also made him angry, and jealous, and frustrated. He cursed himself silently for his failure to uncover the necessary hard evidence to convince others of what he knew in his marrow.

The pain behind the eyes had come on gradually, and, accustomed as he was to the headaches, he had not really taken notice until it had grown considerably in intensity. Now he began massaging his temples with the tips of his index fingers, small, focused circles. He pressed in harder, taking some perverse pleasure in the throbbing pain that resulted, believing that, if so isolated, it could be contained.

The headache was a symptom, a warning of a impending seizure. He knew that, but he told himself that that wasn't necessarily so. Usually, the headaches followed the seizures, and sometimes they came all by themselves. Usually. Two blocks short of the inn, he stopped momentarily. He needed to compose himself. He leaned against a building and closed his eyes for a few seconds, wishing he had just a little bit of his medicine with him.

He was beginning to have second thoughts. What did he really think he could accomplish? What could he say that made any sense? That didn't sound like the fantasy of a sick, jealous fool, desperate to keep Rebecca away from Tremont?

But he had to try. He pushed off from the wall and continued walking, trying to bend the pain inside his head to his will, to master it. He'd had worse. He could manage it. He slowed his pace a bit, taking short, deliberate steps, forcing himself to breath slowly, deeply, and rhythmically. By the time he got to The White Horse Inn, the throbbing remained, but he felt calmer, and confident that he could mask the pain and do what he needed to do.

Maybe he would not try to convince the Boutwells of his suspicions. Maybe he would just confront the man who called himself Tremont privately, warn him off. He had the feeling that the man knew that he suspected him. This would get it out in the open. Maybe he would see the risk of capture as too great and would abandon his mission, and Philadelphia, and Rebecca Boutwell. The man would escape the punishment he deserved, but his assassination plan would be foiled. No other innocents would fall victim to his evil.

Well, not in Philadelphia, maybe, but the man would not stop. There would be other victims, in other places. No, Will would have to find another way, some way to convince Rebecca and her family to take precautions, without revealing information that might compromise the investigation, and his oath of confidentiality. Maybe Joseph Boutwell's natural protective instinct would kick in. Or Martha Boutwell's. She was the first person he saw when he came through the entrance. She smiled at him.

"Hi, Will." Then she frowned. "Are you all right?"

Was it that obvious? Had the blood drained from his face? Was the pain etched in it? He realized he was sweating, and he wiped his forehead with the sleeve of his shirt.

"I'm fine. Thank you. Just a bit under the weather."

The frown didn't leave her face. "You don't look well, my boy. Why don't you sit down?" She motioned to a chair against the wall.

Will shook his head, which aggravated the pounding in his temples. "Mrs. Boutwell, is Henri Tremont here?"

"I believe he is next door, in the residence with Rebecca and Elizabeth."

"What about your husband?"

"He has gone to the lumber mill."

Will thanked her and headed toward the Boutwell residence, which was adjacent to the inn, connected by a series of gardens and sitting areas the family shared with guests. It was convenient in many ways, though it seemed to Will that you could never get away from your work.

With the mother close behind him, he found Tremont and the Boutwell sisters in the garden. He could feel his face growing hot and he told himself to separate the personal from the professional, to not do anything to create a greater risk to Rebecca and her family. But when he saw the three of them, laughing and playing a board game, he felt his resolve melting.

"Monsieur Tremont, may I have a word with you?" He purposely did not look at either Rebecca or Elizabeth.

Tremont gave him a big smile. "Ah, Monsieur Harrell. So nice to see you again. But how can you be so rude, and blind, not to first acknowledge the beauty before you." He leered at the two sisters.

"Yes, my apologies," He turned to Rebecca and Elizabeth. "Good morning."

They both nodded a greeting. Elizabeth, perhaps sensing the tension, stepped away and sat in the nearby swing. Rebecca smiled, seemingly amused at what she saw in front of her.

Will turned his attention back to Tremont. "A word, please, in private?"

"I have no secrets from the Boutwell women," he said. He nodded at the sisters and their mother who had arrived now upon the scene. "Anything you have to say to me they can hear as well."

No, no, no. This is not how Will had played it out in his mind. In truth, he wasn't sure how it would play out. But not like this. Then again, maybe it was for the best. "I must insist that you accompany me to the sheriff to answer to certain charges."

"Charges? What charges?"

"Well, for starters, two counts of murder and witness intimidation."

Rebecca and Elizabeth gasped, and Will thought she was going to faint, but Tremont placed an arm around her shoulders to calm her. He looked at Will, cold, hard eyes boring into him. "I must protest this joking around, Will. You have upset the ladies."

"It's not a joke, as you well know, but if you would come with me now, they will be just fine."

Tremont released Rebecca and walked toward Will. "I can see that you are serious, Monsieur, but I must decline your invitation, unless you have some official document charging me with such crimes."

From behind him Rebecca said, "Please, Will. You're making a fool of yourself."

Tremont then bent forward then and whispered in Will's ear. "I have had my way with the girl, my young friend. I have managed to accomplish in weeks what you could not in years. And my, what an imagination for one so young, and formerly inexperienced. But then again, a good teacher can make all the difference."

When he spoke to Will, the French accent was gone, and his words had the crisp clip of an English gentleman. But it was only later that this detail came to Will. In the moment, the words themselves seemed to first knock him backwards and then propel him forward. Patches of red clouded his vision and the sound of blood rushing through his veins was so loud it drowned out everything else.

Suddenly his hands were around Tremont's neck and he was squeezing with all his strength. He saw neither alarm nor pain in the man's eyes, but rather some perverse sense of satisfaction. Tremont bent and rolled on his back, bringing Will with him, lifting him with his legs and tossing him over his head. This move, and Will's forward momentum caused him to release his grip on Tremont's neck and use his hands to break his fall. He landed awkwardly, though, unable to get his hands underneath him and landing at an angle on his back. He stood up quickly to face Tremont, who held his hands out in front of him.

"No Monsieur. No more fighting. Not in front of the ladies. If you will give me a time later this afternoon, I will appear before your sheriff to answer to any charges you wish to levy against me. But I will not go with you now."

Will was completely embarrassed and felt the fool. He had played right into his hands and had been unprepared. He looked at the Boutwell women and back to Tremont, but his vision was out of focus. When he started to speak, the words would not come. The odor of sulfur filled his nostrils. His entire body stiffened, and then, the dark abyss.

Philadelphia, June 11
Chapter 26

John Dickinson resided with his wife in her family home, called Fairhill, located six miles outside of Philadelphia. In 1771, he purchased two lots between 6ᵗʰ Street and 7ᵗʰ Street on the north side of Chestnut and built an elegant residence there over a period of four years. But to Will's knowledge, he never resided there as he was never able to convince his wife to move. Will showed up at the Fairhill residence the day after he and Dickinson confronted their client, Charles Rockwood.

When he approached the home, he was greeted by Dickinson's personal servant, a slave called Cato, who acted as if Will had been specially invited. When he dismounted, Dickinson came out of the front entrance, a look of surprise on his face, tempered with a large smile. He embraced his young charge, then separated. "Nice to see you, Will."

"Sorry to come unannounced."

Don't be silly. You are always welcome at Fairhill. Mary and Sarah will be pleased to see you, I'm sure." He paused. "I suspect, though, that this is not a social visit."

Will shrugged and worked at presenting a neutral face to his mentor. "I have come to update you on the investigation and to ask a favor of you."

Dickinson arched his eyebrows, then nodded and led him into the parlor. Will dusted off his clothes but still hesitated to come inside. Dickinson waved in dismissal. "These walls have seen much worse, I assure you."

"So, you have news to report, and a favor?"

Will described his visit with Judith Fleming and the possible connection to the would-be assassin. "I firmly believe that her life is in danger. She needs a safe place to stay until this matter is resolved. If she gets back on the streets, she will end up dead."

Dickinson was silent for a few seconds, as if waiting to see if Will would say more. When he didn't, the lawyer said, "You want her to stay here?"

"Only until the danger passes, which I hope will be soon, or until I can find a suitable alternative."

"Of course," he said without hesitation. "Perhaps the more distance the better, to Poplar Hall?"

Poplar Hall was his family's plantation in Delaware. It was where Dickinson had gone after the May 10th resolution passed. "That would be extremely gracious, and much appreciated," Will said. "One less thing for me to worry about." He started to say that he wished he could get Rebecca out of harm's way as well, but he knew his mentor was still a little skeptical of Will's suspicion of the Frenchman, so he did not voice this thought. More importantly, Rebecca would see no need.

Will also left out the part about him confronting Tremont, and his seizure. He had regained consciousness a minute later, shaken and embarrassed. Rebecca and Tremont were gone, and he was being tended to by Martha and Elizabeth Boutwell. His head felt as if it might explode. He thanked them profusely, dismissed their further concern, and left as soon as he could. A double dose of medicine had reduced the physical aftereffects, but the humiliation lingered.

"One possible development of interest," Will added. "We have intercepted some letters to and from Geoffrey Hamilton and friends in New York"

"Phillip Livingston's secretary?"

Will nodded. "I plan to study them tonight to see if they may be coded. My initial thought upon viewing them is that there may be messages written in between the lines in invisible ink."

"Hmm," Dickinson said, but added nothing more.

They sat in silence for a few seconds. Dickinson crossed his legs and looked out of the bay window onto the front yard where several servants were working. "That John Adams," he said, changing the subject abruptly, "never quits, does he?" There was a hint of admiration in his tone. He shook his head. "And he appears to have the upper hand." He turned back to Will and a small smile creased his lips. "At least for the time being."

Will still didn't understand why his mentor had left Philadelphia when he did, or stayed away, allowing the Independents and their allies in the Congress to get the upper hand. As if reading his mind, Dickinson said, "I had to get away from the city and its politics for a while, Will. I was feeling quite exhausted."

"Then I really am sorry for intruding upon your serenity here."

"No, no, not at all. I assure you am quite refreshed now and eager for whatever comes my way."

"What are you going to do?"

Dickinson uncrossed his legs and sat forward. "I don't know, but I'll figure something out."

* * *

Thomas Jefferson was lost in thought, singing softly to himself as he walked up Market Street.

> I'm lonesome since I crossed the hill, And o'er the moorland hedgy,
> Such heavy thoughts my heart do fill, Since parting with my Betsy.
> I seek for one as fair and gay, but find none to remind me,
> How sweet the hours I passed away, With the girl I left behind me."

His manservant, Bob, trailed just behind him, carrying a bag of apples and two books Jefferson had purchased at the Black Cat Bookstore. It had been hot and humid all day, typical of Philadelphia in the summer, but the sun had grown less intense in the late afternoon, and a gentle breeze moved the sticky air around just enough to make things tolerable.

His new lodgings were on the outskirts of town, located within a three-story brick house on the corner of Market and Seventh. The accommodations at Randolph's boardinghouse on Chestnut Street had been suitable and conveniently located, but he felt a need to escape the noise and heat of the crowded city, to a place where the air was cleaner and more refreshing. And, except for the smell and the flies which accompanied the stables across the street, he had been very satisfied with the move.

The couple who owned the house, the Graffs, lived on the first floor and rented two rooms on the second floor to him, a parlor and bedroom connected by a short staircase, ideal for his purposes. They were friendly and cordial. Jefferson enjoyed their company, and doted on their delightful toddler, but mostly he appreciated their respect for his privacy, his need to be alone.

Thomas Jefferson did not like confrontation. He was uncomfortable with the rough and tumble of the Continental Congress. And although he admired those who could move others with their impassioned oratory, he had neither the innate ability, nor the desire, to compete with them in this respect. Nor did he have the stomach for the behind-the-scenes machinations that seemed to give others so much satisfaction. Truth be told, he'd rather be at his beloved Monticello. He'd rather be in Virginia, helping to craft its constitution.

He had resigned himself, however, to the fact that his junior status in the delegation meant that he would have to remain in Philadelphia while others attended to more important matters in Virginia. And if he lacked the oratorical skills of other delegates, he did have, in his own estimation, considerable skill with a pen. It was an evaluation apparently shared by his fellow committee members as they had asked him to author the first draft of a declaration of independence.

He wasn't so naïve that he didn't understand that there were other reasons, practical and political, for his selection. John Adams, who had seconded the resolution for independence and had pushed for the formation of the committee, was a passable writer. But as he himself had observed, "You are a Virginian, and a Virginian should be at the head of this. I am obnoxious, suspected and unpopular. You are very much otherwise. And, you can write ten times better than I can."

Benjamin Franklin was the elder statesman of the group, well known and respected for his writing talents, but he had just recently returned from an arduous mission to Canada and was mostly confined to his house, still recovering from the boils, sores and gout he had contracted on his journey. "Besides," he had said, smiling, "I always seek to avoid writing anything that is to be edited by a committee."

The other members, Roger Sherman from Connecticut and Robert Livingston from New York, provided geographical balance to the committee. Sherman was awkward and ungainly in appearance and in speaking, a public persona which John Adams described as the "opposite of grace," but he had a reputation for hard work and common sense, and had risen from modest circumstances to a position of political leadership in his colony. Livingston also offered some political balance to the committee since he was still under orders from New York's legislature to not vote for independence, which coincided with his vocal opposition of record to what he saw as a premature move. Despite his opposition, however, he had also made clear that if the majority decided to do so he would go along. He was also considered to be a bright, hard-working member of the Congress who served on numerous committees.

Although Sherman and Livingston professed an inferiority of skill with a pen, Jefferson suspected that they, like Adams and Franklin, felt they had more important assignments which should take priority. For example, Franklin and Adams had both been appointed to a committee to plan for treaties to be proposed to foreign powers; Livingston and Sherman were assigned to a committee to prepare articles of confederation. Jefferson, too, had other duties and assignments, and he could not afford to spend an inordinate amount of time on the document. But though the drafting of the declaration was not seen as the most important or prestigious of assignments, he was determined that it should be done as well as he could do it.

When Jefferson arrived as a delegate to the Congress the year before, one of the youngest delegates at 33 years old, he had arrived in style in his phaeton carriage with four horses and three slaves. He had been sensitive, though, to the criticism of what was seen as the ostentatiousness and haughtiness of the southerners, who were described in a local newspaper as the "Sultans of the South." He had also been shocked that it cost as much or more to stable his horses as it did for his own lodgings. So, this year he had arrived on horseback, accompanied by only one slave, Robert Hemmings. He had inherited Bob from his father-in-law, John Wayles, upon his death in 1773. The boy had been eleven at the time, but quite capable, and by 1775, had become Jefferson's manservant.

He looked back at his servant. "Bob, how are those apples?"

The boy took another bite and shook his head. "Not as good as home, but passable, Mr. Tom."

Jefferson smiled. "That's your second one since we left. Better save some for the Graffs."

"Yes, sir, Mr. Tom, I was just making sure they be all right."

"It took two apples to find out?"

Hemmings shrugged his shoulders. "Best to make sure, you know. Besides, I ain't et since this morning."

Jefferson reached over, retrieved an apple from the bag and took a bite. "Hmm," he said as he chewed. "Not bad, but you're right, not as good as home."

At this point the house came into view, and Will Harrell was standing outside, waiting. Jefferson approached him and extended his hand. "Will, I hope you haven't been waiting long."

"No, sir, only a few minutes. I'm surprised I arrived before you."

Jefferson glanced over his shoulder at his slave. "Bob insisted on getting some apples and candy at the market after we left your store."

The slave smiled at his master's attempt at humor and looked down at the ground. They both knew the apples and candy had been Jefferson's idea.

"Thank you for coming," Jefferson said. "You should have waited in my parlor. Get out of this heat."

Will would not have dreamed of doing such a thing, but he merely nodded neutrally.

"Well," Jefferson said, "come along then." He led the way up the short steps and into the house. They were greeted by a petite young woman with chestnut hair tied in a bun. Jefferson made the introductions and she bowed slightly as she repeated Will's name. "A pleasure to make your acquaintance."

"The pleasure is all mine," Will said. "I believe I know your husband. A brickmaker?

"That's right."

"He has done some work for one of my clients, Mr. Charles Rockwood."

"Yes," she said, smiling. "He is my husband's uncle. James also manages Mr. Rockwood's warehouses for him."

Will wondered if her husband's politics were the same as his uncle's.

Jefferson smiled, pleased to learn there was a connection already. "And where is little Adam?"

"He is taking his nap."

"Well, we have brought some apples for you and your family, and," he said, pulling a small package from his vest pocket, "some sweets as well. I suspect Adam will prefer the latter."

The woman took the proffered gift and smiled. "How very sweet of you," she said, seemingly pleased with the pun. She stole a quick look inside the bag. "Pear drops, too. One of my favorites." She looked back up, smiling again. "There may be nothing left when he awakens."

Her guest nodded, the hint of a smile creasing his lips. "A parent's prerogative," he said, giving Will a wink. "I leave it to your sound discretion."

Then he led the way up the stairs to his lodgings on the second. Bob moved back the curtains in the parlor and opened the two windows all the way, which brought in the sunlight and some of the breeze from outside into the fairly large room. A grandfather clock stood in between the two windows, a fireplace centered one wall and a highboy dresser the other, and a variety of paintings adorned the walls.

Will noted the violin which was propped on a stand in the corner to the right of the windows and next to it a straight back chair. He was reminded of what he had overheard Richard Henry Lee say about his fellow delegate, that as a student at William and Mary, Jefferson had read his books for upwards of fourteen hours a day, followed by violin practice for another three hours. "It didn't leave much time for anything else other than eating and sleeping," he said. Lee's account had been given in support of his somewhat disapproving observation that "Tom has always been a little too serious."

To Will, however, such discipline and dedication to learning were admirable traits, as was the man's quiet demeanor in Congress, and suggested a kindred spirit. And like Will, Jefferson needed his alone time, and preferred quiet discussion to fiery rhetoric. They both loved to read and had good retention of what they had read, which perhaps explained in part why the man had seemed to take a liking to Will. He spent a fair amount of time in the bookstore, perusing the volumes and discussing philosophy, politics, science and other subjects with the younger man. They were even similar in physical appearance, both tall and slim, freckled, with reddish blond hair.

"This is quite nice," Will said, looking around.

"Yes," Jefferson said, "I have found it comfortable." He explained that the adjoining bedroom, which was up the half flight of stairs, was roomy and comfortable as well, though he did not offer to show it to him. Instead, he suggested they sit. He walked over to where his swivel Windsor chair sat in the corner and folded himself into it. He slouched and leaned to one side, crossing his right leg over the left as Will took a seat in a nearby straight chair.

Jefferson lifted a small wooden object from a side table and placed it on his lap. "My writing box," Jefferson said by way of explanation. "I designed it myself and had my former landlord construct it for me."

"Mr. Randolph does nice work," Will said, "and it is a clever design, sir."

Jefferson nodded, acknowledging the compliment. "It is plain, neat, convenient, and takes up no more room on the writing table than a moderate quarto volume, and yet displays itself sufficiently for any writing." He then reached over to the side table which held a supply of paper, ink, and pens and withdrew a document which had been underneath the lap desk. He handed it to Will.

"This is my first draft of the declaration. Please read it over while I pen a message to Dr. Franklin and tell me what you think."

"I would not presume, sir, to edit your writing or to offer an opinion on it." It occurred then to Will that perhaps his host had not meant to suggest otherwise. "But I would be honored to read it."

Jefferson picked up a pen from the side table, dipped it in the inkwell and began writing on a piece of paper. He spoke as he wrote. "I have organized it into three parts: a preamble, a set of charges against the king, and a conclusion. After a moment he added, "And I would value your comments, Will."

Will shrugged and began to read.

"When in the course of human events it becomes necessary for a people to advance from that subordination in which they have hitherto remained, & to assume among the powers of the earth the equal & independent station to which the laws of nature & of nature's god entitle them, a decent respect to the opinions of mankind requires that they should declare the causes which impel them to the change..."

Will read the remainder very quickly, aware that his host had finished writing the note to Franklin and was staring at him. Will could have offered a few criticisms, asked some questions, suggested some changes, but his intuition told him that, that like most writers who took pride in the result of their efforts, Jefferson was most likely a little thin-skinned when it came to criticism of his work. Best to let his colleagues take that role.

"Masterful, sir," Will said when he put the document down. "The prose is strong and flows easily. I'm sure Mr. Franklin will have little to suggest."

Jefferson's nod and slight smile told him that he had made the right decision.

"We shall see." He stood and handed the note to Will, who took a glance at it, reading it quickly.

The enclosed paper has been read with some small alterations approved by the committee. Will Dr. Franklin be so good as to peruse it and suggest such alterations as his more enlarged view of the subject will dictate?

Will placed the note on top of the document, which he folded from the four corners and reattached the wax seal that had held it together.

"Thank you, Will, for delivering this to Dr. Franklin, as well as my best wishes for a speedy recovery from his maladies. Tell him I will anxiously await his response."

Will went right away to the address on Market Street. He had thought he would leave the document with a servant and be on his way, but the old man had called out from his parlor when he heard his voice at the door. The servant led Will into the parlor where Franklin read Jefferson's note quickly while he motioned for Will to take a chair. Then he looked up and said, "If you have a minute, I'd like to speak to you about something. It concerns the man who calls himself Henri Tremont."

Philadelphia, June 12
Chapter 27

"I don't know what you're talking about," the man said again. His eyes darted around the room and he drummed his fingers nervously on the small table, betraying his lie. Geoffrey Powell Hamilton, personal secretary to Phillip Livingston, looked up at Will, then to his employer as if for affirmation, for defense against the accusation. None was forthcoming. Livingston, sensing the attempt at deception, hardened his stare.

The three of them were crammed into the man's small room at The White Horse Inn. He was sitting on the bed. Livingston and Will were standing over him, as there were no chairs or other place to sit. Outside, the afternoon sun was low in the sky but still fierce, the air a muggy blanket over the city, the temperature hovering in the mid-eighties. Inside, it seemed even hotter, the room having efficiently captured and stored the heat and the humidity of the summer day, the air still and stale. It didn't help that the room now had to absorb the warmth of two more bodies. Beads of perspiration popped out on the secretary's forehead, which he wiped at with his shirtsleeve.

Will shook his head, indicating his disappointment at the man's answers. "It's no good, Geoff, no use in denying it. We have the letters."

"What letters?"

The ones between you and the known Tory spies in New York; the ones with the secret messages written between the lines in invisible ink."

The man was sweating profusely now. "If its invisible ink, how can you have read it?" It was a stupid question and he slumped noticeably in regret for having uttered it.

"Not the right answer, Geoff." Will waited a few moments to let him stew in the soup of his own deception and denial. "Perhaps 'invisible' is not as precise as it should be, nor "ink" for that matter."

He turned to Livingston and explained, "Probably used a little lemon juice, maybe vinegar. They are mildly acidic, and when used as a writing medium they weaken the fibers of the paper." He turned back to Hamilton, holding up a handful of letters. "When heat is later applied to the paper, which is what I did to these, the treated part, the weakened part, turns brown more rapidly."

Hamilton looked down at the floor, saying nothing.

Livingston, too, was quiet. When Sam Adams and Will approached him earlier in the day with their concerns, he had been skeptical. But when Will laid out the evidence Cecil and his boys had collected pointing to his secretary as a spy, or at the very least a British sympathizer who was aiding and abetting more active players, he went from astonishment to anger.

So, Livingston took Will to the man's room, introduced him as a deputy clerk for the Continental Congress. "He is investigating a matter of great importance and would like to ask you a few questions. I trust you will cooperate fully." Then he was content to have Will take the lead in questioning the man.

"We have reliable information," Will said, "that you have been assisting a British spy who has come to Philadelphia."

There it was, plain, unvarnished and directly to the point. It threw the man off guard. He sputtered and tried a dismissive snort of a laugh, but it strangled in his throat. All he could manage was "I don't know what you're talking about."

Then Will laid out the evidence against him, piece by piece, letting each bit of it sink in before going to the next: his expensive clothes and other tastes, his gambling losses, the unexpected way he ended up substituting for Livingston's regular secretary at the last moment, his frequent association with known Tories in Philadelphia, including

Charles Rockwood. And now, the coup de gras, his intercepted letters from "friends" in New York that alluded to a coordinated plan that would coincide with the arrival of the British fleet in New York.

Will had not mentioned sightings of him and Tremont together on several occasions, to either him or Livingston. He would wait to ask specifically about him. But what Ben Franklin had told him the day before solidified Will's suspicion of the man.

Franklin told him of Tremont's visit to his home, of his gnawing feeling that he had met the man before. "Upon reflection," Franklin said, "there were a couple of things that bothered me. I am by no means fluent in French, but I have spent some time around the people of that country, and I generally have a fairly good ear for languages. His accent seemed unauthentic, non-native. Excellent, mind you, but just a little off." He paused a moment. "His English, on the other hand, seemed a little too good, his awkwardness with it feigned. He also seemed very knowledgeable about all things British, and in particular the details of my rather trying time in London—which seemed to give him some measure of satisfaction, I might add."

Franklin removed a document from a pile next to him. "When I was in England, I occasionally wrote reviews of plays for the *London Times.*" He held the document up. "This is a review I penned for a staging of Mr. Shakespeare's play, '*Much Ado About Nothing.*' My conclusion concerning the performance of the lead actor was 'much ado about nothing.'"

He handed the document to Will who began reading. "The actor was Edward Collingsworth, the eldest son of a wealthy aristocratic family in the Manchester area. He was quite bright as I remember, accomplished in several areas, including all manner of weapons and combat. From all accounts he was a much-pampered young man with a temper and violent tendencies, especially toward the opposite sex, and whose father continually bailed him out of the trouble that invariably resulted. He took up acting as a lark, and it showed. My assessment of his performance and his abilities was, I admit, a bit harsh. It earned me a nasty letter from his father and death threats from the actor himself."

Will was reading quickly as Franklin spoke, and now read aloud some of the descriptive terms in the review, "Narcissistic, melodramatic, egotistical, and delusional in his opinion of his acting abilities." He looked up.

Franklin smiled. "Not the sort of thing easily forgotten."

Will nodded his agreement.

"At any rate," Franklin said, "I believe that the man who calls himself Henri Tremont could be, in fact, Edward Collingsworth. I'm not at all certain. I could be wrong. It has been quite some time. But that is my best explanation of why he seemed familiar."

For Will, though, it was the confirmation he was looking for, and he was determined to get solid evidence against the man.

Hamilton had offered off-the-cuff responses and innocent explanations for the circumstantial evidence against him: The regular secretary had grown ill just before departure, nothing more sinister than that at play. His political sympathies were not a secret and he neither apologized for his opinions nor made any attempt to conceal them. Moreover, his views were in line with most of the New York delegation, including his employer. It made perfect sense that he would associate with, and correspond with, like-minded men. Yes, he enjoyed cock fights and bull baiting and other forms of entertainment available in Philadelphia. Sometimes he lost, but mostly he won, and it afforded him some extra income by which he could afford a few nice things.

"And more to the point," he said with a huff, signifying his disdain for the insinuations, the baseless accusations, "it's none of your business, and you have no right having me followed and reading my personal mail."

Will pursed his lips and frowned, acknowledging his points, but countered with the fact that the man had no real explanation for the letters. "They contained hidden messages, written between the lines with invisible ink."

"Assuming what you say is true, I didn't know anything about some message in invisible ink."

"You have a couple of problems there, Geoff." Will could tell that the use of his first name, abbreviated, bothered him, so of course he made a point to keep doing it. "First, as you just said, these were private letters, addressed to you. Why would the sender insert a coded message for someone else in a letter to you?"

"Someone could have intercepted any letters to and from me." He looked over at his employer then as if suggesting the most likely person to have done so.

Will nodded. "That's possible, but not likely. It would be a lot of extra trouble for no more secrecy or security."

Hamilton said nothing.

"And, in fact we also intercepted letters from you to your friends in New York, which also had messages written in invisible ink."

"How dare you..." he began, but the protest died in his throat, and he looked down at the floor again. At this point the man turned defensive, a transformation not unlike what Will had witnessed with Charles Rockwood. He railed against the invasion of privacy, pointed to it as an example of the lawless mob mentality that permeated the rebel movement. He looked to Livingston for support and snarled that he was the real patriot here. He was doing what he could to end a fruitless, lawless rebellion to avoid more bloodshed.

"No," Livingston said, "You did it for the money. Your lavish spending on entertainment, clothes and other conveniences was not made possible by gambling winnings, but by blood money, bribes from a coward who does not fight openly and honorably on a battlefield, but in secret, against civilian targets, and with little direct risk to his own safety. No, we do not wish to hear your whining, your false claims of patriotism. What we wish for are the names and locations of the men with whom you have been plotting, and the details of your plan."

He waited a couple of beats to let the message sink in. "If we are satisfied with your answers, our conversation will stay in this room. If not, I will inform the head of the committee of safety in Philadelphia of my findings. The committee, as you know, has its own manner of meting out justice to those it sees as traitors to the cause."

There was some more protesting and expressions of righteous indignation from the secretary, but in the end, self-preservation kicked in with his realization that his best course of survival now lay not in defiance but rather in cooperation. He gave a long, deep sigh, and then said, "What do you want to know?"

When Will asked him what he had done to assist the spy in his planned attack in Philadelphia, he looked genuinely surprised and said, "I don't know anything about a planned attack in Philadelphia. All I know about is the plan for New York."

Livingston arched his eyebrows in surprise. Will, too, was taken aback by the answer but did his best to not show it. "Yes," he said, neutrally, what about the New York plan?"

"You don't know anything about it, do you?"

Will slammed his hand down on the nightstand, surprising everybody, including himself. "Enough of your games. I know plenty, and if you fail to confirm what I already know and tell us everything else you know about it, I will turn you over to General Washington and have him deal with you as the spy you are. This is your one and only chance to prove yourself, if not loyal, at least useful enough to spare you from what you most assuredly deserve. Your choice."

The secretary again looked from one to the other for several seconds. Then, he gave a sigh and started. "The plan is to kill General Washington. It is to be coordinated to occur at the time the British fleet arrives in New York."

"Details," Will said. "How is the assassination to take place? Who is involved? And in what way?"

The conspirators, Hamilton said, included the mayor of New York City, David Mathews, and his brother, Fletcher, the governor, William Tryon, and other highly influential citizens. He didn't know the details except that it was to be an inside job. They had infiltrated Washington's inner circle, including members of his personal bodyguard. "I don't know their names or exactly how it is supposed to happen, whether he is to be shot or stabbed or poisoned. All I know is that the preference is to do it just as that rag tag band of rebels begins to quake at the display of the British navy, sailing up the Hudson, unimpeded."

A trace of smugness had crept back into his voice. "That's the plan anyway, but the timing would have to be flexible, of course, depending on the opportunities." He gave them a surly little grin then and added, "My best guess, and that is all it is, a guess, is that they will place a bomb at his headquarters and at the right time detonate it. And then, in the chaos and confusion, amidst the smoke and noise and panic, it will be a simple matter to put a bullet in the old man's brain and escape undetected."

Although pressed, Hamilton could not, or would not, provide more details, professing to have no further knowledge. Will couldn't tell if the man was telling the truth or not. Even if he was, his information might not be reliable. Perhaps he was hiding the extent of his own involvement. Perhaps he was engaging in a little misdirection, appearing to cooperate but in reality, pointing them in the wrong direction. Could he have been wrong all along about the coded message? Had Washington been the target all along? Or were there two separate but related missions? His instinct was that there was at least a grain of truth in what Hamilton had said, and if so, General Washington should know about it as soon as possible.

Will fixed a hard stare on the man. "And what role does Henri Tremont, or whatever his true name is, play in this conspiracy?"

This time Hamilton's surprise did not appear as genuine as before. "Tremont? The Frenchman who lodges here at The White Horse Inn? I have no idea what you are talking about."

Will noted the line of perspiration forming on the man's upper lip. The man was lying.

He was about to press him on the subject when Livingston said, "Tremont?" Will turned to face him. "You suspect his involvement in the plot against Congress?" Will had neither the time nor the inclination to explain in front of Hamilton the basis for his suspicion, so he simply nodded.

Livingston shook his head. "Pity. He seemed like a good fellow. At any rate, if he is involved, he may have eluded capture, or maybe simply lost interest."

Will gave him a questioning look.

"Yes," Livingston said, "he left the city this morning."

Reading, Pennsylvania, June 13
Chapter 28

The man whose code name was Incognito reined in his horse, stretched in his saddle for a few seconds and wiped his brow with a handkerchief. The June sun, though partly blocked by the canopy of trees along the road, was fiercely hot and the air was like a wet blanket around him. His shirt and britches clung to him, bound by a thin layer of sweat. His horse, the Narragansett Pacer, had worked up a good lather as well. He was impressed with the fleetness of the animal, and its hardiness, well-suited to traverse the muddy, rutted pathways generously referred to as roads by the locals. He patted the horse on the side. In general, he found animals more companionable than humans, and certainly more reliable. "At the next stream or body of water, we'll both take a break and cool down."

He removed the sack of water from its pouch and took a long swig. He had been warned about the water, told that beer, wine and whiskey were safer choices, and he was becoming fond of a drink particular to the colonies called rum. But he found that water, if you were careful, was not a health danger and quenched the thirst much better—and without the mind-numbing effect of alcohol. Of course, that might have been the idea, and fear of illness just an excuse for the vast quantity of alcoholic beverages consumed by the colonials.

He calculated that he was still a couple of hours away from his destination. The man he sought lived on the outskirts of Reading, in Berks County, some 60 miles northwest of Philadelphia. It was named after Berkshire, the English home of William Penn's family. Lovely country, as he recalled, though he had not visited there since his childhood. He didn't think this colonial namesake could measure up, but he was not going for the view.

He left Philadelphia before the sun was up and made very good time. His plan was to conduct his business in Berks County, then make another 30 miles or so before stopping for the night. He wanted to reach New York by noon the next day if possible. He had mixed feelings about leaving Philadelphia just as the cowardly snake, Franklin, had arrived back in the city, and, his taunt to Harrell notwithstanding, just as he was on the cusp of seducing the Boutwell girl.

But the timing had been right and fit his plans. The vote of the rebels in their Congress for independence had been postponed for a month for delegates to consult with their home colonies and get direction on the issue. He wanted to coordinate his actions in both New York and Philadelphia to have maximum psychological effect on the traitors. There was no urgency, no reason to rush things, to act rashly from personal motivations. No, so far, his plan was coming together nicely, and he would stick with it.

Rebecca Boutwell had been particularly distressed at the news. She had pouted and batted her large blue eyes at him. "You no longer find our city and my company pleasing?" She regretted that she had been so accommodating to the man's advances. She felt like a fool, worried that he might never return. He could see it in her eyes, smell it on her skin.

He took her hands in his and gave them a light kiss. "Oh, my dear, nothing could be further from the truth. I have very much enjoyed both. The fact is that I have family business in New York that will require me to travel there for a week or two, three at the most. I intend to return to you and your fine city as soon as I can. There are exciting things happening here and I wish to witness it firsthand." He told her that he adored her and promised that he would expedite his business to return as soon as possible. "I will be thinking of you constantly, my dear."

Her parents offered to store his personal items at no charge and assured him they would find a room for him upon his return, but he had insisted on keeping his room as it was, and paid three weeks of rent in advance. The Boutwells, rent money in hand, had not argued the issue further.

News of his departure was taken in stride by his new friends and acquaintances in the city. They understood the need to go where a man's business required. As for the young Mr. Harrell, a bit of distance might be a good thing. Perhaps his suspicions would be allayed by his departure, maybe not. At least he wouldn't have to worry about being followed and having the boy snooping around in his business.

Two hours later, with one additional stop at a stream for water, he made it to the small village of Reading. Following the directions he was given, he found the place, a residence with a detached workshop next to it along the banks of Wyomissing Creek. Both buildings were framed in unpainted wood but appeared well kept and in good condition. The surrounding yard was neat and tidy. A small, unadorned, wooden sign beside the double door opening to the workshop read, *Martin Meylin: Blacksmith, Farrier & Gunsmith,* the lettering burned into the wood.

An old woman with a thin, angular face sat in a rocking chair on the front porch, shelling peas. She eyed him carefully from head to foot as he approached and dismounted, taking in the expensive clothes and horse. Incognito bowed in her direction and she nodded slightly but did not speak as she continued her shelling. He was just about to introduce himself and ask if her husband was around when a man appeared in the doorway to the workshop, hands on his hips. He was a large man, six feet tall and easily 200 pounds, with broad shoulders and a square jaw. The man, like the woman, took the measure of the visitor quickly, and his face was neutral when he inquired, "*Ja?*"

"*Guten morgen.* You are Mr. Meylin?"

"*Ja.*"

My German is a little rusty. Do you speak English, or perhaps French?"

"I speak English," the man said, the heavy accent noticeable even in those few words.

"Good," Incognito said as he walked over to the man. "My name is Henri Dubois Tremont." He extended his hand and Meylin took it. The spy noted that the hand felt small for such a large man, but the grip was exceedingly firm.

"Yes, the Frenchman from Philadelphia. I was told to expect your visit. You wish to purchase one of my long rifles?"

"Perhaps. May I see the product?"

"Come into my shop," he said as he turned to go back inside.

The man calling himself Tremont followed, taking note of the variety and orderly organization of tools and materials inside the building. He noted the forge with a hearth to heat the metal, and a nearby tank of water for cooling, bellows to blow on the coals to make the fire hotter, and long-handled tongs to hold the hot metal over the forge and to shape it on the anvil, hammers and swags to force or bend the hot metal into different shapes. There were also the typical tools of the farrier: the rasp, cat's head hammer, farrier stand and other files and hammers.

He saw a variety of long metal files with wooden handles, used to file down metal while making and repairing guns, with different coarseness for work ranging from rough shaping to fine, smooth finishing. He noted a vise used to hold a gun or rifle immobile while one worked on it, hand drills and augers, which turned manually by twisting the wrist. There were also saws, planes, rasps and chisels to fashion a handgun's grip or rifle's stock, or to add ornamental decoration for an extra flourish.

Tremont liked what he saw, a virtual cornucopia of quality tools, neatly arranged. It suggested an orderly mind, suited for detail and preciseness. He explained to Meylin that he had heard about long rifles but had never fired one and was very interested in their characteristics and the method of manufacturing.

Meylin seemed to appreciate the interest and the opportunity to display his knowledge. He pointed out the specific tools used for the rifling, and their functions. "This is the boring bench," he said. "I use a hand crank to propel the borer as it cuts through the length of the barrel, adjusting to the proper caliber." He moved over a few feet to what he described as his rifling bench. "This holds the barrel while I use a spirally grooved cylinder to cut the rifling grooves uniformly inside the barrel."

When the man completed his description of the manufacturing process and the tools used, Incognito said, "Fascinating." And he meant it.

The man handed him a rifle. "This one, it is my personal rifle, the first one I make, many years ago."

Tremont turned it over in his hands, examining it closely as he listened intently to Meylin's explanation of the advantages of the long rifle over the musket, superior accuracy mostly, while acknowledging that the rifle took longer to reload. "Would you like a demonstration?"

"I would, indeed."

Meylin took back the rifle and the two men repaired to a nearby open area that fronted the creek. Meylin pointed to several metal objects that hung in the branches of a tree on the opposite bank of the creek southward of their position, a distance Incognito estimated to be about one hundred yards.

Meylin expertly loaded the rifle with gunpowder and ball. He looked at the targets once, then to Tremont, then back at the targets. He placed the rifle barrel in the crook of a tree branch "You can get better accuracy if you have something to rest the barrel on. My eyes, they are not so good as they used to be." He shrugged. "The one to the right. I will give it a try."

Incognito watched as the man took a comfortable stance, steadied the rifle, took aim and pulled the trigger. Then he watched the metal object about the size of a man's head dance in the air and clang loudly, confirming that the rifle's bullet had found its mark. Meylin looked over at his potential customer. Incognito smiled and nodded. "Quite impressive, Monsieur Meylin. Quite impressive, indeed. Shall we discuss terms and details?"

Meylin explained that he would take measurements of Tremont and make the rifle to fit him, like a tailor makes a suit to fit. He recommended a half inch bore size as it was less expensive in terms of the cost of ammunition and asked if he wanted any special ornamentation on the stock. He gave him the price.

"Will you include in that price the personal training in its use that I will need?"

"*Naturlich.*"

"How soon can you have it ready?"

"I will need four to five weeks. I have another order I am working on now."

Tremont frowned. "I really need it done by the end of the month." When Meylin started shaking his head, Tremont said, "I will pay a premium for the extra effort. Perhaps your other customer will be willing to wait a little longer?"

"*Veilleight,*" he said, "for a premium." He gave him a small smile. "The man, he will wait. I concentrate on your rifle."

The spy wondered if the man might use this to leverage his other customer or raise the price. It didn't matter, though. He would get a rifle, maybe two, before he went back to Philadelphia. "I understand and appreciate the courtesy."

Meylin rubbed his chin with his thumb and forefinger a few moments before quoting the new price.

It was less than Tremont had anticipated. "Agreed," he said, and the two shook on it.

Manhattan, June 15
Chapter 29

It was mid-afternoon when the ferry completed its crossing of the
Hudson River from New Jersey and docked on the New York side, on
the island called Manhattan. The smell of salt and decay at the wharf
was comforting to Will in its familiarity. The seagulls darted about in
the cloudless sky, diving close to the churning, greyish green water then
up again, circling the vessel, screaming their greeting. Or perhaps it was
a warning. The salt breeze created by the movement of the ferry had
now subsided, and as the passengers waited to disembark, the air was
still and hot, and heavy with humidity. Will's clothes clung to him.
Sweat beaded up on his forehead and collected under his shirt.

The ferry crossing was the final one of several the mail coach had
made along the way as they travelled from Philadelphia to New York,
via Trenton, Princeton, New Brunswick, Newark and Hackensack. The
trip had taken a little more than a day and a half, the drivers pushing
the horses steadily, their stops brief and efficient, including the few
hours overnight spent at a small inn in Princeton.

His companions were two men who shared the job of driving and
tending to the mail deliveries. They normally did not take passengers
on the mail coach, but John Dickinson had prevailed upon their
employer to make an exception. He could have travelled by horseback,
with the specially designed harness device he used when riding that kept
him upright in the saddle if he suffered a seizure. But a coach was
certainly a safer, more comfortable alternative, and it could make better
time. The drivers did not seem annoyed that they had been pressed
into taking a passenger and had not asked him the purpose of his
journey. He found them companionable.

270

Their manner toward him changed, however, when he had a seizure early that morning. It came with very little warning, just a few seconds of excruciating pain in his temples, then the familiar blackness. When he awoke, the coach had stopped and both men were staring at him. After he recovered, he explained what had happened. They both expressed sympathy and concern, but he noticed that they kept their distance after that, were not quite as friendly as before, afraid that perhaps whatever he had might be contagious. It was silly, of course, but he was used to it. It was not an uncommon reaction.

It was his second seizure in three days, and fairly major ones. This concerned him, but he didn't know what else to do. He had been taking his medication regularly. Three or four weeks might pass now before another attack, maybe longer, or he could have another one tomorrow, or sooner. It was the random nature of the affliction.

Still, even though the drivers didn't know why he had been put on their coach, they knew his mission must be of some importance, and they continued to treat him with appropriate courtesy. He suspected, though, that they were glad to be rid of him now, at least temporarily. He collected his small bag from the coach, thanked the drivers, gave them a small gratuity, confirmed the schedule for the return trip, then stepped out onto the wharf.

This was Will's first visit to New York, but he had familiarized himself with the city's layout somewhat by reviewing a map of the area they had at the bookstore, and which he brought with him. Phillip Livingston had also been very helpful in giving him directions and advice and letters of introduction to persons on whom he might call upon for assistance.

His first impression of the city as he embarked was not overly favorable, at least in comparison with his home city of Philadelphia. New York had a much smaller population—approximately twenty-five thousand versus forty thousand—crammed into a much smaller geographical area. The streets were paved but much narrower, the buildings taller and closer to the edge of the streets, making it seem even more crowded, and allowing less sunlight through.

The buzz of commerce, of constant activity and a sense of irrepressible energy, people scurrying about all reminded him of Philadelphia, but it all seemed more frantic. He checked his map, got his bearings, and headed toward his destination, a residence located at No. 1 Broadway, currently serving as the headquarters of General George Washington.

Will had reported to the security committee what Hamilton told him about a planned assassination of General Washington in New York, and of Tremont's purported departure for that city. He also told them of Franklin's tentative identification of the man they had come to know as Henri Tremont as a British actor. This latter bit of information was the first bit of corroborating evidence he'd discovered to confirm his suspicions. The others weren't quite ready to declare him the assassin, but they seemed to be coming around to that conclusion. All agreed that Washington should be notified immediately. It was also agreed that Will should be tasked with this assignment. Tim would make sure that all leads were followed up in Philadelphia and all precautions taken for the security of the Congress. Will could hardly wait to get on the road.

And now, after about a ten-minute walk, he reached his destination. The residence, mansion really, fronted Bowling Green. There was no mistaking that he was in the right place as the grounds were crawling with soldiers around the perimeter and patrolling the grounds. Ironically, Bowling Green featured a large equestrian statue of King George III, a constant reminder, perhaps, to the soldiers and their general of why they were there.

Will presented the sealed letter to the sentry at the front gate and said, "I am William Harrell, here to see General Washington. This is a letter from the president of the Continental Congress, Mr. Hancock, for the general's consideration."

The man frowned. "I don't know you. You are not the usual messenger." He held the letter aloft. "How do I know this is what you say it is?"

Will returned the frown. "I suspect this is not the first time the general has received a letter from Mr. Hancock. I'm sure he or someone on his staff will determine its bona fides." Will didn't like the man's surly attitude but told himself he was just being cautious. "I'll wait right here."

The man puffed up with importance and handed the sealed letter to a soldier just inside the gate. "Take this to Mr. Baylor." He was too important to leave his post apparently. The other man nodded, took the letter and hurried off toward the residence.

* * *

The Kennedy Mansion, used by the general as his headquarters in New York, was an elegant residence with a grand stairway and banquet hall, and a garden to the rear that reached down to the Hudson River. From the rooftop cupola one could see for miles in all directions. Washington stood now in the cupola, using a spyglass to survey the territory he must defend against a sure and pending attack from the British.

He saw the three islands clustered close together, each emerald green with nearly impenetrable growth of oak and maple and foliage. The island called Manhattan was a narrow finger of land running north and south, dividing the Hudson and East River. Broadway, the main thoroughfare was straight and broad-lined with shade trees and fine houses and churches. Queen Street, close to the crowded East River wharves, was the business center. City Hall was on Wall Street. Approximately twenty thousand souls and four thousand buildings were crowded into an area less than one square mile, surrounded by a busy, deep-sea harbor, an area thus very vulnerable to the British navy.

The mainland to the west was New Jersey. Close to the southern end of Manhattan was Staten Island, irregular and oblong. To the east and closer was the larger island called Long Island. The Dutch settlement they called Breukelen, or in English, Brooklyn, meaning marshland, lay to the southeast on Long Island. To the north was a mix of woods, small streams, marshes, and great rocky patches interspersed with a few small farms and larger estates. Known as the Outward, the area ran all the way to King's Bridge, connecting it to the mainland over the Harlem River.

If Washington had been unimpressed with the New Englanders he had encountered thus far, he considered them exemplary human beings compared to the natives of New York. He agreed with the observation of one of his officers, Henry Knox. "They are magnificent in their carriages, which are numerous, in their houses and furniture, which are fine, in their pride and deceit, which is inimitable, in their profaneness, which is intolerable, and in the want of principle, which is prevalent, and in their toryism, which is insufferable."

In addition to the inherent difficulty of defending the city against an assault from the British Navy, Washington had to contend with the large number of loyalists, or Tories, in the local population, those who professed ardent support for the king and more importantly those who feigned loyalty to the rebel cause. He also worried about the smallpox, syphilis, and other diseases to which the men were exposed, and the many distractions to weaken discipline, of which the prostitutes ranked high on his list. One section of the city, referred to as the Holy Ground, so named because it was owned by the Trinity Church, was a foul slum and brothel district west of the commons with a high crime rate. It contained, he felt certain, the largest concentration of whores in all the colonies, and they plied their trade with abandon.

His men were under strict orders to treat the locals with respect, to not harass or abuse them, but it had proved difficult to enforce. Less than a week after they arrived in April, the mutilated bodies of two soldiers were found concealed in a brothel on the Holy Ground, one of which had been castrated in a most barbarous manner. In retaliation, soldiers had gone on a rampage, destroying property and exacting revenge on one suspected whore, whose rotting remains were later discovered in a privy. But men were men, and business was business, and his soldiers continued to frequent the saloons and the brothels in the city, and the whores continued their lucrative trade. He doubted that it could ever be fully controlled.

To defend against an approach on the East River the army had built Fort Lee on the Jersey side and Fort Washington on the Manhattan side. Fort Stirling has been erected on a bluff called Brooklyn Heights, from which one could look down on all of New York City, the harbor, the rivers and the long low hills of New Jersey beyond, one of the grandest panoramas to be seen on the entire Atlantic seaboard. On the eastern side of the hamlet of Brooklyn they had built Fort Putnam and Fort Greene and Fort Defiance, all of which were connected by a line of entrenchments. Earthworks and gun placements had also been built on Governor's island, in the direct path of the entrance to the East River. Barricades had been erected in the city itself. He had done what he could to ready the city and his forces for the attack he knew was coming. In his heart, he knew it would not be enough, but no matter, he would do his duty.

He turned when he heard the soft rap on the captain's hatch. the upper torso of George Baylor, one of his aide-de-camps, was visible through the opening.

"Yes?"

"Sorry to disturb you, General. There is a young man from Philadelphia here to see you, with a message from Mr. Hancock."

"Does the young man have a name?"

"William Harrell, sir."

The news surprised him, but the general's face remained passive. "Bring him to my office in five minutes. See if Colonel Reed is available to join us."

* * *

As he waited, Will paced the street in front of the building. After about twenty minutes, the guard returned, accompanied by a man he recognized. Joseph Reed was a Philadelphia lawyer who had served as Washington's personal secretary, and now as adjutant general. Reed smiled warmly and extended his hand. "Will, how nice to see you. It has been a while."

Will griped his hand firmly and smiled back. "Yes, Mr. Reed, nice to see you again as well. I understood that you had left your practice to serve the general. I saw you briefly, and from a distance, when the general came to Philadelphia to consult with the Congress but didn't get to say hello. How do you find it?"

"It's Joseph, please, and yes, I have left my practice but more importantly my family, in service to the cause. For no compensation, I might add. But as you know, or will learn, it is difficult to say no to George Washington." He shook his head, smiling. "That being said, I consider it an honor."

Will nodded. Remembering how he had felt in his presence in Philadelphia. He could understand the desire, the need, to gain the man's approval.

"The general is waiting for you," Reed said, and with that turned and walked toward the residence, Will following behind. Reed looked back over his shoulder. "How are things in Philadelphia? Anything new in Congress?"

There was of course the resolution to declare their separation from England, and he was sure news of this had been conveyed to Washington, but if the general had not seen fit to advise Reed, it wasn't Will's place to depart from the confidentiality expected of those who worked in the Congress. "Nothing really," he said.

"I did enjoy our short visit recently," Reed said, "and would have liked more time with my family, but General Washington was anxious to get back. He arranged for fresh horses to be stationed all along the way between Philadelphia and New York so that he could get back as soon as possible after his consultations with congressional leaders, so by June 6th we were back here, going full speed." He frowned his disappointment, then shrugged as if to acknowledge the futility of complaint.

"The general and his wife, Martha, have set up residence two miles north of the city, along the Hudson, but he spends much of his time here at the Kennedy residence, which makes a passable headquarters," Reed led Will to a room just past the foyer, on the right. Reed nodded to the two guards who stood on either side of the entrance and knocked lightly on the door.

"Enter." came the voice beyond.

Reed opened the door and led the way into the room, a fairly large space, nicely adorned. On the wall to their right, a large fireplace was framed by two floor-to-ceiling windows. On the opposite wall, George Washington sat behind a large walnut desk. He looked up from his writing, expectantly, placing the quill pen in its holder. On the desk in front of him was the letter from John Hancock.

"Thank you, Joseph," he said, holding up the letter. "Mr. Hancock has sent Mr. Harrell with a message that is for my ears only, at least initially."

Reed bowed in acknowledgment, his face passive, a very slight frown the only hint of hurt feelings at not being included. "Of course," he said, and turned to leave.

"If you could stay close by, though, I may have need of your assistance."

Reed nodded. "Of course," he said again. He looked at Will briefly, the frown gone, then left them alone.

Washington motioned for Will to take a chair opposite him and allowed himself the barest of a smile, a slight upturn at the corners of his mouth. It was well known that the general had lost most of his teeth at an early age and had difficulty getting man-made ones that fit properly, something that made him extremely self-conscious about smiling. So, a small smile was all one could expect. Yet, his manner was warm and Will believed him sincere and not just being polite when he folded his hands together on the desk and said, "Will, so nice to see you again."

"You as well, sir."

"I assume that what you have to tell me is somewhat urgent, enough to prompt a trip to New York to deliver it personally."

"I think so, sir, but of course you will be the judge of that."

"Well, spit it out then, boy. Does it pertain to your investigation of the supposed assassination plot against members of the Congress?"

"Actually, sir, it involves a possible plot to assassinate you."

If his words surprised him, the general didn't show it. He asked for details and sat calmly as Will laid it all out for him as thoroughly and succinctly as he could, the evidence he had gathered, the confession of Livingston's secretary, Tremont's supposed travel to New York on business, and Franklin's revelation. When he finished, Washington made a tent of his fingers, elbows resting on the desk. "So, you suspect this same man, this Mr. Tremont, or Collingsworth, is involved in whatever is planned here?"

"Whatever is his true name, yes, I believe he is the spy known as Incognito, and I think it is too much of a coincidence, sir, that he is now here in New York."

"How reliable is your information, in your estimation?"

Will shrugged. "I believe it wise to be skeptical of any confession given under duress or the hope of some gain. That being said, I, we, thought it sufficient to bring to your attention."

"Come, lad, what do you think," he said, a bit of impatience creeping into his voice.

Will cleared his throat. "I think Hamilton was telling the truth, as he knew it, if perhaps using some embellishment to foster his own importance and improve his position. He was a little too arrogant to discount it entirely."

Washington stood then and walked to one of the windows and peered out, his hands clasped behind his back. There was about the man a regal presence, an intangible quality supported by his very tangible height and sturdy frame, by the grace with which he moved, and the way he held himself, resplendent in his immaculately tailored uniform.

"It is true," he said, "that I am beset here by Tories and spies, and I have long suspected the governor and the mayor of actively supporting the British. I am sure this group would like nothing more than my death or capture." He turned then to face Will. "It is most concerning and disheartening, however, to hear that those within my personal guard might be involved in such a plot."

Will nodded but said nothing.

"Thank you for bringing this to my attention, Will. What are your plans now? Do you intend to search for this Tremont person?"

"My specific instructions from Mr. Hancock were to make myself available to you to assist in any manner you see fit regarding this new information." The general nodded, seeming to consider the offer. "I had hoped, however, to be able to make inquiries, to check on his story if I had the opportunity. Discovering his whereabouts and activities could be important both here and in Philadelphia."

Washington nodded but gave no response.

"Also, General Washington, there is a couple from Boston who I believe may be in the city, at the home of the woman's parents. I have information that the couple shared a coach from Boston to New York with a man very similar in description to the man who calls himself Tremont. This was right about the time the suspected spy escaped from Boston. They may have useful information."

The general nodded again and pursed his lips. "Given your background and knowledge of the circumstances, it would be appreciated if you could lend your assistance here for a few days to investigate the matter further."

"I am at your service, General," he said, sitting up a little straighter in his chair.

The general stood, as did Will. "Anything else, son?"

"Well, sir, my brother. I understand that he volunteered to accompany Colonel Benedict Arnold on a mission to Canada. The last letter we received from him was in April. I was wondering if there was any word of the company."

Washington shook his head. "I am awaiting word myself, which I hope is soon."

Will suspected that the general knew more than he let on, but he also understood why he would choose not to share his knowledge with him. "I see."

The general then walked across the room, opened the door, and had one of the guards summon Joseph Reed. His adjutant-general appeared at the door in less than half a minute. The three of them stood in the middle of the room as Washington summarized the information Will had conveyed. Then he asked Reed, "Did we not receive word day before yesterday that a man being held in jail said he had information useful to General Washington that he wanted to trade for his freedom?"

"Yes, sir. Our people at the jail sent a message to that effect. The man's name, I believe, is Ketchum. He didn't say what the information was and insisted on speaking only with someone who had authority to speak for you. He is there on a charge of counterfeiting." He waited a couple of moments before adding, "We didn't think much of it." He turned to Will. "We often get people who claim to have useful information, either for money or something in trade. It is almost always a waste of time as they really have nothing more than the open gossip we can obtain anywhere from just about anybody." He turned back to the general. "There was nothing about this man that suggested his offer was any different."

Washington looked up at the ceiling before bringing his gaze back to Reed. "Don't we have a couple of our men who have gotten themselves in trouble with the local sheriff, for counterfeiting as well?"

"I believe so, though I don't recall their names."

"Hickey and Lynch," the general said, frowning at Reed, as if suggesting some failure on his part that he could not also recall their names. "Perhaps," he said, "you and Mr. Harrell might have a talk with this man, see if there is anything to it."

New York City, June 15
Chapter 30

The man whose code name was Incognito was disguised this time as an elderly gentleman. He sat on a bench in Bowling Green, some fifty yards away, his cane beside him and his gaze fixed on the Kennedy residence. He had observed Will Harrell, that meddling, too-clever-for-his-own good lad from Philadelphia, enter twenty minutes before. "Damn," he muttered under his breath. What was Harrell doing here? None of the possibilities were appealing.

He had taken up similar positions for surveillance on several occasions in the last few days, watching the comings and goings, evaluating the pros and cons of an attack against the general at this location. Every time Washington entered or left, he was surrounded by a large contingent of bodyguards. If he had one of those long rifles, he might be able to pick him off from one of the nearby rooftops. But he didn't have a rifle.

In fact, he'd rather capture the man than kill him. That is what he had counseled. But those with the means, those upon whom he had to rely, were a bloodthirsty lot, and he had known when to defer. Either way, though, captured or killed, he had concluded that this was not the place. The risk of failure, and of his capture, was too great. He was in this for the long term. He was a professional, and a professional didn't get caught. No, he had concluded that the job was best accomplished from the inside rather than the outside.

The man rose slowly from the bench and ambled away, his cane tapping on the sidewalk. Eventually, he took a coach out to the Flatbush residence of the Mayor of New York City, David Mathews. He was admitted entrance and immediately taken to the large study where the mayor was dictating a letter to his secretary. Mathews dismissed his employee, instructing him to close the double doors on his way out, and beckoned his guest to take a seat.

The mayor was a tall man, thin, and made to seem taller by the erect manner in which he sat. He was immaculately dressed in a dark blue coat and breeches. He looked at his visitor who had not said a word since he entered the room. He offered him a glass of wine, but the man shook his head. Business only, apparently, which was fine with Mathews. Something about this man made him uneasy. "So," he said to his guest, "what is your decision?"

"I agree that you should proceed as planned," he said simply.

The mayor smiled. "Good. Everything is in place."

"There is one small concern, however, that should not escape our attention."

Mathews arched his eyebrows. "Yes?"

"There is a young man, boy really, who seems to have followed me from Philadelphia. He's remarkably intelligent and perceptive for one so young, and he has just recently arrived at Washington's headquarters. I have nothing really to confirm it, but he might be here to warn the general of the plot."

"How could he know?"

"Do you not have persons in Philadelphia who are aware of your plans?"

The man thought for a moment. "Well, yes, but I have no reason to doubt their loyalty."

Incognito smiled inwardly at the naiveté, or perhaps it was arrogance. He shrugged, "As I say, I have nothing more than a feeling, but I would recommend that you double check the people you have on the inside." He nodded, then rose to leave. The two shook hands.

"Will you be returning to Philadelphia now?" The mayor asked.

His visitor frowned. "I will remain just to make sure you don't bungle it from this end."

Mathews nodded amiably but Incognito knew he was seething underneath, could imagine what he was thinking. Who was this man to chastise him? He was taking no risk but would be sure to take the credit when the plan was executed successfully. It was Mathews and his co-conspirators who had put in the hard work, who were taking all the risks. The mayor held in his rage, kept his face neutral. He knew that Incognito had the absolute backing of General Howe, and he did not want to get on the wrong side of Howe. Who did?

"Don't worry," he said to his guest, "nothing will go wrong."

Incognito frowned and shrugged but said nothing. In truth, he found that he was ambivalent about the plan's success. He didn't like the mayor, or the governor, or some of the leaders of the loyalists in New York. They were a bit seedy in his opinion and in the end probably untrustworthy as a result. Besides, he found he had begrudging respect for George Washington, a real gentleman who deserved better. Well, he had given his warning. If it was heeded or not, he decided he would wash his hands of it. He turned and walked out of the room.

* * *

Will turned down an offer from Phillip Livingston to stay in his personal estate while in New York, but on the strength of his letter of introduction, he found quarters that afternoon at the Merchant Coffee House. His room on the second floor was more than adequate and had a balcony that offered a view of the masts and riggings of boats in the harbor which lay at the end of Wall Street.

After a quick bath and change of clothes, and armed with another letter of introduction from Livingston, he made his way to the address on Nassau Street, a short walk from his lodgings. It was the home of Charles and Winifred Carlisle, parents of the Boston woman in whose company the suspected spy may have travelled. It was a stately, elegant home with a brick walkway from the street past a small, immaculately landscaped front yard, enclosed by a black iron fence and gate. He used the brass knocker on the door to announce his presence.

Momentarily, a short, fat servant appeared at the entrance. "Yes?"

Will handed him the letter from Livingston and asked him to deliver it to the master or mistress of the house. The man gave him a skeptical look and did not ask him to wait inside, but he nodded and closed the door, presumably doing as requested. But as he waited on the front stoop and the minutes went by, Will began to wonder. Finally, the door opened again, and the servant gave him a nod, then said, "Mrs. Carlisle will see you now."

He stepped inside the door and was greeted by a small, round woman with dark hair and a curious expression. "Mr. Harrell?"

He bowed.

"I am Winifred Carlisle," she said. "Mr. Livingston, who is a dear friend, has requested that I give you an audience."

"If this is a good time."

"Certainly." She motioned for him to follow and led him into a sitting room off to the right. He took note of the furniture and furnishings and the architectural details and concluded quickly that the interior was even more elegant than the exterior of the home. Mrs. Carlisle took a seat on a sofa and requested that he take one of the upholstered library chairs across from the coffee table. She inquired if he would care for tea. He thanked her but declined the offer.

She accepted the cup from the servant who then discreetly stepped into the adjacent room. She took a sip. "Well, Mr. Harrell, I sense that you wish to attend to your business without delay. And Mr. Livingston seems to think it quite important. So, how may I be of assistance?" She looked at him expectantly.

Will cleared his throat and glanced in the direction of the room in which the servant had gone. He assumed he would be listening, so he chose his words carefully in explaining the purpose of his visit, which for obvious reasons was not entirely truthful.

"I am looking for a gentleman, a business associate of Mr. Livingston, who was in Boston but travelled to New York around the same time that your daughter and son-in-law did. Despite repeated efforts to contact him, he has received no reply, and Mr. Livingston is concerned. Knowing that I was coming to New York, he asked me to see if I could locate him or find out what happened to him. I have learned that your daughter and son-in-law shared a coach with a man on their trip here. The driver of your daughter's coach has given a description of the man which seems to match that of the gentleman in question."

Mrs. Carlisle listened politely and when Will had finished, she gave him a small frown. "It appears that you may want to speak with my daughter." She summoned the servant and told him to ask her daughter to please join them, if convenient. The way she said it suggested that her daughter should find it convenient. She explained to Will that her son-in-law had recently returned to Boston, but her daughter and newborn were still there. "I did meet the man as he accompanied them to our home, but he stayed only a few minutes. I don't even remember his name, though he seemed very nice and my daughter found him to be agreeable company on their trip."

While they waited for her daughter, Will discovered that Mrs. Carlisle knew more about the man than she thought. She remarked that he was a handsome man with impeccable manners, a real gentleman. "John, my son-in-law, said he was related to the Howe brothers. Oh, and now I remember, I think his name was James Howe."

Not Henri Tremont, Will noted. When he didn't respond she explained that William Howe was the commander of the British Army in North America and his brother, Lord Richard Howe commanded the British Navy. Will knew full well who the Howe brothers were but she seemed so proud of her knowledge he didn't wish to deflate her, so he simply said, "I see."

At this point, a pretty young woman appeared at the doorway, an infant in her arms. She looked at Will and then to Mrs. Carlisle. "Mother?"

"Hello, Annabelle. Dear, this is Mr. William Harrell. He is inquiring into the whereabouts of a man who he thinks might have travelled with you and John from Boston. The man is apparently a friend and business associate of Phillip Livingston, and there is some concern, as I take it, that something may have happened to him. I thought perhaps you could provide helpful information, at least more than I could."

Will bowed in her direction. "Ma'am."

She nodded at him. "Mr. Harrell."

"Your mother has told me she thinks that the name of the gentleman who accompanied you and your husband from Boston is James Howe. Is that correct?"

The young woman seemed a little skeptical, suspicious perhaps. "Is that the name of Mr. Livingston's friend, the gentleman you seek?"

It was a good question, and a fair question. If that wasn't the name of the man about who he had come, there would be no need to make further inquiries. Or he would have to explain why the man might be going by a different name. If he lied and said it was his name, but her mother's memory was faulty, he would have the same result.

Will opted for the lie. "Yes. And he is described as tall, just shy of six feet, with dark hair, squared shoulders and jaw?"

She nodded, much to his relief. "Yes, that describes Mr. Howe. A very nice gentleman. He made the trip much more interesting. I hope that he is all right."

"As does Mr. Livingston, which is why he asked me to locate him if I could. Did Mr. Howe say where he was staying in New York?"

She shook her head. "He came to visit his aunt who was ill. He called her Aunt Marianne, but I don't think he ever gave her last name. I think he said she lived in Flatbush, but he never gave a specific address that I recall. There would be no reason I suppose."

"Did he mention any friends or acquaintances in New York? Or how long he planned to stay? Or where he was heading after his visit?"

To all these questions, she shook her head and said, "No, not that I recall."

"Tell me what you remember from your conversations. He must have revealed something about himself, his business pursuits, his hobbies, his interests, anything that might give me a clue as to where he might have gone in the city."

She seemed to think hard on this for several moments, then said, "I am embarrassed to say that I was not nearly as polite and gracious in inquiring of his interests as he was in inquiring of ours. He talked about horses, I remember, comparing and contrasting some of the breeds prevalent in the colonies to those in England. He had travelled widely on the continent and recounted some of his experiences, giving his impression of the various countries and their peoples. He spoke French and Italian and Spanish as I recall. He talked about fencing and I got the impression that he was quite knowledgeable about and proficient with various weapons. Much of this conversation was over my head and beyond my interest and knowledge but my husband seemed to enjoy the discussion." She paused a moment or two, then smiled. "I also remember that he loved the theatre."

Will stifled an instinctive flinch and a desire to follow up with a specific question. As it turned out, it wasn't necessary.

"Yes," she said, "that seemed to be a favorite form of entertainment for Mr. Howe. I suspect that he frequently attends plays wherever he is, so you might wish to direct your inquiries to the local theatre houses." She smiled again. "I remember that he lamented the lack of quality productions in the colonies as compared to England, and the offerings in New York are not as plentiful or varied as he might desire. But if he is still in the city you might find him there any given evening."

"Did he seem to have a favorite playwright?" It was an innocent inquiry, suggesting mere politeness or mild curiosity, but it was a key question for Will, the answer to which might confirm his suspicion.

"Oh, yes," she said without hesitation. "He just adored William Shakespeare."

* * *

That evening Will took the young woman's advice to heart. The proprietor of the Merchant Coffee House gave him the location of two playhouses he said had performances scheduled that evening. So, around six o'clock Will made his way to the corner of Pearl Street and Maiden Lane, where both playhouses were near each other. He alternated his attention from one location to the other, observing the persons who entered the buildings. It was an imperfect system, and he could have missed someone. He prevailed on the managers at both places to allow him to step inside and look around before the plays began, "to see if I can locate my friend." But no luck.

When he returned to his hotel, he had developed a very bad headache. He took a light meal downstairs, took a good dose of the medication Marshall had prepared for him, then retired early to his room where he fell asleep quickly. When he awoke in the morning, the headache was gone, and he felt refreshed. After a quick breakfast, he stationed himself just outside the front entrance where, at a quarter to eight, Joseph Reed, accompanied by two uniformed soldiers, arrived to escort him to the city jail. He thought an armed escort unnecessary, but had not protested when the general ordered Reed the day before to find "two trusted guards" to come with them.

In retrospect, he could see the logic of having a high-ranking officer along to ease access at the jail and to suggest the importance of the visit. After all, he had neither rank nor position nor any gravitas to lend to the situation. And he supposed that the two soldiers added to the imagery of formality and authority the general wanted to project to better ensure cooperation from the local officials in charge. Still, he felt more than a little self-conscious as their entourage walked along the streets.

Washington had also decided that the matter was not so urgent that the visit could not wait until the morning. In the meantime, security protocols could be reviewed, and a closer inspection or investigation of staff could be conducted. The general was also sensitive to Will's desire to pursue matters related to "your other investigation" which, he noted, might very well be interrelated. It was best to be as fully informed as possible before interviewing the prisoner.

It made sense, the general explained, to limit the number of people privy to this new intelligence. Still, they were able to accomplish a great deal in a fairly short time with a small circle of trusted staff. Will learned that there had been an incident two weeks before, an attempted poisoning of Washington via a plate of peas, that had subsequently killed some chickens. Suspicion had fallen naturally upon the cook, a man named Pincock, who had strenuously denied any involvement. Nothing was proven, but the cook was let go for safe measure.

In addition, an inventory of food items for the pantry at headquarters revealed extra barrels of what were marked as either salted cod, or flour, but when examined, turned out to contain gunpowder. Investigation determined that they had been delivered at night and placed directly above the room Washington used as his office.

In general, because of the large numbers of Loyalists throughout New York, suspicions of citizens ran high, and there was a constant concern with espionage and infiltration of the ranks. Will learned that two weeks before, Washington had ordered a stepped-up search for suspected Tory spies who were reported to be supplying British warships moored off Sandy Hook. There were supposedly plans to sabotage canons and other armaments of the Continental Army. And it was rumored that the efforts were being directed by the agent known as Incognito, and supported by high-ranking public officials, including the mayor, David Mathews, and the governor, William Tryon, who was to issue royal pardons to any defectors.

Those charged with crimes were housed at the City Hall, located on the corner of Wall and Nassau Streets. It was a two story, brick building that, like many of its neighbors, was a little shabby looking. Reed explained that they relied on patriots employed at various city government facilities for information. "We can never be sure of the political loyalties of those in charge, given the fact that they may be dependent on the loyalist mayor or governor for their positions. They must tow the political line, so to speak. But they also know better than to openly oppose or confront the general whose army occupies their city."

True to this observation, they were treated courteously upon their arrival and received full cooperation in arranging to meet with the prisoner, whose name was Isaac Ketchum. He was a short, dirty little man in a dirty little cell with a surly attitude and a sense of entitlement wholly unjustified by his circumstances. Will disliked the man before he even opened his mouth and his initial impression just grew stronger the more the man talked.

"Mr. Ketchum, my name is Joseph Reed. This is Mr. William Harrell," he said, nodding in Will's direction. It has been reported that you indicated to the guards that you have information for General Washington."

Ketchum looked around and said, "Well, where is he?"

Will wanted to slap him right then and, he expected, so did Reed. "Listen, Ketchum," Reed said, "we don't have time to play games. You said you had information, let's have it. We will decide if it is useful."

Ketchum snorted contemptuously. "Oh, it is very useful information. I want a guarantee, in writing, that my charges will be dropped."

Reed looked at the man for a few seconds, then turned to Will. "Come on, let's go."

Will began to rise, and Reed called out to the guard.

And that was all it took.

"Now, now, no reason to go off in a huff. You look like reasonable men. I guess I can rely on your good graces."

Reed waved the approaching guard away and looked at Ketchum. "Well?" he said.

The prisoner looked around, then leaned in close and said, "There is a plan by certain persons to kill General Washington."

In stops and starts, he told his story, confirming much of what had been rumored, and suspected among Washington's officers. And he gave them several specific names of persons involved in the plot, including the mayor, David Mathews, and the governor, William Tryon. He said that a gunsmith named Gilbert Forbes had been assigned to pay off turncoats with money supplied by the mayor. The most distressing, however, was his claim as to those on the inside. "Thomas Hickey and Michael Lynch are up to their necks in this," he said. "They both have important roles to play, if they ever get out of jail." He explained that, like him, they had been charged with counterfeiting.

Will turned to Reed and whispered, "Are these the men the general spoke of yesterday? Do you know these men, Lynch and Hickey?"

Reed nodded. "They are both members of General Washington's personal guard."

New York City, June 18
Chapter 31

Incognito was disguised as Henry Belmont, complete with walking cane and clay pipe. The former rested against the wall next to his chair, and the latter he puffed on occasionally as he looked out the bay window onto Flatbush Avenue. The house belonged to Fletcher Mathews, brother to David, mayor of New York City, whose summer residence was just down the street. The three men were sitting in the parlor, which seemed to Incognito to be a duplicate of the room in the mayor's house. Indeed, the two brothers also shared similar physical features, short and thick around about the middle, with dark, wavy hair.

The spy looked out onto the street, half listening to the brothers prattle on about the "damn rebels." He drummed his fingers on the arms of the leather chair in rhythm with the tick tock of the grandfather clock which stood against the opposite wall. It registered the time at ten minutes after eight o'clock. William Tryon, Governor of New York, was late, as usual. It was childish, really, and arrogant, this desperate attempt to assert his presumed importance, his essential role in the plot, to make others wait for him. But Incognito was determined to not let his irritation show. He took another puff from his pipe.

The governor's carriage pulled up to the front entrance five minutes later. Incognito watched with a mix of distaste and mild amusement as Tryon emerged, straightened his coat, spoke briefly to the driver, then walked up the front steps. He listened as the servant opened the door for him and led him back to the room. The brothers moved toward him in anticipation. Incognito remained seated.

William Tryon had just celebrated his birthday on the 8th of June, and he looked every bit of his 53 years. He was a slender man with rounded shoulders, a slight paunch, a double chin and huge bags under his eyes. In his mind, however, he was still in his prime, both physically and mentally. When he looked in the mirror, he still saw the young Lieutenant Colonel who had fought in the Seven Years War, still fit and ready for battle if necessary.

Incognito had researched the man thoroughly and had to acknowledge, begrudgingly, that he had certain administrative skills useful to their joint purposes. He had developed those skills before coming to New York, as governor of North Carolina from 1765 to 1771. While there, he expanded the Church of England's presence, established a postal service, and put down a rebellion. He demonstrated loyalty to the crown and deft political skills during the Stamp Act crisis, finding a balance between enforcing the law and appeasing the strong opposition to it. He dissolved the Assembly for a period to prevent the passage of a resolution opposing the Act, but also offered to personally pay any tax on papers on which he would be entitled to fees. He also managed to have the taxpayers construct an elaborate and opulent mansion as his official residence. And though many derided the building as Tryon's Palace, the governor considered them shortsighted and petty. Good government, he reasoned, required the expenditure of funds.

The challenges in New York had been similar but more intense of late as hostilities between the rebels and the crown had escalated. He had needed his political pragmatism even more. When opposition to the tax on tea became rather hot, he had first proposed to land the tea and store it at Fort George. The Sons of Liberty were opposed and there were chants from mobs to "prevent the landing and kill the governor and all the council". When news of the Boston Tea Party arrived on December 22, Tryon gave up trying to land the tea. He told London the tea could be brought ashore "only under the protection of the point of the bayonet, and muzzle of cannon, and even then, I do not see how consumption could be effected".

At one point, in 1775, the Continental Congress had issued orders to put Tryon under arrest, and he was compelled to seek refuge on the British sloop-of-war *Halifax* in New York Harbor. But when passions cooled a bit, George Washington had ordered Philip Schuyler, the commander in New York, to leave Tryon alone. In 1776, back in control, he dissolved the pro-independence assembly and called for new elections in February. This man, Incognito conceded, was no meek or weak-willed politician. He knew how to organize and to motivate.

Tryon had been the one to take the initiative in devising the plan of sabotage and assassination, and he seemed to have the necessary resources and willing participants to follow through. Incognito's role was that of consultant. Tryon was confident, he said, that he would be rewarded in the end when the British put down the rebellion. He winked then and added, "I just have to keep up pretenses of, if not neutrality, at least passive resistance regarding the rebels and that arrogant, pretentious Virginian who calls himself Commander-in Chief."

The sentiment seemed to Incognito somewhat ungrateful, given that Washington could have had him arrested, but chose not to. When he mentioned this to the governor, Tryon dismissed the idea. "He wouldn't dare."

Tryon had confided to Incognito that he didn't really like or trust the mayor, David Mathews. "He is corrupt at his core with not an ethical bone in his body. But I am forced to gather allies where I can, and Mathews' self-interest is sufficient motivation in the matter. It was one of the reasons why, against my better judgment, I appointed him mayor in February." He frowned and shook his head. "And he has, in fact, proved useful."

If Incognito did not like or trust the governor, he was sure the feeling was mutual. But the spy had the ear and strong backing of the Howe brothers, and Tryon knew how to play along. Normally, the governor would have insisted that they come to him—a matter of principle—but he had come to Flatbush as summoned for the hurriedly called meeting. He took his gloves off, accepted a cup of tea from Fletcher and nodded toward Incognito, who was still sitting.

"I was told you have new information."

The spy motioned for Tryon to take the chair opposite him. When he did, and the Mathews brothers took the chairs on either side, Incognito leaned forward and said, "I have had the Harrell boy followed." He looked briefly at the other two men before returning his attention to Tryon. "It was reported to me that this morning Harrell visited the city jail in the company of two uniformed soldiers and a high-ranking officer in Washington's army. They spoke to one Isaac Ketchum."

Incognito looked once more at the other two men, then back to Tryon. "The prisoner had requested an audience with Washington, claiming he had valuable information for the general. We also know that Ketchum has recently shared a cell with Thomas Hickey."

Tryon's eyes arched sharply at the mention of Hickey's name. "Do we know what this man, Ketchum, said?"

David Mathews shook his head. "We can't know for sure but we can make a fairly good guess."

"And I suspect it does not bode well for your plan," Incognito added, barely disguising the annoyance he felt. The inescapable truth was, the more people who knew your plan, the more the risk, the more likely you would have to rely on unreliable people, and with a resulting greater chance for failure. And he did not like failure.

On the other hand, he had become philosophical about such things as of late. It was the nature of the beast, so to speak, that your chain was only as strong as its weakest link. He had been ordered only to assist and advise what had already been planned. If he had been consulted from the beginning, things might have turned out differently, but he wasn't, and he was already distancing himself from what he thought would be a colossal failure. He looked around the room at the three men. "I suggest that you get this Thomas Hickey out of jail and take care of him before he talks."

"Hickey won't talk," Fletcher said.

His brother looked at him as if it was the stupidest thing he had ever heard, but he said, "No reason to panic. We don't know what this Ketchum told Washington's men, or if they gave it any credence. And they haven't paid Hickey a visit."

"Not yet," Incognito said.

Tryon nodded. "See what our people at the jail can tell us about what this Ketchum said. I'm sure there were ears at the door."

"I think you need to be prepared to call off the plan. I suspect arrests of Hickey and others in the general's personal guard are imminent. And if Hickey or any of the others talk, you can expect arrest warrants for each of you as well. Indeed, they may already be in the works."

The governor's face reddened. "You can't possibly know that."

Incognito shrugged. "I know this Harrell boy. He is a persistent son of a bitch, and smart." He did not tell them that Harrell was also observed visiting the Carlisle home, and that later he had been snooping around the theatres. He knew that the boy had been searching for him. The two of them were headed for a confrontation. He knew this, too. "It's only a matter of time," he said, "before he puts the puzzle together. You might consider taking a trip out of the city for a time, to see how things work out."

The three men scoffed in unison, and the governor said, "Washington wouldn't take such action. On the word of a criminal? If he thinks he does not have the support of the people here now, watch what happens if he arrests the governor of the colony and the mayor of the city."

The two Mathews brothers nodded in agreement with Tryon and the three men began discussing their next move in light of this new information. What fools, Incognito thought. The sooner he could distance himself from them the better. He gazed out the bay window again and took a couple of puffs on his pipe. From across the street, the glint of metal, reflected in the moonlight, caught his attention. He focused his eyes on the spot just in time to see a man duck back around the corner of the house across the street. The movement had been quick and he had only an instant to observe, but he thought the glint had come from a sword by the man's side.

In a matter of seconds, he devised a plan, and began acting on it. He stood. "I think I have need of your privy," he said to Fletcher. "I believe it is at the rear?"

Fletcher looked up and nodded.

Incognito took his cane and walked down the hallway. He opened the back door, looked back once more toward the front parlor, then stepped outside, quietly closing the door behind him. He walked around to the front of the house, on the northwest corner, stopping behind a large clump of azalea bushes and peering back out across the street, surveying the entire area. Though he could see no movement, he sensed that the one man he had glimpsed minutes before was not alone. And his furtive movement suggested they wanted to see without being seen. He also suspected that their purpose was not simply surveillance.

Incognito angled his course and walked over to the governor's carriage and approached the driver, who was leaning against the front wheel, smoking on a pipe. Hopefully, his movements had not been detected by whomever was positioned across the street, and he was now hidden from sight by the carriage. "Good evening, my good man," he said as the driver looked up. "Governor Tryon has been gracious enough to offer me the use of his carriage and driver back to the city as I am not feeling well. Shall we be on our way?"

The driver regarded him skeptically. No doubt such kindness in his employer would be unusual in the extreme. "I'll have to check with Governor Tryon, sir."

Incognito shook his head. "I was afraid you might say that," he said as he suddenly produced a six-inch bladed knife which he drove into the man's stomach with such force it almost knocked him down. The spy pulled the knife up through the driver's chest, twisting its blade as he did so. The look of surprise, then panic on the man's face quickly turned into a blank stare as the life rushed out of him and he slumped in Incognito's arms.

The spy opened the door and placed the driver's body inside. He removed the man's hat and placed it on his own head, then climbed up to the driver seat in the front of the carriage. With a gentle prodding of voice and a snap of the reins, he coaxed the horses to move, guiding them to reverse direction and head back the way they had come shortly before, headed back to the island of Manhattan.

* * *

From their position across the street, hidden behind the house and the shrubbery at its corner, Will Harrell and Captain James Gardner, and the five soldiers who had accompanied them from headquarters watched as the carriage maneuvered its turn on Flatbush Avenue. They had received intelligence by persons placed near the governor that he was scheduled to travel to Flatbush sometime this evening. They first stationed themselves near the mayor's residence, assuming this would be the location of any meeting, but when the mayor was observed walking to his brother's house at about 7:30 p.m. they re-positioned themselves accordingly.

Will's heart had raced when an elderly gentleman came walking slowing down the avenue shortly before eight o'clock, puffing on a clay pipe and walking with the assistance of a cane. Will strained to see the man's face, to see if he was, as he suspected, the man he had known as Henri Tremont in disguise, the British spy and assassin known as

Incognito, but the distance was too great. Had the man been staying in Flatbush? If not, he must have been let out of his conveyance from the city some blocks away, perhaps to keep confidential the address that was his final destination. Will thought probably the latter explanation the most likely.

At twenty minutes past the hour, the governor arrived, and the men began preparations to approach the house. The orders from Washington were to take into custody the governor, the mayor, and anyone else present at the time, "for questioning," he had specified, though everyone assumed arrests would be forthcoming. No one had seen the old man, or anyone else, approach the carriage after the governor entered the residence, and all assumed it carried no passenger. "Should we stop the driver, Captain?" one of the soldiers asked.

Gardner seemed undecided in the matter.

Will sensed that somehow, the spy he sought had entered the carriage unseen, and was getting away. "With permission, Captain," he said, "I can use one of the wagons we left by the church to follow the driver, just in case it contains a passenger. If no one is inside the coach, no harm. You and your men will have detained everyone inside the residence. But if someone has sneaked inside—and our sight is limited, obscured in that area—we will not lose them."

The urgency in his voice and registered on his face was apparent to the captain, who hesitated only a couple of seconds before nodding his head and saying, "Very well. Be on your way then, and quickly."

New York City, June 18
Chapter 32

Will sprinted diagonally across the lawns of three houses and arrived at the Old Dutch Reformed Church in less than sixty seconds. and out of breath. He approached the two soldiers who had remained behind to look after the horses and wagon while the rest approached the residence on foot.

"Sergeant Simpson" he said, "Captain Gardner's orders are that you and I follow the governor's carriage which should be coming this way in a few moments." He looked at the other man. "You are to bring the horses to the Flatbush address as the occupants are being taken into custody as we speak."

Those were not the specific orders of the captain, of course. Will had extrapolated a bit, and the two soldiers looked at him for a few seconds, as if trying to decide whether to take this civilian at his word. But he had spoken with authority and urgency and the hesitation gave way quickly to action. The one soldier began to gather the horses together and Simpson jumped up onto the driver's seat of the wagon just as the governor's carriage made the turn off Flatbush Avenue and onto Parkside. Will climbed up beside him. As the carriage headed toward Prospect Park, he put his hand on the driver's arm. "Let's let him get a bit of a lead. I don't want him to know he is being followed." After a brief delay, he gave him the go ahead and Simpson pulled out.

From all appearances, when the carriage left the Flatbush residence there had been only the driver with it. No passengers. But the view had been blocked by the carriage itself, and someone certainly could have boarded without being seen. Will thought it peculiar that the driver would stay parked for some time, then take off without his passenger, and he had the sense that the unexpected and sudden departure was not at the behest of Tryon. He would have walked out the front door to speak with his driver. But neither the governor nor anyone else had spoken to the driver before he departed, at least not that Will had seen.

He thus suspected that someone had come out the rear of the house and walked around to the front, and persuaded, perhaps forced, the driver to take him away. Of course, it could have been with instructions from Tryon, but that was doubtful. Either way, he felt certain the driver was not alone.

The route back to Manhattan was a fairly straight one, and they kept the carriage in view but at a great distance. They almost lost it when the carriage took a ferry across the East River. They couldn't take the same ferry or risk being discovered. Fortunately, a second ferry came shortly thereafter, and the driver seemed to be in no hurry, as he kept a leisurely pace travelling up Broadway. Soon, they were within sight.

The carriage pulled onto a side street near Trinity Church and stopped. With their wagon about fifty yards back on Broadway, Will motioned for Simpson to pull over to the side and stop. "I'm going to go take a look, follow on foot if necessary. If I'm not back in twenty minutes go ahead and leave. I'll walk back to my inn."

Simpson looked doubtful but did not voice an objection as Will jumped down and began walking toward the carriage. As he walked, he realized where he was—the southern boundary of the land owned by the church, ironically known as the Holy Ground, described to him in vivid detail by Joseph Reed. It was almost a square mile in size, bordered by the Hudson River on the west, swamps to the north, and Broadway to the east. Reed had described it as "a seething slum of shacks and portable houses, a foul district of gin shops, bawdy houses, and gambling halls, and where over five hundred prostitutes ply their trade." It was a short stroll away for the students of Kings College, he'd said, or the wealthy residents of the lavish homes on the other side, east of Broadway.

Will strained to make out who was at the carriage, but it was parked just around the corner so that his line of sight was partially blocked. He hastened toward the intersection, and just as he rounded the corner, he saw an elderly man with a cane walking away down Barclay Street. No sign of the driver.

When Will made it to the carriage, he looked inside quickly, then stopped. He glanced once more toward the man walking away then returned his attention to the man inside the carriage. He opened the door and an arm flopped out. The driver's hat was on the ground, next to the front wheel. Blood had pooled on the floor and was dripping down the side and onto the ground. He took one look at the man and knew he was dead, beyond any help he could give him.

He started off after the man with the cane before he could get out of sight. The man, who Will was convinced was Incognito, had not looked back, seemingly unconcerned with what he had done or who might have seen him, or whether he might be followed.

The street was thick with people. In the space of three blocks Will was propositioned by at least two prostitutes, aggressive women with foul mouths who he had to literally fight off. The suspected spy had a similar experience, and Will watched as the man knocked one of them down with his cane, stand over her for a moment or two, then walk on.

The man veered right at the next intersection, and when Will turned the corner, he did not see him anywhere. He walked quickly down the narrow street, stopped at the next intersection and looked both ways, up and down the street. Nothing. He looked behind from where he had come, checking for some building or other place he might have ducked into. Had the man known, or suspected, he was being followed? As Will stood there in the middle of the street, four men walked toward him. They began to fan out as they got closer.

They were not particularly large men, though the two taking positions on his side were the larger of the four, muscled and with the look of men used to hard labor. One was dark haired and the other a

303

redhead. The two in front were tall and thin, wiry looking. All were unkempt in their appearance, their clothes dirty and ragged, their faces unshaven. A foul, sour odor emanated from them that pervaded the space around them and caused Will to involuntarily wrinkle his nose. They stopped about five feet away.

"Evening, mate." The man most directly in front of Will gave him an unfriendly smile. Will figured him to be the leader. He was a stick of a man at about five eleven, maybe 130 pounds, with a long, scraggly beard. The other thin man wore only a stubble on his chin.

"Evening," Will said. The men on his side shifted a little, moving a little more to his rear.

"You may not have known it, mate," the bearded stick man said, "but this here is a toll road."

"Toll road?"

"That's right. And we are the toll collectors," he said, looking around at his buddies. They all smiled and nodded.

Will looked past him and caught sight of the man with the cane, peering around the corner of a building to his right. Will focused his attention back on bearded stick man and his friends. He didn't particularly like the odds and would avoid a confrontation if he could. But he had also grown up with constant teasing and intimidation because of his condition and had learned at an early age how to defend himself against bullies. He was prepared either way. "How much is the toll?"

"How much you got on you?"

This brought a few chuckles from his friends.

"Never mind. I'm sure I don't have enough. I'll just go the other way." Will turned to leave but the other two larger men behind him now blocked his way. He turned back to face bearded stick man. "I suppose you will tell me the toll applies in both directions?"

The man gave him a grin. "That's right, mate."

Will saw that the elderly man he was following, the suspected spy, had come closer now and he stood, puffing his pipe and watching. The two locked eyes then and Will recognized the man he had first met as Henri Tremont. And he saw in those eyes a cold-blooded killer. The spy no doubt saw that flicker of recognition in Will's eyes. Perhaps, it was what he had intended.

Will evaluated his options and conceived a strategy. If all they wanted was his money, he could just hand it over. But something told him it would not end there. And besides, there was a matter of principle involved. He figured he had one thing going for him— overconfidence on their part. He thought he could use it to his advantage.

The two muscled men to his rear grabbed him at the elbows and pulled him close to them. "Let's see what you have, mate," bearded stick man said as he came toward him.

Using the arms of the two men as leverage, Will raised both his legs and kicked out as hard as he could. He caught bearded stick man square in the face and heard the sound of breaking cartilage. Blood spurted from the man's nose and a yelp of pain from his throat. He put his hand to his nose and yelled, "The bugger broke my nose."

His three companions were momentarily frozen in place, unsure of how to react to this unexpected deviation from the plan, perhaps waiting for some direction from their leader. Will turned slightly to his right, squatted, and swept his leg forward, catching the dark-haired muscled man just above his heels, throwing him off balance, making it easy for Will to pull him backward, and onto the ground. In a continuous motion, Will ducked and pulled the red-headed muscled man over his back and on top of his friend on the ground.

Will stood then and faced the remaining stick man, who was now brandishing a knife. The other three were only momentarily out of commission and Will knew that his best option was to flee, to put some distance between him and the toll collectors. But he didn't want to lose sight of Incognito. He glanced quickly in his direction, but the man had gone.

Will focused back on the man with the knife. He seemed nervous, twitchy and Will sensed that he didn't really want to have a fight. But his friends were beginning to get to their feet and the broken-nosed stickman had adjusted to his pain and was now seething. He too now had a knife in his hand. Very well then, flight it would have to be. Maybe he could double back and pick up Incognito's trail. He started to run but felt temporarily paralyzed, as if his feet were in concrete. His body would not respond. And a faint, familiar, and feared smell of sulfur filled his nostrils. No, not now, he thought.

Broken-nosed, bearded stick man came at him, brandishing the knife, but though he willed himself to do it, Will found that he just could not move. He felt the sting of the blade as the man plunged it into his gut. He smelled the man's sour breath man as he leaned in close and whispered something he couldn't quite make out. But still, he couldn't move.

He was beginning to slip into that familiar nether world, the blackness only moments away. He waited, helplessly, for the next thrust of the knife. Suddenly, bearded, broken-nosed stick man flew away from him, like a fish being pulled from the water. And indeed, the man had been pulled, Will saw, by Sergeant Simpson, who moved with speed and dexterity, and power, dispatching each of the assailants with cold and deadly efficiency. He used the butt of his pistol to revisit the broken nose with a sharp smack, which set off another round of howling, quickly silenced by a blow to the side of the head that knocked the man unconscious. The other thin man edged away, as did his companions. Simpson waved his pistol at them and patted the sword that swung by his side.

"I suggest you gentlemen leave before I get mad."

And they did.

By this time, Will's knees had begun to buckle under him, but he remained standing, for how much longer he did not know. The expected seizure had not come. Or more precisely, it had been a partial seizure. Already, he could sense feeling returning to his limbs, though considerably weakened now by a loss of blood. A group of on-lookers had begun to gather, but they gave the soldier wide berth as he stepped toward Will.

The tingling in his lips gave warning of another seizure to come. Now, his knees buckled completely, and he fell to the ground. His muscles began to tighten, and his vision blurred, but he remained conscious. Simpson tore a sleeve from his shirt and pressed it against the wound. Then he placed Will's hand on the make-shift bandage. "Hold this tight," he said. "I need to get you to the wagon."

Will wanted to thank Simpson, to tell him he was glad he had ignored his advice to leave and had come after him. He wanted to tell him about Tremont, to ask him to see if he was still around, pondering why the spy had hung around when he could have easily escaped. Had he just wanted to watch Will die? Had he somehow instigated the incident? Next time he saw him, Will thought, he'd ask him. If there was a next time. But as he tried to speak, it came out hopelessly garbled, as if his tongue had swollen to twice its normal size and filled his mouth.

The next thing he knew, he was being carried by two men down the street. His vision was blurred. He was aware of a dull pain in his stomach where the stab wound oozed blood, and the beginnings of a monster headache, but he was still conscious. The men placed him in the back of the wagon—tossed would be more accurate—and he winced in pain at the jolt. Sergeant Simpson jumped up into the driver's seat, then whipped on the reins, and the horses took off quickly down the street, pedestrians making way as the wagon passed, and every bump in the road bringing a sharp, painful reminder of his injury. Then every muscle in his body began to stiffen at once. He struggled uselessly against the tide that washed over him, involuntarily surrendering moments later to the total darkness that came with it.

New York City, June 27th
Chapter 33

Will was in and out of consciousness for two days. As with most knife wounds, the real danger had not been from the loss of blood, but from the secondary infection which often followed. He realized this immediately and had begun his own treatment by rinsing out the wound with a flask of whisky reluctantly volunteered by Sergeant Simpson.

For reasons known only to General Washington, Will was brought into his protective zone, and as a result, had the good fortune of being attended to by his personal physician and assistants, who were scrupulous in their attention to maintain sanitary conditions. They cleaned the wound and closed it, kept it dry and clean, changed dressings regularly and were alert to possible signs of infection. His fever dissipated after a couple of days, and he was on the path to complete recovery, though he remained weak for several days.

Washington insisted that he convalesce at the residence he shared with his wife, Martha, just north of the city on the Hudson River. The general's wife was even more gracious than her husband and saw to it that Will was properly attended to. It was a lovely and peaceful setting, maddeningly so for Will because he was afraid that Incognito was getting away while he lay helpless in a bed. But after a few days, and with the general's permission, he began to supervise a city-wide search for the man.

With some of the general's personal guard, headed by Sergeant Simpson, they scoured the city, looking for anyone fitting the description of Tremont, and of the elderly man who had been known as Henry Belmont in Boston. Men were placed near the theater houses, at the docks and ferry landings, and all venues for public transportation out of the city. Patriot contacts were questioned and told to keep an eye out for the man. But after several days, they had nothing. No sightings, no word of anyone who may have seen or talked with such a man. No intelligence concerning the suspected spy at all.

When Will was well enough, he paid another visit to the Carlisle residence. The mother and daughter were happy to be able to inform him that James Howe was indeed among the living. He had visited them only two days before, they said.

"Do you know where he is staying in New York, or how I may get in contact with him?"

Mrs. Carlisle tittered briefly, then answered, "Oh, I am afraid you may have just missed him. His visit was to bid us farewell. I doubt he is still in the city."

"He was so nice," the daughter added, "to make a special trip to see us, and my new baby."

"Do you know his aunt's name or her specific address?"

Both women shook their heads. "No, sorry," the daughter said. I feel ashamed that I didn't even ask. But he was leaving, and it didn't occur to me that you would come by again looking for him."

Did he say where he was going?"

The daughter smiled and looked at her mother, pleased to be able to provide some specific information. "Yes, he was heading back to Boston, to conclude his business there, he said."

Will thanked the women and left soon thereafter. He didn't know if the spy they knew as James Howe had told them the truth. He might still be in city, in fact. But his gut, and the negative results of the search for the man, told him that he probably had fled the city. His instincts also told him, though, that if the man was no longer in New York, he was en route to Philadelphia, not Boston.

Will reported his findings and his suspicions to Washington that same day in his office at the Kennedy residence on Broadway. The general listened intently, tenting his fingers in front of him on the desk.

He stood when Will finished and paced briefly. He stopped and looked out the window upon the vast expanse of gardens. Then he turned back to Will. "I believe your instincts are right on this. We need to get word to Philadelphia, to the Congress, of the danger. We now have sufficient evidence to arrest this man who calls himself Tremont, in connection with the conspiracy that has unfolded here in New York."

"I can be ready to go in the morning."

Washington shook his head. "No, my boy, you are not yet in a condition to make that journey"

"I am fine, sir."

"No, not yet," he said with a firmness and finality that cut off any notion of disagreement. "I will send a rider at once with a letter and a request for an arrest warrant to issue for this Tremont fellow, whatever his true identity. I will send word to our people in Boston as well, just in case. Besides, I would like you to witness the execution of Mr. Hickey, as you were instrumental in foiling the plot.

* * *

Incognito had remained in New York for several days, trying to see if he could salvage the plan, but it had been too late. The best he could do was to escape capture himself. He assumed that Washington's men would be scouring the city for the elderly gentleman seen at Fletcher Mathews' house, and the Frenchman calling himself Henri Tremont, as well. So, he had mostly stuck with his lesser-known Irish sailor disguise as he moved about the city. Finally, he disguised himself as an elderly woman and took a carriage to Long Island, where he had stashed his horse with a loyalist contact. He changed back to his Tremont disguise and headed out toward Philadelphia, with a stop in Reading along the way. He made it to the gunsmith's shop outside of Reading mid-afternoon on his second day out of New York.

Several days before, he had followed Harrell to the Carlisle residence, and he wondered at the time if it had been a mistake to let the young couple live. He decided to pay them another visit before leaving the city, to revisit that decision. He came, of course, in his James Howe disguise. He had come to bid them farewell as he was headed back to Boston on business. He thanked them for their kindness, and asked to see the new baby, about whom he made a big fuss. He congratulated parents and grandparents alike on their "beautiful boy."

Annabelle Fleming and her mother told him about the young man from Philadelphia who had inquired after him on behalf of their friend, Phillip Livingston. They talked Tory politics, as the parents were staunch loyalists. They talked about their disappointment at the foiled plot against Washington, and their mutual hatred for the French.

"I told him of your expressed love of the theatre," Annabelle said.

Yes, he thought as he smiled at the woman. That explained Harrell's presence at the First Nassau Street Theatre that night. After their conversation he concluded that they really had no additional information that would be useful to Harrell. The family was no threat to him. Killing them now would be counterproductive. So, he had let them live, again.

But that meddlesome bookworm. The little piss was too clever, and too damn persistent for his own good. Harrell no doubt was partially responsible for foiling the plot and causing the arrests of some of the conspirators. Perhaps if they had moved up the schedule, or if the others had been more discreet. But it had all fallen apart.

He could have killed the boy and was thinking about it when the street thugs intervened. It looked as though they would do the job for him and he watched with mixed emotions. The boy was a thorn in his side, but he respected the lad's abilities and he liked the way he handled himself facing four-against-one odds. Indeed, the hoodlums would not have gotten the upper hand if Harrell had not had one of his fits. He was a worthy adversary who deserved more than death at the hands of low-life ruffians. He thought about injecting himself, if only to give the lad a dignified death, by one who could appreciate excellence in one's opponent. But the army sergeant had arrived on the scene just as he was about to move in.

He thought the boy might die from his wound, but he didn't, and he found to his surprise that he was relieved. In truth, Incognito enjoyed a challenge and he would take satisfaction in neutralizing Harrell in his own way, in his own time. Their eyes had met for a long moment in that street, and he was sure that the boy had seen through his disguise. Well, no matter. The lad had already fit that piece into the puzzle and had concluded that Henri Tremont was not who he claimed to be. But he had only his suspicions, no real evidence with which to convince others, and Incognito would use that to his advantage.

The plot against Washington had failed, and he couldn't say he was surprised. Some of it was just bad luck, inopportune timing, an unfortunate series of unanticipated events, but a good part of it was the result of the inadequacies of his co-conspirators. That was nothing new, either. He had been plagued with incompetents, from top to bottom, from the beginning of his mission, surrounded by those whose estimate of their abilities never measured up to reality.

And that included William Howe, the commanding general. He had warned Billy in Boston to take Dorchester Heights, but he sat by, and let the rebels sneak up there in the middle of the night. Stupid, stupid, stupid. When the decision was made to make a direct assault on the rebels' position on Bunker Hill, he warned against it. Yes, the British had ended up taking it, but at tremendous cost of lives, prompting one member of Parliament to observe, "With many more victories like this, we will lose the war."

Incognito had done his part in New England and done it well. He set up and operated a network of spies and sympathizers. He recruited and trained Benjamin Church, the physician for the army, who had provided valuable intelligence, until he had gotten careless, and captured. He told them where they could find John Hancock and Sam

Adams on that fateful date in April, and where they would find the stored firearms and ammunition. But they had squandered the opportunity. They had been humiliated by a band of farmers who shot at them from behind trees and stone walls like cowards.

If they had just arrested the leaders early on as he had advised, much of that humiliation and loss of men could have been avoided. The rebellion would have died an early death for want of leadership, and a healthy respect for the might of the British army. Yes, the city of Boston had been awash with rabid rebels, but there were many who remained loyal to the king. They were weak, however, and easily intimidated by Adams and his thugs.

And that's the way it has always been. The reasonable, peaceable and civil sort end up on the losing side because they are unwilling to do what they need to do to win. They do not possess that tendency toward intimidation and coercion, or downright physical violence if necessary, to achieve one's political ends.

Incognito firmly believed that he was worth every shilling he was paid. And he was paid handsomely for his work, regardless of results. Truth be known, he would have done it for his expenses. It was an opportunity to play the role of a lifetime. It was the supporting cast that was bringing down the production.

Howe was a soft-hearted fool who couldn't set aside his sympathies for the colonists and his hope for a reconciliation. But the only way to handle a rebellion was to crush it. Howe was a brave and skilled military man who would eventually realize this truth. But he couldn't afford to play with them forever. The French might just decide to join in their farce, just to distract the British while they increased their influence in the West Indies.

Incognito couldn't worry about such things. He had his mission. He had his plan, and his role to play. He was an actor after all, and a damn good one, despite what that infuriatingly ignorant Franklin thought. And this was as good a role as one got. Part of the appeal was that it was make-believe in real life, with the highest of stakes. A successful performance brought the audience into that make-believe world, manipulating their emotions and their actions, a most satisfying result. A poor performance, though, could result in more than just a bad review or boos from the audience, but rather capture, and death.

He was thinking about this and digging deep into his role as Henri Dubois Tremont when he rode up to the residence and workshop of the gunsmith, Meylin. And, once again, the thin, raw-boned woman was sitting in her rocker on the front porch, whittling this time rather than shelling peas. She looked up, and as the last time, did not speak, but rather nodded in the direction of the workshop. Momentarily, Meylin came to the entrance and stood, hands on his hips as Tremont dismounted.

"Monsieur Tremont, you have returned sooner than expected."

"I completed my business in New York and did not wish to linger there."

Meylin nodded his approval of this evaluation of New York. "But I am happy to tell you that your rifle is ready. I believe you will be pleased."

He turned then and walked back into his shop. Tremont followed. Meylin retrieved from one corner the rifle, which he had wrapped in a thin wool blanket. He removed the covering and handed it to Tremont. "I do think it is the best one I have ever made, next to my own, and I made it in half the time. I have test fired it and it works perfectly, accurate up to two hundred yards, maybe more, but I have only tested it to that distance."

Tremont held the rifle up, turned it in his hands. It felt solid, though remarkably light. The stock was smooth, and made from a lighter shade of walnut, with silver decorative accents near the bottom of the stock and near the flint lock mechanism.

"Shall we give it a try?" Tremont asked.

Meylin nodded once, wiped his hands with a rag, then picked up his own rifle. *"Ja."*

The gunsmith handed his customer a horn of gunpowder and an oiled leather bag, which he said contained lead balls and any other items he might possibly need, appropriately named a "possibilities bag," Meylin said. They walked again through the forest and into the meadow, down to the edge of the creek, where Meylin had his targets—metal pans and wooden boards in different sizes, hanging from fishing line tied around the tree branches. Then they walked back to a staging area at the edge of the meadow. There were three shooting sites, as Meylin called them, one at 50 yards from the targets, one at 100 yards and another at 150 yards. They stopped at the first shooting site.

Meylin showed him how to load the rifle. "You want to use just the right amount of powder," he said. "usually just enough to cover your ball." He held out a ball in the palm of his hand, cupped it and sprinkled powder from his horn onto it. "Like so." Meylin then poured the powder back into the horn. "I use a hollowed-out hammer tip as a measuring devise. Makes it more precise." He held it up for him to see.

Meylin took the lead ball and a piece of cloth he called wadding, which he used to pack the ball and powder into the barrel. Then he took the ram rod which was attached to the underside of the barrel and used it to pack it all down the cylinder.

"You move the cock back and put a little powder in the pan there between the frizzen and the cock, to prime it."

Incognito understood the basic concept. The cock held a piece of flint in place, then struck the flint against the frizzen, which created a spark, and which in turn ignited the powder in the barrel and propelled the ball through the barrel and toward its target.

"If it doesn't ignite, you get what we call a flash in the pan."

Not what you want in the heat of battle," Tremont observed.

Meylin nodded. "It means, usually, that you haven't packed the load sufficiently."

"It seems that it takes longer to load than a musket."

"Ja, but it is so much more accurate, and at a greater distance," he said. "And with practice, you get faster. I can fire and reload two to three times in sixty seconds."

Meylin coached him on how to steady the rifle and sight his target, using the intersection of a tree branch and trunk. Then they practiced without anything on which to rest the barrel. Tremont took to it quickly, and after a fairly short time, was hitting his target and reloading quickly.

"You have good instincts, the gunsmith said, "a natural ability."

Tremont nodded. *"Merci.* And you are a fine craftsman. I have handled a variety of weapons before, including many firearms, but never a long rifle. I am quite impressed."

They moved back to the next shooting site and repeated the process, then to the final site, 150 yards back from the targets. Meylin checked the accuracy each time now with a long glass. He seemed pleased and impressed with his quick-study student. "If we could move back farther, I do believe you would have the same result," he said.

"Merci, Monsieur." He pulled an apple from his pocket. "Perhaps this might make a good target. Would you be so kind as to affix it to the branch for me?"

The gunsmith nodded approvingly, took the apple and began walking toward the creek. Tremont watched him as he began to reload the rifle. He reflected on their conversation as they passed through the woods. Incognito had learned that Meylin's father settled in Pennsylvania in the 1720s, first in Philadelphia and then to a small village called Heydelberg, which was about thirty miles to the south of Reading.

"All my family is still there," Meylin said. "I came here to Reading about twenty years ago. Too many gunsmiths in one small village." He smiled, and Tremont smiled back.

"I noticed in your workshop a pamphlet titled "Der Alarm."

"*Ja.*"

Incognito had read the same pamphlet in its English version. It had been penned by Thomas Paine in Philadelphia and presented the argument in favor of ousting the current colonial government.

"Do I assume you are in favor of this push toward independence?"

Meylin gave him a look over his shoulder, then said, "*Ja, naturlich.* It will bring more freedom for people like us, people who are not English. They have met already to draw up a new constitution." He waited a moment or two before adding, "We were ready for the Tories when they came to town to get signatures on their *Remonstrance*, as they called it, a loyalty oath to the current government. We burned it."

The gunsmith seemed like a good and honorable man, Incognito thought as he now steadied the rifle barrel in the V of the tree branch. He sighted down it to the back of the gunsmith's head. When the man placed the apple on the branch, in between two metal pans and turned to face him, Tremont fired. The flash of the muzzle would have been visible to Meylin, but would the bullet fly faster than the image? The gunsmith's face may have registered his surprise, his fear. From such a distance, Tremont could not tell. He saw the man's body pitch backward at the impact, though, confirming that he had hit his target.

He reloaded the rifle and walked to where the man lay prone on the ground. His lifeless eyes stared upward. Bits of bone and blood and brain matter littered the grass around the body, some as far as six feet away. He then retrieved the apple from the branch where Meylin had placed it, took a bite, and began walking back to the gunsmith's residence and workshop.

He expected to find the wife still on the porch. He would tell her that her husband would be coming along very shortly, as he had wanted to adjust his targets. It was a pretty lame explanation, and she might be suspicious, but by then it would be too late.

She was not, however, on the porch when he arrived, and he didn't like that. He did a quick survey of the outside and didn't see her. A quick glance into the workshop confirmed she wasn't in there, either. He went to the door of the cabin and knocked. No answer. He knocked again and called out, "Frau Meylin?" Nothing.

He stepped back to the edge of the porch and looked back in the direction from which he had come from the field. He realized that, from her vantage point, she could see persons walking across the meadow at some distance. If she had looked up, she would have seen him walking, alone, on the path. He was running through the implications in his mind when he heard a click behind him. He turned to see the woman standing in the doorway, a pistol in her hand, pointed at him.

He had just enough time to feign left and dive right before the pistol fired. He could hear the whistle of the bullet as it flew past his head, barely missing him. He jumped back to his feet and faced the woman. Her expression was one of surprise, replaced by anger, and then fear. She threw the pistol at him, which he fended off with his forearm. Then she grabbed the door and tried to close it, but he blocked it with his foot and pushed it back, knocking her to the floor.

She let out a cry of pain when she landed. She crawled backwards, her eyes darting around the room, then, showing remarkable strength and flexibility, sprang to her feet and ran toward the kitchen area, toward a large butcher knife resting on the counter. But he had seen the knife as well, and guessed her intention, and moved faster. He picked up the knife and gave her three quick stabs to her stomach as he held her close to him with his other hand. Then he twisted the blade upwards, noting with admiration how extremely sharp it was. He expected nothing less from a master craftsman like Meylin. Then he let her fall to the floor.

Earlier, he had confirmed with Meylin the necessity of keeping their transaction a secret. It was possible the man had been indiscreet, but he thought not. There was little risk, he thought, that the death of the man and his wife would be traced to him. And even if it was, it would be too late to do anything about it.

He went out to the workshop. On the way, he picked up the pistol from the porch and tucked it into the waistband of his breeches. In Meylin's workshop, he took the gunsmith's personal rifle as well as two more pistols, powder and shot, all of which he loaded into gunny sacks and attached them to his horse's saddle. Then he mounted his Narragansett Pacer, and with one more look around, rode off toward Philadelphia.

New York City, July 1

Chapter 34

The execution of Thomas Hickey, the arrogant member of Washington's personal guard who was at the center of the assassination conspiracy took place on the 28th. The mayor and the governor had been arrested, along with two more members of Washington's personal guard. There were practical and political reasons for downplaying the matter, prime of which was the embarrassment to Washington of having members of his personal guard involved in an assassination plot against him. But the general also thought it important to send the appropriate message to those who might have similar traitorous thoughts. Thomas Hickey thus became the face of the conspiracy and the conduit for that message.

Will had no desire to witness the event, but he had no real good reason to decline the invitation from Washington, which was a good bit stronger than an invitation anyway. It was considered an honor, he supposed, but Will didn't see it that way. On the appointed date he walked over to the place of execution, near Bowery Lane, and joined a large crowd, at least ten thousand, which included a good number of prostitutes and pickpockets, aggressively plying their trades. The mood was a strange mix of somberness and celebration.

They carried Hickey there in a horse-drawn cart. A rope was tied to a large maple tree, and Hickey was made to stand on the cart while the noose was placed around his neck. He was asked if he had any last words. He did not. He also declined the tendered blindfold. Upon the signal from the sergeant in charge, the driver pulled away.

From his training with Dr. Rush, and from independent reading, Will had a fair understanding of the mechanics or physiology of hanging. Essentially, the jugular vein is blocked by the compression, resulting in a stoppage of cerebral circulation, causing a rapid rise in venous pressure in the head. His attempt at objective analysis was pushed away, however by its visceral effect. There was a sharp crack as Hicks body fell, the weight of it providing the constriction that tightened the noose around his neck. After a momentary collective gasp from the crowd, there were murmurs of approval, even cheering as Hickey struggled violently for what seemed a long time. His face grew distorted and livid, and his eyes protruded grossly from their sockets. After about ten minutes, he was dead.

* * *

Two days after the hanging, Will departed for Philadelphia. He rode with the same two men on the mail coach. News of his participation in foiling the plot against Washington had apparently spread, gaining him additional esteem in their eyes as a result. The return trip seemed to pass more quickly, and by early morning of July 1st, they arrived.

He went straight to the State House where Matlack and the assistants were completing the morning security check and preparing the chambers for the day's session. He found Tim in the bell tower.

"Welcome back, stranger. And congratulations. We got the news about the foiled plot against General Washington. When did you get in?"

"Just a few minutes ago."

He took in the lad's disheveled appearance. "I appreciate your dedication, but you have time to go home and clean yourself up."

"I wanted to get the update on Tremont. Did he return here? Has he been placed under arrest?"

Matlack gave him a puzzled look. "Why. yes. Tremont has been back a few days now. But why would he be under arrest? I mean, we know he is under suspicion, and I've had Cecil and his lads watching him, but we still don't have anything concrete on him."

"He was implicated in the plot against Washington. Didn't you receive the warrant? The general sent it by messenger a few days ago."

Tim shook his head. "Hancock received messages from Washington by rider, about the plot, the arrests of the mayor and governor, but that was several days ago. There was no mention of Tremont, and no warrant. There has been no messenger since then."

How was that possible? This was not what he expected at all. He thought that the spy would return here, but not in his Tremont disguise. The spy knew that Will had recognized him on the street that night, and that it was likely that word would be sent to Philadelphia of his involvement in the plot. Why would he risk coming back as Tremont? What Will expected to hear was that they had received the warrant but had yet to locate the man. "But he is here?" he asked.

Matlack nodded. "He's staying at the White Horse Inn again."

Will banged his hand on the wall. "I will go get him myself, then."

"Not a good idea, Will. That's a job for the militia or the sheriff. Let's meet with Hancock and Adams, explain what's happened. I'm sure your word will be good enough to have the man taken into custody to await official confirmation from General Washington. We'll find out what happened to the rider, and the warrant."

Will frowned. "Incognito no doubt had intelligence on what was happening and either killed the rider himself or had him killed so he would not deliver the message. He knew I would be along shortly, so it was just a delay. It means he plans to attack very soon. He needs to be apprehended now, not later. And I need to at least go warn the Boutwells."

Matlack shook his head. "I don't know that you have a lot of credibility for that mission. They think you are just jealous. They won't believe you. And if this man is as proficient with weapons as you say, it would not be wise for you to act alone."

Will pondered this, remembering what happened last time he confronted the man. "He won't do anything out in the open. Not yet. It

323

would spoil his plan. He already knows I'm on to him, and I'll wager that he has been told of my arrival from his sources. Look, you stay here and update the committee. If Tremont is at the inn, I will speak to him and ask him to come to the State House to sort things out. If he declines to come, I will leave it at that."

Again, Matlack shook his head. "Let's get the members together. It will only take a couple of minutes. We do work for the Congress, not the other way around. We should get their direction before taking further action. Perhaps they have received information I have not been privy to."

Will reluctantly agreed, and Tim quickly assembled the committee members to receive Will's report. There was some reluctance to act without official confirmation from General Washington, but they all agreed to rely upon his verbal assurances and to issue an order to take Tremont into custody.

"Tim," Hancock said, "You will arrange for some of your militia fellows to take care of the matter?"

He nodded.

"The session is about to begin, though, so take care of it at our first recess."

Will started to protest. Incognito's arrest was crucial to the security of the Congress. It should be done now. Time was of the essence. If he knew of the rider from Washington, he probably knew of Will's arrival. He would know that his ability to move freely about the city was at an end. He would take steps to avoid capture.

Upon reflection, though, Will realized that the man who called himself Tremont was most likely no longer a lodger at the White Horse Inn and had probably already gone in hiding. He would not leave the city, though, as he would want to see things through. Will felt confident that he would find him, and perhaps more of those who were assisting him, before he could complete his mission. And it was obvious that Hancock was determined to get the session started, to resume the debate on Lee's resolution for independence. So, Will bit his tongue and followed Hancock and the others into the chambers.

As usual, the members took up the routine matters first—letters from generals and officers in the field and reports from various colonial assemblies. One letter from Washington advised that the militia supposedly coming to help defend New York had not yet arrived. With his characteristic understatement he added, "I hope their tardiness will not cause disagreeable circumstances during our defense of the city."

Hancock then broached the subject of Tremont. "There has been a recent development relevant to the security of the Congress. The man many of you have come to know as Henri Tremont is a suspected British spy. He has been implicated in the assassination plot against General Washington."

A collective gasp passed through the room, followed by a murmuring buzz. When it abated, Hancock continued. "There is reason to believe that he may also have plans to assassinate members of this body. I have directed that he be taken into custody. But until then, we should all be alert to a possible attack." He paused a beat. "And be aware that the man may be disguised." He then described the other known personas used by Incognito, asked the members to report anyone or anything suspicious they saw or heard, or any information they thought might be useful, to Tim or Will. "And," he said, "be especially careful during any recesses."

There was a stunned silence for several seconds, then questions from members, and expressions of skepticism. Will felt sure that they were chagrined, many of them, embarrassed at how they had been fooled by the man. Some openly scoffed, declaring that they were not afraid, but he sensed real concern underneath. Good. They needed to be concerned. But in the end, most members were in no mood to worry about spies among them. They were preoccupied with what most saw as probably the most momentous moment in the assembly's history, a vote to declare their independence from England.

Most of them thought a favorable vote was a foregone conclusion, based on the behind-the-scene negotiations spearheaded by Sam Adams. Even John Dickinson, who rose to speak in opposition to the resolution seemed aware of the futility of his effort. This would perhaps be his last speech to the body as he had announced that he would resign if the resolution passed. It was rather sad to see one of the most revered men in Pennsylvania brought down by his inability to change with the times. Some thought it was because of obstinacy or stubbornness, but Will knew it was the result of integrity and an unshakable faith to his principles.

"I am very much aware of the great burden that rests upon my shoulders in speaking on behalf of my colleagues who resist this ill-advised sailing into uncharted waters with neither a compass, nor any precise notion of where we are headed, except somewhere over the horizon."

It was late morning now and the outside temperature was close to ninety. Inside it was a sweatbox and Will's mentor seemed even more frail than usual as he spoke from his notes. "I know that what I have to say will not be popular with many, and perhaps it is useless to attempt to persuade minds already made up. But I have to try. To sit back and do nothing would be sinful.

"The resentment we feel toward British policies and actions is natural, and legitimate, and the present tyranny of the British government should be resisted with everything we have. But independence is not in America's long-term interest. Rather, we would be better served by reconciling on fair terms with England."

He repeated many of his same old arguments. A war for independence would take longer than a war for reconciliation, and a long war would plunge the colonies into debt. The populace was still divided, and the Congress lacked the full-throated support necessary in such an endeavor. The chances of success were limited. After all, the British military was the best in the world. Without the connection to

England, they would be perceived as weak and vulnerable, and foreign nations would make a play on the continent. The colonies had no governmental structure to replace what was now in place. Civil war was a real possibility as differences among the colonies had yet to be resolved.

Although it was indeed an interesting and historic debate, Will found that his mind wandered. He was anxious to get about the business of finding Incognito and eliminating the threat. After a while, he excused himself to carefully examine the entire building again, checking closets, looking for loose boards in any of the floors, peering under stairs, and under the steps at both entrances. He stuck his head inside the metal grates to each side of the steps that allowed access to the crawl space underneath the building. He was looking for explosive devices, or anything out of the ordinary. He found nothing.

In the bell tower, he looked out again over the surrounding rooftops and upper floor windows, searching for the most likely spots from which to fire on the State House with a long rifle. But Tim and he had already checked the most likely spots, even the least likely ones. Interviewed building owners about recent tenants and checked roof tops. Nothing promising. He wondered if his assumptions about the manner or method or timing of attack were wrong. The assassin might very well be planning something less dramatic, perhaps killing members away from the building. The truth was, they had to consider and try to anticipate any of the possibilities. "Damn," he said aloud before heading back to the chambers.

An intermittent rain began late morning and toward the end of Dickinson's remarks, the members had to strain to hear him over the rain that pelted the windows. He concluded somewhere around one o'clock. John Adams rose to answer Dickinson, but Hancock gaveled a recess, much to the relief of the members. Will planned to put the time to good use.

Philadelphia, July 1
Chapter 35

Will had no illusions that Incognito would still be roaming the streets of Philadelphia disguised as Henri Tremont, and certainly, he would not be hanging around The White Horse Inn, waiting to be arrested. So, while Matlack went off with his militia friends in search of Tremont, Will went in search of Cecil O'Conner.

He found him easily enough, at his regular haunt at the corner of Market and Second Streets, working another street hustle. When the game was over, he caught his eye and Cecil came over.

"Master Harrell. When did you get back?"

"Just this morning. Listen, Tim said you and your lads have been keeping an eye on Tremont since he returned. I'm anxious to know what he's been doing, where he's been going and who he's been talking to."

He nodded and grinned. "Would you care to step into my office, sir?" He gave a large sweep of his hand then moved over about four feet, creating a little separation from the crowd. Will moved with him.

"Well, what can you tell me?"

"Tremont arrived three days ago. I've had one of me lads on his tail most of the time"

"Most of the time?"

"He's a slippery sort, as you know. We lost him on occasion. And didn't think you wanted to pay to watch him sleep."

Will made a circling motion with his hand. "Go on."

"He checked out today, telling them he was headed back to New York. But his horse is still stabled and no indication that he hired a private coach, nor that there were any passengers on the mail coach that left town this morning. He could have bought, borrowed or stolen another horse, but that seemed unlikely, as there was no compelling reason he wouldn't use his own horse. My conclusion, he is still here in Philadelphia."

Will nodded. "So, what's he been up to these last three days?"

"The man spent a lot of time in the taverns, buddying up with the members of Congress. Nothing real suspicious. But something you might find interesting." He paused a couple of beats. "Tremont visited the Black Cat Book Store a couple of times," he said, arching an eyebrow. "Both times, he talked with your father a bit, went upstairs for a few minutes, then left. Don't know what he was doing up there, but it wasn't buying books. Both times he left without having made a purchase."

Nothing all that unusual, Will thought. Many of their customers just browsed the shelves and rarely bought anything. He wasn't sure he liked the implication in Cecil's tone. He stared at him expectantly.

"It gets better," Cecil said. "Tremont was followed to the riverfront, where he was seen entering a side door to a warehouse. Approximately twenty minutes later, another man emerged from this same door. He was a red-headed man, dressed like a sailor. He was followed to a tavern on Chestnut Street, just around the corner from the State House. When he didn't come out after a good long time my lad, Toby, went inside. The man was nowhere to be found, so Toby went out the rear door and checked in the alley there. Nothing. So, we assumed he knew he was being followed and this was his way of shaking the tail. He hasn't been spotted since then. That was last night."

"What's the name of the tavern?"

"The Black Swan."

"And do you know which warehouse he entered, to whom it belongs?

He nodded and arched his eyebrows again. "The sign above the door says 'Black Cat Storage.' I believe it is owned by one Patrick Harrell."

Will stared at him, open-mouthed for a few seconds, then recovered. "Thanks, Cecil. I may have an errand for you later, a special assignment, but now, I have to get back to the State House."

* * *

Adams was not the orator that Dickinson was, but he was an effective advocate. He referred to no notes, and didn't need them, he said, "as there are no arguments for or against that have not already been made several times already."

He detailed the British policies and actions that had led them to this point. Nothing seemed to deter that government from continued abuse. And yes, Britain was powerful militarily, which was one reason they needed to seek alliances, particularly with France, to even the odds a bit, and they could only do that as an independent nation.

He minimized the supposed calamities of moving forward without a constitution. "All of the colonies have constitutions and people able and willing to lead the people. This Congress has done much hard and conflicted work for over two years now and there is no reason to believe we cannot devise a way to resolve any differences that may arise."

And he spoke of unflinching confidence in victory. "There is no way that, in the end, the British can suppress the entire populace. The geography and the population of the colonies virtually guarantees eventual defeat of the British. It is only a matter of time and will."

Adams' speech was at least as long as Dickinson's. And as the afternoon wore on the rain turned into a thunderstorm. It grew very dark and candles were lit in the chambers. As he was just about to conclude, four of the five recently appointed delegates from New Jersey arrived. They requested that he start over, so they could hear the entire speech. Adams obliged, remarkably repeating it almost word for word.

330

Yet no one left the chambers. Four o'clock came and went with no sign of Tremont. No surprise there. Finally, close to five o'clock, Adams finished and sat down.

Although pretty much everything that could be said on the subject had been said by these two advocates, Dickinson and Adams, the delegates all wanted to record their words for posterity, hoping no doubt to make their own mark on history. So, one delegate after another rose to speak. It was night before they finished. In all, they had been in session nine hours, and they were tired and famished.

When the vote was taken, it was nine colonies in favor, three against, and one abstaining. New England and the southern colonies were solidly behind it and voted yes. New York abstained pending new instructions from its assembly. Pennsylvania voted no, four to three. South Carolina no, and Delaware split. Ed Rutledge of South Carolina requested an adjournment so that his colony's delegates could discuss matters over the evening, hinting that South Carolina might change its vote in the interest of unanimity. Everyone understood the problem with only a majority voting in favor of the resolution, so Rutledge's motion carried, and the body adjourned for the night.

When the session ended, James Wilson approached Will and Tim. "Gentlemen, may I have a moment?"

"Of course," they said in unison.

The three men stepped over to the side and Wilson said, "I received word just this afternoon of the death of two of my friends and clients, near Reading."

"Yes?" Matlack prompted.

"Martin Meylin, a well-regarded gunsmith and his wife were found murdered. Meylin was shot in the head out in the field, apparently with one of his own long rifles. His wife was stabbed to death in their home."

"How awful," Tim said.

Will nodded his agreement. "And you figure it has something to do with our situation here?"

"Well," Wilson said, "Martin had confided in a neighbor that he had just completed working on a long rifle for a Frenchman. Showed it to the neighbor." He paused a couple of beats. "No money or other property was found missing, except for the newly made long rifle, and Meylin's own personal weapon." He paused again briefly, then said, "So, yes, I think it might very well have something to do with the plan to attack the Congress."

Both men nodded in agreement.

"Thank you, James," Matlack said. "This is very useful information."

"And sorry to hear of the death of your friends," Will added.

Wilson nodded. "Is there anything else I can do."

"Not at this time," Matlack said. "Just keep an eye out and report anything or anyone suspicious."

Wilson nodded and left the room. When they were alone, Matlack commented that they needed to pay another visit to "that little Tory who owns the Emporium."

Will nodded. "And the other buildings, too."

Matlack then reported that the men from the militia had not found Tremont.

"No surprise there," Will said, then he recounted his conversation with Cecil, leaving out the part that seemed to tie his father to the spy. "It's possible," Will said, "that he hired a private coach, but I doubt it."

Tim nodded. "He's gone underground somewhere, and he'll be disguised now. We shan't see Tremont as Tremont again, I'll wager."

"Perhaps we should split up here, cover more territory. If you will get Cecil and his boys, maybe some of your militia friends, to help you in the search, I have a couple of leads to follow up on."

Matlack didn't ask him what leads, but he gave him a questioning look. When Will did not volunteer any additional information, he nodded and said, "Let's meet up at The City Tavern at say ten o'clock and compare notes."

Will nodded.

"Ten o'clock it is." And the two men went their separate ways.

Philadelphia, July 1
Chapter 36

Incognito took the back streets, avoiding the raucous crowds that flowed in and out of the many taverns, or gathered at one of several gaming enterprises. People were animated more than usual with talk of a resolution calling for independence, so the city streets were more crowded than usual.

He was disguised this night as an itinerant cutler, a role easily within his artistic reach as he had always had an affinity for knives and all sorts of blades, proficient in their uses, and fairly competent in their making and repair. His clothing was plain and unassuming—worn and baggy muslin shirt and trousers. He sported long brown hair and a full beard, both streaked with grey. A leather strap held his hair back on his neck and a floppy, brown wool cap kept errant strands in place. He carried over his shoulder a plain canvas sack, which purportedly carried his wares and the tools of his trade, but in fact had something completely different underneath. His body language—hunched over and looking down as he walked, careful not to make eye contact with anyone he passed—did not invite unsolicited conversation.

The new disguise had been necessitated by the arrival of the Harrell boy back in the city. He had learned from his contacts in New York of the warrant issued by Washington. The interception and killing of the messenger had given him the few extra days he needed to set things in place and cover his tracks, and he couldn't afford to be captured now. So, he had hastily checked out again from the White Horse Inn, removing what he needed to the warehouse and to his room. And, he had his plan for the meddlesome book clerk.

He walked down Third Street behind the City Tavern, over to Chestnut Street, then three blocks west to the corner of Chestnut and Fifth Street, to the courtyard entrance at the rear of the State House. He continued slowly to sixth Street and turned right, taking note of his surroundings, and of any persons nearby. He circled the building but didn't notice any eyes on him. The ground was wet, the streets muddy and dotted with puddles from the late afternoon thunderstorm. His shoes made a sucking sound when he veered into the street or its shoulder. The rain had stopped mostly, with only an occasional sprinkling, or water drops knocked free from the leaves by the wind. The air was heavy, subtlety menacing, encouraging the dark rain clouds that blocked the moon and threatened another storm.

The courtyard of the State House was empty, as he expected. He had surveyed the building carefully for weeks, and knew there was no business conducted nights, nor was security posted on the premises. He walked the length of the block, then doubled back to the iron gate in the center, glancing around to make sure no one was watching him, then entered. He moved quickly along the perimeter, keeping close to the shrubbery. On both sides of the entrance steps were two openings for ventilation of and access to, the building's crawl space, covered by slotted iron grates. He went to the one on the right side of the entrance first. He crouched in front of the metal grate and placed his sack on the ground. From the sack he removed a narrow iron wedge and used it to pry the grate from the opening, then crawled through, pulling the sack behind him.

He stopped just inside to let his eyes adjust to the blackness. What little illumination there was came from the half-hidden moon which penetrated only a few inches past the opening, and he felt more than saw his way along the side of the wall. Fortunately, he didn't have to go far, and at least the dirt here was not the soggy mess it was outside. He stopped just beyond where the steps ended, squatted in the small space between the dirt and the floor joists, reached into the sack and removed one of the bombs.

He wedged the device securely into the space between the edge of the steps, the floor joist, and the subflooring. He then crawled the width of the steps, removed a second bomb from his sack, and placed it in the corresponding location on the other side of the steps. For each device, he uncoiled the fuse and laid it on the ground along each side of the steps and up to the grated openings on either side, so that each could be reached for the purpose of lighting, but would not be visible from the outside unless one got right up to the grate and looked in. When he replaced the grate, he stepped back and examined the area on both sides, confirming that the fuses were not visible.

Next, he walked up the steps to the back door, removed the key he had obtained from his contact, inserted it into the lock and heard the satisfying click. He turned the handle, pushed the door open, and stepped inside. He stood in silence for several seconds, listening for any sound indicating the presence of anyone else in the building. He had expected the place to be empty, but he did not abandon prudent caution. He wanted to be sure. If there was another person there, it wouldn't derail his plan, thwart his mission, but it would be an inconvenience he didn't need. But he heard only the tick tock of the grandfather clock which stood against the wall next to the chambers in which the Congress met, and the light, drizzly raindrops blowing against the windows, precursor perhaps of another storm to come.

Even though he was certain he was alone, he took the stairs to the second floor as quickly, but quietly, as he could. Force of habit. He did likewise when he came to the narrow spiral stairwell that led to the bell tower. When he reached the tower, he pushed his sack through the opening and placed it on the unfinished wooden floor, then pulled himself after it. He stayed low, crouched below the four-foot wall, even though he doubted anyone would happen to be looking out of an upper story window, or from the rooftop of one of the surrounding buildings. Then he moved to the other side of the bell, which did a complete job of hiding him from sight. He removed the remaining two explosive devices from the sack, together with the ring of thin rope, which he used to fasten the bombs to either side of the support timbers which helped to hold the large, heavy bell in place. He used additional rope to wind the fuse around the support timbers for the width of the cupola.

Remaining in the shadow of the huge bell, he looked across Walnut Street to the rooftop of the Philadelphia Emporium, and to the window of his room on the third floor. He would be better able to confirm his viewpoint when he was actually standing there, but it seemed as though he would have a clear line of sight to take a shot from either location. He didn't want to waste a shot but if for some reason the fuses didn't ignite one or both bombs, or his confederate didn't do his job properly, he could detonate one of them with a rifle ball, the explosion of which would set off the other.

Satisfied, he retraced his steps to the first floor and out the back door, locking it behind him. He checked once more to confirm that the fuses to the bombs beyond the vented grates on the side of the stairs were not readily visible. With his now near-empty sack in his hand, he went through the back gate of the courtyard onto Chestnut Street, turned right, and circled around to the front of the building on Walnut Street. He encountered only a few people, none of whom gave him much notice. He crossed the street and walked down Fifth Street, which ran to the side of the Emporium, then right again at the end of the block to the front entrance to The Black Swan Tavern.

It was crowded, as usual, with patrons spilling out into the street. Many of these persons knew him as Henri Tremont, or maybe as Dutch MacGregor, the Irish sailor who was an occasional customer, or maybe as Henry Belmont, the jovial old man from Virginia, none of them suspecting they were all the same person. He was that good of an actor. It wasn't arrogance. It was just a fact, and it allowed him now to enter in this new disguise, which only the proprietor knew concealed the same man, with little apprehension. To be sure, there were a few looks as he walked through, but only of mild curiosity, not recognition, and no one spoke to him. He gave a nod to the owner/bartender and two other customers whose acquaintance he had made earlier in the day as he walked back toward the rear entrance. To one man who waved him over, he mouthed, "I'll be back shortly," grabbing his crouch and pointing to the rear, to indicate he was going outside to relieve himself.

Outside, he noticed two men who were doing just that, on the side of the building to the left of the door. He pretended to do the same thing on the right side, and nodded to each as they finished and headed back in. He took one more look around to confirm he was again alone, then he quickly scaled the metal ladder up to the roof of the tavern. There, he retrieved the two by twelve board he had leaned against the chimney and slid it out across the space between the tavern's roof and that of the Emporium building.

He had taken to coming and going to his rented room this way instead of coming in through the side entrance of the Emporium building, to avoid any connection between his new persona and the building from which he would launch his attack. Certainly, he didn't want his landlord to see him. It was a little tricky because the tavern's roof was not quite as high as the other, creating an incline for him to walk across, but, as he had done many times now, he walked across the space quickly, then pulled the board across after him. He laid it on its edge and against the far wall of the rooftop, where he stood a few moments looking toward the State House, confirming what he had surmised minutes before in the bell tower, that he indeed had a clear line of sight to where he had secreted the bombs.

He took the stairs down to the third floor and to the room he rented. The emporium closed at six o'clock, but Patterson and his wife often stayed late to take inventory, update the books of account, and do some minor cleaning. That was two stories below him, though, and the second floor housed a surveyor and a lawyer, neither of whom had a habit of keeping night hours. And no other tenants were on the third floor. He would not be disturbed.

He unlocked the door to his room and stepped inside. It was, like the rest of the floor, hot and stuffy, and he quickly opened both windows to get a little fresh air in the room. He walked to where his landlord had placed the desk and chair. He stood first on the chair and then the desk itself. He reached up and pushed up on the plank which he had loosened soon after renting the room and placed it to the side. He reached in and felt for the two long rifles he had secreted there, as well as the bag with ammunition and other implements and tools. He took the rifles and bag down and for the next thirty minutes cleaned and oiled both rifles and checked to make sure all parts were operable and in good condition. He wanted no malfunctions, no missteps.

As he worked, he envisioned what would happen tomorrow, the fruition of his plan. He had once thought he would come to the State House himself, in disguise, and light the fuses, but he needed to be on the rooftop. There was not enough time to do both. Plus, he didn't want to risk being stopped as someone suspicious. So, he had recruited the boy. No one would suspect him. No one would stop him. Once the session began, he would climb to the bell tower. The bombs there had longer, slower burning fuses, so he would light them first. Then he would light the fuses of the explosive devices at the rear of the building and make his escape before the explosions. The bombs at the rear entrance would detonate first, followed shortly by those in the bell tower. The explosives at the rear entrance would make a rather sizable hole in the floor of the foyer and, more importantly, create a ball of fire that would quickly begin to lick the floor and walls. This would certainly get their attention and create panic in some, who would immediately head for the front entrance. But most he thought, would remain to fight the resulting fire.

Hence the secondary explosion in the bell tower, the sound of which, reverberating against the bell would be deafening. The extremely heavy bell itself, its supporting timbers destroyed, would drop through the floor of the cupola, and perhaps even all the way to the ground. Regardless, even those who had lingered would not be so foolhardy as to remain and would flee out the front entrance. Amid the smoke and confusion and panic, he would be free to pick off his targets, if not at leisure, then rather quickly before anyone registered what was happening. When his mission was completed, he would escape back across the roof to the tavern, and onto the street and away from the scene, and Philadelphia.

After he put away the rifles in his room, he made his way back across to the roof of the tavern, down the ladder and inside the building. As he made his way to the entrance, he spotted the Harrell boy at the bar, speaking with the proprietor. What was he doing here? The sight of the book clerk, and its implications unnerved him, but just for a moment. He kept his eyes forward as he walked by. Harrell glanced at him but didn't stare and quickly returned his attention to the bartender. The spy known as Incognito exited the tavern, turned left and headed back toward the river.

Philadelphia, July 1
Chapter 37

The bartender at The Black Swan Tavern wiped down the bar with a soiled towel as he spoke. "Tremont? Sure, I know the Frenchman. A fine gentleman he is. Comes in here from time to time." He looked up at Will. "Ain't been in tonight, though."

"What about an elderly man, walks with a cane and smokes a pipe, calls himself Henry Belmont, or a red-headed sailor, goes by the name of Dutch?"

The man pursed his lips and proclaimed that each had been in a few times, though, again, neither had been in that night. "Been a few days for either of them. And I have an eye for my customers, so I would have noticed if they had been here. Why do you ask?"

Will knew the owner/bartender of The Black Swan to be a Loyalist in his political leanings, though his customers were a mix. The owner could be covering for Incognito. "Congress business," Will said, as if that was all the explanation needed. He ordered a beer, then made his way around the room, making inquiries. After a few minutes he concluded that the bartender had probably been truthful, as none of the customers reported seeing Tremont, as himself, or in one of his known disguises, that night.

After a bit, Will made his way out back into the narrow alley behind the tavern, where Tremont had presumably evaded his tail two nights ago. There was only one way out of the alley, east onto Sixth Street. He was about to walk that way when he noticed the metal ladder attached to the back wall of the tavern, leading to its roof. He climbed up.

The view from the roof allowed only a glimpse of the State House through some trees and over the building next to it. He walked to the edge and peered over at the roof of the adjacent building. The distance between the two roofs was about six feet, a manageable leap, he thought if you got a running start, but not something you'd want to try if you didn't have to. Then he caught sight of the board, in the shadows, flush with the wall.

Its length and width suggested its use. He retrieved it and placed it between the two roofs, took a deep breath and walked across. The adjacent building Will knew to house The Philadelphia Emporium. It was one of the buildings he and Tim had inspected when considering the likely spots from which a man with a rifle might position himself for an attack on the State House. Indeed, Will had thought, the most likely choice. It was the building owned by a known Loyalist, Eric Patterson.

Patterson had been quite sure that no one had access to the roof other than he and his wife, his two employees and his tenants, all of whom were long term. He had not rented any space recently, and specifically not to the Frenchman named Henri Tremont. Maybe he was telling the truth. Maybe not. Will had been suspicious but they found no evidence to contradict his story. Either way, it was now clear to Will that one could access the roof without going through the building. He looked around, searching for any weapons or other signs to confirm his suspicion, but found nothing. He tried the door leading inside the building, but it was locked.

When he made his way back over to the roof of the tavern, he pondered whether he should let the board fall into the alley, and then haul it away. If, as he suspected, Incognito planned to use it to travel between the two roofs, that would certainly put a crimp in his plan. On the other hand, if he made another dry run, he would discover the missing board, replace it, or come up with an alternative. And, he would be alerted to the fact that his secret was no longer a secret.

No, best to allow him a false sense of security and then catch him in the act. They would just station Cecil's boys, or the militia men, or both, at points to observe both roofs and entrances to the buildings. He returned the board to its hiding place, climbed back down the ladder and headed toward his next destination, The Black Cat Storage building on Front Street.

He walked hurriedly, propelled by both a sense that he might be close to getting the answers he needed in order to capture the spy, and by the apprehension, or dread, as to how those answers might lead to his father. As he walked, he found himself coming up with an explanation that led elsewhere. For example, the warehouse was owned by Patrick Harrell, true, but he had hired a manager, Owen Green, to run things.

Will had never liked the man. He considered him shady, prone to cut corners and bend the rules if it increased profits. And he wasn't at all sure he wasn't cheating his father out of some of those profits. But the business made so much money for him, Patrick Harrell was apparently content to look the other way and not question how Green made it. Will was hoping any connection between Incognito and the warehouse was through Green, not his father.

It was after eight o'clock when he drew near to the building, yet there was still much activity on or about the place, evidenced by the profusion of lamps and people going in and out. Men were hauling merchandise and materials from a nearby ship docked on the river. Green, who was just outside the main entrance, observing and directing the men, looked surprised to see Will, and annoyed. He put a smile on his greasy face that was as insincere as it was large.

"Master Harrell, to what do I owe this honor?"

Will got right to the point. "I have information that a man, wanted by the authorities for various crimes, has been seen frequenting this warehouse."

"What sorts of crimes?"

"Serious crimes." Will didn't feel the need to be specific.

Green gave him a look filled with animus and dismissiveness. "Serious crimes, huh? What makes you think he has been here?"

343

"That's unimportant," Will said. "suffice it to say that I'd like your cooperation in the matter."

The man bowed deeply. "At your service, Governor. How may I be of assistance?" There was a mocking tone to his words.

"Has there been such a man who has used a portion of the space here, who can enter through a separate entrance, who has his own key?"

Green looked at Will for a long few seconds before responding. "Yes, there has been such a man."

Will was surprised by the frank and quick admission. He did not speak, waiting for the manager to elaborate.

"The man is the Frenchman, known as Tremont. Under orders from your father," he said, pointing his chin at Will. "Patrick gave him a key to one of the side rooms there, to come and go as he pleased. I was not to concern myself with his business and was directed to stay out of the room." He turned then and Will followed his gaze to a part of the building with a low roof, which jutted out about ten feet and ran the length of the building. There were three separate rooms or attached sheds which were sometimes rented as storage space to individuals if the business did not need them. "Tremont has the second one down," Green said.

"What has he stored there?"

Green shrugged. "As I say, this was all Patrick's doing. I don't know the man's business."

"You've never looked inside?"

"I was told not to."

That was not really an answer, Will observed, and gave him a skeptical look.

"I got more important things to worry about, like getting this cargo inside before the rains come again. It was none of my business. I only met him the one time, and I haven't seen him in several weeks now. He is free to come and go as he pleases, and maybe it pleases him to come here in the night, when nobody else is here." He gave Will a conspiratorial glance.

"You do have a key, though?"

He pulled at the metal ring attached to his trousers. "You know I do, laddie."

Will held out his hand. "I need to take a look."

The man looked as if he was about to protest, but he searched on his key ring and removed a key. "Mr. Harrell gave me strict instructions not to go inside, but I suppose it's all right, given that you are his son. I guess he wouldn't mind." He handed the key to Will.

"I'll just take a quick look. May I borrow one of your lamps?" Will looked in the direction of oil lamps hanging on either side of the wide entrance.

Green nodded. "Help yourself. Then, if you please, I will return to supervising these miscreants." He gave another greasy grin. "Some of 'em will rob you blind if you don't watch 'em close."

Will unlocked the door and stood a few moments, anticipating and dreading what he might find. Then he pushed open the door and stepped inside. Using the lamp for illumination of the small space, it was obvious right away that whatever may have been stored in the shed, it was now gone. The space was empty. He did find, however, a trace amount of gunpowder and fuse material. There was no way of knowing how long it had been there, and it wasn't unusual to store such material in warehouses, but Will thought it was one more important piece of the puzzle. It seemed that Incognito was planning an attack by both long rifle, and explosives.

Will closed and locked the door behind him and returned the key to Green, thanking him for his cooperation. Green grunted his acknowledgement and Will took off for the book store. His mind toggled again between dread and anger, racing through all the possibilities, struggling to latch on to one that didn't end with his father a traitor to the rebel cause, a cause for which he had lent his very vocal support for this past year. He wanted to think that Green had been lying, that if Incognito was using the warehouse, it was without his father's knowledge. Or if he knew about it, he had been too trusting of the Frenchman.

Tremont could be charming and persuasive. That was true. Hadn't he won the heart and confidence of Rebecca and her family? Christ, he had members of the Congress eating out of his hand, at least until recently. Yes, that could be it. His father had been just helping the man out, not realizing what he intended. An innocent pawn. Maybe Green was too. The warehouse manager had to know that Will would check with his father and discover if he had lied.

Will couldn't ignore the evidence, though, evidence that had been right in front of him but that he had refused to see. The frequent visits to the bookstore by Tremont and his collaborators suggested it was being used as a meeting place or message drop off. His father had pretended not to have met Tremont before when he and Rebecca came into the store together. But Tim had seen the two together at a cock fight, days before. He had serious money problems due to gambling losses that might give him motivation to look the other way for a price. Will hated to think that his father could be so cynical, so opportunistic, but in his heart, he knew it was possible.

He had witnessed his father's bitterness over his wife's death lead gradually to increased gambling, and drinking and drugs to self-medicate against the grief, and the guilt. Never mind that there was no reason for guilt. That rarely matters in such things. His father's natural sarcastic wit and fondness for parody in poking fun had turned more and more into a black cynicism. He covered it well, but Will had clearly noticed. No, the circumstances required that he confront him with the information he had.

He was rehearsing in his head what he would say to his father as he rounded the corner of Market and Arch, the store in sight, and spotted his father through the large front window, speaking to a man whose back was to him. Will stopped and watched. The man was dressed plainly, even shabbily. And there was something familiar about the him.

After several seconds, the man turned and went through the door. He was carrying no books or other merchandise. He looked up and down the street, and as he did so, Will got a better look. The man wore a baggy muslin shirt, beige in color and brown, wool trousers. His hair was also brown, and thick, as was his beard. A quick, darting image flickered across his mind's eye and he placed him, a patron at The Black Swan earlier that evening.

Will strained to see more clearly across the street. The man looked his way and Will backed up against the wall and into the shadow. But the man had seen him, and he stopped and looked in Will's direction. Will stepped forward out of the shadows then, and their eyes met. He knew in a cold instant that he was looking into the eyes of the spy known as Incognito, in a new disguise, to be sure, but one and the same man he'd first met as Henri Tremont. As the man began walking down the street, Will had to make a choice, go and confront his father, or follow this man.

It wasn't really a choice.

Philadelphia, July 1
Chapter 38

Will fell in behind the man, keeping his distance, as he made his way down Arch Street, then to Front Street. The man hesitated a few moments in front of the Red Bird Tavern, as if deciding whether to enter, but then continued on to Market Street, where he turned and headed west. The man walked slowly, leisurely, puffing on his pipe, stopping occasionally to look in shop windows. He didn't look like a man who knew he was being followed, but Will thought it an act. He must have seen Will, must have known he might have recognized him.

When the man got to the intersection of Market and Third Street, he suddenly picked up his pace for the remaining half block, then darted down the alley on the east side of The White Horse Inn. Will hesitated a moment before also picking up his pace. When he made it to the corner, he saw no sign of the man.

He eased down the alley, aware that it might be a trap, that the man might be hiding, waiting to ambush him. He realized, too, to his dismay, that he had no weapon on him with which to defend himself. He had seen firsthand the results of Incognito's handiwork, and no desire to become his next victim. He spotted a glass bottle on the ground, picked it up and hit it on the iron post of the fence, holding it at the neck. The result was a make-shift knife, with jagged edges. It would have to do.

Thus armed, he continued down the alley, alert to any movement on either side of him. He made it all the way to the back corner of the inn's property without being attacked, but with no sign of his quarry, either. It appeared that no ambush was planned, just escape, and he had lost valuable time, being so cautious. He cursed under his breath, looking up and down the street, searching for any sign as to which way the man had gone. To the left he saw fresh footprints in the mud alongside the street. He followed them, this time not as cautiously. Halfway down the block, the footprints disappeared at the brick walkway that led to the back entrance of the inn, and to the private quarters of the Boutwell family. He looked up toward the building, and to the window of Rebecca's bedroom. The shade was drawn but the silhouettes of two figures were illuminated against the shade by the candlelight inside the room.

* * *

What a stroke of luck, Incognito thought, then reconsidered. No, he made his own luck. He hadn't planned it, not precisely, but he had anticipated this development, had prepared for it. He knew the Harrell boy would be looking for him, urgently, aware that he might be disguised. He also knew his investigation would eventually bring him to the bookstore, to a confrontation with his father. He didn't know when, but he thought it might be tonight.

So, he had strolled around on the streets near the store, hoping for the inevitable chance encounter, a side long glance, a meeting of the eyes and the flicker of recognition, and the game would begin. And what a charming coincidence that it should happen just as he was leaving the bookstore. Yes, he knew Harrell would follow him if he got the chance, and that was just what he wanted. He had made arrangements with the girl earlier in the day. If he had not miscalculated, she was even now anxiously awaiting his arrival. And now, he took his time, walking down Market Street. But when he got to the intersection with Third Street, he doubled his pace as he turned the corner, headed to the back entrance of The White Horse Inn.

* * *

Rebecca Boutwell sat on her bed, her hands clasped in front of her. She stared at the clock on the wall. He said he would come this night, but he didn't say when. She had retired early, just in case, to be ready to receive him. That was at eight o'clock, and it was almost ten. She dressed in her night shift, with nothing underneath it. She had tried to keep herself occupied. She had sat at her dressing mirror and brushed her hair, a hundred, then two hundred times. She had paced back and forth the width of the small bedroom. She had tried to read, but she couldn't concentrate. She was extremely nervous, excited but also apprehensive, eager but also fearful. Their conversation this morning had started the emotional whirlwind that now threatened to consume her, to whisk her away from herself.

He had taken her aside, in the garden. "Can you keep a secret?"

"I love secrets."

"I'm not really leaving Philadelphia today, but I have to pretend to leave."

She gave him a puzzled look. "But why?"

"Your friend, Mr. Harrell, has made some vicious, false accusations against me concerning certain matters that occurred in New York."

"What? Will?"

He nodded, frowning. "I need time to prove that his so-called evidence is made up."

"What evidence? What allegations?"

"It's better you do not know the details, and I am loath to repeat it in your presence anyway. Suffice it to say that his words are defamatory, and I will have my satisfaction from him, but first I must convince the authorities that they are false before I can be arrested."

"But Will Harrell? Why?

"My dear, isn't it obvious? Jealousy can cause people to act out of character, or perhaps display their true character. At any rate I will need to go undercover for a few days, but I will come to you tonight, my love, to your room, though in disguise. Will you wait for me?"

Her mind swirled with a thousand thoughts. She nodded. "Yes, I will wait for you."

"You must tell no one what I have confided in you."

She nodded again. "Of course."

And now, as she began to pace again, her doubts beginning to outweigh her excitement, she heard a light knock on her door. She froze.

"Rebecca?"

It was him. She rushed to the door and opened it. The gasp, the quick intake of breath was involuntary, as was the reflexive recoil at the sight of the stranger in her doorway. The man put his finger to his mouth.

"Rebecca, it is me, Henri." He stepped inside and closed the door. "Listen, we don't have much time. I was followed here."

"By whom?"

"Harrell."

"Will?"

He nodded then went to the window, parted the blinds and peered outside. "Here, come to me." He motioned with his hand for her to draw near. When she did, he pulled her to him and kissed her, hard and long. It was what she had been waiting for, longing for all day. The thought of it would not leave her, exciting her with guilty pleasure at the anticipation of their clandestine, dangerous rendezvous. But now, somehow, it didn't seem right. In fact, it seemed all wrong. Instead of excitement, of arousal, she felt more anxious, more fearful.

"We are going to play a trick on Mr. Harrell, my love. I suspect that at any moment now he will charge through that door. When he does, do exactly as I tell you." He drew her closer to him, and from somewhere he produced a large knife, its blade shimmering in the candlelight. He put it to her throat.

* * *

This time, there was no hesitation on Will's part, no caution. He opened the gate and ran toward the back entrance of the inn, which served as the private residence for the Boutwell family. He yanked the door opened and entered, took the stairs to his right two at a time to the second floor and rushed down the hallway to the last room. He hesitated a moment, listening, heard a very soft cry from Rebecca from inside, then tuned the handle and entered.

Will stopped abruptly just inside the room and took in the scene. The man he had come to know as Henri Tremont, stood behind Rebecca, next to the window. He had a knife to her throat and a hand on her shoulder. She was trembling. It was a sight that was instantly seared in his brain forever, returning from time to time to haunt him, to bring forth self-doubt and regrets. If he had reacted differently. If he had not hesitated in the alley, too afraid for himself, too cautious.

Incognito put a finger to his lips, then said, "This is a very sharp knife, Will, so let's not do anything to panic Miss Boutwell, or to make me nervous for that matter, as the slightest movement by either me of the lovely lady might have catastrophic consequences." He looked at Will with eyes that suggested amusement.

"No need to involve the girl, Tremont, or whoever you really are. This is between you and me. Let her go and we'll settle this like men."

"Don't be silly, Will. She is an integral part of the plan now. And it is you who has involved her. You must have known that if you persisted something like this was bound to happen."

Then he whispered something in Rebecca's ear, which made her begin to tremble. "There you go now, girl," he said, moving the knife a couple of inches away from her throat. "Go ahead. Let's hear you give a big scream."

She turned her head slightly to catch a glimpse of him, perhaps trying to understand, but then she did what she had been told, what was a natural reaction to her situation, what she had been holding in at the threat of the knife to her throat. The scream was loud, and genuine, carrying the raw fear that compelled it, and it seemed that she relaxed just a little.

Two things happened then at once. First, Will began moving toward them, correctly reading his adversary, sensing what was about to happen, fearing that he would be too late to stop it. And second, Tremont moved the knife back to her throat and pulled it across, opening a large gash. Rebecca's face registered only surprise, the knife so sharp that she didn't comprehend what had happened, nor felt pain really, until she put her hand to her throat and felt the blood spurting.

Tremont dropped the knife to the floor, and as Will advanced across the room, Tremont shoved the young woman toward him. Will caught her before she could fall to the floor. He could see, looking into her eyes that the life was quickly draining from her, and he knew in an instant that she would die in his arms. But even though he knew it was useless, that his focus should be on subduing Tremont, he found he couldn't let her go. He watched helplessly as Rebecca's blood poured all over him. Tremont went to the window and opened it. He gave one more look at Will, then scrambled out and onto the roof.

Will could hear voices and footsteps out in the hallway and momentarily the door flew open and he was staring into the horrified faces of Joseph Boutwell, his wife, Martha and daughter, Elizabeth. They had all stopped just inside the door, the scene before them one that they were not prepared for, that did not seem real. They let out a collective "Noooh!" the anguish in their voices filling the room.

"Out the window," Will said, pointing with his chin. "Tremont went out the window."

Joseph Boutwell looked in that direction but did not go to the window. Instead, he went to his daughter and took her from Will's grasp, cradling her, stepping back a few feet as if to protect her from him. It was obvious, though, even to her family, that Rebecca was beyond protecting now. They all stared, unbelievingly, at her lifeless body, limp in her father's arm, the blood still flooding from the wound at her neck but slowing now as the heart had stooped pumping. Will stared, too, unsure what to do. He knew what it looked like, sure that is just what Tremont had counted on.

The father handed Rebecca to his wife who laid her on the floor and hovered over her. Joseph then walked toward Will, his face registering doubt, then anger, at what he thought must have happened, though his mind didn't want to believe what the evidence before him showed.

"I didn't do it, Mr. Boutwell. It was Tremont." He didn't resist, though, when Boutwell grabbed him and pinned him against the wall. Nor did he resist or flinch when the man drew back his fisted hand, preparing to strike him.

"Joseph," Martha Boutwell said.

The man looked over his shoulder at his wife, then lowered his hand, but still held onto Will with the other one.

"He went out the window," Will said again.

A small crowd of guests and employees had gathered outside the room now, and Boutwell called over his shoulder, "Jonathon, go fetch Sheriff Dewees." The employee hesitated a moment then backed away quickly and his footsteps could be heard running down the hall. He released Will but pointed a finger at him. "You stay right there." As he walked toward the open window he said over his shoulder, "Martha, is Monsieur Tremont a current guest of the inn?"

"No," she said, giving Will a look that one might to a child caught in a lie. "He checked out earlier today, headed back to New York."

"I know how it must look," Will said, "but you must know I would never harm Rebecca. He tried to explain how he had followed Tremont, who was in disguise, and saw him through the window in Rebecca's room, how he had come in just as Tremont sliced her throat and left by the window. But even as he said it, he could hear how ridiculous it sounded. He knew that any professions of love for the victim only highlighted the motive for the murder, jealousy, and why he would try to blame his crime on the foreigner, who from all appearances, had no motive to harm the girl.

Joseph stood before the window, examining it. He stuck his head out of the opening and looked around briefly, then brought it into the room. He turned back to Will. "You would think that a man who had just done what you say he did, would have blood all over him, that he would leave a trail of it as he left out the window, as you say occurred. But there is no blood either on the floor next to the window, nor on the sill, nor on the roof outside. And that is a very steep roof. Difficult to manage it without falling to the ground." He paused. "No, the only one with my daughter's blood all over him is you. You are the one I find holding her lifeless body, moments after hearing her scream, the blood drenched knife next to you on the floor. You are the one who had a reason to be angry, perhaps enraged, at her because she did not return your affections as you wished."

Will was about to explain how Tremont had stood behind Rebecca, and held her out from his own body when he slit her throat, sending the blood spurting forward toward Will, and how he had thrown the knife and shoved Rebecca toward him. Very little blood would have gotten on him under those circumstances, though he thought that upon closer examination, some blood drops would be found near the window or on the roof. But before he could say anything, Will heard the voice of Sheriff Dewees saying, "All right, let me through."

Those in the room turned their heads to see the sheriff as the spectators parted and he entered the room. He quickly took in the scene and, remarkably, registered some of the same mixed emotions of doubt, confusion and anger Will had seen on Boutwell's face.

He looked at Will and asked, "What's happened here?"

It was Joseph Boutwell, however, who answered. "This boy has just murdered my daughter."

Philadelphia, July 2
Chapter 39

The Walnut Street Jail was by most measures as humane as any in the colonies, but it still was not a place anyone would want to be. Will had slept, what little he could manage, on a hard, wooden bench with no cushion or blanket. He now sat on that same bench, ten hours after his arrest, staring at the stone walls and floor. The small cell smelled of urine and vomit and sweat—not much different than many of the pubs in the city—though without the alcoholic beverages that made those places more convivial, nor the lively conversation the heavy drinking encouraged.

Not that he wanted lively conversation. Indeed, he was glad he had a cell to himself, left with his thoughts for company, as dark and depressing as they may be. He could not get the image out of his mind, of Rebecca's startled, helpless, hopeless eyes as the life rushed out of her. He could not escape the feelings of guilt that enveloped him, paralyzed him for much of the night. Will had asked him to let her go, said that it was between the two of them? *Don't be silly, Will. She is an integral part of the plan now. And it is you who has involved her. You must have known that if you persisted something like this was bound to happen.*

But he hadn't known, had he? Should he have known it? Suspected it? Anticipated it? While his reason told him there was only one person to blame for the death of Rebecca, the doubts haunted him. But that was just what the spy wanted, to neutralize him, not only physically, but psychologically. Incognito had outmaneuvered him. And in a most horrific manner. All the explanations in the world seemed unconvincing, even to himself, in the face of the evidence against him.

But Will would have to find an effective counter. And every minute he spent in this cell was another minute Incognito had to carry out his plot. Will felt certain that whatever the man had planned would take place today. It was why he wanted Will out of the way.

His efforts to convince the sheriff to release him had been fruitless. Will told him about Tremont being a spy, of the planned attack against members of the Congress. Confidentiality had lost its value in Will's mind at this point. He urged the sheriff to confirm it with Franklin and Dickinson.

"Would have been nice to be informed of this earlier," the sheriff said, frowning, "but it doesn't matter who this Tremont really is, or what he has planned. You were the one with a knife in your hand and Rebecca's blood all over you."

"But I didn't do it. It was Tremont."

"So you say. But listen, son. I got you out of there for your own safety, not because of my confidence in your guilt. I've known you all your life and what I saw in that room was not you. But no telling what Joseph might have done if I hadn't arrested you right then. I'll go back over there when it's light and see if I can find something to support your story. In the meantime, I'll see if I can go wake up your father, tell him what's happened."

"Don't bother going to the house. He won't be there."

The sheriff nodded. "I know his usual haunts. I'll find him. Maybe he can make arrangements with the judge to have you released in the morning."

"But I need to get out now."

He shook his head. "Not gonna happen, son. Make yourself comfortable. I'll be back first thing in the morning."

But it was eight o'clock and the sheriff had not yet come to the jail. A few minutes later, though, he heard footsteps out in the hallway, two sets. They stopped outside the door, a key was inserted in the lock and the door opened. Deputy Thomas Barr stood aside and allowed Will's father into the room, then closed the door. Patrick Harrell walked over and sat down next to his son, rested his hands on his knees. Neither said anything for several seconds. Finally, the father broke the silence.

"They told me what happened. I know you didn't, couldn't, have done that to Rebecca. I'm going to get you out of here as soon as I can."

"It was the Frenchman, father."

Patrick Harrell nodded.

"And you were helping him." His father said nothing in response, his silence as good as a confession.

Finally, he said, "I needed the money. I had run up a good bit of gambling debts. I just needed to get out from under. I didn't see the harm. I had no idea he was capable of such violence."

"That's it? You needed the money? Father, the man is a British spy and assassin. How much of his plan do you know?"

"I thought he was spying for the French. And what do you mean he's an assassin?"

"Didn't Dewees tell you?"

He shook his head. "I haven't talked to him. Barr found me at the shop this morning."

Will stared at his father, trying to decide if he was lying or telling the truth. He cross-examined him, as a lawyer at trial. He posited certain facts as established and gauged his father's reactions and responses, testing them against what he knew. He wanted to believe his father would tell him the truth, but he knew he had to remain objective. In the end, he concluded that the man's words rang true, that he was more a dupe than a willing co-conspirator—though some of it was willful blindness to the truth rather than pure ignorance. Will weighed his options and decided to disclose what he knew, and suspected, of Tremont's activities and present intent.

When he was through, his father said, "I had no idea. I had no idea."

"Father, I need to get out of here, now. Your friend, Tremont, will certainly strike today, perhaps this morning, during the continued debate in Congress."

"And you think it might involve explosives or attack with long rifles?"

"Or both. Tell me you have arranged to have me released."

He shook his head. I didn't have time. I just came right over. It will take some doing but I'll get you out."

"When?"

"Soon." He hesitated a few moments, then said, "I'm going to make things right, Will."

"Don't try anything on your own. The man is a vicious and efficient killer. Best to get me out first and we can work together, utilize the militia. At least get in touch with Tim Matlack. He can get word to President Hancock. They may want to cancel the meeting today, until we can locate this man."

His father nodded and said, yes, he would do that. He told Will not to worry.

But he did, and for quite a while after his father left. When Patrick Harrell said he would make things right, he knew his father meant that he would clean up the mess he had made.

Will called vainly for Barr but either the man had left him there or he was intentionally ignoring him. He paced back and forth, becoming more anxious as the time went by. Then, a little before ten o'clock his jail cell door opened once again and Sheriff Dewees stepped inside. Behind him stood John Hancock, Ben Franklin, and Joseph Boutwell.

"You're free to go, Will," the sheriff said, without preliminaries. "The charges against you have been dropped."

Will could hardly believe he had heard correctly. He stared at the men.

Franklin spoke after a few moments. "We can explain everything to you as we walk, my boy, unless you would rather stay in these accommodations a while longer. Perhaps the sheriff may change his mind."

Will needed no additional prompting. He stood, grabbed his coat and walked with them out of the jail and into the street. The sheriff closed the door behind them, with a "Good luck."

Will looked at Franklin and asked, "My father got in touch with you, then?"

The puzzled looks gave Will his answer, but Hancock confirmed, "No, but we were able to present additional information to the sheriff this morning that put a different light on things." He turned to Joseph Boutwell.

"Yes," the innkeeper said, looking directly at Will, as was his nature. For better or worse, the man would let you know just how he felt. "I owe you an apology, Will. And you really have Elizabeth to thank for the change in circumstances. This morning she went back up to Rebecca's room. She spotted a few drops of blood near the window. She climbed out on the roof and found more." He paused a couple of moments, looking down at the ground before he faced him again and continued. "You can understand what I thought, what it seemed like from what I saw when we came in the room last night. I should have known that you were not capable of such an act. I should have taken what you said more seriously."

Will put his hand on the man's shoulder. "Yes, I understand. I would have reacted the same way if the roles were reversed."

"And you tried to warn me. I should have listened." He turned to Hancock and Franklin. "Any word on the whereabouts of our Monsieur Tremont, or whoever he really is?"

"Unfortunately, no." Franklin said, but his real name, I believe, is Edward Collingsworth, an English aristocrat who fancies himself an actor."

"And now a spy," Hancock said.

Franklin explained about the visit from the man, and how something about him had seemed familiar, about his eventual recollection of the reason.

Will said, "It all makes sense, the disguises, the fluency in French, the knowledge of plays. The man is an actor." He looked over at Franklin. "And perhaps not as bad as your review might suggest."

"It was only one play. I do admit that. But he was god awful in it."

Will nodded. "Well, whoever he is, we need to stop him. I fully expect he plans to attack the Congress sometime today. I need to get to the State House. We need to examine every inch of the building for explosives. We must inspect every other building close by that has a view of the entrance, from which a man with a rifle might fire on persons leaving the building."

"We also have an important debate to resume," Hancock said.

Philadelphia, July 2
Chapter 40

Hancock did not want the members to be unduly alarmed, certainly not panicked by this new information, but he had an obligation to tell them. And he did. It was the first order of business.

"The man we have come to know as Henri Tremont, the British spy and assassin whose code name is Incognito, is still at large. He is suspected in the brutal murder of a young woman last night, and we believe that he is poised to attack this body and its members today. It has been recommended," and here he looked over at Will, who was still wearing his bloodied and disheveled clothing, "that we postpone our session until he is captured."

The reaction was immediate and predictable. No, they would not be cowed or frightened into hiding away. They had important business to conduct, and they would do so regardless of the threat to their own safety. Will wasn't sure how much of this was bluster, or whether the sentiment expressed was the consensus of the body, but not one voice was heard in opposition. They would just have to double their efforts at security. Indeed, continuing the session might allow an opportunity to trap the spy if he did try to attack.

Word was sent to summon some of Tim's militia members. They would be posted outside the building and at the entrance to the chambers. Some would inspect the surrounding buildings. Presumably, Cecil and his lads were also stationed as lookouts near The Philadelphia Emporium building and The Black Swan Tavern, which were of particular interest to Will.

He and Tim took the doormen aside and grilled them as to their inspection of the building and grounds that morning. The two on early duty this day were Jonathon Zeigler and Thomas Beal. They both assured that a thorough inspection had been conducted, as they had been instructed, and nothing out of the ordinary had been discovered. The third doorman, Jeremy Owens had only recently arrived.

"Jeremy," Will said, "you stand guard at the doors to the chamber until the militia arrive. Jonathon, you go with Tim to the second and third floors. Examine every room, every closet and cubby, and all windows. Check under all the desks, tables and chairs. Take special care to inspect the bell tower and while there search the surrounding rooflines. Thomas, you and I will take the first floor and the grounds of the building."

"But we've already checked everything, and thoroughly," Thomas said. "Why do we need to do it again?"

Will wanted to slap the lad, but he held his temper in check and calmly stated, "Simple, Thomas. First, I don't know how good a job you did first time around. Never hurts to have a fresh set of eyes look at things. Second, your examination of the premises was conducted when you first arrived, between seven and eight o'clock, most likely. It is now almost ten. How many people have come into the building or onto the grounds in the interim? And of those persons, could one have been our assassin, in disguise?"

Thomas still wore a look of petulance, but he said nothing in response and nodded his head in acquiescence. As Tim and Jonathon took off for the stairs, Will said to Thomas. "Let's start out back."

Just outside the rear entrance, down the steps, Will paused, looking back at the building, and then doing a quick survey of the walled space between the building and Chestnut Street. "Check the perimeter," he said to Thomas, and then turned to face the back entrance again. As he got closer to the steps, he noticed what appeared to be a flickering light behind the grate, just to the right of the steps. "What's this?" He moved toward the spot.

Thomas moved in behind him. "What? What do you see?"

Will quickly removed the iron grate and crawled inside. In the semi-darkness of the space he could see that the light was coming from a lit fuse. He followed it to where it connected to an explosive device lodged between the subfloor and the joist. The fuse was slow burning, a delayed detonation apparently planned, but there was only a couple of feet of fuse left. Will immediately cut the fuse, disconnecting it from the bomb, and it burned harmlessly in the dirt. Then he crawled to the other side of the steps where he found a similar device and in turn neutralized it, as well.

When he crawled back out, Thomas was standing nearby. Will stood and came toward him quickly. "I thought you said you checked this area thoroughly."

Thomas took a couple of steps backwards. He was visibly nervous, sweating profusely and looking around as if searching for the best escape route. "I did check it. Those two bombs weren't there earlier. Like you said, maybe someone came in afterwards and placed them there."

"How did you know there were two bombs and not just one? Or three or four? Or any bomb at all?"

"I could see them. I saw you defuse them." His voice had gone up in pitch a bit, and he seemed even more nervous.

Will shook his head. "No, I could barely make things out in that space. No way you could see what was what from out here."

"I don't have to put up with this. If you are going to impugn my character, I will just resign my position. Besides, they don't pay me enough to hang around and get blown up." The petulance had returned to his tone of voice, but the words were said without conviction. "Please tell Mr. Thomson, I'll come back later for my pay, when things have cooled down a bit."

But when Thomas turned to leave, Will grabbed him on the sleeve and pulled him to him. "No, Thomas. Not yet. We're not finished with our inspection. Let's go inside."

"No. I want to leave. You have no right to keep me here against my will." He pulled against Will's grip, frantic now to get away, but Will held on tight, pulling him closer. He could smell the fear on the man's breath.

"If there are any more bombs in that building, you and I are going to find them together. And if one of them blows up before we can defuse them, then I guess we'll get blown up together."

"No, no, no. You can't. I mean, it's too late."

"How many, Thomas? And where?"

"Let me go," he said, more frantic now.

"How many? And where?"

"One," he almost shouted. "In the bell tower. But there's no time. It's set to go within a minute of the blast of those underneath the building and they should have already gone off. We need to get out of here."

Will quickly weighed his options. He could drag Thomas with him into the building, but that would take much effort, and time he didn't have. He could let him go and hope to bring him to justice later—if he didn't die in the next minute trying to defuse a bomb. No, he thought, he'd go with the third option. A compromise. He stood Thomas up straight and hit him square on the jaw with a round house punch, the force of which knocked the lad unconscious, and probably broke his jaw as well.

He left Thomas sprawled on the ground and rushed into the building. As he did, he weighed his other options. Try to make it to the tower and defuse the bomb before it went off? Try to get everyone out of the building before the explosion? Both were fraught with risks if he failed. Despite Thomas' warning, he couldn't be sure exactly how long before the other bomb detonated. But clearly, time was of the essence, and he couldn't afford to waste any of it.

He quickly settled on another compromise. He stopped briefly inside the entrance and got Jeremy's attention. "There's a bomb in the tower. Get everyone out of the building, including anyone upstairs, take them out the back, not the front." He headed toward the stairs then stopped and turned back to Jeremy. "And if Thomas wakes up outside," he said, pointing with his thumb toward the courtyard, "tie him up. Don't let him leave." Then he was off, taking the stairs two at a time.

* * *

Will made his way up the spiral stairwell and onto the floor of the bell tower. He quickly spotted the bomb. No, not just one, as Thomas had said, but two, one on each side of the bell, lodged into the support timbers. Were there more devices in other parts of the building? He couldn't worry about that now. The fuses on both were lit, and perilously close to the point of detonation.

He started with the one whose fuse appeared to be shortest. He pulled out his knife and attempted to cut off the fuse, but he could not obtain purchase, to hold it still so the knife would cut. He only succeeded in moving it around with the knife. There was not enough length of non-burning fuse to grab. He tore off his shirt and tried to put out the fuse by smothering it, but to no avail. It just caused his shirt to begin smoldering.

He then stomped out the fire on his shirt, wrapped it around his hand several times, then grabbed the burning part of the fuse with his covered hand. The heat from the burning fuse was intense and penetrated the layers quickly, but Will held firm and cut the fuse, dropping it to the floor. He did the same with the other explosive, then unraveled the make-shift glove and dropped it, as well, to the floor.

He allowed himself a moment of self-congratulation as he sat on the floor, breathing heavily. When he stood, he looked out across the street and surveyed quickly the roofs of the surrounding buildings. The glint of metal reflecting the morning sun caught his attention. It was coming from the direction of the roof of The Philadelphia Emporium building.

The reflective metal was that of a Pennsylvania long rifle, and it was pointed right at him.

* * *

Incognito cursed under his breath when he saw Will Harrell in the bell tower. What was he doing out of jail? He hadn't expected that the charges would stick but figured it would take some considerable time for the sheriff to uncover the necessary exonerating evidence. But here he was, again.

The spy had waited on the roof for the expected explosions at the rear of the building, intended to scare more than kill the delegates, to spur them to exit the front of the building in a panic, followed by the explosion of the devices in the bell tower, to complete the task. Amid the confusion, he would pick off his targets with the rifles. The timing of the explosions was not precise, only an estimate, but after some time passed, he began to wonder if something had gone wrong. He looked through his spy glass and saw that the fuses on the bombs in the tower were burning, slowly but steadily, but the two devices he planted under the back entrance should have gone off by now.

And then, Harrell appeared and quickly began attempting to defuse the devices. He thought about trying to kill him with a shot, thought the lad was too late, vacillated between shooting at the boy or at one of the bombs. As the former was a moving target and the latter a fixed one, and as a detonation of the bomb would most emphatically kill Harrell while also dislodging the bell, causing it to crash through the building, he chose the second option. This choice was reinforced when the boy somehow managed to cut both fuses. He now had no choice in detonating the bombs. He would have to do so with a rifle ball. He had sighted his target down the barrel and was just about to squeeze the trigger when he sensed movement behind him.

* * *

Will immediately ducked behind the bell tower wall when he saw the rifle pointed in his direction. It occurred to him that the target might be

367

not him, but one of the bombs. Could he remove them fast enough? He waited a few seconds, moved to a different position and then cautiously peered over the wall toward the building. What he saw made him stand up straight—Incognito and his father, engaged in a struggle on the roof, and then both falling out of view behind the roof's wall.

With no more than a moment's hesitation, he scrambled down from the tower, down the stairs to the first floor, and out the front entrance. He was surprised, and alarmed, to see quite a few delegates milling about. He had told Jeremy specifically to have them exit to the rear of the building. Now they were easy targets for Incognito. "Go to the rear of the building," he shouted, but couldn't take the time to make sure he was heard or heeded. He raced across the street and into the Emporium. He ignored the startled looks from Patterson and his wife and flew up the stairwell. He paused just before the small door that led onto the roof, then cracked it open just a bit and peered out.

No sign of either his father or Incognito. But then again, the door opened on the side away from Walnut Street. He did spot the board which traversed the space between the building and that which housed The Black Swan Tavern. He opened the door enough to ease himself out and he crouched, listening for sounds of a struggle. Nothing. He stood and inched around the corner of the enclosure for the stairwell, toward the Walnut Street side. After a few paces he caught sight of his father, sitting on the roof, legs splayed out in front of him, leaning against the north wall. He was alive, and conscious, but barely, and in obvious pain. He held both hands to his stomach, trying to stem the flow of blood from what looked like several knife wounds. As Will rushed toward is father he caught a glimpse of movement behind and to the left. In the split second before it made contact with the back of his head, Will thought it might be the barrel of a rifle. Pain exploded in his head for one brief moment, then everything went black.

* * *

After some time—he had no idea how long—consciousness began to return, slowly, gradually. The pain in his head was intense, throbbing, and it hurt just to open his eyes, even more when he tried to blink away the vapor-like cloud that obstructed his vision. He started to become oriented now as to where he was and what had happened. As his vision began to clear, he saw Incognito standing at the roof's wall, using it to steady his rifle barrel as he aimed it across the street. Patrick Harrell had not moved from his spot and seemed weaker still. The two of them made eye contact and Patrick mouthed "I'm sorry," and Will shook his head in response, the movement causing a burst of pain.

Incognito fired the rifle and a split second later the bell in the tower of the State House erupted in a tremendous clang. Will realized the man was trying to hit one of the bombs with a rifle ball and detonate it that way. The explosion itself might kill anyone standing close to the building as the bell tower collapsed, but it might also prompt more of the delegates to venture out into the range of Incognito and his rifle. He had to stop him. The head pain was receding but still, every movement exacerbated it.

Incognito looked in Will's direction as he put down the one rifle and picked up the other. Will pretended to still be unconscious. Satisfied, the spy turned back and began to sight the rifle again. Will got to his knees, then slowly rose to his feet. He stood, waiting to get his equilibrium as things spun around for several seconds. Finally, the spinning stopped. He kept his eye on Incognito as he crept slowly toward him, looking around for something he could use as a weapon. He was too weak, too unsteady on his feet to take him on without one.

But there was no weapon. Only the rifle the spy had set aside, and it was unloaded. It could be used as a club, but he would never be able to get to it before Incognito noticed him. He'd have to try. The man was preparing to fire again. Will was about to attempt a quick dart across the six or seven feet that separated them when Incognito suddenly turned and faced him. He leaned the rifle against the wall and from somewhere produced a knife. A big knife, stained with the blood of Patrick Harrell. He had a smile on his face.

When Will glanced over toward his father then, he was surprised to find that the man was now half standing, leaning against the wall for support. He had a pistol in his hand pointed at Incognito. The spy's face registered his surprise as well just before the pistol fired. The ball found its mark, exploding into Incognito's shoulder. The blow turned him a quarter and caused him to drop the knife. Before he could recover, Will girded himself against the expected pain of movement and rushed at Incognito.

He made contact at his chest, just below the wounded shoulder and he yelped in pain. There was surprisingly little resistance from the man and the force of Will's body blow sent the man against the wall. Will bent and pushed up with all his strength. Incognito, clutching, scratching at him, teetered on the edge of roof's wall before Will's final push sent him over.

Will heard his scream, the crash as the cloth canopy below crumpled under the force of the fall, and then the thud when he hit the sidewalk below. He looked over and saw the man, sprawled and motionless. After a few seconds, he then turned back and walked over to where his father had now eased himself back into a sitting position, leaning against the wall. He took the man in his arms and told him he would be all right. But he knew, looking at the wounds, and into the man's eyes, and listening to his labored breathing, that he wouldn't be. And indeed, seconds later, as the man mouthed again, "I'm sorry," he closed his eyes for the last time.

Will sat there for a minute with his father cradled in his arms. Then he wiped the tears from his eyes, laid him gently on the roof, and stood. He went once more to the roof's wall and peered over, just to satisfy himself that the spy was dead.

But the man was gone.

"What?" he said aloud to himself. He couldn't believe it. The fall should have killed him. Certainly, he had been seriously injured and was unconscious on the ground. He hadn't been moving. Will looked up and down the street and saw no sign of him. Maybe the body had been moved.

He rushed down the stairs, and when he got down to the sidewalk below, he followed the blood trail inside the Emporium. The owner, Eric Patterson, seemed to have been expecting him.

"Where is he?" Will demanded.

"He said you tried to kill him."

So, he wasn't dead. The canopy must have broken his fall just enough. "I did. Now, where is he?"

"He's not here. You can check if you'd like," he said, waving his arm around.

"Where did he go?"

"He grabbed some clothing to clot his wound. He was also limping badly."

"Where did he go, Eric?"

He pointed to the rear of the building. "He left out the back a couple of minutes ago."

Will didn't know whether to believe him or not. Incognito might have headed back up to the roof to extract revenge, to finish him off. But he saw the blood drops on the floor, not of the volume as outside, but noticeable. And they did, indeed, lead him to the rear of the store, then to and through the Black Swan Tavern, where, despite the physical evidence of his presence, no one remembered seeing the man. He followed the trail of blood out the front entrance, but it disappeared after about fifteen feet, at the place where horses were tethered.

And that was where the trail ended.

New York City, July 9
Chapter 41

Will stood among the soldiers and civilians gathered on the New York Common at six in the evening to hear a reading of the Declaration of Independence. Will had delivered the document to General Washington the day before. It was one week from the date it was passed, one week from the date Rebecca and his father had been murdered, one week from the date that the spy, Incognito, had escaped. It was a date which would carry for him none of the positive feelings destined to be associated with it for the new nation.

An urgent and thorough search of the city and its environs turned up nothing on the spy. No physician had treated his wounds. No one reported seeing any one of the multiple personas the man had used. Inquiries revealed that his horse was missing from the stables—without the bill having been paid. There was no way of knowing where he had gone. Perhaps the man had died somewhere in the country. His wound was serious after all. But there had been no bodies found anywhere near the city. Maybe he was hiding out with one of his Tory collaborators until he was well enough to travel. Will's best guess, though, was that he was headed to New York as soon as he could. And Will had resolved to follow him there.

He was not at all certain that they had identified all the collaborators in the assassination plot but all who had been identified were awaiting their punishment. Protestations that it was no crime to refuse to support the rebel cause were met by the observation that conspiracy to commit murder was a crime, regardless of one's politics. Protestations that they didn't know what the man had planned were met with a collective we-don't-care shrug. Will's father had suffered the ultimate punishment for his participation, and Rebecca too, though she was guilty only of naiveté and a need for attention.

When Will made his report to the general upon his arrival, Washington was quiet for a long time, then he said, "I suspect that is on your mind now, a search here in New York for the would-be assassin?"

Will nodded. "And when I find him, I will kill him." He said this with a certainty, and coldness, that surprised him.

A long silence passed between them, finally broken when Washington said, "I understand that the citizens of Philadelphia, some of them, are not entirely convinced of your innocence in the matter."

"That is so. I have been cleared of any charges and I believe I have the confidence of those whose opinion I value. But for some people, I may always be under a cloud of suspicion."

The general turned his chair and looked out the bay window. "Terribly unfair to you," he said. "Yet, there may be some advantage to the ambiguity of your situation." He turned back to face Will. "If you are willing to be of further service to our cause."

His service to the cause thus far had resulted in the deaths of two people close to him, and probably others as well. What had started out as a distraction, another puzzle to solve, had turned very personal, and deadly. Perhaps it was best to cut his losses. Nevertheless, he heard himself say, "Of course."

Washington began to pace the room. "You are an extremely bright and resourceful young man, with skills and talents very much in demand in our current situation. I would be honored, and pleased, if you would agree to assist us." He stopped and faced Will.

"What is it that you want me to do, sir?" In fact, he could think of only one reason why doubts as to his loyalty to the patriot cause might be of value, which was confirmed by the general with his next observation.

"Information about one's enemy, accurate, timely information, is one of the most powerful weapons to have in any conflict. I need men who can obtain, interpret, analyze, and evaluate such information. By the same token, we also have to be constantly vigilant in keeping our secret information secret."

It was clear the man was not quite finished, so Will did not respond. The general then requested that Will be his "special envoy and assistant" which, when it came down to the details, meant to be his secretary, intelligence analyst, and all-round trouble shooter. He would divide his time between his work for Washington and the practice of law and his family's businesses in Philadelphia.

Will had much awaiting him in Philadelphia. His father's death had meant that his children had to take over running the businesses, which wasn't that big of a change as they pretty much did already. But now it was management by committee, and he was an important part of the team. They would have to get a new manager for the warehouses. That was agreed. But who would replace him? Anne would soon be married, and he wanted to be present for that.

And then there was Elizabeth. She had been the first and strongest of his defenders in the death of her sister, the one who had found the evidence to convince her father. She had been a great source of comfort in the aftermath of the deaths. She had shown herself to be a true friend. And though it seemed a little disloyal to the memory of Rebecca, he had allowed himself to think that perhaps, after a respectful period of mourning, that friendship might grow into something more.

But, despite his desire to return to Philadelphia as soon as reasonably possible, he found himself telling the general, "I am at your service."

And as he stood now, some fifteen feet away from where the general sat astride his great white stallion, Will had no regrets over his choice, but rather, a sense of purpose. A relative quiet descended on the troops and the numerous civilians who had gathered at the common as one of the officers, one with a booming baritone, began.

The unanimous Declaration of the thirteen United States of America:
When in the course of human events, it becomes necessary for one
people to dissolve the political bands which have connected them with
another, and to assume among the powers of the earth, the separate
and equal station to which the Laws of Nature and of Nature's God
entitle them, a decent respect to the opinions of mankind requires that
they should declare the causes which impel them to the separation.

The crowd listened in respectful silence as the document was read.
Will found himself searching the faces of the crowd, wondering if
Incognito might be among them. An elderly woman, aided by a cane,
crossed in front of him. She dropped a scarf on the ground and Will
retrieved it for her.

"Thank you kindly," the woman said.

Will tipped his hat. "You are very welcome."

The woman ambled off and Will returned his attention to the
reading and scouring the crowd. When the document had been read in
full, the troops shouted out three huzzahs. A group then proceeded to a
statute of King George. They tied ropes around it and pushed and
pulled until it toppled over, resulting in more shouting. Will looked on
with mild amusement. Washington looked on with disapproval, as he
did not wish to encourage lawlessness. But he was unwilling to attempt
to curb their enthusiasm. Besides, the lead in it could be melted down
and made into ammunition, a fitting symbolic end.

The crowd was still shouting and parading around the common in
high spirits when a skinny, dark-haired lad of about fourteen
approached Will. He had a piece of paper in his hand, folded and
sealed.

"Are you Mr. William Harrell?"

"Yes," Will said, surprised, and curious.

"This is for you." He handed Will the paper.

"What is it?"

The boy shrugged. "I think it's a message. I was just given two shillings to deliver it to you."

"From whom? Who paid you to deliver it?"

He looked back over his shoulders as he spoke. "The old woman over there." He started to point then stopped, turned fully in that direction. "She's gone," he said, scanning the area. He turned back to Will, frowning. "She gave me the one shilling and said, 'one now, the other when you have delivered it.'"

Will opened the document and read the contents: "To weep is to make less the depth of grief." He recognized right away the quote from Shakespeare's *Henry VI, Part III.* He looked up at the boy, reached in his pocket and produced a shilling coin. He held it in the air. "I'll cover the other shilling, for the right answers. What did this woman look like?"

"Like I said, she was old. Had grey hair, bent over."

"Did she walk with a cane?"

"Yeah, a nice one with a horse head."

An image of the woman, earlier, who had dropped her scarf, flashed across his mind. "What's her name?"

"She didn't give me no name."

"Ever seen her before?"

He shook his head. "Never seen her before. Don't know nothing about her, what I haven't already told you. Now can I have that shilling?"

"I am staying at The Merchant Coffee House. I will double this if you bring me information on where I can find this woman." Will handed the coin to the lad, who pocketed it, smiled and nodded, then walked off, whistling as he went.

Will looked out over the crowd again, searching, without success, for someone who matched that description. But he knew two things. Incognito was alive, and he was in New York.

CPSIA information can be obtained
at www.ICGtesting.com
Printed in the USA
JSHW022213250321
12947JS00004B/22